William Alexander Hammond

Robert Severne, His Friends and His Enemies

A Novel

William Alexander Hammond

Robert Severne, His Friends and His Enemies
A Novel

ISBN/EAN: 9783337030575

Printed in Europe, USA, Canada, Australia, Japan

Cover: Foto ©Andreas Hilbeck / pixelio.de

More available books at **www.hansebooks.com**

ROBERT SEVERNE

HIS FRIENDS AND HIS ENEMIES.

A NOVEL.

BY

WILLIAM A. HAMMOND.

——

PHILADELPHIA:

J. B. LIPPINCOTT & CO.

1867.

CONTENTS.

ROBERT SEVERNE.

CHAPTER I.

A DEN AND ITS OCCUPANTS.

In one of the most crowded thoroughfares of New York, there stood several years ago an old brick building black with age, and altogether, in an architectural point of view, far behind many of its more pretentious neighbors. It was not ornamented with brownstone or marble columns and cornices; the windows were small and not overclean, and many years had evidently elapsed since the carpenter, the mason, or the painter had given it any touches of their respective arts. Doubtless at one time it had been fully as presentable as any other house in the row; but it had year after year been losing caste, until now it was regarded as an eyesore by most of the passers-by. Many a sharp and calculating glance was cast at this old house by eager speculators, who wondered why it was allowed to occupy such valuable ground—ground which could be advantageously used for far more active business operations than appeared to be transacted within the walls of the structure by which it was encumbered.

As has been said, the windows were not overclean. In honest truth, it must be admitted that they were positively dirty. The panes were small and the sash was heavy and clumsy. The distorted images which reached the eye through the twisted glass of which the windows were composed appeared to possess no attractive features for the great mass of pedestrians, and consequently no crowds were collected, such as blocked up the sidewalk in front of many of the neighboring shops, where curious works of art or utility were displayed in profusion.

And yet at times it was very manifest that the windows of the old building we have referred to were not altogether devoid of interest, for occasionally persons of more than ordinarily thoughtful mien would stop, scrutinize them very closely, and finally either enter the door or else pass on with a sigh of regret. In addition to the other obstacles to distinct vision, the panes were so mottled with rain and dust that it required good eyes to perceive the articles they almost concealed rather than allowed to be seen. Still, the earnest and loving and appreciative seeker for knowledge by dint of patient observation could discover objects more precious in his eyes than the bronzes, Sevres china, or manifold house-furnishing articles so conspicuously exhibited behind plate-glass in the palace-like shops of the vicinity.

There was no sign gorgeous with paint and gilding such as can be read a quarter of a mile distant. In fact, it required a not inconsiderable amount of perseverance to find out what kind of wares the old house contained, so unobtrusive and modest is true worth. But, as in the case of the contents of the windows, the solution could be obtained by persistence in the attempt, for on one of the brick columns which supported the doorway was painted on a ground which had once been white, and in a text which not one half of the passers-by could read:

John Holmes.
Old Books—Rare Books—Curious Books.

Within, to the indifferent observer, the aspect was still more discouraging than that of the exterior. A long, narrow room, dark and dismal looking, contained thousands of still more dark and dismal-looking books ranged around the walls on common deal unglazed shelves, and piled on tables of similar material placed in the middle of the gloomy area. There were no luxurious morocco, calf, or Russia bindings glittering with resplendent tool-work; no gaudy sheep and cloth covers enveloping the ephemeral literature which comes to-day and to-morrow is forgotten;

but there were parchment and vellum and black musty calf
and worm-eaten wood, within which were to be found treasures which made the heart of the poor bibliomaniac beat
with an envious throb, and even caused the wan, pale face
of the mentally exhausted student, to light up with renewed
excitement.

It seemed to be a matter of the most supreme indifference
to all concerned in the establishment whether any sales were
made or not.　No anxious clerk rushed forward with bows
and smiles to greet the customer ere the tip of his nose had
fairly passed the threshold.　On the contrary, he was permitted to thread his way among the tables to the back of the
room, perhaps passing on his route several individuals, who,
unattended and unwatched, were standing in front of the
shelves, gleaning a little from this and a little from that
volume, or else in unrestrained bibliophilogical liberty,
walking along the ranges of shelves, seeking by themselves
for what they might require.

At the extremity of the room was a high desk and a high
stool, upon which latter would probably be found seated a
tall and thin gentlemanly-looking and elderly personage,
wearing a broad-brimmed hat and gold spectacles, whose
whole demeanor was remarkably quiet and reserved, and
who, unless he was addressed directly, never took his eyes
from the book he was studiously perusing, but left the intruder with full license to follow the examples of those he
had passed on his way.　If asked whether or not the book
wanted was on hand, he would either answer shortly but
politely in the negative and resume his scarcely interrupted study, or else would descend from his elevation, and
going straight to the spot where it stood, would hand it
with undoubted but half suppressed reluctance, as if dread-
ing the prospect of its passing beyond his control.

The reader will make a mistake if he supposes we have
been describing Mr. John Holmes.　Very few of the visitors
to the old book-shop got beyond the high stool and its occupant, Miles Standish Goodall, Mr. John Holmes's part-
ner, and friend of forty years' standing.　There was an inner
temple, beyond the precincts of which the head of the establishment seldom emerged, except when he left it to go to ·
his residence, which he did every day at five o'clock with

sidereal punctuality. Into this *sanctum sanctorum* or "den," as Mr. Holmes preferred to call it, casual buyers were not admitted. None but the regular frequenters of the establishment, who, from long acquaintance, had become recognized as true bibliophiles, were allowed to enter its limits, and thus to the great majority of those who were courageous or earnest enough to visit Mr. John Holmes's book-shop, his existence was not only unknown, but was even unsuspected.

The whole appearance of the "den" was much more genial than that of the outside room. Not only was the light better, but there was a warm and comfortable carpet on the floor, and, in winter, a grate full of blazing cannel coal gave additional cheerfulness to the scene. Instead of the plain pine shelves of the shop, the walls were lined with handsome walnut book-cases, filled with elegantly but not gaudily bound volumes. There was a sofa, covered with green leather, half a dozen arm-chairs to match, and a large green cloth-covered table, at which, with several books and numerous half sheets of paper covered with writing before him, on the afternoon of December 31st, 1858, sat Mr. John Holmes, bookseller, looking as intensely comfortable as a good conscience and a fair share of this world's goods and learning could make him.

Mr. Holmes, although very comfortable, was evidently very busy. At times he would write hurriedly several lines on one of the half sheets of paper, and then stopping, would lay down his pen and look meditatively at a portrait of Scaliger, which hung on the wall before him. There was nothing in this picture which could, by any direct association, aid him in the subject of his present reflection. It was simply a way of his whenever he was in deep thought to fix his eyes abstractedly in that direction. As he does so now, we may take advantage of the opportunity to inspect his appearance more closely.

Though fully sixty-five years old, Mr. John Holmes would have passed for at least ten years younger. There was but little hair left to form an opinion from, and what he had was as white as snow, for John Holmes disdained a wig as well as all other shams. His face was, however, full, and comparatively free from wrinkles, and his complexion was as blooming as that of many a maiden of one-fourth his age. His large blue eyes, wide apart and not very deeply set, were overhung by a brow which could only have belonged to a person of no common mind. His head was ample in size, without being what is called massive, and was firmly set upon a pair of broad shoulders, which had as yet scarcely begun to droop. His nose and mouth were both large, and the lines of the latter, though strongly drawn, were expressive of as much good nature and kind feeling as of firmness and decision. As he sat in his arm-chair, Mr. John Holmes would have been taken for a man of more than the average height; had he stood upon his feet, however, it would have been seen that though his body was long his legs were short, and thus he was rather below than above the medium standard. For all that, his appearance was decidedly imposing and eminently respectable. His hands and feet were remarkably small, and the former were graced with wristbands of unimpeachable whiteness, while the latter were set off by well-fitting and well-polished boots. If there were any parts of his person that Mr. Holmes was especially vain of, those parts were his hands and feet.

A skillful analyzer of expression observing John Holmes, as he sat and gazed absently at the portrait of Scaliger, would have detected a latent gleam of sadness on his countenance. It was not thrust prominently forward, for he felt that he had too much to be thankful for, to let the marks of any trouble obtain a firm seat on his features. But though at ease all the year through, on this the last of its days, the traces of a long passed and sorrowful event which lingered in his heart, forced themselves to the surface and gave a tone of subdued seriousness to an expression which usually was one of unalloyed happiness.

He sat in quiet meditation for a few minutes, and then, looking at his watch, rose from his seat, took off the short black velvet coat which he habitually wore in his den, and putting on one of thick cloth, together with a stout overcoat, a black beaver hat, and a pair of woolen gloves, was fully accoutered for the street. By the time he had completed his preparations, the sun was just about sinking behind the hills on the west bank of the Hudson, and on looking at his watch he found he had yet nine minutes to spare.   He had ascertained by long experience that in good weather it took him precisely three-quarters of an hour to walk from his shop to his house.   His dinner was always served at precisely six o'clock, and thus he was allowed full time to reach his residence and get ready for his repast.

As he stood with his back to the fire smoothing his ample gloves over his small hands, there was a knock at the door. Upon Mr. Holmes saying "come in," Goodall entered the room and assumed a position in relation to the fire similar to that of his senior.

"I suppose, sir," he said, "the shop will not be opened to-morrow, as it's New-year's Day?"

"No, Goodall," said John Holmes, "and I shall be glad to have you take your dinner with us.   This is not only my invitation, but Margaret's also. If you were a younger man, Goodall," he continued, smiling, "I should be half disposed to think you had got possession of her heart. Do you know, she told me last night—me, John Holmes, her grandfather, and a man who has lived all his life in an atmosphere of books —that she believed you had more solid information in your head than any other man in New York? So far as I can see, the only ground she had for that reckless assertion was the fact that you alone were able to give her the history of old Mother Piggot, who some two hundred or more years ago was burned as a witch."

"I was very glad," replied Goodall, seriously, but evidently pleased with what John Holmes had said, "to be able to tell Miss Margaret all I knew about Mary Piggot. My reading has been a great deal in the direction of superstitions of all kinds, and therefore Miss Margaret has taken too favorable a view of my acquirements. Now, sir, though perhaps I know more about witches than you do, I am certain that I do not possess a tenth part of your——"

"Stop, stop, Goodall!" exclaimed John Holmes, laughingly, "you know no such thing, and on the last day of the year too, when you ought to be forming resolutions to lead a new life, you should be ashamed of yourself for making such speeches. But come, I must be off. You shall tell me all about Mary Piggot to-morrow at dinner; and in the mean time I wish you a happy New Year and a great many more of them. Ah, my old friend," continued John Holmes, taking Goodall's hand and pressing it warmly, "I don't believe you know, with all your knowledge, how much I love you! How many years, Goodall, have we been together in this old shop?"

"Forty years the tenth day of last November," replied Goodall, his eyes glistening with moisture. "Forty years, and in all that time you have never spoken a cross word to me, nor done me an unkind act. You have enabled me to live in comfort, have given me opportunities for acquiring knowledge, and have in every way been my friend."

"Well, well, Goodall," said John Holmes, his own eyes beginning to show evidences of the state of his feelings, "you have more than repaid me for any little friendly offices I may have done you. Why, what would the shop have been without you? You have been the life and soul of it. You have as much knowledge of books in your head as Brunet, Wood, Lowndes, and Dibdin have in all their combined volumes. Perhaps that is rather too strong language, Goodall, but you know what I mean. God bless you, old friend,—God bless you! To-morrow we'll have a good time of it. Till then, good-by!"

So saying, John Holmes shook Goodall's hand again, and, buttoning up his overcoat to the chin, walked out into the shop and began his journey through the devious passage between the tables of books. He had not gone far, when he turned around and addressing Goodall, who had followed him as far as the high stool on which he was already perched, exclaimed:

"By-the-by, Goodall, do you know anything of an alchemical work written by one Kieser some two hundred and fifty years ago? I met with a reference to it to-day, but I do not recollect to have heard of it before."

"Kieser! Kieser!" said Goodall, musingly. "Oh, yes, I recollect now; he wrote three tracts, which were bound together and published at Frankfort in 1606. They were entitled Cabala Chemica, Concordantia Chemica, and—really," he continued, after a pause, "I cannot just now recall the name of the third. The volume is very rare. There is a copy in the Bibliotheque Imperiale, and another in the library of the Archbishop of Vienna."

"Please write at once to my agent at Leipsic, and direct

him to get me a copy," said John Holmes; "I must have it at any price in reason." With which words he opened the front door, and passing out into the street was soon lost in the crowd, which at that hour was always unusually great.

CHAPTER II.

WHICH IS RETROSPECTIVE OF GOODALL.

FOR several minutes after John Holmes left the shop, Goodall remained seated on his stool deep in the reflections which crowded upon his mind. He thought how, some forty years ago, he had been literally picked up out of the street by the man who had ever since been his firm and constant friend. How, little by little, painfully and with incessant labor, he had been able to acquire such an amount of knowledge as rendered his services valuable to his benefactor, and he felt no small degree of pride that he had been successful in his efforts. He was proud, too, that he had been able to lift himself from ignorance and low associations to a position of education and to the society of many refined and intelligent persons. At fifteen years of age, having been left an orphan, he had come to New York to seek his fortune. The small sum of money he had brought with him soon became exhausted, and he had as yet found no settled occupation. There was very little besides mere manual labor that he was fit for. His education had not been carried beyond the very rudiments of the branches then taught in the public schools, and when in the course of his applications at counting-houses for a situation, his acquirements were examined into, he was invariably dismissed with an intimation that his services were not required. He was honest and correct in his deportment, but he soon made the painful discovery that virtue, unaccompanied by business qualifications, meets with little consideration from the great mass of the population of a commercial and manufacturing

city. To be sure, he was a mere boy, and an ignorant one
in addition, but he was possessed of good natural abilities
and excellent perceptive faculties. He saw, therefore, that
he must take his proper level, low though it might be, and
trust to his own exertions to rise to a better position. He
accordingly, when reduced to the last extremity, became an
assistant to the bar-keeper of a restaurant.

In this situation there was very little time allowed him
for study, but he made good use of every leisure moment.
All the money he was enabled to save from his small wages
was spent at a neighboring book-stall, and thus at the end
of a year he had obtained possession of a score or so of
elementary volumes on various branches of knowledge, the
contents of which, by repeated perusal, he had almost learned
by heart.

No doubt Miles Standish Goodall would in time have
emerged from obscurity by his own unaided exertions. He
was strong of heart like his illustrious namesake, and Providence always takes such persons under special protection;
but he was materially assisted by an event which occurred
about this time, and which determined the direction which
his course through life was to take.

One morning, having come to the conclusion that he
ought to study Latin, he obtained holiday for an hour, and
with a dollar in his pocket started out in search of a Latin
grammar and dictionary. None within his means were to
be found at the book-stalls he was acquainted with; but,
persevering in his search, he came at last to John Holmes's
shop, which had been opened that day for the first time.
Holmes had not long before returned from England and the
Continent, bringing with him a rare and valuable collection
of old books, which he had spent much time and money in
getting together. Goodall was the first customer who had
entered his shop; and as John Holmes, then a young man
of twenty-five, who had been blest with all the advantages
of a university education, and had, moreover, a snug little
property of his own, looked at the thin pale-faced and poorly-
clad boy who inquired if he had a cheap Latin dictionary
and grammar for sale, he divined that a noble spirit dwelt
in that overworked body, and he instantly determined to
render all the aid in his power toward its elevation.

"Yes, my lad," he answered, "I have. So very cheap that you shall have them for nothing if you will promise to make good use of them."

"Oh, thank you, sir!" replied Goodall, "but I am able to give a dollar for them."

"Do you read Latin?"

"No, sir; but I want to learn it."

"What is your name, and what do you do for a living?"

"My name is Miles Standish Goodall, sir, and I am the assistant bar-keeper at Mr. Rider's eating-house."

"Are you very anxious to learn Latin?"

"Oh, yes, sir, very anxious!"

"Then, Miles, listen to me. You look like a good boy, and I think you have something in you. As you see, I have a great many books here, and I want some one to help me to take care of them. Now what do you say to becoming my clerk, having the free range of the books, being taught Latin, and paid a fair compensation, which shall be increased as you become more proficient in your duties?"

Goodall could scarcely believe his ears, but at last found words with which to express his thanks. But a difficulty occurred to him:

"What would Mr. Rider do for a boy, sir, if I were to leave him? he has been very kind to me."

"That is a very creditable thought of yours, Miles; but don't let it trouble you. I will go at once and see Mr. Rider, and, if necessary, get him another boy."

The next morning, everything in the mean time having been satisfactorily adjusted, Goodall became a part of John Holmes's book establishment. The latter soon saw that he had not made a mistake in his estimation of the boy's character. Ere many years, Goodall, with his employer's assistance, not only became a good Latin scholar, but had mastered Greek, several modern languages, and had acquired a most profound knowledge of books and literature in general. At the end of ten years, John Holmes admitted him to a third interest, and after five more years increased this to a full partnership. Such was the condition of their relations when our story begins, although the style of the firm had not been changed by Goodall's entrance into it. His thorough scholarship was well known and appreciated, and several offices of honor and profit had been offered him. Nothing, however, could tempt him to leave the shop. He was nowhere so happy as when in the midst of those "masters who teach without scolding and chastise without stripes." His only ambition was to acquire knowledge, and to show his appreciation of John Holmes's friendship. In these objects, as has been seen, he was eminently successful, and if there could have been a thoroughly happy man in the world, that man, but for one thing, would have been Miles Standish Goodall.

The events of his past life fled by in rapid succession before him, as he sat on his stool, his elbows on the desk and his face buried in his hands. For forty years there had not been many very striking incidents to disturb the methodical existence he had led, but the same cause which on the last day of every year made John Holmes sad, never failed with each returning anniversary to excite a pang of sorrow in his own honest and truthful heart.

"Oh, Margaret! Margaret!" he exclaimed, scarcely above his breath, "it might have been different if you had loved me. Seventeen years ago to-night, Margaret, since your pure spirit fled to another world. Seventeen years since I pressed your little hand, and read in the last look of your eyes that at length you knew I loved you. No one else knew it; no one knows it now but you and I, Margaret; and if you had loved me, if in that glance there had been one ray of love, I should not despair. There was pity, Margaret, but there was no love. You belonged to another, and you were faithful to the end, though he did not deserve it of you.

"He did not deserve it of you, Margaret, but it was his legal due. You were lost to me when you vowed to love him while life should last. You kept that promise; but in that other world where you now are, and whither I must soon go, is it to be the same? Are you to be forever his, and is there no hope for me? Can I do nothing, Margaret, to win the love which in your lifetime was denied me?

"She is wondrously like you, Margaret, though she is his child," he continued, after a pause of several minutes. "Your eyes, your hair, your mouth. When she speaks to me, her voice brings back your gentle tones; and then,

Margaret, I lose myself in the fancy that I am once again
in your presence. Dear, sweet child ! is she not dear to me
because she is yours ?"

"Is it time to close, sir ?" said a stout, good-looking man,
who, unobserved by Goodall, had approached within a few
feet of him.

"Yes, Thomas, close the shop, and tell Jane I shall be
ready for dinner in ten minutes." So saying, Goodall proceeded up stairs to his apartments. But before going to
dinner, he opened a little cabinet, which stood on his dress-
ing-table, and took from it a small morocco case, which he
unclasped. It contained one little glove, which he raised
reverently to his lips, and then carefully replacing it in the
casket, sat down to his solitary meal.

"I wonder what is the matter with Mr. Goodall ?" said
Thomas the porter to his wife Jane that evening. "I
hope he has not lost any money by that bank which stopped
payment yesterday. I passed by there this morning, and
there was a great crowd waiting to see if it was going to be
opened again."

"I guess that's it," rejoined Jane; "he did not eat any
dinner but a little soup and a piece of bread, though he
likes stewed chicken, and I had taken so much trouble with
it to-day, too ! But when men lose money, they lose their
senses, too, which is very misfortunate, because they com-
monly hasn't got much to spare,—I mean money, though I
might have said sense neither, for all that."

CHAPTER III.

WHICH INTRODUCES THE READER TO THE CHIEF HEROINE, AND
SHOWS WHY JOHN HOLMES AND GOODALL WERE UNHAPPY ON THE
LAST DAY OF THE YEAR.

JOHN HOLMES, as was his habit, walked rapidly through
the streets toward his residence, situated in the upper part
of the city, in a quiet but very respectable neighborhood.

It was just such a home as a wealthy, sensible, refined, but not fashionable man might have been expected to make for himself.   Nothing that could conduce to the comfort of the occupants, whether as regarded the gratification of correct taste or ministration to the merely physical requirements of life, was wanting, which his means allowed him to obtain.   It was a plain brick building, not overlarge, but yet of ample size, with ground enough belonging to it to afford its owner sufficient opportunity to indulge his horticultural inclinations to a reasonable extent.   Within, everything was comfortably and tastefully arranged.   There was a good-sized parlor, a large library, well stored with literary treasures, a nice little suite of apartments for his granddaughter, upon which he had been profuse in his expenditure of money, and a more sedate but grander set of rooms connected with the library, which were especially his own.

Besides himself and granddaughter, there was the housekeeper, the cook, the chambermaid, a gardener, a coachman, and a man who was half servant and half companion, whose particular duty it was to attend to a somewhat mysterious room, in which John Holmes spent a great portion of the night, and to which the reader will be introduced in proper season.

As John Holmes was arranging his toilet preparatory to dinner, he could not avoid thinking of the twofold character of the emotions which this day was calculated to awaken in his heart.   Seventeen years ago his daughter died in giving birth to the one who now filled her place, and who was the light and life of his existence.   Margaret Leslie had thus grown up under his own immediate care, nurtured by her grandfather as tenderly as though she had been his own child.   Her mother's sad history and her father's misdeeds had never been narrated to her, but John Holmes had come to the conclusion that he had no right to keep her longer in ignorance, and had resolved, now that she had finished her seventeenth year, to make her fully acquainted with all the events which so intimately concerned her.   It was a task which he knew would give him great pain, and which could not fail to cause distress to one who was very dear to him; but he was not the man to shrink from a clearly-defined duty because of any trouble it might cause him, nor even to spare his dear Margaret when a matter of right was in question.

As he crossed the hall which separated the library from the dining-room, he heard a soft step in the passage above, and in a few seconds Margaret Leslie, his dear grand-daughter, was at his side.

"So you are seventeen to-day, my darling," he said, putting his arm around her waist and drawing her into the room. "Come to the light and let me see how beautiful you are."

Margaret blushed, and, smiling, allowed him to lead her to the window.

"Yes, grandpapa, seventeen. Don't you think I am tall for my age?"

He stood before her with her little hands in his, and looked lovingly into her face. It was a very beautiful and intellectual and truthful face. There were masses of golden hair, a pair of soft, large violet eyes, a delicately chiseled, but not a meager mouth, teeth of dazzling whiteness, and a complexion which, while it rivaled them in brilliancy, allowed the color of the rich blood to be seen as when in sympathy with her emotions it came in greater profusion to her dimpled cheeks. She *was* tall for her age, but her full, round bust and unconstricted waist showed that development in that direction had not taken place at the expense of her vitality. There was a natural refinement of manner about her too, which was very different from the studied and artificial elegance which so many affect, and which, though perhaps more imposing to the superficial observer, is infinitely less charming in the eyes of those who know the false from the true. Her dress of simple, tasteful, but not common material, set off her graceful form to advantage, and altogether no one could deny that Margaret Leslie was one of the most beautiful of the daughters of men.

But there was something more than beauty in her countenance. There was an expression of frankness, of trustfulness, and depth of feeling which cannot be described in words. Everybody saw it, but few were capable of analyzing and appreciating it in all its immensity of truth and faith and love.

As John Holmes looked at her long and affectionately, he

saw that there was nothing in her face that did not express purity and goodness.   He pressed his lips to her fair brow.

"God forever bless you, my darling," he said; "you are very beautiful, and you are as good as you are beautiful. You are so much like your dear mother, that I can almost believe that these are her hands I am holding. But you are taller than she was, and your hair is a shade or two lighter, and I think that perhaps you have more strength of character than she had.   But she was very good, Margaret."

Never before had her grandfather talked to her so freely of her mother, and Margaret, seeing that he always avoided the subject, had never persisted in inquiries which evidently pained him to consider. She knew that in good time she would be fully enlightened, and she saw with her quick perception that the time had come.

"You are going to tell me all about my mother?"

"Yes, darling, after dinner we will go to the library and you shall then know all. It is a sorrowful story, Margaret, but not one to make you blush with shame for any crime of hers. You will love her more dearly, my child, and you will learn one more lesson which cannot fail to be of service to you in the life upon which you are now entering."

With this prelude, it was impossible that the dinner could be a very joyous feast to either John Holmes or Margaret. Both their hearts were full. The meal was therefore finished in almost complete silence, and the dishes upon which Mrs. Markland the housekeeper, and Susan the cook, had expended their combined culinary efforts were scarcely tasted. Even the old Madeira, of which John Holmes usually drank three or four glasses, remained untouched. Before the library fire, with Margaret's arm resting on his shoulder, John Holmes thus related the story of her mother's life and death.

John Holmes's Story.

"I have had but one child, my darling, and that one was your mother. She was left at an early age to my entire charge, for her mother died before we had completed five years of our married life.

"Margaret was as lovely a child as I have ever seen. I think I say this without being biased in my judgment. It was the opinion of all with whom she came in contact. Her disposition was affectionate, gentle, and confiding. In her education I had taken the utmost care. I could not bear the thought of intrusting the development of her mind to strangers, and therefore, with the exception of her music and drawing, which she learned at home from competent teachers, I took upon myself, with the assistance of my friend Goodall, this duty, which was at the same time the greatest pleasure of my life.

"And yet I did not keep her in seclusion. I knew well the dangers of such a course. Margaret's beauty and education, to say nothing of her prospective wealth, readily gained her many friends among refined and educated people; but she was not disposed to indulge to excess in the frivolities of a fashionable life. Her early associations had not been without influence upon her, and she never lost that love for her own home and for me, which made the gayeties of the world more irksome to her than pleasing.

"Among the families with which Margaret was most intimate was one named Sedgefield, consisting of a widow lady, her son, and daughter. Between Margaret and the latter a warm friendship existed. They were constantly together, their dispositions appeared to be very similar, and as Mary Sedgefield was a good girl, I was pleased that she and my child had become attached to each other. Of course the intimacy of these two gave many opportunities for Mary's brother, Matthew, to be thrown in Margaret's society, and as time wore on, I became aware of the fact that a stronger feeling than friendship actuated him in his attentions to my child. Still, even this was not displeasing to me. Matthew Sedgefield's previous history had been closely inquired into by me. I had carefully studied his character, habits, and disposition, with all a father's anxiety, and there was nothing with which I could find fault. On the contrary, high as I had placed Margaret, I was forced to admit that he was worthy of her, and therefore, had she reciprocated his affection, I should have given her to him with the certainty that her happiness in this world was secured.

"But with a father's watchful eye, I soon perceived that Margaret's attachment to him was no more than such as was the offspring of her friendship for his sister. For Matthew Sedgefield personally, I doubt if she had any very strong feeling, at least she never gave me the slightest reason to suspect such to be the case, and I often noticed her conduct under circumstances, when, if she had loved him, she could not have avoided giving evidence of her emotion. From what little I could gather from her, she appeared to think him wanting in manliness, but I was very certain she was mistaken in this opinion.

"One evening, as Margaret and myself were sitting in this room, Matthew Sedgefield entered, accompanied by a gentleman, whom he introduced as his friend, Mr. Leslie. He was a very handsome young man, with an easy, careless manner, and a fund of conversation, which made him very agreeable. I did not observe him with much particularity, but I was certainly pleased and amused with him, and Margaret also was struck with his vivacity, his extensive information, and the charming way in which he discoursed upon the most varied topics. There appeared to be no book that he had not read, no place he had not visited, no celebrated living personage whom he had not met, and about whom he could not relate some amusing anecdote. It may well be imagined therefore that my dear child was dazzled and bewildered. Mr. Leslie was quite a different person from Matthew Sedgefield."

Margaret Leslie had listened to her grandfather's recital without uttering a word. She knew he was talking of her father, but she dreaded asking a question, for she also perceived, what she had for years intuitively divined, that there were some painful circumstances connected with his career that it had been deemed proper to conceal from her. Her grandfather's last words were spoken with a depth of feeling and a bitterness of expression that left no doubt on her mind; still she said nothing. She dared not trust herself to speak, but she quietly stole one of her hands to his and motioned to him with her head to proceed.

"Again and again Richard Leslie came to the house, sometimes with Matthew Sedgefield, but often alone. From all that I had been able to ascertain in regard to him, I could perceive no reason why he should not visit my daughter. He was gentlemanly, apparently of good habits, and, as I have said, well informed above the generality of the young men met with in society. Still, as I became better acquainted with him, I acquired an inconceivable dislike for him. I resolved to conquer this because I deemed it unjust, and therefore I placed no restrictions on Margaret's intimacy with him. Would to God I had heeded my mysterious monitor !

"As I have said, I made due inquiries in regard to Richard Leslie's early life. From Matthew Sedgefield I ascertained that he was the son of a wealthy merchant, residing in Glasgow, in which place Sedgefield had met him two or three years previously; that he had been sent on a matter of business to this country; that he had always borne a high character at home, and that since his residence here his conduct had been unexceptionable. To my great regret, however, for I could not overcome my repugnance to Richard Leslie, I saw that he was deeply interested in Margaret, and I feared also, from many little signs, that she was pleased with him. Finally, one morning, he requested a few minutes' conversation with me, on, as he said, a matter of great importance. I knew what was coming, but I resolved to hear him through.

"He told me of his attachment to my dear child, and asked my formal consent to address her. He said he had not mentioned the matter to Margaret, for he desired to lay it before me first, and would abide faithfully by my decision, though he believed she was not altogether indifferent to him. In regard to his previous history, he told me precisely what I had learned from Sedgefield, and exhibited several letters to me in support of his assertions; among them was one from his father, addressing him as his dear son. I was pleased with what I considered his frankness and honor, but told him that before giving him an answer, I preferred to ascertain Margaret's views from herself, and that in no event could I consent to any engagement till his father had been communicated with and his approval asked. He expressed his entire acquiescence in my determination, and I was so much ashamed of my former-feeling of dislike for him, which I now was convinced to be utterly without foundation, that I gave him to understand, that if Margaret loved him, and no reasonable objections were urged by his father,

my full consent would be granted.   I will not dwell upon
this part of my narrative.   Suffice it to say that Margaret,
in her modest and quiet manner, gave me every reason to
know that she returned his love, and that in due time I received, through Richard, a letter from his father, expressing
his cordial approval of his son's marriage with my daughter.
There was therefore no longer any valid reason for withholding my consent, and yet I dreaded giving my dear Margaret to Richard Leslie.   To add to my uneasiness, I saw
that Goodall had also conceived a dislike to him.   As you
know, he and I have been friends for many years.   He is
one of the most honest, truthful, and faithful men I have
ever known, and I have always trusted very much to his
judgment in all matters of importance.   He had been very
fond of Margaret.   For several years he had taken great
pains to instruct her in many branches of learning, in which
few in this country possess anything like his proficiency;
and he had acquired a knowledge of Margaret's character
and disposition fully as profound as that which I had.   He
had also seen a good deal of Richard Leslie, and although
he never said a word calculated to prejudice me against
him, I knew from various evidences that Goodall disliked
him as much as it was possible for him to dislike any person.   Still I did not see my way clear to interpose any objection, especially as I could not shut my eyes to the fact
that Margaret thought her happiness depended on her union
with Richard Leslie, and therefore the marriage took place
when my dear child was in her twenty-first year.

"It was arranged that, after spending a short time with
me in New York, Richard Leslie and his wife should make
a visit to Scotland, and then returning to this country, he
should go into mercantile business for himself.   His father,
he said, would furnish him fifty thousand dollars capital.   I
had already settled this sum on Margaret; so that, as far as
pecuniary matters were concerned, everything looked promising.

"For several weeks after their marriage, I saw no reason
to regret the course I had pursued.   Nothing could exceed
Richard Leslie's devotion to his wife, and she was only
happy in his presence.   No one appeared to be dissatisfied
but Goodall and Matthew Sedgefield.   The former said or

did nothing which bore even the semblance of unkindness. He was often at the house and tried to look pleased at witnessing the happiness of her whom he regarded with so much affection; but it was impossible for him to conceal from me the fact that his mind was ill at ease. Sedgefield, after endeavoring, without success, to conquer his unrequited passion, went to Europe with his mother and sister. I have never heard from them since, though I believe they are still somewhere on the Continent.

"Week after week passed, and Leslie said nothing about going to Glasgow. I thought it strange, though I was very well pleased to have my daughter in the same house with me longer than I had expected. I observed, too, that he was not so constantly in his wife's society, and that sometimes he did not come in at night till very late; but he always, so far as I could judge, treated her with kindness and respect, and generally seemed sorry that she should fatigue herself sitting up for him. He excused himself for his late hours by alleging occupation with his father's business. Margaret's eyes were occasionally red and swollen at breakfast, as if she had been weeping, but I attributed this to want of sleep. Finally, I began to perceive that my poor child was unhappy. Leslie became more and more indifferent to her society, and once I was sure he had been drinking to excess. Still I did not think it expedient to seem to notice what was causing me great uneasiness. I knew there was no more thankless task than that of mediating between husband and wife unless the necessity was very apparent. I determined, however, to find out where Leslie spent his nights, and, one evening, when he left the house, I followed him. I tracked him to the most notorious gambling-house in New York."

John Holmes paused, overcome with the force of the recollections he had called up. Margaret covered her face with her hands, unable longer to restrain her grief. Her grandfather tenderly put his arm around her waist and drew her closer to him. They sat thus for several minutes, the silence only broken by Margaret's sobs, and then he continued:

"I stood on the pavement opposite the gambling-house for some time, trying to make up my mind in regard to the course to be pursued. I thought at first of entering, and accusing Richard Leslie of his wicked conduct in presence of his assembled companions; but upon reflection I determined upon a milder, and what I trusted would prove a more effectual procedure. I resolved to go home and wait for my son-in-law's return, and then as mildly and as persuasively as possible to point out to him his faults, and beg him to change a course which could only, if persevered in, cause us all unlimited sorrow, and him certain ruin.

"Nearly a year had now elapsed since my poor Margaret's marriage. I had written to Leslie's father in Glasgow, informing him of my views relative to his son establishing himself in New York, but had received no answer. From many circumstances needless to refer to, I was convinced that Richard's assertions in regard to his father's business in New York were unfounded. In fact, I was trembling with apprehension when I made the discovery I have just mentioned, and then my worst suspicions were confirmed.

"When I arrived at my home I came to this room and waited in sadness, not unaccompanied with anger, for my son-in-law's return. I resolved not to inform Margaret of what I had found out till after I had appealed to Richard himself; but after I had waited several hours, Margaret entered the room. She was very pale, and had evidently been weeping. I went forward to meet her, and she threw herself into my arms and sobbed as though her heart would break. I tried to comfort her, but in vain. The long pent-up anguish of many months had at last burst its bonds,—and where could it be so well discharged as on the heart of her father, now her best, and with one exception, her only friend? What added greatly to my distress was the fact that my dear Margaret was soon to become a mother.

"I led her to a sofa, and continued my efforts to calm her. I told her that there was yet hope of saving her husband; that come what might she still had her father's love to depend upon, and I begged her to remember her situation, and not to imperil the life of one whose existence would be so dear to her and to me; but for a long time she could do nothing but sob and moan. I saw that her hopes of happiness had fled, and that she knew how fruitless would be all attempts to reclaim Richard Leslie from his criminal

ways.   She knew how thoroughly false, wicked, and depraved he was, while I was not without hope that he had as
yet only reached the threshold of vice.

"Still, my last appeal to her had its effect, and she became
more composed.   As delicately as I could, and with every
appearance of entertaining hopes for a better future, I drew
from her the intelligence that Richard Leslie had obtained
from her the whole of the fortune I had settled upon her,
and that it had all been gambled away.   The last thousand
dollars had been given to him that day.   Though she stated
nothing directly on the subject, I saw that this was not all,
and that her husband had ceased to care for her.   It was
this, not the loss of her money, which was breaking my poor
Margaret's heart."

John Holmes's emotion now became so great that he was
unable to proceed for several minutes, while Margaret gave
unrestrained expression to her intense distress, as her head
rested on her grandfather's breast.   "My poor mamma, my
poor, dear mamma!" was all she could say.

"It was a sorrowful time that my dear child and I spent
waiting for her husband's coming, and we began to despair of his return that night, when we heard the front door
softly opened and shut, and the sound of footsteps in the
hall.   I had scarcely time to say a few words of encourage-
ment to her when Richard Leslie entered the room, accompanied by two other men whom I had never seen before, and
whose appearance was such as showed them to be even more
depraved than my son-in-law.   He looked very angry when
he saw Margaret; his face was flushed, his hair and clothes
in disorder, and his gait unsteady.   I saw a stormy time before me, but I was prepared for it, and had resolved to be
determined in the course I thought right.   Motioning to his
companions to be seated, Richard Leslie staggered to where
I sat with my arm around my Margaret's waist, and looking
her in the face, but without paying the least attention to
me, said, in hoarse and passionate tones:

"'What are you doing up at this time of night? Hatch-
ing a conspiracy against me, I suppose. Go to bed!' Then,
seeing that Margaret did not raise her eyes or obey him, he
strode up to her, and shaking his clinched fist in her face,
shrieked out: 'Go to bed, I say, or by the living God I'll
be the death of you!'

"Before the words were fairly out of his mouth I sprang to my feet and dealt him a blow in the face which sent him reeling to the floor; I then reached out my hand, opened the table-drawer, and took from it a pair of small pistols, which had been loaded for many years, but which were in good order, and holding them in readiness, awaited any assault the gang might make.

"When Richard Leslie fell, his two companions raised him from the ground, and a hurried consultation took place between them. I saw I had the advantage of them and I did not intend to lose it; I therefore cocked one of my pistols, and pointing it toward the one who appeared to be the leader of the party, ordered them to leave the house instantly. Leslie was completely stupefied with liquor and the blow I had given him, and was incapable of making any further attack, and I felt myself more than a match for the other two, especially as I perceived that they had no fire-arms with them. The one whom I addressed replied that he was sorry any trouble had taken place, and that they had come to see me to collect a draft which Leslie had given him for five thousand dollars, which if I would pay they would leave peaceably. Of course I refused, and advancing toward them with my pistol in my hand, I again ordered them to leave or I would fire on them. Muttering many curses, they laid Leslie, who was now almost insensible, on the floor, and hurriedly departed. I followed them into the hall, and locking the front door after them, returned to the room where I had left Margaret. I found that she had fainted, but the blood was returning to her face, and in a few minutes she recovered her faculties. I left her on the sofa, and calling the servants, directed them to go for the physician and Mr. Goodall, with whom I wished to advise. Leslie was still on the floor, breathing heavily. I then had my dear child carried to her room, and directing a man-servant to watch Leslie, I sat by her bedside till the doctor and Goodall were announced. I saw that she was going to be ill, and a few words with the physician, after he had seen her, confirmed my apprehensions. Leaving her in his care, I returned to the library, where Goodall awaited me. Leslie had so far recovered as to be able to comprehend what was said to him. He was sitting on the floor, looking very angry, and tried, though unsuccessfully, to get up when I entered. I hastily informed Goodall of what had happened; and then addressing Leslie, I ordered him to leave the house and never again to set his foot inside of it, and told him that so far as my influence would prevail, he should never see his wife again.

"He answered that he never wanted to see her again; that he had only married her for her money; that he not only did not love her, but thoroughly hated and despised her; and then, with a degree of *sang froid* which showed how hardened he was in crime, he said that he had been obliged to leave Scotland for having forged the signature of the firm to which his father belonged; that all the letters he had shown me were forgeries, and that ere long I would learn something more about him which I did not then know. He then left the house, and I have never seen or heard of him since.

"To say that I was horror-struck by these revelations, would not fully express the state of my mind. I was over-whelmed, stupefied, and filled with sorrow for the wrongs my poor Margaret had been obliged to endure, and for the blight which had been cast over her dear life. Goodall tried to soften the shock to me,—but what are words at such a time? Even as he was speaking, a severer and still more agonizing blow was being prepared for me. He was utter-ing language of promise and comfort, and Margaret was dying in the chamber above! I was unprepared for this ad-ditional affliction, although I knew that my dear child's condition was such as required the most tender care, and therefore when a message came from the physician request-ing my presence, I obeyed with a strong feeling of hope in my heart that he had good news to communicate. But the moment I saw the expression of his face, all hope vanished. In a few hurried but solemn words, he told me that though you were born, the life of your poor mother was slowly but surely ebbing away."

Again John Holmes stopped. Margaret made no at-tempt to speak. Her agitation was inexpressibly painful to him, and yet he felt that he ought to continue on to the end.

"I approached the bedside," he resumed, "and wiped her pale cold brow. She turned her eyes on me—those dark-blue eyes, my darling, which the good God has permitted me still to see in you—and tried to speak. She was too weak, for no sound came from her pallid lips. A little wine, which she was able to swallow though with great difficulty, somewhat revived her waning strength, and she whispered in my ear a few words, commending you to my care and begging me not to blame her husband too much for what had occurred. Even in her dying moments, her thoughts were of him who had treated her so cruelly. She was always very fond of Goodall, and therefore I was not surprised when she requested to see him. By the time he entered the room, she was again too much exhausted to speak, and could no longer swallow the wine which was held to her lips. 'She saw him, however, and as he took her hand and knelt by her side, her face was lit up by an expression of ineffable interest, and then the soul of my dear Margaret was no longer of this earth—she was dead. She gave her life to you, and now you know why I said that you would love her more after hearing the story of her death than you ever did before.

"There is not much more to tell, my dear child. I was very wretched; but why should I try to represent to you how bitter was my distress, how lonely and miserable I felt without the society of her who was all in all to me? In you, however, I found something to hope for, and thus in time I came to appreciate the fact that God rarely sends us a great sorrow without giving us something in compensation.

"As to Richard Leslie—I cannot bear to call him your father—fresh proofs of his wickedness came to my knowledge. A few days after your mother's death, two drafts for large amounts, having the forged signatures of my name, were presented to me. There was no doubt but that they had been uttered by him. I paid them without a word rather than let the world know the full measure of his depravity. A letter received from his father expressed the greatest regret at his falsehood, and gave me a full history of my unworthy son-in-law's criminal conduct in Scotland. It is needless for me to state any further particulars of it. My only fear is that he may still be alive and may some day attempt to take you from me. If that should ever come to pass, do not forget how he treated your poor mother, and how in every way he is unworthy the love of my darling."

Margaret's heart was too full for words, but she put her arms around her grandfather's neck and pressed her soft cheek to his.

"Do not try to talk to-night, darling," he said; "to-morrow you will feel more calm, and then I will answer any questions you may have to ask. In the mean time, thank God that neither in body nor in spirit do you bear any resemblance to Richard Leslie, but that your dear mother lives again in the person of her daughter. You will hereafter feel as if you knew your mother; you have heard a sorrowful story, but you will not regret it, inasmuch as it has been the means of revealing to you events which will seem as the framework for a new ideal world, from which she who gave her life for you will never be absent."

"Yes, grandpapa," said Margaret, through her tears, "I shall constantly see my dear mamma and feel that she is watching over me. Oh, if I could only be as good as she was! But how can I, grandpapa, when my father was so very wicked?" and again she burst into a flood of tears.

"God has made you unlike him, my darling, and in His goodness will keep you so. Since your poor mother's death you have been the chief joy of my life, and I feel that such you will always be. One thing more, dear child. I have something for you which you will prize above all earthly gifts. For seventeen years I have worn it next my heart, and now I give it to you." So saying, John Holmes took from his neck a gold chain, to which was attached a miniature set in a locket, which he put in Margaret's hand. Margaret's heart fluttered with joy as she gazed long and with intense emotion at the fair young face of her mother. She saw that she was strikingly like it, and, as she raised it reverently to her lips, she inwardly resolved to keep the image of her mother's person and virtues, which her grandfather's words had created, always fresh in her heart. Then thanking him for his precious gift, she kissed him good night, and, going to her own chamber, sat for several hours with her mother's miniature in her hand, deep in the reflections which her grandfather's story had awakened.

After Margaret left the library, John Holmes lit a cigar and paced the floor as was his custom. He liked a good cigar, and he liked to walk up and down the room while he

smoked it. He smoked, perhaps, somewhat more energetic-
ally than usual, and his pace was a little faster, for the smooth
course of his evening thoughts had been ruffled. He had
probably been thus engaged for half an hour, when a single
stroke of a bell interrupted him. He looked at his watch.
"Ten o'clock!" he exclaimed. "I had no idea it was so late!
I am afraid Joshua has had trouble again, or he would not
disturb me on this evening when he knows I am not in the
humor even for my favorite science." With these words,
John Holmes passed through the door at the farther end of
the library, crossed his bed-chamber, then a narrow passage-
way, and finally entered the room which formed the last of
the suite appropriated to his own special purposes.

CHAPTER IV.

JOHN HOLMES AND HIS MAN.

As John Holmes opened the door of the room in question, a scene was presented, which if not a strange one to
him, would certainly have been so to most people who witnessed it. The room was not large, being scarcely more
than twelve feet square, and was filled to its utmost capacity with apparatus of various kinds, furniture, and books,—
most of the latter, with their black calf bindings and brass
clasps, giving evidence of possessing a degree of antiquity
which no scholar could regard with indifference. At a large
table, which occupied the middle of the room, and which
was covered with retorts, beakers, flasks, and several forms
of electrical apparatus, sat the half servant, half companion
who has been already mentioned. He was a short, thick-
set man, perhaps forty-five years of age, with a bright, black
and rather good-natured eye, a nose strongly aquiline in its
character, and a wide mouth, which was tightly closed, and
which, when he spoke, he opened to a very slight extent,
and apparently with as much difficulty as though he were

laboring under the lock-jaw and a surgeon were forcing the
rows of teeth asunder with a lever to allow his words to
come out.   If ever a mouth expressed firmness, that of
Joshua did.   On his head was a skull-cap of black velvet,
trimmed with tarnished gold lace, which looked as if it
might at one time have done service as John Holmes's
smoking-cap, and his coat was very similar, both in material
and shape, to the one worn by the bookseller in his den.
Altogether, he was about as odd a looking old fellow as
one would desire to see, and though there was a lurking expression of good humor about his face, it was very evident
that he had a will of his own, which, when once aroused into
activity, could not easily be diverted from any pursuit in
which it had engaged or yield opinions which it had
formed.

As he sat at the table busily occupied, he did not observe
the entrance of John Holmes.   He held in his hand a small
test-tube containing a colored liquid, which he was examining with great care, holding it between his eyes and the
lamp, and occasionally shaking it violently.   Apparently
he was very much disappointed that the reaction he expected did not take place; but it would have been difficult to
have ascertained this from his face, his hurried manner
alone indicating any mental disturbance.   John Holmes
stood behind him unperceived, and also closely scrutinized
the contents of the test-tube.

"I hope I may be blessed forever and ever!" exclaimed
Joshua, at last, enunciating each word in a spasmodic sort
of way, as if his jaws objected to being opened for the purpose of allowing him to speak.   "I hope I may be blessed
forever and ever if I understand this at all!   It ought to
have turned blue, but instead of that it has turned red.
'Vanity of vanities, all is vanity, saith the preacher,' and
the greatest vanity of all the vanities is chemistry, or
rather alchemistry or alchemy, for that's just what it is,
neither more nor less.   Ah, my worthy friend, Henry Cornelius Agrippa, Knight, etc., you were right when you called
it a 'composition of trifles and inventions of mad brains.'
I don't think I ever appreciated your grand work 'On the
Vanity of Arts' till now.   Who but a madman would sit
here night after night boiling his brains over furnaces and

blowpipes, and inhaling all sorts of abominable fumes like I do? What is the use of it? What am I tryiug to do? Suppose some one should say to me, 'Joshua, what are you working at in the laboratory every night till twelve o'clock?' If I told the truth I should answer, 'Trying to make 197.' That is just it. Trying to make 197—neither more nor less. I have been at this job now till those figures are burnt into my brain, cooked in with the heat of oxyhydrogen blow-pipes and galvanic batteries. I never shut my eyes but I see two big fiery rings with 197 in blazing figures in the centers.

"I am sorry I rang for the master; but what was I to do? I have followed his directions, and it will not turn blue. We never shall make 197, depend upon it."

"Yes we will, Joshua, if we work hard," said John Holmes, coming to the table, and taking the test-tube out of Joshua's hand. "Why, see! it has turned blue while you have been talking."

And sure enough the fluid was now of a deep-blue color, when but a few minutes since it was dark red.

"Well, I hope I may be blessed forever and ever!" exclaimed Joshua. "So it is. Ah, sir, we will make 197 yet, and then we will be the greatest men in the world. Princes and kings will worship us, fair maidens will smile on us, and even such snap-dragons as Mrs. Markland will think well of us."

"Don't be a fool, Jóshua," said John Holmes, smiling at his companion's earnestness. "Don't be a fool, but attend to the matter before us, which is now at the most interesting stage of its progress. I see you have followed my directions."

"Yes, sir," replied Joshua, resuming his usual sedateness and spasmodic articulation. "I took every precaution, and, as you see, the result is just what you said it would be. I am very sorry though, sir, that I disturbed you; but I was at my wit's end when the color did not change."

"Well, never mind, Joshua. It was my own fault; I ought to have told you that it would not change for several minutes. You need not stay any longer to-night. You never talk about our work here, do you, Joshua?"

"Never, sir. No one knows from me what we are doing.

I never say what our work is outside of this room, unless it be in my sleep."

" 'That is right, Joshua. Of course we have the reputation of being chemists, and that we do not care for; but if the world suspected that we were alchemists, we should be laughed at, and considered crazy. Good night, Joshua,—good night!"

Joshua took his departure, and John Holmes was left alone. The test-tube, with the blue liquid, which had interested them both so much, was still in the stand where the former had placed it. John Holmes raised it from its position and held it close to the light. As he gazed at it a smile of intense satisfaction came over his countenance. "This," he said, musingly, "convinces me that I am on the right path. I have now proved that iodine is not a simple substance, but a compound of bromine and chlorine; that manganese and iron are isomeric conditions of one substance just as are the various forms of carbon; and that iridium and platinum, likewise, do not differ from each other except in atomic arrangement. More than this, I have advanced far toward showing that gold is a compound of several bodies, which are called elementary; and when I finish this demonstration, I shall bring my labors to a close. I will have done enough, and can be content to leave to others the glory of proving that there is but one substance in nature, and to others after them the awful duty of demonstrating this one and indestructible matter to be self-creative and godlike, if not Deity itself. The number of so-called elements must first be reduced. Newton and Davy did their parts well, and I will emulate them. There is but one substance. It is a bewildering thought, but it is true. All things living and dead are but modifications of it. Newton proved the diamond and charcoal to be identical. What is more strange than this fact? If he had announced it without proving it, people would have called him crazy, just as they would me if I were to say in public what I have said to-night in this room. Balthazar Claes, that grand creation of Balzac's mind, was mad. He was the victim of a single idea, and that makes one insane. He wasted his property and his life in searching for the absolute. I shall never carry my thought to such a state of exaltation as he did his. I love science, but I love my dear child more. Poor Margaret, how bitter must be her anguish when she recalls her mother's wrongs and her father's crimes! I would have spared her, had it been right. She knows all now, and should Richard Leslie ever make his appearance again, she will know how to regard him. I fear he is not dead. Why, I cannot tell. If he had lived, I should doubtless have heard of him in some way or other during these seventeen years. Yes, he must be dead, and yet I cannot avoid the apprehension which forces itself upon me.

"God knows I did not exaggerate his wickedness to Margaret. Many acts of unkindness to her poor mother were left untold. What I revealed was all true. I suppose she will be thinking of marriage some day, and then her mother's fate will not be lost upon her. I must take care, too—better care than I took when I allowed Richard Leslie to enter my house. Ah—well, well, time enough for that yet!

"Now, let me see how stands this subject of the compound nature of gold. First I must show that it is composed of different substances, or rather different forms of one substance. Next I must take these several constituents, and combining them in proper proportions, make gold. I shall thus have proved my point by analysis and by synthesis. Thus far I have obtained from pure gold, lead 104, silicium 22, sulphur 16, and nitrogen 14. The sum of their equivalents is 156. As gold has an equivalent of 197, I have still to separate those forms of my universal substance, the sum of whose equivalents amounts to 41. I assume the probable fact that oxygen and hydrogen are present in the proportions necessary to form water. I have several indications that this is so. If I am right, I have to recognize a form of matter the equivalent of which is 32; or, perhaps, two or more forms the combined equivalent numbers of which amount to 32. The former was more probable till to-night, but now I am sure that more than one form of matter is present. Copper, phosphorus, yttrium, and zinc have the same atomic weight of 32. This little test-tube contains the evidence that neither of them enters into the composition of gold. I think that will do for to-night. In truth, I must admit that I am unstrung by the memories I have recalled. Other thoughts than those of a scientific character occupy my mind. To-morrow, however, will find me more composed, and then I shall go to work with renewed ardor. I wish I had Kieser's book, not so much for any valuable information it contains—for those old alchemists were great humbugs—as for its value as a curiosity. Even if Goodall orders it to-night, it will be a month before it can arrive."

With these words, John Holmes, after arranging the apparatus on the table in the order in which he would probably use it at his next period of study, quitted the laboratory, and in a short time was sleeping as soundly as though nothing had occurred to disturb his mental quietude.

CHAPTER V.

IN WHICH THE HERO AND HIS NEXT FRIEND APPEAR UPON THE STAGE.

On the last day of the year, in a fashionable quarter of the city, and at about the time John Holmes was telling to Margaret Leslie the story which had caused her so much pain, but which had also revealed to her mental vision the image of her mother, and had thus opened in her bosom a new source of love, two gentlemen were sitting at a dinner-table, in a luxuriously furnished room, sipping their claret and carrying on a most animated conversation. Judging from the appearance of the side-table, the repast had been one with which the most exacting *gourmet* would have been fully satisfied, and the wine which they carried to their lips, in glasses as thin as an egg-shell and almost as fragile, coming as it did from the sunniest spot in the vineyard of the Chateau Lafitte, and being as it was of the vintage of one of the sunniest years, would have softened the heart of any anchorite capable of appreciating its delicious fragrance and flavor.

The one who appeared to be the master of the house was somewhere in the neighborhood of thirty years of age, and considerably above the average stature. His chest was

broad and full, and his whole frame gave evidence of great
physical strength. The expression of his features was intellectual; but few would have pronounced him handsome,
because few are able to see beauty unless there is a turn-
ing-lathe regularity of the lineaments, which may indicate
anything at all but force of character. The forehead was
both broad and high, and overhung the eyes, which were
rather deeply set, were large, and of that indescribable color
which sometimes appears to be black and at others dark blue.
His nose was neither large nor small, and though the outline was not Grecian, it was not *retroussé*. Some would
have called it aquiline and others Roman. The mouth
was larger than is regarded as altogether becoming, and
the lips, though somewhat full, could scarcely be considered
sensual, although they indicated warm and genial feelings.
His head was of full size, broad, but not so high arched as
to give evidence of weakness and superstition in its possessor, and there was an abundance of dark-brown curly hair,
which, however, like his beard, was kept short, and which
therefore allowed the contour of his head to be seen in all
its beauty of high mental development.

Though, as we have said, few persons would have pronounced Robert Severne handsome, scarcely any would have
denied that there was something about his face which rendered it worthy of more than a casual ·glance. Intellectu-
ality, quiet composure, self-reliance were there, so well
marked that they could not be overlooked; but there were
evidences of more impetuous and more passionate characteristics, which flashed up as he became interested in the
conversation, or as some exciting thought passed through
his mind, and then faded away, so that only the adept in the
study of the human countenance could have detected them.

Nor was this all. It needed no very careful scrutiny of
Robert Severne's face to be assured that he was not a
happy man, and it was this perhaps which excited so greatly
the interest of all with whom he came in contact. It aroused
a spirit of curiosity, it became a mystery; for why should
not he be at ease who apparently possessed all the cards
necessary to win in the game of life? Yet so it was; with
high physical health, with far more than ordinary mental
abilities, with correct ideas of his duties to God and to his

fellow-men, with habits and traits formed by a thorough moral and intellectual education, and with wealth which enabled him to gratify almost every wish, Robert Severne was unhappy. Hopes had been unfulfilled, desires had been ungratified, troubles had been endured, till little by little they had left their marks upon his countenance in lines and expressions so deep, that time and every element of material prosperity had been powerless to efface them.

It would have been strange, indeed, if Robert Severne's mind had not exhibited some traces of what his face so clearly revealed. He had learned to distrust others, to see through their pretensions, to discover motives when their owners thought them most securely hid, and to unveil the lies, the subterfuges, and the meannesses by which men seek to obtain their ends. Yet true and high toned himself, no one was more capable than he of appreciating in others those qualities which adorn the soul, and which, as it were, are the seal of divinity stamped upon an immortal spirit.

Had it not been for his literary and scientific tastes, Severne would have found, at the commencement of his trials, but little in life to give him pleasure. He had studied human nature, and had discovered its shortcomings; he had trusted in so-called friends, and had experienced the hollowness of their professions; he had seen those whom he regarded as upright and honorable men, shrink from their duty when right and expediency came in conflict; he had suffered outrage and indignity, when those who knew his innocence, and who should have vindicated his good name, kept silence rather than side with a losing cause. But in his books he had always found consolation; in his science he had always found truth, and thus he had been able to surround himself with a new atmosphere in place of the old from which he had fled, and to obtain enjoyment from sources which never failed to respond to the demands made upon them.

But experience showed him that this was not enough. As Aristotle has said, no one not a beast or a god can take pleasure in solitude. Severne had tried to isolate himself from the world, and he had failed. There were some friends who would not be cast off, who clung to him when misfortune was at its height, and with whom, consequently, when the bitterness of his grief had in a measure subsided, he delighted to hold intercourse.

Among those few who, having known Severne in former prosperity, had adhered to him in adversity, had never lost faith in his honor, nor from fear of any consequences to themselves had failed to espouse openly the cause which had nothing but its righteousness to recommend it, Edward Lawrence, who now sat at the table with him, stood first. There *are* those in the world who are faithful and true, who place their friends above themselves, who add to the joys, lessen the griefs, and yet never become the mere blind adherents, seeing perfection in every thought and act of those to whom they bind themselves. Such a one was Edward Lawrence. He could rejoice, sympathize, and advise with his friend. He could appreciate both excellences and defects of character, and never underestimated the one nor overrated the other. His influence with Severne had been and was very great. He had softened the cynicism which the latter was beginning to show, and though his mental power was not so ample as that of his friend, nor his education so extensive, there was so much good sense in all his thoughts, and they were urged with such moderation, and yet with such force, as to give them great weight with one who, like Severne, knew how loyal and true was the heart from which they came.

Lawrence, though not wealthy, obtained a sufficient income from his profession to enable him to enjoy the comforts and many of the luxuries of life. He was a physician, one of those who, not content with the science of medicine as they find it, seek with unceasing labor to enlarge its boundaries, and thus to render it more and more worthy of its divine mission. He was not what is called a genius, but he had a well-balanced mind, one fruitful in resources, and which never faltered in the face of dangers and difficulties of any kind. His thin, slight figure and pale countenance were not indicative of much bodily strength, nor even of robust health, and his features expressed thoughtfulness rather than vivacity. He was certainly not a "good-natured man,"—such are almost always weak,—and yet he never wantonly said a word or did an act which was calculated to wound the feelings of any one. On the contrary, his time, his services, and his money were given unstintedly to those who required and deserved them of him. In all these ways he had befriended Severne, and the latter never forgot the debt, nor ceased to remember that when others stood aloof, this one had been to him more than a brother.

"And so you think I ought to marry?" said Severne, poising his claret glass by its straw-like stem, and looking admiringly at its ruby contents. "For once, at least, I am able to answer you in a way which, as a native-born Yankee, you will doubtless appreciate in all its force. Why don't you get married yourself?"

"I intend to do so," replied Lawrence, with gravity.

"Oh, you do! You do not appear to be overjoyed at the prospect. Why, my dear fellow, your tones are as lugubrious as though you were telling me you feared losing your head instead of your heart."

"Are they?" replied Lawrence, smiling. "Perhaps it is because I really think one is about as serious a matter as the other, though certainly much more agreeable. I speak earnestly because I feel the importance of the step I contemplate. Having definitely made up my mind that I shall increase my own happiness, and perhaps that of another mortal, by marrying, I am naturally desirous of indoctrinating you with my ideas, and therefore, my dear Severne, I have given you at least ten good reasons why you should follow my example."

"And what is there in marriage so pleasant that I should again voluntarily bind myself in its chains? Do you think, Lawrence, that I have forgotten the bitter experience of the past; that all its torturing lessons have been in vain, or that love with me is a passion which, when once burned out, can, phœnix like, rise again from the ashes of my heart? Can I look back upon my married life and find one single spark of light in the abyss of darkness? Do not, therefore, urge me to do that from which my whole soul revolts. I am well enough as it is, and cannot hope to be happier than I am now, blessed as I am with your friendship."

"And yet, my dear Severne, you are not happy. You overburden yourself with the memories of sorrows which have long since been dissipated. You brood over the past as if it were a thing of to-day, when, in fact, no one element of it remains. Your circumstances, your position are altogether different. You married mainly to please your father, and from what was an exalted but mistaken sense of duty; now you would do so to please yourself, and with the soberness arising from a mature mind. You were then too young to appreciate the importance of the step you took, and consequently you ventured upon it rashly, with no thought of the future. Now you are of riper age, with both more reason and more experience to guide you. Heed the lessons which the past teaches you, but take them at their proper value. Unless you have made up your mind that there is no hope of your finding a good and true woman who will be your wife, your ideas are unreasonable, and if you have formed such an opinion, you have done so on a very insufficient basis, and the sooner you get the notion out of your head the better it will be for you."

"And I have very nearly arrived at the conclusion which you denounce so positively. Since my sojourn in this country, I have seen but one woman I would have been willing to make my wife, and of course I have no idea of trying my fortune again in England. As I say, there was one I might have loved, but I could not permit myself to yield to the allurement, for I had nothing then to offer her but a life of poverty and hardship. Besides, I do not think she cared particularly for me, and since then she has married, and is happier far than I could have made her. Why should I make it longer a secret? You, Lawrence, must know to whom I refer."

"My sister Mary? I never suspected this," said Lawrence, sadly. "You should have confided in me, my dear friend, and perhaps it might have been as you and I would have wished. I think Mary at one time was interested in you; but you seemed to shun her society, and I know she acquired the idea that you disliked her. I knew better than this, but I attributed your avoidance of her to another cause. How little we both understood you then! As to the poverty, believe me, Mary would not have minded that when shared with one she loved."

"I think I might have loved her," said Severne, musingly. "She was like you, Lawrence, though cast in even a more delicate mould. She was very beautiful, too, when I saw her last, just before she went to Europe; very proud of her husband, and very happy. Don't distress yourself over it," he continued, addressing his friend; "Gilman is a good fellow and worthy of her. Remember, too, that I did not actually love her, except as your sister, and as a noble and true-hearted woman should be loved by her brother's friend. That she was interested in me I believe, but it was the interest excited by sympathy and by your attachment, not by any particular regard or admiration she had for Robert Severne. In fact, Lawrence, I doubt very much if I am capable of exciting the emotion of love in the heart of any sensible woman. I suppose if I were to try, I could get married without much difficulty; any man with fifty thousand dollars a year can. But, as you know, such a marriage would not suit me. I must have true, unaffected, devoted love—the love that shrinks at nothing, that sees in its object a divinity which it worships, in which it trusts, and for which it is ready to die if need be. You see I expect a good deal. I do not even make friends readily. I dislike to form new acquaintances. People say I am haughty and over-bearing in my manners. Perhaps I am so to some persons. To those I like I try to be the reverse; but sometimes I am painfully conscious of failure It is unreasonable, therefore, to expect that a young, beautiful, intellectual, and warm-hearted girl, with a soul as fresh as a May morning, could ever love so seared and wearied a mortal as I am; one who takes nothing on faith, who is suspicious, who has lost the bloom of youth in a precocious maturity, and who is therefore unfit to have his life bound up with that of an innocent, hopeful, trusting woman. In place of a heart, she would find a cinder; in place of confidence, caution. In time she would lose all her artlessness. She would become experienced. An experienced woman! What that is unfeminine or unlovely is not embraced in the phrase? It is bad enough when applied to men—to woman it is disgusting. And so, my dear Lawrence, I think it would be wicked for me to entrap such a one as I have described into a life-long union. Do not, therefore, urge me further. You know how influential your arguments are with me, and how in the end I generally yield to them. Perhaps it is because you are so often right. You may be so in this instance, and therefore

I ask your mercy. Let me alone at least for the present. Time may bring me to see the matter as you do; but I can conceive of nothing more repugnant to my sense of delicacy and to my whole nature, than setting out deliberately in search of a wife, with as much self-possession as though one were going on a hunting or fishing expedition. Take a cigar, my dear fellow, and tell me who is to be Mrs. Lawrence. I would rather talk about you than about myself at any time."

"I think you do yourself great injustice," replied Lawrence. "There are many women worthy to be your wife, who would regard you with more favor and more fairness. You are distrustful of your own powers, and unconsciously exaggerate the difficulties of your position. I think I know you better than you know yourself, with all your experience and all your study. You have a degree of self-will and strength of character which few possess. You have only to resolve that you will break through this dark wall which shuts you out from society, and my word for it, you will be successful. You have no right to seclude yourself from the world. You have intellect, good looks, education, a love for art, wealth, and many other qualifications which men and women regard with favor. You can take any position in life that you choose. As it is, you spend your days and nights in reading musty books, or in working in an ill-ventilated and overheated laboratory. Even your physical health, magnificent as it has always been, is beginning to suffer, and your brain cannot long withstand the influence of such a pernicious system. Be warned in time."

"My dear fellow," said Severne, laughing, "I am sure I ought to be very much obliged to you for the extremely flattering character you have given me. I see now that I have only to announce myself as in the matrimonial market, to be inundated by applications for the honor of becoming Mrs. Severne. Your last two arguments are almost irresistible. Let me see; suppose I send an advertisement to the newspapers somewhat in this style: 'A gentleman, thirty years of age, good looking, of high intellectual development, superior education, refined tastes, and considerable wealth, to say nothing of many other endearing characteristics, is desirous of making the acquaintance of a worthy

young woman, who will regard him with a more favorable
judgment than he can conscientiously give to himself. He
takes this step, not from any particular desire to be married, but because his health has been broken down by excessive literary and scientific labor, and fears are entertained by
his medical advisers that his reason may likewise soon give
way. It is hoped by his friends that the change of associations incident to the condition of matrimony would lead to
his complete restoration. A lady experienced in taking care
of invalids preferred.' To be sure, some far-seeing people
might say, 'Poor fellow, the anticipations of his physicians
have been already realized!' but it would make no difference. I should get a wife, my life would be saved, my reason preserved, and I should be happy. Now, Lawrence, I
have taken a fair view of your proposition and opinions,
and I must say, with all due respect, that I think they are
very ridiculous. I don't overexert myself with my books
and laboratory. My health was never better, and as to my
mind, it may not be much to boast of, but it is at least as
good as it ever was. Besides, it is preposterous for you,
one of the hardest students in New York, to find fault with
me for spending a large portion of my time in occupations
which are not only congenial, but which I trust make me a
better and a wiser man every day."

"My dear fellow, I am glad to have amused you, but
should have been much more pleased if you had taken my
remarks more seriously. You may not now feel any ill consequences from your mode of life, but be assured they will
come. It is only a few days since that a well-known literary
gentleman consulted me in regard to his case. 'For God's
sake, put me to sleep,' he said, 'I have not closed my eyes
for two weeks!' He was too late; yesterday he was taken
to Bloomingdale. Flesh and blood and brains are strong.
With care they wear well; but they are not stone and iron,
and some of these days you may perhaps discover it for
yourself."

"But I am not like your literary gentleman," replied
Severne. "I go to bed late, but I sleep well. As soon as
I feel the least symptom of giving way, I will get you to
put me on my pins again; and in the mean time, as you
wish it, will think seriously of what you have said. As you

say, I am not happy. It wonld be strange, indeed, if I were. Would to God that my flesh and blood and brain were stone and iron, or something else as unimpressionable! Then I might enjoy a sort of idiotic contentment, which would be preferable to my present condition. But enough of this. You have not informed me yet who is to be Mrs. Lawrence."

"I do not know yet myself. I am looking out for her with as much deliberation, to use your idea, as though I were hunting for a wild duck or trying to hook a fine trout. I have simply made up my mind to marry some one, and don't intend to be in a hurry about it. By-the-by, now that you have come into possession of a large estate in England, will you not find it necessary to return there for a short time?"

"No, I think not. Freeling manages all my business matters for me. I sent him over a short time since, and he reports that my presence will not be required. There was no dispute in regard to the property. My father's will was perfectly in form, and all the real estate was entailed. I have no very near relatives, the next of kin being a second cousin, residing somewhere in Cornwall, whom I have never seen, and to whom the legacy my father left him having been paid, there is no necessity for my making his acquaintance. A visit to England would be very distasteful to me in every way. I do not think I shall ever again see the land of my birth."

"You ought not to say so," said Lawrence. "It appears to me that you ought to make it a point to return, if only for the sake of letting those who formerly annoyed you see that you have not only lived, but have prospered in spite of them. Doubtless the pretended friends who once cast you off would now be the first to assure you that they always trusted and believed in you."

"Of course they would, as Pompey reminded Sylla, 'more people worship the rising than the setting sun.' It may be very wicked, but it is very human to love your friends and hate your enemies. I am afraid I do both right cordially. An open, undisguised, and persistent enemy claims my respect as well as my hate; but for the fawning sycophants who crowded around me, smiling when I smiled, frowning when I frowned, who appropriated my thoughts, ate my dinners, drove my horses, borrowed my money, and then, at the first shock of disaster, held up their hands in pious horror, and by their innuendoes and silence gave a coloring of truth to the wicked lies of my persecutors,—for them I cannot express the extent of my loathing and disgust. It would be very pleasant, certainly, to meet these people in my changed fortune, and to witness the chagrin they must feel and could not conceal. My dear Lawrence, if I should conclude to return to England, will you go with me?"

"So there is an emotion which can be excited in you!" said Lawrence, smiling. "Although it is very different from the one I hoped to arouse, it is far better than the state of passive indifference to everything into which I fear you are drifting. You wish to triumph over your enemies? A very worldly, but not a very Christian wish. You know that I have never thought you perfect, and this last revelation of your thoughts confirms my judgment. However, I shall not scold you for it. As to going with you to England, how can I? Unlike you, I am obliged to work for my living. No, no; go by yourself, and leave me here to take care of my patients and find a wife."

"I don't think I shall go in any event, but if I should you must accompany me, and more than that, you must allow me, as the expedition is entirely for my benefit, to look after all the expenses. My physical and mental condition is so very critical, you know, that it will be impossible for me to travel without a physician. Well," he continued, lighting another cigar, "I'll think it all over. There may be something in what you say, but really, I never felt better or stronger in my life. Labor comes natural to me; I should not be able to exist without it, so that like you, my dear Lawrence, I too am obliged to work for my living. I almost wish I had to work for my bread again, for now one of the chief inducements to exertion, one from which there was no escape, is removed, the consequence is that my work is not so effective as it used to be, and I am consequently afraid of degenerating into a state of superficial amateurism from which it would be difficult for me to extricate myself."

"No fear of that. Why, Severne, you are one of the

most constant and steady students I know anywhere. I
have seen many men, in Germany especially, who carried
their labors to a very extreme point, who would write a vo-
luminous treatise on the digestive organs of an earth-worm,
or on the difference between free agency and free will, or
on the presumptive qualities of some hypothetical substance,
but I never met with one so thoroughly capable of exhausting a subject as you are. That is the trouble with you. If
you would be less persistent, and resolve to leave those who
follow you something to do, you would not cause so heavy
a drain upon your vital powers, a drain which you may not
feel now, but which is exhausting you slowly but surely.
You need relaxation, change. A wagon driven always in
the same rut wears the road away. I am not such a fool as
to wish you to give up your studies, and become a mere
loiterer in drawing-rooms, with no thought above the fit of
your gloves or the color of your neck-tie. Even such a life,
however, would in many respects be preferable to yours, for
people who lead it never lose their minds at any rate. Give
yourself a respite every now and then. Go to a ball occasionally, subscribe for a season at the opera, take a run to
the prairies, or make your trip to England, and your studies
would be far more profitable to yourself and the world, too,
than they are now. Do you know why I am boring you
with my presence so long this evening? Simply because I
know that as soon as I am gone you will go to your library
and write till three or four o'clock in the morning. It is so
seldom that I get a chance at you like this, that I am determined to take full advantage of it."

"Do so, my dear Lawrence," laughed Severne. "If you
will promise to dine with me every evening I shall be perfectly willing to forego that much from my literary labors.
As to going into society I cannot. I am unfit for it. I
know nothing about the last fashions in music, dancing, or
perfumery. I have no small talk, and women don't care for
men who have not. Where should I go to find a thoroughly
educated and sensible woman, one who, without being a blue,
could talk intelligently upon something above crochet and
the lancers? I know there are such, but where do they live?
Not in Fifth Avenue to my knowledge. Find me one, my
dear fellow, and I will make her acquaintance immediately."

"It would not be difficult to find a dozen or more even in Fifth Avenue," said Lawrence; "and if you are serious in giving me a commission to seek one for you, I may safely promise that not many days will elapse before you will be gratified by having one pointed out to you. But you must give me the requisite facilities, otherwise I can do but little. My friend Mrs. De Lisle gives a ball next Thursday. Her daughter Alerta is a very pretty and sensible girl, and there will be many others there still more beautiful and intelligent. Leave a card there to-morrow, and you will receive an invitation. Let me manage the rest."

"Very well, Lawrence, I yield. Have it as you will. You always conquer me, I believe, outwardly at least, though I seldom change my opinions in consequence of your arguments. I am an obstinate, unreasonable fellow, I know, but I can't help it. However, if not convinced, I, at any rate, place myself in your hands to be managed and shown off to the best advantage. You are my keeper, and I promise to be as docile as a lamb or an ass, whichever you choose. Will you ring that bell by your side? I feel that I need another cup of coffee after this discussion. However, I must ask your permission. It might interfere somewhat with certain faculties of my nervous system, and consequently do discredit to the high-colored portrait you will draw of me. You must give me some idea of how I am to behave; am I to be grave and silent, waiting to be attacked, or am I to be gay and voluble, making my onslaughts with vigor as soon as I get the cue from you? Am I to be a man of the world, skilled in all the subtleties of human nature, especially the nature of women; or am I to be fresh and verdant, a student whose whole life has been spent in meditations in philosophy, and who knows no more of actual life than a snail does of the pragmatic sanction? Am I to be like myself— a fool, or am I to sail under false colors like a knave? The fact is, I shall be both fool and knave. Bah! I am ashamed of my weakness in having consented to such an unnatural proceeding. I know how it will end, however, and that is the only consolation I have in regard to it. I shall become ten times more firmly set in my opinions of the world than I am now. I shall hate the sight of women, with their twaddle, their schemes, and their hypocrisies, their silly laughs, their artful glances, their conventional exclamations, their artificial ways, stripped as they are by a false system of education, extending from generation to generation, of almost every beautiful attribute of their intellectual and physical natures. As for the men, imbeciles that they are, I cannot despise them more heartily than I do now."

"Well," exclaimed Lawrence, "what a tirade! One would think you had just been jilted, to hear you talk. My dear fellow, be reasonable, leave all to me, hold me to a strict responsibility, and act like the true, noble-hearted man that you are. Come, drink your coffee (no more for me, thank you), put on your hat and cool your brain by a walk in the moonlight. You certainly must require it after that ferocious ebullition."

"Just as you please," said Severne, with an accent of supreme resignation. "I am yours, body and soul. Faust was never more completely sold to the powers of evil than I am to you, and, like Mephistophiles, your bribe is a woman. That contract, however, turned out rather disadvantageously for all concerned. Let us hope this will have a happier termination."

The moon was shining brightly, but the night was intensely cold, and they consequently met but few persons on their way down Fifth Avenue. As they approached Madison Square, a thin, squalid figure darted out of one of the cross streets, and in most piteous tones begged for a little money. Lawrence gave her a small piece of silver, but Severne looked at her with attention. He saw that she was scarcely seventeen years old, that she was rather pretty, and that her whole appearance betokened the most abject poverty. He asked her several questions, and then, apparently satisfied with the result of his examination, took out his purse and put a ten-dollar gold piece into her hand. The child looked at it stupidly for several seconds, as if doubting the evidence of her senses, and then, stammering out her thanks, darted away in the direction whence she had come.

"That girl is honest, I will wager my life," said Severne. "I have a great mind to follow her. Did you notice with what perfect artlessness she answered my questions? She has trouble at home, depend upon it, for the tears came into her eyes when I asked her about her mother. I tell you, Lawrence, I would have a much better chance of getting a good wife if I were to take that girl, educate her, bring her up as a lady, and then marry her, than I would by looking for a wife in any of these grand houses."

"Perhaps," said Lawrence, quietly. "A friend of mine tried that once, and his dear ward ended the matter by running off with his coachman. The chances are ten to one yours would do likewise, and it would certainly be a dangerous experiment for you to try."

Severne made no reply, and at the next corner the two friends parted, Lawrence to visit a patient and Severne to retrace his steps homeward. He did so slowly, for his mind was occupied with what Lawrence had said during the evening, and he was deliberating with himself as to the probable termination of the plan the latter had proposed, when he heard voices and laughter, and the next moment a man and woman turned into the Avenue from a cross street, immediately in front of him.

Both were apparently in a state of great glee, the man especially, who kept up a continued chuckling over something which seemed to give him intense satisfaction. They were so close to Severne that he heard every word that was said by either, but it was some little time before he caught the thread of their conversation.

"Well," said the man, "that's one of the best things I've heard for many a day. Won't Bill laugh when he hears it? My Lord, how green some people are! How was it, Sal? Tell me again, you do it so good. Ha! ha! ha! A gold X! Lord, but you are sharp, Sal! I guess you must have been to school on Sunday."

"Well, you see, Jack," said the woman, laughing immoderately, "it was right along here when I saw two chaps a coming down the street arm-in-arm like, as if they was sweethearts. I had just started out on a lark, because you see we was all hard up, and I told Jim Terry to order the drinks and something hot, ready by the time I came back. When I went down stairs, I just took off my petticoat, pinned up my frock, tied an old piece of carpet over my head for a shawl, and then you see I was all right. Well, who should I see but the two coveys as loving and green as two pigeons. I said to myself, now I'll get a half, perhaps. I went right up, and says I, 'My mother is sick, we've no work, and I've had nothing to eat to-day, please give me a little money.' Well, the little one—I think I know him, and a good fellow he is, too, if he is the man—put his hand at once into his pocket and pulled out a quarter dollar, which he gave me, but the big one looked mad-like, and I thought I had waked up the wrong customer.

"'What's your name?' says he.

"'Sarah Tompkins, sir,' says I.

"'What's the matter with your mother?' says he.

"'Oh, sir!' says I, 'she's got the consumption so bad she can't work, and Mr. Barton, the minister, who used to come to see her and bring her things to eat, and pray with her, is sick too.'

"'Have you no father?' says he.

"When he said this I hung down my head as if I were ashamed, and said nothing.

"'Have you no father?' says he again.

"'Oh, yes,' says I, putting my hand to my eyes, 'but father is very unkind to us all, and we haven't seen him for a long time.'

"'Well, well,' says he; 'I know Barton. He is sick as you say, my poor girl, but you shall not suffer in consequence.' And then he took out his purse and put a ten-dollar gold piece into my hand.

"'Here,' says he, 'take this. Get something to eat, and I'll see Mr. Barton about you all, and send a physician to see your mother.'

"Of course I took it right off. At first I thought it was a penny, but it was too heavy for that, and besides, I saw it shine in the light. So I said 'God bless you, sir!' and off I ran as fast as I could. Wasn't that a smart dodge of mine about the preacher? You see, I found out this morning that he was sick from a girl in our street that goes there to get cold victuals. That settled the matter with my cove. He thought he was mighty smart, but I guess Sal Tompkins is as sharp as any of them."

"Smart! Lord bless you, Sal, I should think you was," said the man. "But won't we have a jolly time of it? Who's going to be there, Sal?"

"Well, Jim Terry—that's my man you know, Jack—and Bill and you and the Dumpling and Betsy and——"

Severne wished to hear no more, and therefore slackened his pace till the two had passed far up the street out of ear-shot. He was mortified that he who prided himself on his penetration should have been so easily deceived by the transparent piece of deceit that had been practiced upon him.

"It will only serve to put me on my guard against more refined and therefore more dangerous deceptions," he thought, as he entered his house. "And if it does that, the lesson will be a thousand times worth the cost. The young hussy, to think that she should have humbugged me so easily! I, who have run the gantlet of the most scientific beggars of the world, to be taken in at my time of life by a child like that! Falsehood and deceit on every side," he continued, as he entered his library—"everywhere but here. Here at least nothing passes for more than it is worth. And here I almost feel as though I would be content to pass every hour of the life that remains to me."

CHAPTER VI.

IN WHICH THE READER IS MADE ACQUAINTED WITH SOME OF SEVERNE'S THOUGHTS AND DESIGNS.

NEW-YEAR'S DAY had come and gone. Goodall had dined with John Holmes and Margaret, and had told the whole story of Mother Piggot, who, rather than allow her little granddaughter to be burned as a witch, had voluntarily confessed herself to be in league with the devil, and to have inflicted all the torments upon the boys and girls of the village which had been ascribed to little Susan, a bright, blue-eyed child, over whose head but twelve summers had passed. Mother Piggot was seventy years old, gray-haired, wrinkled, and toothless. Yet she had a noble and a self-sacrificing spirit in her decrepit body, so she resolved to save her little grandchild, with the certainty of being deprived of her life for being a witch, and the risk of losing her soul for telling a lie. The place on her body which the devil had touched when he made his covenant with her was found; pins and needles were stuck into it, and she did not wince. Of course, therefore, she was a witch, and so she was burned at the stake. "O man, man! to what a pitch will not thy folly and stupidity carry thee!" Little Susan Piggot was left homeless and friendless. However, after many trials and troubles she did very well in the world, and had numerous descendants, among whom, to his great pride, was Goodall himself.

Mrs. De Lisle's ball had taken place, and Severne had so far yielded to Lawrence's entreaties as to accept the invitation sent him. It had passed, however, wearily enough for him, and left him tenfold more disgusted with life, especially the fashionable life he saw there, with its pretensions, its inanities, and its ridiculous assumptions, than he had been before for many a year.

He had kept to himself the knowledge he had acquired from Miss Sarah Tompkins relative to the swindle she had successfully practiced upon him. In the first place, it would not have been pleasant to expose what he could not but regard as an act of weakness, even to so intimate a friend as Lawrence, and in the second, he was considering in his own mind the expediency of endeavoring to obtain a further insight into that young woman's character and associations.

The more he reflected upon the matter, the more attractive it became. That this young girl was hopelessly depraved, he did not believe. To find out and to develop the good that was in her; to subdue, if not altogether eradicate the evil; to educate her mind to a knowledge of those things that ennoble the soul; to kindle into a flame that latent spark of divinity which God has implanted in the breasts of all mankind,—this were indeed a task worthy of him: an object to which he could devote his energies with unchanging ardor until the end should be reached, and he should find his reward in the consciousness that he had been the means of redeeming a fellow-mortal from a life of ignorance and crime.

What was there in life to promise him half the pleasure that the contemplation of this measure unfolded? What joy could equal that to be derived from watching, day after day, the growth of new feelings, the awakening of new thoughts, the springing up of emotions which had never yet been excited, the birth and expansion of all that was lovely, the destruction of all that was vile, and to feel that it was his work? There was happiness in all this; there was a purpose to be accomplished, one that would engage his best thoughts for years to come, and which of itself would expand his contracted heart and light up again the hopes which long years of disappointment had well-nigh crushed out.

He might fail, however, and it were well to consider the subject from this point of view. That this young woman's associations had been and were of the lowest kind, there could be no doubt. That she was bold, brazen-faced, immodest, unchaste, false, ignorant,—in short, so low in the social and moral scale of humanity, that even he, with all his worldly experience, could scarcely conceive of any lower grade, he had the evidence of his senses to prove. Through the precocious development of the worst impulses of human nature, she had become so debased that the difficulty of bringing her to virtue would prove almost insurmountable. There would doubtless also be trouble in getting her to accede to his wishes. The paths of vice are often as pleasant as those of virtue, and this young woman was probably very well contented with her lot. Why then should he, for the gratification of what was in a great measure a selfish wish, seek to induce her to undertake the drudgery and submit to the restraint inseparable from her novitiate in the new life to which he contemplated introducing her? If it had been altogether a matter of self-gratification, Severne would have abandoned it at once, but with every disposition to regard his own predilections with the most complete impartiality, he at the same time was forced to admit that, entirely aside from any pleasure he might derive from the success of his plans, he should be doing a good service to one of God's creatures. Severne had very high ideas relative to his duties to his fellow-beings. He was perhaps not what the world calls a philanthropist. He would have declined giving a contribution toward translating sectarian tracts into the Timbuctoo language; but the misery, the want, and the ignorance which he saw on all sides, he was always ready to alleviate by every means in his power.

Thought with Severne always led to definite results, and that too without delay. The more he pondered in his mind his schemes relative to Sarah Tompkins, the more he was pleased with them. He had not considered the subject more than a few hours before he had formed the resolution of at once making the attempt to reclaim that young woman from her evil ways, and the next thing, therefore, was to devise a plan for getting her within the range of his influence. This was a matter which really required more consideration than the first, and he did not as yet feel himself at all qualified to deal with it to the best advantage. He had no difficulty in arriving at the determination to conduct in person all his negotiations with Sarah; but how to find her, was a question he was not prepared to answer. However, he set about the task with a good deal of energy. The little beggar girl, from whom Sarah had obtained the information that Mr. Barton, the clergyman, was sick, had not made her appearance at the house of the latter for several days, but Severne left word that when she came again, she was to be brought to him at once. Day after day passed, however, without any intelligence. In all his walks and drives, he kept a sharp look-out for the young woman he was in search of, but he never obtained so much as a glimpse of her. He always had the alternative of the police to resort to, but this was reserved till other means should be clearly proved to be ineffectual, as he had a great repugnance to asking the aid of these gentry in an affair which, for the present at least, he was desirous of keeping as quiet as possible. Without therefore abandoning his purpose or relaxing his personal efforts in the search which he daily made in localities likely to be frequented by such characters as the one he was so anxious to find, he betook himself with renewed diligence to his literary labors.

The work to which Severne devoted himself was of a kind demanding most intense thought and the most constant application. A train of reasoning once entered upon, could not be interrupted without detracting from the unity

of design and thoroughness of execution which he was desirous of making prominent features in the new system of
philosophy he was constructing; many of his ideas required
demonstration of their correctness, and hence difficult and
delicate experiments were necessitated. Severne never did
anything by halves. A subject which he undertook to in-
vestigate was always pursued with a degree of ardor and
perseverance which was truly astonishing. No part of it
was left untouched, no source from which it was possible to
gain information was unheeded. He not only made himself
acquainted with what others had done, but he went over
the ground for himself, followed their reasonings, repeated
their experiments, modified and extended their researches,
and struck out many paths which led to new and often un-
looked-for discoveries.

It was not without cause, therefore, that Lawrence had
admonished him to be less studious—less persistent in the
one direction to which his labors led. His friend knew well
the danger attending long-continued concentration of the
mind upon one line of thought; how the brain, feeding as
it were upon the products of its own decay, wears itself
away little by little, but with awful certainty, till either nothing but the shadow of its pristine greatness remains, or
else the reason, utterly breaking down, finally becomes ex-
tinguished in a condition of hopeless insanity.

Nor was Severne disposed to question Lawrence's arguments. He knew they were correct; but, like others who
have their hearts in their labors, he was not to be easily
diverted from them. Probably no inducement, based upon
purely personal considerations, would have proved strong
enough to cause him to change his mode of life. The episode
of Sarah Tompkins had therefore been doubly beneficial.
It had reawakened emotions which had slept for years, and
it had in a measure been the means of abstracting his
thoughts from subjects to which, with almost unceasing
resoluteness, they had been devoted.

But the relaxation was not of long continuance, and,
though he every day for an hour before dinner continued
his search for Sarah, he more than made up for this slight
respite by extending his studies further into the night. Having arrived at a decision relative to his course toward that

young woman, he ceased to occupy his mind to any great
extent in regard to her or her future life. What he did in
the way of endeavoring to find her, was a mere mechanical
fulfillment of his views so far as he was then able to fulfill
them. He had no doubt in his mind but that he would ere
long meet with her, and, until that event occurred, he had
no wish to change the great current of his thoughts. There
were occasionally moments of uneasiness and of irresolu-
tion—as there are in the lives of the most devoted students—
but they were only moments, and were as nothing in the
long hours he gave to the studies which had for years engrossed so large a proportion of his mental energies. Nothing would have persuaded him to give them up altogether;
but had he been successful in finding Sarah Tompkins when
he first conceived the plan which, in its freshness, had seemed
to him so attractive, it is very probable the time given
to his philosophical pursuits would have been materially
abridged. As it was, he was becoming more and more absorbed in them. Day after day, and night after night, found
him in his library or laboratory, working at those problems
which have engaged the attention of the mightiest intellects
the world has ever seen, and which even yet are apparently
as far from solution as when, ages ago, man emerged from
barbarism and began to inquire into the laws which govern
his intellectual and physical existence.

Never before had Severne labored with so much ardor;
and at last he began to show evidences of the state of body
and mind which Lawrence had predicted with so much posi-
tiveness. The latter urged him with renewed earnestness
to abate a little in his zeal; but he might as well have addressed his arguments to the wind, for Severne was not in
the slightest degree influenced by them. He still continued
a passive search for Sarah Tompkins, but it was more because he felt that his faith was pledged to find her, and to
give her the opportunity of rising in the world, than from
any particular interest he took in her.

Both Severne and Lawrence were frequenters of John
Holmes's book-shop, and held this worthy old gentleman,
and his coadjutor Goodall, in high estimation. Before
Severne had become so deeply enraptured with his studies
as at the period he is introduced to the reader, it was his

daily custom to spend an hour or two in "the den," to which place Lawrence also usually repaired about the same time. Latterly, however, he had become less regular in his attendance, and although he did not altogether discontinue his visits, it was evident that his attention was given to other pursuits, from which he could not divert it. Neither Holmes nor Goodall, however, gave themselves any uneasiness on this score. They knew that Severne was a hard student, and being students themselves, they were able not only to excuse his apparent neglect, but even to feel proud of the devotion he manifested, and which they had so largely aided in exciting and continuing, by furnishing much of the material by which it was kept alive.

One morning, as John Holmes sat at his table busily writing on the little half sheets of paper which nearly covered it, Goodall came to the door of "the den," with an open note in his hand.

"Here is an order," he said, "for some twenty or more books from Mr. Severne, not one of which we have in the shop. We shall have to procure them all from Europe, and I fear there are several which, from their great rarity, we shall not be able to obtain."

"Twenty books, and not one of them on hand!" exclaimed John Holmes; "I scarcely thought, Goodall, that we should be caught in this way. Let me see the order."

"There is not a bookseller in the world who has a third of these books in his stock," replied Goodall, as he handed the note to his senior. "Mr. Severne knows too much about books to order those which cannot be had at all; but if he had deliberately set out to make a list of twenty books which it is possible to find for sale, and yet are extraordinarily scarce, he could not have succeeded better than he has in this instance."

"Why, what can the man be thinking of!" exclaimed John Holmes, as he looked over the list. "I never heard of any of these books except Camfield's Theological Discourse of Angels. I am afraid Severne is perpetrating a joke on us *a la* Count de Fortfas. If he collected books from any bibliomaniacal propensity, I should not be astonished at his wishing to obtain such rarities and out-of-the-way productions; but I have often heard him say, he only bought books for use, and if that is his principle, I cannot conceive what benefit he can derive from some of these. Magic, secret poisoning, hallucinations, and such trash, are not very edifying subjects in these days."

"Mr. Severne wants to use them at once, he says," remarked Goodall. "There are three of them which I have in my private collection, and which I will lend him with pleasure; but he will be obliged to wait some time for the others. I do not see anything strange in his wanting these books. You know he is writing a New System of Philosophy, and with his usual thoroughness he is desirous of covering the whole ground."

".No; I did not know anything of the kind. How was I to know it? He comes here now so very seldom, and is so uncommunicative, that I have not been able to form an idea in regard to the present direction of his studies. I knew a year ago that he was deep in philosophy, but I thought he had finished that long since."

"No; he is carrying his labors far beyond the point he at first contemplated, and has even yet a task before him which would appall most literary men. But he is so assiduous that I am very sure he will complete his project, and that we shall, in the result of his labors, possess a rich mine of thought and information."

Scarcely had Goodall uttered the last words when he heard the door of the shop opened and gently closed, and a soft step approaching "the den." It was not often that women came to the old place. The books which were kept there were not of a character to interest the sex. A few there were who knew all about the shop; where the Elzevirs, the Aldines, and the Pickerings were to be found; who could talk learnedly of Plato, Spinoza, and Stewart; who read the Lusiad in the original, and sympathized with Urban Grandier in good French; but they were few, and if the truth must be told, lamentable though it be, of scrawny figures, scraggy necks, orange complexions, and not over-young. Why is it that so few pretty women delight in literature? What is there incompatible between beauty and learning? Here is a subject worthy of the profound attention of the psychologist and the physiologist. Ill-natured and ignorant men might say that only those women who have learned by experience that they are not sufficiently beautiful to command the attentions of the sterner sex take to books. But this is not the true reason. Facts do not sustain it. Sensible men do not regard mere beauty in a woman as the one attractive feature. A truer explanation may be found in the circumstance that nature very seldom so highly favors her creatures as to endow them with both personal beauty and a love for learning. She sometimes ventures on the combination, and then those whom she thus befriends, be they men or women, are irresistible.

Goodall, as soon as he heard the light step and the musical and measured rustle of a silk dress, looked into the dismal shop with a brighter face than he had exhibited that morning. No woman who visited the shop trod with so firm, so gentle, so youthful a gait as Margaret Leslie. Before he could do more than advance a few paces toward her, she was close enough to give him her little hand.

"Ah, my dear Miss Margaret," said Goodall, "it is not often we see you down here. If we did, we should be obliged to remodel the old place and make it more suitable for so charming a visitor."

"So you think I am really a charming visitor, do you, Mr. Goodall?" said Margaret, smiling. "Do you know, I think you are trying to bribe me into coming here more frequently! Now, if you would only make half a dozen windows in that long wall, whitewash the ceiling, clean the paint, and dust the books, perhaps I might be induced to pay you a daily visit. But I heard you talking to grandpapa as I came in; I want to speak with him for a few minutes, and then I am coming to get a book from you."

John Holmes met Margaret at the door of "the den," his face radiant with pleasure at the sight of the beautiful and joyous girl who was so dear to him. It was not often that she came to the shop, for it was a long way "down town," and the journey involved no small risk of life or limb in treading the narrow and crowded thoroughfares which led to it. John Holmes knew, therefore, that it was a matter of importance which brought her to see him that morning, and after greeting her with his warm-hearted manner, and leading her to a seat on the sofa, he awaited with some anxiety the disclosure of the object of her visit.

Margaret did not allow him to remain long in suspense.

"Dear grandpapa," she said, still letting her hand rest in his, "I do not know whether I am overanxious or not, but I cannot help fearing that you will be very much inconvenienced by what has happened this morning. I thought it best, however, to inform you at once of all that has occurred, because the mischief may not be irreparable. It is my fault, too, which of course does not make it any better."

John Holmes felt a pang shoot through his breast while Margaret was speaking; his first idea was that her father had made his appearance again at the house, but this was dissipated as he observed Margaret's feeling to be rather one of annoyance than of apprehension.

"I hope, my dear child," he said, "that whatever has happened has not distressed you. As for me, I am too old and hardened to be much affected by any ordinary trouble."

"I am annoyed on your account, dear grandpapa, and vexed at myself. I went into your laboratory after breakfast, a place into which, as you know, I rarely venture, and seeing a flask containing a liquid of the most beautiful purple color, I took it up to examine it more closely, when to my great surprise it suddenly became perfectly solid. I did not know what to make of the transformation; but Joshua said I had destroyed the labor of two years, and made me feel so badly about it that I came down to tell you of my meddlesomeness. I hope, dear grandpapa, it is not so bad as that."

"And is that all you have to worry you, my darling?"

"Yes, grandpapa, that is all, and if I have made your work of two years fruitless, as Joshua said, I am sure it is enough."

"Joshua is an ass; what business had he to tell you any such nonsense?"

"He is very much distressed, dear grandpapa. He sat down on the floor and cried and muttered over the mishap for an hour and more. You know he is almost as much interested in the laboratory as you are."

"Poor Joshua!" said John Holmes, musingly; "he is very faithful and very devoted. But give yourself no uneasiness, my darling; the accident is not irreparable, nor even very serious. If anybody else had done it but you," he continued, smiling, "I might have been somewhat irritated; but what could make me angry with my dear child?"

"Oh, I am so glad you forgive me!" said Margaret, putting her arms around his neck; "I will never again touch anything in the laboratory, or even go into it, unless you are there. You know, dear grandpapa, that I am sorry, very sorry, and if I could do anything to atone for my thoughtlessness I would do it at once."

"Then never open your lips upon the subject again," said John Holmes, kissing her forehead, and thus deranging her *coiffure*, which was as pretty and tasteful a piece of hairdressing as one would wish to see. "All will soon be right. Why, if you were to destroy the whole laboratory and all its contents, instead of merely hastening the crystallization of one of my solutions, I should not mind it a very great deal."

"But if you go on destroying my bonnet, I shall mind it a great deal, for I am not so generous as you are," said Margaret, smiling, and laying her face against his. "Of what importance is a whole chemical laboratory compared to a bonnet? You see, dear grandpapa," she continued, earnestly, "that you have made me very happy again. I know that I have disarranged and retarded your studies, but I also know that I should give you real pain if I did not accept your forgiveness as freely as you offer it. Now I shall never say anything more about it, but you will not therefore think that I am not truly sorry for my heedless act, or incapable of appreciating the kindness which makes you underestimate the extent of my mischief."

"And is there nothing else I can do for my darling?" said John Holmes. "It seems a great pity that you should come all the way down here through dirty streets and money-making men for such a trifle. By-the-by, talking of money. How are your own finances?"

"Oh, I am as rich as I want to be," replied Margaret. "I have only spent half of the hundred dollars you gave me last month. If it were not for the few deserving people whom I am able to assist, I should never be able to get through my allowance. I think I must have over sixty dollars in my *porte-monnaie*."

As Margaret spoke these last words, she put her hand

into her pocket and felt for her *porte-monnaie* to show her grandfather how much money she had; to her surprise it was not to be found. "I am afraid I have lost it," she continued; "but I do not see how that can be, for I certainly had it a few minutes ago. A young woman asked me for a little money for her sick mother just as I reached the door, and I took it out and gave her a half dollar. I recollect distinctly putting it back into my pocket, but it must have slipped out of my hand in some way or other."

"My dear child," said John Holmes, smiling, "the probability is that the young woman whose imaginary necessities or those of her fictitious mother you relieved, seeing that you had a well-filled purse, picked your pocket of it."

"Oh, grandpapa, I can scarcely believe that of her; she had such a good face and looked so sick and miserable that I asked her where her mother lived, for I intended to go and see her and do what I could to relieve her wants. Do you think the girl, who was not older than I am, could have been so wicked as to steal my pocket-book, and yet look so honest, too?"

"I do not know, my dear child. Perhaps I wrong her; but there is so much precocious depravity in a large city that it makes us wary of all young beggars. Did she tell you where she lived?"

"Yes, she gave me her direction. Dobbin's Court, Baxter Street, and told me her name was Sarah Tompkins."

"I will send Thomas to ascertain if any such persons live there, and to make inquiries about your pocket-book. The latter is almost a useless undertaking, however. I have a great mind to send a policeman with him."

"Oh, do not, dear grandpapa. At least not yet. Let Thomas go first and find out what sort of people they are, and whether or not she told me the truth about her mother."

"Very well, my dear Margaret, it shall be just as you wish; and as you are now bankrupt, you must take this to aid in repairing your broken fortunes." With which remark, John Holmes took from his pocket-book a hundred dollar note and put it into Margaret's hand.

"Thank you, dear grandpapa," she said. "I think I have had a great deal of conceit taken out of me by my

day's proceedings ; and now good-by till dinner. Do not
forget to send Thomas to Dobbin's Court in time for you
to tell me all about his discoveries when you come home."
And then, declining the carriage which her grandfather was
anxious to send for, Margaret went into the shop, and after
getting the book she wanted from Goodall, passed into the
busy throng in the street. She had scarcely got out on the
pavement, when a gentleman, whom she did not know, but
who regarded her with a very anxious and with as much of
an admiring look as was respectful, made way for her, and
passing by her, entered the door she had just closed.

<hr>

CHAPTER VII.

THE MEETING OF MARGARET AND SARAH, AND THE EFFECT UPON
THE LATTER.

MARGARET cast a glance toward the spot where she stood
when our young friend Sarah Tompkins asked her for
money. Of course her pocket-book was not there ; at least
a thousand people had passed in the hour that had elapsed,
and even if she had dropped it, some one, whether honest or
dishonest, had picked it up. If the former, it would be advertised ; if the latter, it was vain to expect it to be returned.

She had not gone far, when a voice by her side said :

" Will you let me speak to you for a moment ?"

She knew it in an instant, and turning, saw, as she expected, Sarah Tompkins; but looking even more miserable
than when she had first accosted her.

"I cannot say all I want to say here in the street," continued Sarah, "and it does not look well for a young lady
like you to be seen walking with one of my kind. I've been
waiting for you to give you your pocket-book which I stole
from you. Here it is, with all the money, just as it was."
So saying, Sarah placed the *porte-monnaie* in Margaret's
hand.

"And did you really take it?" said Margaret, sorrow-fully.

"Yes; I took it out of your pocket."

"You must tell me all about it," said Margaret. "Per-haps this is the first time you have done such a thing."

"No, it is not the first, nor the second, nor the third. I am a very bad girl, I know, but I am not bad enough to do you an injury in cold blood."

"Why did you bring my pocket-book back to me?"

"I don't know. Perhaps it was because you spoke kindly to me, and are so beautiful. It was not that alto-gether, either, for others before you have been kind, but I never felt as I did when I found your pocket-book in my hand. It seemed as if I was holding a coal of fire."

"I am not ashamed to be seen with you. Walk with me a little farther, and tell me something more about yourself. I cannot think you are as bad as you represent yourself to be. Have you never felt sorry before when you have taken what was not yours?"

"Never."

"Is your mother sick, as you told me this morning?"

"I have no mother."

"Do you not live in Dobbin's Court, Baxter Street?"

"No."

"All false?"

"All lies."

"And yet, Sarah, you do not look like a bad girl."

"Then my face lies as well as my tongue."

"Will you tell me where you really do live, so that I can come and see you? Perhaps I can do something for you. I am very much obliged to you for giving me my pocket-book again. I am sure you must be very poor or you would not have taken it."

Sarah hesitated. She knew that her home—if the house she lived in deserved so holy a name—was not one that Margaret could come to. But though hardened in vice, Sarah had a warm and generous heart, and as she looked into her companion's face, and met her kind and sympathiz-ing expression, the tears came into her eyes.

"You must not come to where I live," she said, with emotion. "It is not a fit place for one like you; but if you

will let me, I will come to you.   You are very good to me,
and some day I may be able to serve you.   Whenever you
want to see me, send a note to Sarah Tompkins, at 110
Wayne Street, but do not come yourself."

"Have you no brothers nor sisters, nor any one to take
care of you ?"

"I have no relations ; but there are plenty who, so long
as I am useful to them, treat me kindly enough.   But you
must not ask me any more questions now.   Perhaps some
other time I will tell you more. God bless you ! This street
leads to where I live, and I must go."   With these last
words, Sarah grasped Margaret's hand, and pressing it,
turned hastily down a side street, and was soon lost in the
crowd.

Margaret pursued her way, thinking over this last adventure, which had made the day one to be remembered by
her.   Before forming any plans for the future with regard
to Sarah Tompkins, she determined to submit the whole
matter to her grandfather for his advice ; but at the same
time it was impossible for her to avoid feeling very much
interested in one who, acting from some uncontrollable impulse, had restored the money she had stolen.

In her conversation with Margaret, Sarah had dropped
the swaggering tone and the slang phrases she had used
when her language was heard by Severne as she walked up
the Fifth Avenue before him several months previously.
Sarah was sufficiently impressionable to be affected by the
beauty and refinement which Margaret possessed.   She was
a shrewd, sensible girl, too, and knew perfectly well that
there would be an incongruity between the fulfillment of her
moral obligations to Margaret and the ordinary tenor of
her speech, which would be out of place.   She was perfectly
sincere in all the feeling she had exhibited.   She had taken
Margaret's pocket-book without stopping to reflect, and
probably as much from the influence of habit as any other
cause.   But when she had it in her possession, she began
to think.   Margaret was apparently about her own age, and
the most beautiful girl she had ever seen. This last circumstance of itself had great influence with Sarah.   Women
generally, unless actuated by jealousy, admire beauty in
their own sex fully as much as men do, and are as easily led

by it. Margaret had spoken very kindly to her, and had given her money, trusting in the story told to her. Sarah had probably not been influenced much by these facts. She had withstood them before, and had frequently laughed at the simplicity of those who had been duped by her wiles. And yet she felt unpleasantly with Margaret's property in her possession. She had hurried off to an unfrequented alley, had opened the pocket-book, and had found it to contain a greater sum of money than she had ever before possessed at one time. The temptation to keep it was very great; but something· made the act very repugnant to her. Sarah was not sufficiently trained in the habit of self-examination to be enabled to probe her motives to their source in this instance. She simply knew that she should be happier by returning the pocket-book than by keeping it. That was enough for her. And so she replaced the notes, closed the *porte-monnaie*, and started back toward the place she had seen Margaret enter. When she reached the door of the shop, she was uncertain whether Margaret had gone or not, or whether it would be expedient for her to enter and inquire for her. While pondering these questions in her mind, she further occupied herself by reading the words painted on the sides of the entrance ; and though she found it a rather difficult task to decipher the old English text, she managed to make out that the establishment was one where books were kept for sale. Turning then to the windows, she put her face close up against the glass and endeavored to make out the interior of the shop. This was even a more laborious undertaking than the other ; but after receiving many erroneous impressions she succeeded in getting an idea of the arrangement within. She could see the tables of books, the door of "the den" far in the background, and, as it was open, could see into the *sanctum* itself. There was no sign of Margaret, however, and Sarah was beginning to despair of meeting her, when she saw the flutter of a woman's dress in the more distant apartment, and recognizing the color as like that of Margaret's frock, she sat down on the door step to wait for the exit of her of whom she was in search.

Sarah had not been long seated when, happening to turn her eyes toward one of the windows, she perceived a gentleman looking very intently at something within which seemed to afford him a great deal of pleasure. She was so much struck by his manner and expressions, that she did not scan his features very closely at first; but when at last she did so, she was somewhat annoyed to find that he was the same who had given her ten dollars nearly six months since in the Fifth Avenue. There was no cause known to Sarah which could disturb her equanimity at meeting with Robert Severne, except the consciousness that she had perpetrated a fraud upon him. She was unaware that he had heard the conversation between herself and her male companion, which took place shortly afterward, or that he had been looking for her ever since that occurred. Had she known these circumstances, she would have been still more anxious than she was to avoid Severne's observation. It was impossible for her to rise from her position without running a greater risk of attracting his attention than she did by remaining seated and averting her face, and so, turning her head aside, she waited impatiently for his departure.

But Severne did not appear at all disposed to "move on." He had evidently found something which interested him, and having, by the most strenuous exertions, caught the run of the sentences on the open face of the books which were displayed, did not seem inclined to relinquish his position till he had read them through. At last, however, he apparently discovered a book which gave him extraordinary pleasure.

Sarah could not distinguish what he said, but it was very evident to her that he was both surprised and delighted. Why he should be so much excited over an old musty book was a mystery to her. She turned her face toward him in order to observe his demeanor more closely, for she was becoming interested. But though she saw that he was speaking, she could scarcely hear his voice, much less distinguish his words, and as to the book, she could not see it at all.

Having finished his scrutiny, Severne turned to enter the shop, and Sarah, seeing that if she remained she would certainly be discovered, started suddenly up and ran rapidly in the opposite direction. Just as she passed the door, she saw Margaret come out, and, almost at the same moment, Severne entered without having had his attention specially attracted by the meanly-clad girl who flitted away at his approach.

As soon as he was fairly within, Sarah turned, and by dint of fast walking shortly overtook Margaret. The result of the interview is known to the reader. Sarah's good intentions had not been interfered with by the fact that she had recognized Severne as the gentleman whom she had swindled out of ten dollars. On the contrary, her determination to refund Margaret's money was strengthened. Why, was not very clear to her mind, for she certainly felt no such disposition toward him; and had the opportunity offered, she would in all probability, if she had thought herself secure from detection, again have made him the victim of her artful proceedings.

Sarah walked rapidly down the cross street after leaving Margaret, until finding that the latter had continued her course toward Broadway, she turned and took the same direction. She had been much impressed by Margaret's demeanor. There had been no long harangues on the sin of stealing, no offers of tracts, no appeals to her to change her mode of life. And yet every tone had sunk into her heart, every word was fixed indelibly in her memory, every look spoke to her of sympathy and love. For the first time in her existence she began to form for herself an ideal of goodness. She had no definite thoughts of changing her mode of life; such a thing did not even occur to her. She merely saw and acknowledged the fact that Margaret was far above her in the possession of the power that virtue gives, and she began therefore to experience a feeling for her approaching to adoration.

In the possession of what is called "worldly wisdom," Sarah Tompkins was very far the superior of Margaret Leslie. She was perfectly aware of the fact that she was not a proper person for Margaret to be seen walking and talking with in one of the most frequented streets of New York, where at any moment she was liable to meet acquaintances. At the first opportunity, therefore, Sarah had taken her leave, intending however to follow Margaret, unobserved, till she discovered where she lived.

With this view she continued on in the direction she had seen Margaret take, and soon caught sight of her. She kept far enough away to avoid all risk of being discovered, should Margaret chance to look back, and thus followed her till the latter, leaving Broadway, finally entered her own house and closed the door after her. Allowing a safe interval of time to elapse, Sarah resumed her course till she also arrived at the house she had seen Margaret enter. She merely stopped before it long enough to read the name on the door and to fix the number in her mind; and then, retracing her steps, crossed Broadway, and hurried away toward the western part of the city.

"I could not bear to let the night pass without finding out the name, and where she lived," said Sarah to herself, as she walked along. "I don't know though why I should think so much about her. It isn't very likely her father will let her have anything to do with me. She knows where I live, and I know where she lives. Holmes; she must be the daughter of the man who keeps the book-store she was at this morning. I wonder what her first name is! I hope it's prettier than Sarah. Holmes, though, isn't much prettier than Tompkins."

"Halloa, Sal, where are you going so fast that you don't see your friends?" said a big, burly, red-faced, but good-looking man, who had opened his arms and caught Sarah in his embrace, as with downcast eyes she pursued her way. "Lord, but you are a precious armful, Sal!" ·

"Let me go, Bill, and don't do that again. Where I'm going, is none of your business. You just mind your own concerns and I'll mind mine."

"Well, you are one of 'em, Sal, and no mistake! Why, Lord bless you, what's the use of you getting mad with me?"

"I ain't mad, Bill; but I won't be stopped by any fellow when I don't want to be stopped. I've got other things to think of besides you."

"Yes, Sal, you are a regular college gal, I know, deep in learnin' of all sorts. You know what kind of cheese the moon's made of as well as any other gal in New York. I heard this morning that you was going to run for Congress. Is it true, Sal?"

"Not quite so true as that you are running for Sing Sing."

"Good for you, Sal.   I always said you could hold your own with any man, even with me.   Now, I'm going to tell you a nice little secret, just by the way of showing my confidence in you.   There's to be a big lay to-night."

"Where, Bill?"

"Oh, over there at the house of a rich old codger, who has more money than he knows what to do with."

"Over where, Bill? In what street?"

"Well, I don't exactly know the place. Jack Duggan got it up.   He says it's the best thing he's found for a long time.   What luck have you had to-day, Sal?"

"Not much. I got fifteen dollars out of a fellow's pocket in Wall Street, but that's all."

"Not much that, Sal. Now as for me, I never feel quite right unless I make my fifty dollars a day. I expect to make a thousand to night."

"Who are in besides you and Jack Duggan?"

"Only Jim Terry."

"Is Jim in?"

"Oh, yes; we could not do without Jim.   He's one of our best men, you know; and besides, he's always the life of any crew he's in. He has his joke about everything. I don't see through half of his fun, but the other fellows do, and so I laugh with the rest of 'em. Just now I asked him where he was a going to-night, and says he, ' We're going to our old homes,' and then Jack and Betsey laughed fit to kill themselves, and I laughed too, but just to keep them company; for blowed if I see anything funny in telling a fellow that asks a civil question, which he has a right to know, that he's going home, when he ain't going to any such place."

"Going to your old homes? Why, what did he mean by that, Bill?"

"You'll have to ask him, Sal, for his jokes are too deep for me."

"Homes! Homes!" repeated Sarah.   "I don't see anything to laugh at in that. My God!" she continued, a sudden light seeming to burst upon her mind.   "Can it be possible?"

"Well, I'm all mystified completely with Jim Terry's jokes. You know, Sal, I'm not a fool by no manner of means. Nobody ever said I was. I may not have much high sense; but when it comes to things in my line, I'm just about as sharp as any of 'em. But Jim Terry's jokes just take all the starch out of me. First one party laughs like a lot of monkeys, and then another party goes off into fits, and says, 'My God, can it be possible?' And all because of Jim Terry's joke."

"Never mind, Bill, it will all come right, I guess. I was thinking of something else just then, something I forgot all day, and just recollected. As you say, I don't see anything funny in Jim Terry's jokes, and, to my mind, he makes too many of them. I'm going home now, and I'll tell him he's a fool."

"Good-by, Sal! We don't start till about two o'clock, and I'll see you again before we go. You'll have something hot for us, won't you?"

"Oh, yes, Bill! I'll get you up something nice before you go, and have a good hot drink ready for you when you come back."

The two separated; Sarah to proceed on her way home, and Bill Smithers to complete an errand upon which he had been sent. Sarah knew that it was not worth while to attempt to find out from him any particulars of the proposed expedition. Although perfectly trusty, so far as his intentions were concerned, Bill was too loquacious and simple-minded to be trusted by the gang to which he belonged with any information except that of the most general character. His chief value to them consisted in the facts that he was possessed of immense physical strength, and was always ready to obey all orders which were given him not involving any great restriction on his faculty of speech. Sarah was certain, therefore, that Bill had told her all he knew, and that any further details must be obtained from the other members of the party. She felt very sure, however, that she had discovered the true meaning of Jim Terry's joke, and the fact that the young girl, whom she began to regard with so much love and admiration, was an inmate of the house to be visited, gave her a great deal of uneasiness. She was fully cognizant of the fact that the gang of which her particular friend, Jim Terry, was captain, and Jack Duggan a prominent member, was one of the most desperate and determined of the many similar organizations existing in the city. Gamblers, burglars, and pickpockets by profession, they were not likely to stop at murder, if the perpetration of this crime should become necessary to accomplish their ends or secure their safety. It was not without reason, therefore, that she was alarmed.

As Sarah hurried toward her home, one thought was uppermost in her mind, and that was how to prevent the success of the burglarious scheme which had been conceived by her associates. It would have been very easy to stop all further movements by going to the nearest police station and causing the whole party to be arrested, but with all her desire to save Margaret from any possible injury, it was not a part of her plan to bring her friends into trouble. There was still plenty of time, however, for her to obtain additional knowledge relative to the proposed robbery, and to resolve the whole subject further in her mind, before the necessity for taking action would arise. To find Jim Terry was therefore her first object, and as her relations with this gentleman were of the most intimate character, she had no doubt in regard to complete success in getting from him all the information she required.

CHAPTER VIII.

MENS INSANA IN CORPORE INSANO.

On the evening before Margaret's visit to her grandfather's shop, Severne sat in his library almost concealed from view by the piles of books which covered the table, and even the floor around him. He had stopped his labors for the moment; and was leaning back in a comfortable armchair, indulging in thoughts altogether foreign to the subject of his studies, and which were doubtless rendered far more vivid by the highly-flavored Cabañas cigar he was smoking.

No one who had seen Severne six months previously, and who looked at him now, would have failed to perceive the great change which had taken place in his appearance. He

had evidently been "losing ground" physically.   His whole
frame was less compact, his countenance was pale and hag-
gard, and betokened a degree of mental anxiety very foreign to the indifference which prevailed when Lawrence
had endeavored to arouse him into activity. With even
greater rapidity than Lawrence had predicted, the mental
and physical ill health, against which he had deemed it his
duty to warn his friend, had become established, and at last
even Severne could no longer shut his eyes to the certain
termination, if he continued to outrage the laws of his
being.

Within the last two weeks certain symptoms had occurred
which gave him uneasiness.   He had had several attacks of
vertigo, and on one occasion had almost lost consciousness.
The page he was reading, suddenly became blurred; the
words ran into uninterrupted lines; he heard a buzzing
noise in his ears, and his head fell forward on his breast.
It was not for long, however. In a few seconds he was himself again, or rather almost himself, for he felt a degree of
lassitude which convinced him that his system had received
a serious shock. In addition, he was tormented with almost
constant headache, and at night scarcely closed his eyes in
sleep.

As has been said, he was beginning to be alarmed, when
an event occurred which determined him to lay his case
before Lawrence, and to ask his advice. He had still at
least six months' steady labor before him ere his present
studies could be brought to a satisfactory conclusion. To
break off, leaving them unfinished, would have been to subject himself to a great trial, and yet in his present frame of
mind he could not so collect his thoughts as to weave them
into a connected train of reasoning, for a misfortune had
happened to him so great as to take precedence in the sorrowful list of all those which had been allotted to him. For
five days and nights he had not been out of the house, and
in all that time had scarcely tasted food of any kind. The
future, never very brilliantly painted, which he had hoped,
however, might be at least unmarked by more than ordinary
trouble, was now darker than it had ever been in his most
despairing moments. What could he do? To think was
maddening, for there was one thought he could not banish

from his mind, and yet it would force itself upon his attention. He had resolved, therefore, to send for his friend, to unburden his mind to him, and to have, at least, the consolation of sharing his sorrow with one who would not fail to comfort him to the utmost of his ability.

For five days, however, he had not been able to bring himself to the point of asking Lawrence to come to him. As soon as he had concluded to do so in the first instance, he addressed a note to him, but when he came to read it over previous to inclosing it, he found to his sorrow that he had written words conveying a far different meaning from what he had intended. So great was the shock which this event gave him, that he dared not trust himself to write again, but had waited, hoping that Lawrence would drop in of his own accord. Day after day passed, and Lawrence did not come. Severne felt that he could not much longer endure the torments of his position. He had tried to write, but his pen refused to obey his wishes, and he had thrown it down, and, taking a cigar, was endeavoring to get that solace from "the weed," which those who approach it, with due recognition of its power, so rarely fail to obtain. But this also failed him. He had consumed at least a dozen cigars that day, and there is a limit even to the benevolence of the goddess Nicotia. He smoked on, however, till the cigar was finished, and then rose from his chair and rang the bell. It was answered almost immediately by his valet, Wilson.

"I wish you would send some one around to Dr. Lawrence, and with my compliments request him to call here this evening as soon as he can."

"Yes, sir," said Wilson, with a bow, and was about leaving the room when his master said:

"Stop a moment, Wilson,—what did you understand me to say to you?"

"To send some one to Dr. Lawrence with your compliments, and to ask him to call here this evening as soon as possible."

"Yes, that is right;" and then, when Wilson had closed the door behind him, Severne threw himself on a sofa. "Thank God!" he exclaimed, "I can yet say what I intend. How long this power will be granted to me, He only knows. When I think of what I have suffered during the last few days, I am tempted to wish that He would take away this miserable life. Surely there can be no troubles beyond the grave equal to those which have been visited upon me here. Can it be possible that I am in my right mind,—that I have seen a reality and not a phantom of a diseased imagination? I know there are instances in which men who have overworked their minds have fancied they saw images of various kinds. There was too much real life about my vision, however. It was a true, substantial piece of flesh and blood. I know it too well to be deceived. My God! my God! what does it all mean? Am I to have no happiness, not even rest, for the little remnant of life that remains to me? I must do something at once for temporary relief or I shall be in no fit condition to talk to Lawrence. How my head throbs!"

He rang the bell, and Wilson again obeyed the summons.

"Has Dr. Lawrence been sent for?"

"Yes, sir, James has just returned. The doctor was not at home, but he left word for him to call here as soon as possible."

"Very well. Bring a bottle of champagne (Clicquot), a bowl of ice, and some glasses. Have some coffee made, and bring it up after Dr. Lawrence comes. I do not wish to be disturbed by other visitors while he is here."

Wilson bowed and left the room. In a few minutes he returned, accompanied by another servant, with the articles Severne had ordered, which he placed on a side-table. He had cut the wires which restrained the cork of the champagne bottle and had placed the latter in a heavy silver wine-cooler, ready to be opened as soon as its temperature should be sufficiently reduced. Further than this he did not go, as he knew his master's ways too well to ask him whether or not he should open it and pour him out a glass. There were few things that Severne disliked more than suggestions from his servants. When he wanted anything he asked for it, and Wilson knew exactly how far to go in meeting his wishes, which was to do precisely what he was told to do, neither more nor less.

For some time after the two men left the room, Severne sat at the table with his face buried in his hands. He had not seen Lawrence for more than a week, and he was conscious that even in that short period his appearance had changed very much. At their last interview his friend had made him promise that as soon as his "System of Philosophy" was completed he would give up all literary labor for a year, and spend that time in travel and recreation. Since then this intention had been placed with many others which had been formed, and abandoned from the force of circumstances beyond his control. As matters now stood, it was impossible for him to give his mind to his studies; and as to travel, could that or any other resource make him forget what he had learned within the last few days?

A half hour had elapsed and Lawrence had not come. Severne rose from his chair, and crossing the floor to where the table with the wine stood, opened the bottle of champagne and poured out a goblet of the foaming liquor, which he drank off, without removing the glass from his lips till he had drained the last drop. Again he filled the glass to the brim, and was raising it to his lips a second time when there was a light knock at the door, followed almost immediately by the entrance of Lawrence.

"My dear fellow," said Severne, "you are in the nick of time to join me in a glass of champagne. I have just swallowed a bumper of it. It is the only wine I drink now; all others have palled on my appetite."

"Well!" exclaimed Lawrence, advancing and holding out his hand, which Severne grasped warmly. "You are about as pleasant a vision as it is ever vouchsafed to a physician to see who is summoned in haste and expects to find a moribund patient. Of course I will take a glass of champagne. It is very seldom I refuse it. I am not able to buy it myself, and therefore I drink other people's with more relish."

"I will send you half a dozen cases to-morrow," said Severne, "as your fee for this visit. You never come here now unless I send for you. What have I done that you should desert me in this way?"

"My dear Severne, be reasonable. Did you not tell me the last time we met that you were going to give your time uninterruptedly to your studies for the next six months, and that you wished to see no one till they were finished?"

"I believe I did, Lawrence; but since then I have seen

one person whom I had hoped never to meet again in this
world. I am willing to see the devil and all his angels now
without a murmur."

"Thank you," said Lawrence, laughing; "and therefore
you sent for me. You lack the first element in the temperament of a patient—respect for your physician. If I did
not perceive from your face that you have been misusing
yourself worse than ever since I saw you, I should think
you had invited me over here to draw me into a quarrel
merely by way of a little relaxation."

"I never was more serious in all my life. I would rather
have seen the devil and all his angels than the person I
have met three times in the last five days. Lawrence, my
wife is not dead. I have seen her."

"What!" exclaimed Lawrence, looking fixedly in his
friend's face.

"I have seen my wife."

"Impossible!"

"I tell you I have, and just as plainly as I see you now."

"And I tell you, you have not. Why, Severne, your
wife has been dead these ten years."

"So I thought till a few days ago. Come, Lawrence,
hear what I have to say before you question the correctness
of my visual impressions. Either I have seen my wife three
times, or I am crazy. I wish you to give me your professional opinion on the point when you have heard my story."

Lawrence made no reply. He had no doubt in his own
mind relative to the true character of Severne's vision, but
he resolved to hear him through before attempting to convince him of his error. He accordingly threw himself on
the sofa, and Severne, resuming his seat at the table, thus
related the particulars of the circumstances which had given
him so much uneasiness of mind.

"Last Monday morning I had occasion to visit the Astor
Library to consult a book which I have been trying for
several years to get for my own shelves, and which I had
just ascertained was in that institution. I felt as well as I
usually have done for the last year or so, except that I had
a little headache and had passed a somewhat restless night.
I walked down Fifth Avenue without meeting with any adventure, and passing into Broadway, continued on my way

to Eighth Street. As I crossed over to Lafayette Place, at the point where Astor Place and Eighth Street come together, I observed a lady in front of me a few paces, about whom there was something which irresistibly attracted my attention. What this was I could not at first make out, but by degrees I began to perceive that she was dressed exactly as my wife was the last time I walked down Piccadilly from Hyde Park and saw her come out of Arlington Street with my father. I recollected the bonnet, the frock, and a very fine shawl which he had given her. I regarded this as a very singular coincidence, but nothing more, for of course I did not for a moment believe the lady to be really my wife. She crossed Eighth Street and proceeded down Lafayette Place, still keeping a few steps in advance of me. Gradually, as I watched her with the greatest attention, I recognized the walk and a peculiar swinging of the right arm as being identical in character with similar movements of my wife. In fact, the longer I looked at her the more I became convinced of the great resemblance. The height, the gait, the dress, the *tout ensemble*, were exactly those of my wife. Still I was not alarmed. On the contrary, I was very decidedly amused. It would be affectation, as you very well know, Lawrence, for me at this day, after all that has happened, to profess to feel the least spark of love for my wife. Aside from what I regarded as her sudden and violent death, I am free to confess that I have latterly congratulated myself in being rid of her detestable presence. It did not, even with all the points of resemblance I have mentioned, at all occur to me that the lady I was following was any other than one whose actions and appearance altogether were very similar to those of my wife. If any such idea had flashed through my mind, God knows I would not have been amused, but horrified.

"As she came opposite the library, she turned half round as if about to enter the building, and I caught a glimpse of her profile. To my utter horror and amazement, I saw my wife's features. I stood still, unable to advance a step farther. There was no mistake this time; the whole outline of the face was hers; and as if to place the matter beyond a doubt, I saw hanging around her neck a chain I had given her and which could not be found after her supposed death. I can-

not venture to describe to you, my dear Lawrence, all I felt
in the second or two during which this woman stopped in
front of the Astor Library. The memories of past years
fled like lightning through my brain. I felt my heart throbbing violently, a singularly bright light flashed in my eyes,
and I believe I should have fallen, had she not at that moment resumed her walk. The fear of losing sight of her,
and thus not being able to trace her, inspired me with fresh
strength, and I staggered on after her. She walked now,
however, much faster than I did, and as she reached Great
Jones Street, she quickened her pace, as if conscious of being
followed. As she turned the corner to go toward the
Bowery, I again saw her face. If there had been the least
doubt in my mind before, it would have been dispelled, for
she turned almost completely round for an instant, and I
had a good view of her countenance. She looked about as
she did ten years ago, perhaps a little older, but fully as
beautiful. She did not appear to see me, and I made no
effort to attract her attention. When I arrived at the corner she was no longer to be seen. As you know, the distance is too great for her to have reached the Bowery, and
I was not half a minute behind her. There was no house
either into which she could have gone, for St. Bartholo-
mew's Church extends some distance along Great Jones
Street, and she could not possibly have passed it before I
reached the corner.

"This sudden disappearance added still more to my astonishment. The impression which had been made upon me
by the woman I had seen was too strong, however, to be at
once effaced by any difficulties of time or place, and yet I
could not account for the abruptness with which she had
vanished.

"Certainly I had no desire whatever to meet my wife;
and yet I experienced an unaccountable impulse to ascertain her whereabouts. I therefore inquired at each of the
houses whether or not a lady had entered them within the
last few minutes, but at all I received a negative answer.
There was, therefore, nothing for me to do but to give up
the search for the present, although I was not entirely convinced that all the servants who answered the door-bells
had told me the truth. One of them I saw hesitated before

answering. However, when I stepped off the distance between that door and the corner, I could not conceive it to be possible that my wife could have reached it before I also turned into Great Jones Street. I came home as soon as possible and sat down to think the matter over as calmly as I could. One of three things had happened: I had really seen my wife; I had been deluded by a creation of my own morbid imagination; or her ghost had appeared to me.

"The first, which had been my original idea, became more untenable the more I reflected upon it. I recalled to mind the facts that I had seen my wife dead in her bed, the cause of her death, the opinions of the physicians, the funeral; and that she had, so far as we all knew, rested quietly in her grave for ten years. I then considered the circumstances of her mysterious disappearance in Great Jones Street; and, after a full review of these and many other points, which it is unnecessary to mention, I came to the conclusion that I had not seen my wife in the flesh.

"The second even was still more inadmissible. What was there to create such a phantom of the mind? I had not been thinking of my wife. I was not melancholic or depressed in spirits. On the contrary, I felt comparatively well, and my attention was altogether occupied with a far different subject. I recollect distinctly that I was considering the subject of the contributions of the Arabians and Saracens to science and philosophy, and was on my way to the Astor Library to refer to an edition of Averroes, printed at Venice in 1496, which I had understood was there. There was nothing at all which could associate this subject with my wife. Besides, I had seen her for fully five minutes, perhaps more. It was not probable that a vision would have lasted that long in broad daylight and in a frequented thoroughfare.

"The third idea was therefore forced upon my belief. I have never credited the stories which have been told relative to the appearance of spirits; but I have never questioned the existence of such beings. There had been many philosophical reasons to cause me to doubt that spirits could become visible. I now, however, believed that I had all my life been mistaken on this point, and it was not at all difficult for me to find proofs to sustain the opposite view. There is nothing like personal experience. It is better than all arguments, and if it does nothing more, it brings your mind into a fit condition to be convinced. I had another very good reason also for inclining to this opinion, and that was that I had determined, upon what I conceived to be good grounds, that I had neither seen my wife nor been deceived by a fiction of the imagination. I therefore accepted the conclusion that I had been visited by my wife's ghost.

"Now, my dear fellow," continued Severne, filling his glass with champagne and passing the bottle to Lawrence, who silently did likewise, "you may think this was all very nonsensical, and, in fact, so it was. I soon had reason, as you will learn, to change my opinion. The one I had formed was, however, at the time, the most convincing to my reason and the most satisfactory in other respects. It would have been exceedingly disagreeable to have had my late wife reappear in this world to insult, to mortify me, and to render my whole life a burden to me; and it would also have been very humiliating to my pride to be forced to believe that I had created the phantom in my own brain. For the time, therefore, I was very well contented to believe I had seen a spirit, and I tried to go to work and forget all about the occurrence.

"I found this, however, a task beyond my powers. I could think of nothing but my wife and the spirit I had seen. Presently I began to ask myself the reasons for this extraordinary appearance, and ere long I found that I was reviewing my conduct toward my wife with a severity against myself which I had never before manifested. You know, Lawrence, all the circumstances of my wife's unhappy end, and of my unhappy life while she existed. How——"

"Yes, I know them all, Severne;" exclaimed Lawrence, interrupting him for the first time, "and no one who knows them as I do can find anything in your conduct but the most thorough consideration for her welfare and your own honor."

"I am very glad to hear you say so," said Severne. "I have never been able to reproach myself with my part till last Monday. Then, as I sat here reflecting over what had occurred, and trying to find a reason for the appearance of my wife's spirit to me, the thought passed through my mind that perhaps I had not done altogether right in the matter of her death. I knew her propensity, the threats she had made over and over again to me and others, and I thought that I should have exercised more care over her than I did. This idea increased in strength. I became morbid over it, and finally began to accuse myself of having been the means of her death."

"My dear Severne," said Lawrence, "you should have informed me of this at the time. I think I could have convinced you of the errors in your reasoning. You have brooded over this thing till you have allowed yourself to form false views of your duty and conduct, and you have suffered acutely through the influence of a diseased imagination."

"Yes, I know all that now," replied Severne. "You will hear directly how I became convinced of my error. In the mean time, however, I bitterly reproached myself with having indirectly, at least, caused my wife's death. I tried to rid myself of the idea by resuming my studies. I found this entirely unsuccessful. I saw nothing on the pages of the books I endeavored to read but self-accusations and curses. I tried to write a note to you requesting you to come and see me. Here it is. Can you, after reading that, imagine a condition more deplorable than mine?"

Severne opened a drawer in his table, and taking from it a folded sheet of note-paper, handed it to Lawrence.

"I shall keep it," he continued, "as a memento of what must be regarded, I suppose, as a state of *quasi* insanity."

Lawrence took the note and read aloud, as follows:

"June 28th.

" My Dear Lawrence :

" It is said that an honest confession is good for the soul. I hope my soul will be benefited when I acknowledge to you that I admit myself to be guilty of my wife's death. I am her murderer. I no longer wish to make a secret of it. I am now suffering the torments of the damned.

" Yours, in utter despair,
" Robert Severne."

"Do you mean to tell me you wrote this, intending to write altogether a different note?" said Lawrence, looking very much surprised and interested.

"Certainly; I intended to ask you to come and see me, and thought I had done so, till I came to read over what I had written. My horror at finding that I had accused myself of my wife's death was only equaled by that which I felt at discovering my inability to control my pen or even to be conscious of the thoughts passing through my mind."

"Strange," said Lawrence, in an undertone, "that two such cases should come under my observation within so short a period!"

Without noticing Lawrence's remark, Severne continued his recital.

"All that night I spent in this room without once closing my eyes in sleep. My head ached as if it would burst, and my whole body trembled with the excitement due to my nervous condition. I ate no breakfast, but took my usual cold bath, with the addition of a lump of ice in it. I poured the cold water over my head and face, and felt greatly refreshed after the ablution. But the relief was only temporary, for very soon my head began to throb again. I came back to this room and lay down on that lounge. I felt deadly weary, but my eyes were staring open as if they were about to dart from their sockets, and I could not, with all my efforts, get my mind composed. As I lay on the lounge, my thoughts, of course, ran over the events of the preceding day. And while I was in the midst of my speculations in regard to the past and the future, there was a soft rap at my door. I said 'come in,' and turned half round to see my visitor, when, to my intense horror and amazement, I saw my wife this time face to face, and dressed just as she had been the day before. I sprang to my feet in an instant, and took a step toward what I then regarded as my wife's spirit. The intruder very quietly closed the door, and advanced toward me, holding out her hand and smiling as sweetly as she ever smiled before our wedded life. She did very little smiling in my sight after our marriage.

"'Are you a devil or a spirit?' I exclaimed.

"'Perhaps I am both, my dear Robert,' she replied; 'but, however that may be, I am your wife, Francisca Severne.'

"'Then you are not dead?'

"'Dead! No more dead than you are, my dear husband. I have come a long way to see you, and you ought to manifest more joy at beholding me than to stand there trembling as if you were frightened to death.' ·

"'Francisca,' I said, 'let there be peace between us. There can be no more love. I thought you were dead and buried. How your life has been preserved, I do not know, neither do I care to be informed. I recognize you too well as my wife. Let that suffice. Name the terms that will induce you to leave me, and they will at once be complied with. If you have not changed, you will sell me peace.' .

"'Oh, but I have changed very much. Money is no object to me now. It is your love I want, my dear Robert. The law allows me that, in theory at least. No! no! I cannot be bought for money. Take me back as your wife, and I am very sure we shall be happy.'

"'Never!' I exclaimed. 'False, perjured, shameless woman, never! It is impossible. Do you think I have forgotten your vile deeds, or that I would desecrate my hearth with the presence of such a fiend as you are?'

"'Very well, my dear Robert. Just as you please for the present. But do not, I beg of you, allow yourself to be excited. It worries me, upon my life it does, to see you get angry. Did not the doctor say, my dear, that you had some disease of the heart? I see you are not in a frame of mind to talk to me calmly. I will leave you, to return very soon for your answer. Good-by! Think of what I have said. For me, I still wear my wedding-ring. Good-by, my dear, good-by!'

"And waving her hand to me, and smiling as if I had uttered words of the most devoted love to her, she turned and left the room.

"I rang the bell, and it was answered before my visitor could have left the house. In reply to my inquiries, the servant informed me that he had admitted a woman, who had told him she wished to see me, and had accompanied her as far as the door of the library, as she said it was a matter of importance; that he had knocked at the door and had seen her enter the room. He had also met her on the stairs as she was going away, and she had requested him to hurry up, as he might be wanted badly. She did not, he said, look much like a lady, and seemed somewhat frightened.

"Of course, my dear Lawrence, my ideas underwent a change after this interview. I was now satisfied that I had seen my wife in reality twice, and not her spirit. The whole current of my thoughts changed. It would have been absurd for me to have longer accused myself of murdering my wife when that wife was still alive; but I cannot say that my condition was much improved. The idea of being still tied to a hateful woman, from whom I had long thought myself separated forever, was insupportable, and I resolved to rid myself of her presence by fleeing from the country and spending the rest of my miserable days in some far distant land. I saw nothing before me in any event but a life of the most supreme unhappiness, to be rendered a thousand times more wretched if I remained within her reach. I therefore began to make preparations for my departure secretly, without even letting you know of my intention; and had made some progress in the matter when I was again visited by my wife.

"She came into this room last night about this time, without knocking at the door, but with as much ease and self-possession as if she lived in the house. She took a seat quietly, apparently waiting for me to be disengaged. I was at the time looking over some papers, and making proper disposition of them, as I expected Freeling, my lawyer, here in the course of the evening. I had expected her to make me another visit, and therefore was not surprised at her appearance. I took no notice of her for several moments, and at last she spoke.

"'My dear Robert,' she said, 'I am sorry you continue to treat me with so much coldness; there was a time when your Francisca was very dear to you. Do you not recollect the words you spoke to me by the lakeside in the hills and at Lady Strickland's ball? There was love enough in them to last forever, I thought, and now you will not even say a word to me. I know your plans though, Robert, and I shall never give my consent to them.'

"'Madam,' I answered, 'I am in no humor to enter into an argument with you on any subject. Whatever demands you have to make upon me in the way of settlements, must be made to my attorney. I have already given him instructions on the subject, and he is prepared to accede to any proposition you may make, even to the extent of giving you two-thirds of my estate. I refuse positively ever to live with you again, or to hold any further communication with you, and I have, therefore, to request that you will leave me at once.'

" 'Very well, my dear husband,' she replied, with the most perfect *sang froid* imaginable. 'I will go once more. My next visit will be considerably longer. You need not think to escape from me. I shall remain with you for the rest of your life. I have a power to wield which you little dream of, and I warn you not to force me to use it. Once more, and for the last time, good-by !'

"With these words she made me a profound bow, and left me.

"Again I rang the bell. It was answered by Wilson.

" 'Never let that woman enter the house again,' exclaimed I.

" 'Woman, sir !' he exclaimed.

" 'Yes, woman ! Did you not admit that woman who has just left the room ?'

" 'No, sir. No person has entered the house within the last half hour, for I have been sitting in the hall, and would have seen any one who came in.'

"All the other servants assured me positively that no woman had entered the house that night.

" What to make of this last phase of the matter I did not know. Either all in the house were mistaken, or I had deceived myself with a phantom of the imagination. You may think it strange, perhaps, that I should embrace the first alternative; but so strong was the impression made upon me by what had occurred,—and I may add that the event is still vividly fixed upon my mind,—that it was impossible for me to give any weight to the idea that I had been deceived. I spent the night in reading Fell on Demoniacs, Scott's Demonology, De Boismont's Hallucinations, Madden's Phantasmata, Dendy's Philosophy of Mystery, and dozens of similar works. I have thus come across several cases similar to mine, but none exactly resembling it.

I find to-night, too, that I am still unable to write what I wish. My pen is as erratic as an insane man's speech, and altogether I am about as confused and as wretched an individual as you ever had for a patient. Now what is to be done? Am I insane or not? Have I seen my wife's spirit, or only the creation of a morbid imagination? My dear Lawrence, I have told you all, and I place myself entirely in your hands. Do with me as you will. I have nothing more to say, except to tell you that I have had several interviews with my agent, Mr. Freeling, relative to my wife, and the terms to offer her. I have also partly arranged for my departure from New York, whether she accepted them or not. I think I acquitted myself well in all these conferences. Somehow, intercourse with that man always rouses my faculties into keen action."

Lawrence had listened with the utmost attention to Severne's recital. He had no doubt whatever that his friend was laboring under a hallucination, and that consequently he had seen nothing at all but the unsubstantial images framed in his own mind. He knew well that the overtasked brain is often unable to rest after it has been goaded into straining every fiber to perform labor in a day for which a week should have been allowed, and that at such times it riots amid phantoms and scenes which exist only in its own unfathomable caverns. He had long foreseen to what Severne's habits of application would inevitably lead him, and though he was distressed at what his friend had suffered, he was thankful it was no worse. He perceived that Severne was alarmed and bewildered, that there was a conflict going on in his mind relative to the true interpretation to be placed upon the phenomena which had been manifested. Lawrence, who knew all the circumstances of Mrs. Severne's death better even than did her husband, knew also that it was impossible she could be alive. The spiritual aspect of the question he regarded as altogether ridiculous. He was confident, therefore, that in a few words he would be able to convince his friend of the real nature of his visitations, and that he could also be relieved from any further onslaughts of a similar character. While he was cogitating over the matter, Wilson entered the room with the coffee, which, having placed upon a table, he was about to retire, when his master said :

"You saw the lady who came here last Tuesday ?"

"Yes, sir."

"Would you know her again if you were to see her ?"

"Certainly, sir. She was here a few moments ago; but as you told me you did not wish to be disturbed, I requested her to come again to-morrow."

Severne looked at Lawrence; but the latter, not appearing to notice his glance, said :

"Will you allow me to ask Wilson a few questions ?"

"Certainly, Lawrence; ask him as many as you please."

"Do you knôw this woman, Wilson ?" remarked Lawrence, very quietly.

"Only by sight, sir."

"Does she look like a lady ?"

"Oh, no, sir ! She was quite a common-looking woman, sir."

"Did she tell you her business ?"

"I did not ask her that, sir; but to-night she said something about Mr. Severne being very anxious to get the information she had for him, and that the last time she was here he was ill, she thought, and she did not like to trouble him."

"And you obtained no idea in regard to the character of this intelligence ?"

"Nothing more, sir, than that she was, as she said, the mother of the little beggar girl that used to go to Mr. Barton's for cold victuals, and that she had something to tell Mr. Severne, which he wanted to know."

"Very well, Wilson. I am much obliged to you; that will do."

Severne could scarcely wait till Wilson had left the room, before he exclaimed :

"Why, good heavens ! is it possible she has the information of which I have been in search for the last six months ? She can doubtless tell me all about Sarah Tompkins."

"I have not the least idea who Sarah Tompkins may be, my dear Severne; but this I do know,—that you have nursed a phantom of your own creation. In two instances you have probably seen nothing, and in the other you have mistaken a woman of very different appearance for your wife, and have even misinterpreted her conversation with you. Such things are not uncommon. I have had several cases similar to yours under my professional charge, all of which were clearly traceable to like causes. The most interesting feature, however, in your condition, is the loss of the power to write what you think. It is certainly very remarkable. But even this is not an isolated instance, for I am now attending a gentleman who has precisely the same difficulty, the direct consequence of excessive mental occupation. Now, I regard it as of the utmost importance that you should see this whole matter in its true light. You have misused your intellectual powers, and you are now experiencing the legitimate results of your indiscretion. You will do me the justice to admit that I warned you of the inevitable effects of the causes you put in action. I wish now to convince you thoroughly that you are the victim of your own folly. You see, I am calling things by their right names. It would be mistaken friendship for me to spare you.

"In the first place, then, it is impossible that you could have seen the late Mrs. Severne. The dose of poison which she took was large enough to kill a dozen people. And I need not remind you of what you know, as well as I do, that I was present at the *post-mortem* examination, and therefore know that she is dead. This part of the question does not admit of argument, and we will not, therefore, discuss it further. It was very absurd in you to entertain the idea for a moment.

"As to the spiritual hypothesis, I leave that entirely to your own good sense. Whether there are spirits or not, who are able to make themselves visible at pleasure, is a question we will not now stop to argue. With me it involves a contradiction of terms. It is impossible for me to prove by direct testimony that you did not see a spirit; but it is still more difficult for you to establish the fact that you did. If you have, however, any lingering idea that you have been visited by a ghost, I think you will get rid of it before very long. I promise to cure you of that and of all other phantom visitations, if you will do what I advise."

"I have said, Lawrence, that I place myself entirely in your hands. You will find me as gentle as a lamb. I begin to think I have made an ass of myself."

"That is the most suitable frame of mind for you to be

in," said Lawrence, smiling. "But, my dear friend, let us be serious," he continued, with gravity. " You have had a narrow escape, and it will require your thorough co-operation to extricate you from your difficulty. Without that, I can do nothing for you. Two things are essential on your part. You must stop work, and you must travel. As to the medical treatment, it will be very simple. I shall not drug you to death, depend upon it."

"I took it for granted," said Severne, "that you would insist upon my leaving off my studies. I am prepared, therefore, to submit to this condition. In my present state it is impossible for me to do anything in that direction, and I agree with you entirely in the view that if it lasts much longer I shall lose my reason altogether. As to the travel, I am ready for that, too. The preparations I have made, therefore, will not come amiss. I have one condition, however, to insist upon, and that is that you shall give me the pleasure of your company, and the benefit of your advice, during my wanderings."

"I will not say no, absolutely," replied Lawrence, "but I am not prepared to give an affirmative answer yet. I am very much obliged to you for wishing me to go with you, and I assure you nothing would give me greater delight. We will talk that part of the matter over again, and, in the mean time, I must ask you a number of questions in regard to your condition."

Lawrence examined Severne with great minuteness, and thus obtained a very correct idea of his friend's disorder. There were some symptoms which gave him a little uneasiness, and which it was necessary should be immediately relieved. Every circumstance brought to light, showed the fearfully excited condition of Severne's mind, and more and more confirmed Lawrence in the judgment he had formed. Having given his directions and left a prescription to be filled, Lawrence took his departure, promising to repeat his visit the ensuing day. It was of the utmost importance that Severne should obtain a good, sound sleep immediately, and Lawrence's treatment was of a character to produce this result. Had he evinced the least desire to be enlightened, Severne would have related to him all he knew about Sarah Tompkins and his previous relation to this young woman.

It was no part of Lawrence's plan, however, to allow his patient to excite himself further that night. He saw that there was something which interested Severne very much, and he hoped, when the proper time came, to make use of it to direct his thoughts and energies into another channel.

As Lawrence walked home, he thought of what Severne had proposed relative to their traveling together. Nothing but friendship could have induced Lawrence to think of leaving New York at a time when he was rapidly rising into a large and lucrative practice. But the more he thought of Severne's proposition, the more he was inclined to yield to his friend's wishes in the matter. He knew that he could be of the greatest possible advantage to Severne, both as a companion and a physician ; and besides, he was apprehensive that if he refused, Severne would reject his advice and relapse into those habits which had already brought him into a very critical condition. He therefore resolved that if anything further was said on the subject by Severne, he would accept his invitation. The route to take was still a subject for discussion.

CHAPTER IX.

MRS. WIGGINS SPEAKS.

The following morning, when Lawrence paid his visit to Severne, he found that for the first time in several months his friend had slept soundly the whole night through, and was in consequence very much refreshed both in body and mind. No phantom Francisca had visited the patient, nor had his imagination conjured up any other visions to disturb his slumbers. One step was therefore gained, and Lawrence now felt assured that time and change of associations would give to Severne better health than he had enjoyed for several years. In conversing together relative to past events and future plans, Lawrence discovered that Severne was not disposed to undertake any extensive journey unless he accompanied him. Severne's arguments

in support of his wishes were really so strong, and were
urged with so much warmth and appreciation of Lawrence's
friendship and abilities, that compliance could not be withheld.

The matter, too, was placed in such a position pecuni-
arily, as regarded Lawrence, that he was not able even to
mention the obstacle which he had supposed to be almost
insurmountable.

Relative to the direction in which their travels should be
made, the discussion was long and animated. Both had
overrun Europe pretty thoroughly, and though, on some
accounts, it would have been preferable to other parts of the
earth's surface, Lawrence thought that entire novelty should
be, if possible, secured. The claims of a yacht voyage to
the North Pole, a journey through Mexico, North America, or Australia, were severally considered and rejected for
divers good and sufficient reasons.

"Come," said Severne, "at last I have it. We will go
across the Continent to San Francisco, thence to China and
India, and back through Egypt and Europe to New York.
This will give us an endless variety, and will fully occupy
my probationary six months. What do you say to this
idea?"

"Nothing having the semblance of an objection," replied Lawrence. "On the contrary, it strikes me with a
great deal more favor than any yet brought forward by
either of us. We shall doubtless enjoy it very much. But
consider, my dear Severne, that the journey you propose
will in some parts be tiresome and fatiguing. Are you prepared for all this?"

"Fully," answered Severne. "I wish to be tired and
fatigued in just that way. So we will consider the matter
as settled. Leave all the preparations to me. It will give
me occupation till the time of our departure comes. Settle
up all your affairs, and be ready to start in a couple of
weeks. Is there any objection, in a sanitary point of view,
to my taking a walk down town this morning?"

"None in the least. Do what you please so that you
keep your thoughts far removed from your usual studies.
Don't write more than you can help at present, and read
nothing but novels. By-the-by, talking of writing, what

have you done with that precious confession you wrote the other day? You ought to take care that no enemy gets hold of it. Many men have been hanged on less evidence than that."

"I have it here in my port-folio, and intend to keep it as a memorial of the asinine condition from which I have just emerged."

"You had better destroy it. No man is safe with such a document relating to him in existence. Give it to me and I will take care that it is never seen again."

"Take it, since you insist upon it," said Severne, laughing, and opening his port-folio, he handed a folded note to Lawrence. The latter went to the mantle-piece, and taking a match from a cigar-stand which stood upon it, struck a light, and setting fire to the note which Severne had given him, watched it till it was entirely consumed.

"It is best," he said, "to get rid of all such papers. One never knows who his friends are in this world; and there may be some people about you, Severne, to whom such a piece of paper would have been a treasure. I don't think you have many friends, my dear fellow. I believe you told me once you did not form acquaintances readily. How is it? Do you still confine yourself to John Holmes and me?"

"To John Holmes and you, Lawrence, with the addition of Goodall, whom I never really got to know well till a few months since. He is worthy to be the friend of the best man on this earth, let alone such a miserable, semi-insane wretch as I am. I shall pay them a visit to-day. It is a glorious place, that old shop. And now, talking of friends, I must tell you how I have failed to make the acquaintance of a young woman with whom we were both interested on one occasion."

Severne then related in full his adventure with Sarah Tompkins, six months ago, in the Fifth Avenue, and his subsequent attempts to discover her whereabouts.

"I presume I am about to obtain some knowledge of her," he continued, "judging from what Wilson told us last night of my recent female visitor and her business. If I should succeed in finding her now, I scarcely know what I should do with her. There is no one whom I could in-trust with her education. How would it answer to take her with us ?"

"It would not answer at all, my dear Severne," said Lawrence, emphatically. "What would the world say to see us going all over its dominions with a young girl in our charge ?"

"I don't care a sixpence what the world would say," replied Severne. "I have lived long enough, and seen enough of its wickedness and hypocrisy, to do what I please, regardless of its ,muttered murmurs or open denunciations. Your disapproval of it is quite sufficient for me. As to the world, it may go to the devil. What, then, shall I do with the young woman ?"

"You are the most energetic man, when you get an idea into your head, I ever saw. First, get your young woman. You seem to think that you have only to say 'Sarah, behold the beauties of virtue; see what a delight it is to learn geography and grammar, to stammer in French and Italian, to seek to ascertain the connection between mind and matter, to finger the piano, and to dance gracefully !' to make her rush into your arms and beg to be taught to comprehend the mysteries of science, art, and good breeding. From what you have told me of Miss Sarah, added to what I saw with my own eyes, I am decidedly of the opinion that she is no fool. You will not induce her to enter your net unless you can make the future appear more inviting to her than you are likely to make it look to her through the medium of a boarding-school and the loss of her liberty. If you succeed in enticing her into your snare, she will run away in a week unless you can get her heart enlisted in the affair."

"And that is exactly what I want to do. I neither wish to make her a prisoner nor a slave. I want to gain her good will, perhaps her love."

"Oh! that's it, is it?" exclaimed Lawrence, laughing. "You had better marry her."

"Perhaps I will some day. Who knows? I might do much worse. And if I can mould her disposition and refine her nature up to my standard, I see no reason why she would not make me a very good wife."

"Get her first, my worthy philanthropist, and then we

will discuss what is best to be done with her. In the mean time don't think that I am endeavoring to throw cold water on your schemes for educating Miss Tompkins in the social and intellectual scales of humanity. On the contrary, if I can be of any assistance to you in finding her, my services are at your disposal."

"Thank you, Lawrence. I expect the woman here this morning who has already called twice to give me some information in regard to this girl. She will doubtless be able to tell me where she lives. If I can once get to see her, and talk with her freely, I do not anticipate much difficulty in gaining her consent to my plans."

While Severne was speaking, Wilson entered the room, and, as soon as his master had finished his remarks, announced that the woman in question was then waiting to see him. Severne bid him show her up, and in a few moments a tall, gaunt female was ushered into the apartment. Lawrence, who had known the late Mrs. Severne, could scarcely restrain a smile as he thought of his friend having likened this coarse-looking Amazon before him to the graceful and beautiful figure of his deceased wife.

Severne requested his visitor to be seated, and then inquired her business.

"I came to see you, sir, twice, about a young woman you was wantin' to find. I beg your pardon for goin' away the first time, but I thought you was not well, sir, and——"

"Never mind about that, my good woman," said Severne, interrupting her. "I was not at all well, as you very rightly supposed. Now tell me what you know about Sarah, or Sal Tompkins, as I presume you call her."

"Yes, sir, Sal is the name as we knows her by. I raised that girl, sir, till she was growed up, and so I ought to know her; not to say as she's any kin of mine, sir. My name's Mary Wiggins, sir, and my husband's name John Wiggins; and if you choose to go to Number 479 Watts Street, there's folks there as will tell you we was always honest people, gainin' our livin' by hard work six days in the week, and restin' on the seventh day, as the Lord commanded. We has always been members of the Latter-Day Baptist persuasion, and I told John yesterday, 'John,' says I, 'we ain't got no riches to speak of, nor much learnin', but we has always been rich in grace and learned in the Lord, thanks be praised!' And John said, says he,—John's a cripple now, sir; he got very old in the shoemakin' business, and his bones growed very brittle from age, and so one day he broke his thigh-bone, sir, a hammerin' on his lapstone overhard, and the doctor set it crooked; and since then he had to give up work, and I gains a livin' for him and me and my little girl a sewin', and she—that's Marthy—gets cold victuals around from those as will give them to her,—John says, says he, 'Mary, what you say is true,' says he; 'we are only poor, ignorant servants of the Lord, but our treasures is laid up in heaven, where neither moth nor rust does corrupt, and where nobody breaks through nor steals.' And then says I, 'John,' says I, 'do you know what Brother Jenkins used to say when he came to the house to exhort you and to comfort you in grace when your leg was broke? "Wiggins," says he, "if the sole is all right, the uppers is nothing to nobody."' Which is true, allowin' as it was John's lowers as was broke and not his uppers."

"My good woman," said Severne, impatiently, while Lawrence was exceedingly amused with the loquacity of his visitor, "I am very sorry you have had so much affliction, and are in such reduced circumstances. Accept this as an evidence of my desire to help you, and tell me at once all you know of Sal Tompkins."

"Thank you, sir," said Mrs. Wiggins, as she took the gold piece Severne put in her hand. "I was comin' to that. You see, Sal's mother was no better than she should be; not that I should say anything against her. We is all sinful creatures, and merits eternal fire, as Brother Jenkins used to say; and I always remembers, 'judge not that ye be not judged.' But you see, sir, Sal's mother, that was Julia Tompkins, lived not far from my old man's shop, and she used to get her shoes from him. She always was a good customer, for she got fine shoes, better nor those John made in usual, and he always got French Bill to help him with Julia's shoes. French Bill was a Frenchman, sir, as you might guess from his name, which was Bill. And one day Julia came into the shop, and, while John was a measurin' her—John always said Julia Tompkins had the smallest

foot of any woman as came to him for shoes, and her stockin's was always clean, and I says 'its all nothing but
vanity,' John, says I. 'The Lord is not goin' to measure
our feet when we knock at the door and ask admittance into
His kingdom,' because you know, sir, John was always a
talkin' of Julia Tompkins's foot, and I felt riled like; not as
I cared, you see, neither; for we don't make our own feet,
and them as finds fault with our feet finds fault with the
Lord as made them, and not we ourselves. And as to
stockin's, if my feet was big, my stockin's was as clean as
Julia Tompkins's or any other woman's. And so you see,
sir, while John was a measurin' her for a pair of shoes, says
she, 'Mr. Wiggins, would you like to have a little baby?'
and, says John, 'What?' says he. 'A little baby,' says Julia.
Now, you see, sir, we had been married over eleven years,
and the Lord had not seen fit to give us a little baby of our
own; not as He didn't do so afterward; for after John broke
his leg and could not work at his trade any longer, my little
Marthy was born. And there was no doctor as could be
had in time, but John's sister, Jane Wiggins, as keeps a
boardin'-house in King Street. 'To think as it should be
a stoppin' shoemakin',' says she, 'as did it!'" ·

"Mrs. Wiggins," said Severne, interrupting her, "I
really cannot see what all this has to do with the information I desire. If you know where Sal Tompkins lives, and
will tell me, I shall be very much obliged to you, and will
amply recompense you for all the trouble you have been put
to in the matter."

"Oh, of course, sir, your time is precious to you just as
mine is to me, but I'll come to it at once, sir. John was
staggered, you see, sir, when Julia asked him about the
baby, and, says he, 'I'll ask Mary;' and, says Julia, 'I'm
goin' away, Mr. Wiggins, to a far distant land, and I've got
a little daughter as is named Sarah, and them that takes
care of her till I come back, gets one hundred dollars in
gold, all down cash. Her father's a gentleman, and a rich
one, too!' And John told Julia to call again the next day
for an answer; and that night, as John sat at the table
readin,' says he all of a sudden, 'Mary,' says he, 'would
you like to have a little baby?' and says I, quite quiet-like,
'Yes, if the Lord pleases;' and says he, 'I've got a little

baby for you as is Julia Tompkins's;' and says I, firin' up, for I miscomprehended, you see, sir,—says I, 'Ain't you ashamed to insult me iu my own house?' and then I burst out a cryin', and says he, 'What do you mean?' says he; and says I, 'To think that I should live for this!' But it all comes of Julia Tompkins's foot; and says John, gettin' mad, 'You're a fool, Mary!' and says I, 'I may be a fool, but I'm an honest woman, which is more than you can say for your Julia Tompkins.' And then John saw how my feeliu's was hurt, and he told me all about it, and so we agreed to take care of Julia Tompkins's little girl till she came back, which she never did to this day."

"And you took care of her how long?" said Severne.

"Well, you see, sir, after John broke his leg, and my little Marthy was born, and Julia Tompkins didn't come back, and the hundred dollars was long used up and we was very poor, I took Sal away from school, for you see, sir, she had to work like the rest of us. I sent her to Sunday-school and to day school, too, and treated her just as if she was my own child. And she was a very good child, too, till I had to seud her out to get her own livin', which she did at a bookbinder's, earniu' two dollars a week. And then she learnt bad ways; and a year ago, she said she was goiu' to live at another house of her own, which she did, but she often comes to see me, and brings me a little money now and then, which is very kind in her not to forget her old friends, as has not forgotten her. But I could cry, sir, when I think of Sal's way of livin', which is no better than that of her mother before her. But what can I do, sir, with John a cripple, and my livin' to make, aud a felon on my finger as has given me the misery off and on for seventeen days and nights? Not as I am complainin', sir, but——"

"Did you never hear anything of Sal's father?" said Severne, interrupting her.

"Never a word, sir. Julia left the day after she brought her little baby to us, which was only six months old, and had to be raised by hand, and——"

"Yes," said Severne, "I can understand the trouble you must have had; but now tell me where Sal lives."

"Well, sir, you see," said Mrs. Wiggins, starting off on a new tack with great energy, "my little Marthy, as goes to

Mr. Barton's for cold victuals and such like, took sick with the fever.as Dr. Wimble said was a pneumony on the lungs. I don't know, sir, as you knows Dr. Wimble. He's been our doctor for a long time, and he only charges twenty-five cents each time he comes, and leaves lots of medicine besides. To be sure, I had to get a mustard plaster for Marthy's breast, which cost me six cents; but then the doctor gave her all the calamy and rhubarb and drops which was wanted. He just looked at her once the first time, and says he, 'Mrs. Wiggins,' says he, 'Marthy's got the pneumony on her lungs; it's a awful complaint, and lots of children dies of it, but I understand this disease particular well, and I'll save her. I shall call eight times, Mrs. Wiggins, which is just two dollars.' I gave him the money right off, though I had to take all I had made that week; but Dr. Wimble says he don't bind himself by no rules, for doctors as reads much learns little. He's a seventh son, too, and I knowed he was gifted; but for all that, Marthy got worse, and Dr. Wimble had to go to the country to see an old man as couldn't come to him, and so I took Marthy round to the dispensary, and the doctor there sounded her lungs, and felt her pulse, and asked me a great many questions, but didn't give me any medicine for her, only an order for some wine, and told me to give her plenty of milk and beef tea, too, which he sent me, and Marthy begun to get well right off; and Dr. Wimble says it was the workin' of the calamy and the drops he gave her, and I guess as how he's right, for I got no medicine at all from the dispensary."

"Very well, Mrs. Wiggins," said Severne, who had been laughing with Lawrence at her description of Dr. Wimble. "It is all very interesting indeed. I am glad Martha got well. Now tell me, please, where Sarah lives."

"Well, sir, that's just what I'm doing. You see, Marthy being sick, could not go to Mr. Barton's for cold victuals and such like; but, after she got well, she went back, and says Bridget—that's Mr. Barton's cook—'Marthy,' says she, 'there's a gentleman as wants to know where a girl lives as is called Sarah Tompkins.' 'I don't know no such girl,' says Marthy, 'but I knows one as is named Sal Tompkins.' 'That's her,' said Bridget. 'I don't know exactly where she lives,' says Marthy, 'but I'll ask my mother.' And so she did; and so I just put on my things and started up to see Bridget, and she told me all about what you wanted, and where you lived, and here I am, sir."

"And where does Sarah Tompkins live?" said Severne, impatiently.

"Oh, as to that, sir, I really don't know exactly. You see, sir, last week Sal moved her lodgings somewhere into Wayne Street; but she'll be at our house to-night, and I'll find it all out. I could bring her here, if you like; for, says I to myself, as I came along the other day, 'Perhaps the gentleman's Sal's father;' but the moment I laid eyes on you, I said 'No.' Maybe you're her uncle. Uncles often looks for their nieces. Not long since——"

"No," said Severne, "I am not her uncle, nor any other relative. I have it in my power to render her a great service; but you need not mention this to her, or tell her that you have had any inquiries made of you in regard to her. I do not care to have you bring her here. I prefer to see her at her own lodgings. And now I must bid you good morning. Here is some money for you, and if you follow my directions I will give you more."

Mrs. Wiggins took the money he gave her, and was profuse in her thanks. She would have gone off on another conversational tour if Severne had not rendered it very evident to even her comprehension that he desired her to leave; so making a profound courtesy to him and Lawrence, she took her departure, with the understanding that she was to repeat her visit the following day.

While Severne and Lawrence were amusing themselves over Mrs. Wiggins, and the former was congratulating himself that at last there was a prospect of his meeting with Sarah Tompkins, Mr. Freeling, his attorney and agent, was announced; and Lawrence, promising to drop in again toward night, bid his friend good morning, and resumed his professional rounds through the city.

10

CHAPTER X.

MR. FREELING APPEARS AS A PROMINENT CHARACTER AND BEGINS OPERATIONS.

MR. BAGLEY FREELING was one of those sharp, active, capable, but unprincipled men, met with in the legal as well as in all other professions. Born and educated in an obscure village, he had grown up with all the little meannesses which were engrafted from birth upon his character, and which his pettifogging legal practice was calculated to add to rather than diminish. Finding that the village in which he flourished was not of sufficient importance to afford him full scope for his talents, he had several years ago fixed his residence in New York, where, as a Tombs lawyer, he had many opportunities of still further sharpening his faculties. Having acquired a sum of money which rendered him to a great extent independent of his profession, he had gradually been getting into more reputable habits, and when Severne was in search of an attorney to take the proper legal measures to secure his estate, and to put his property into such a shape as would admit of easy management, Freeling was recommended to him. "Remember," said the eminent legal gentleman whom he consulted, and who suggested Freeling, "I only recommend him on the grounds of capacity, knowledge, and a wonderful degree of astuteness. I do not vouch for his honesty, though at the same time I am satisfied that if you watch him closely enough, and let him understand that you are doing so, he will not prove unfaithful to you. He values his reputation now very much. He is endeavoring to gain a good position in society, and will only steal or commit any other disreputable act when he is certain he will not be discovered in his rascality."

With a tolerably full knowledge of the character of the man he had to deal with, Severne had given Freeling a large fee, and had sent him to England to secure the property which had fallen to him by his father's death. The attorney had managed this business so well, and had subsequently evinced so much sagacity in investing Severne's surplus capital and income, that the latter, though constantly mindful of the advice he had received, had formed the highest opinion of Freeling's legal knowledge and business qualifications, and had retained him as his agent. He had not, however, the least confidence in the man's integrity. Many little incidents convinced him that the attorney was only honest, because honesty, was for the time being the best policy. Severne exercised a sound control over all the transactions which his attorney carried on in his behalf. He hated to be cheated, and rather than be defrauded out of a cent he would sacrifice hundreds of dollars. He therefore trusted his agent no further than he could do so with entire safety, and as a consequence, Freeling received a large salary, and brought all his knowledge and enterprise into action for his principal's benefit.

Freeling's appearance was by no means prepossessing. He was short, thick-set, and slightly lamed from an accident he had met with when a boy. His eyes could not be very clearly perceived, as he habitually wore spectacles, but they were dark, as were also his hair and beard. The latter he wore long, shaving no part of his face except his upper lip, and as his face was large, and of square form, his countenance had rather a massive appearance, but, at the same time, a sharp and vindictive expression, as if he were constantly on the look-out for an enemy to punish.

Freeling was not a worshiper of God, although he regularly attended church, and affected the most devout piety. He found a reputation for being religious useful to him. But there was an attribute of the Deity which he placed far above every other thing, human or Divine, and before which he bowed his whole soul in unaffected humility. It was power. This was his god. Wealth and love and learning, for which most men are willing to labor unceasingly till they stand upon the verge of the grave, were nothing to him but as means for gaining power. All his toils, all his energies, both of mind and of body, centered around this one object, for which alone he lived.

He was perfectly consistent in his adoration of his deity. He stopped at nothing when secrecy could be insured. No

lie was too base, no treacherous deed too evil, no piece of
cruelty too heartless, no fraud too disgraceful, no act of
self-humiliation too groveling to cause him to shrink from its
perpetration, if by committing it he could gain power. To
his superiors he was truckling and submissive, to his inferiors, and especially his dependents, overbearing and ty-
rannical. He had been married, and it was said that his
wife, a gentle, patient creature, whom he had wedded for the
small fortune she possessed, sank into an early grave, unable
to contend with one whose qualities, undisguised as they
were in his own home, were those of a wild beast rather than
of a human being.

It may seem strange that a man like Severne, all of whose
feelings and instincts were those of a high-toned gentleman,
should voluntarily bring such a person as Freeling into intimate association with himself. But, in fact, the contact was
more apparent than real. Freeling knew no more of his
employer socially than he did of the boudoir of the Em-
press of Russia. Severne never treated him with the least
familiarity. His manner toward him was always rigidly
formal and polite, and Freeling dared not overstep the line
which separated him from one whom he felt was his master.

Besides, in keeping Freeling in his employ, Severne was
governed by two chief motives. As a business agent, the
attorney had not his equal in the City of New York. This
of itself, he thought, was a sufficient reason. If Signor
Pappilini has a magnificent voice, and sings with exceeding
taste and expression, people will go in crowds to hear him
in preference to having their sense of harmony outraged by
listening to the incongruous sounds which issue from Mr.
Beethoven Rohrer's throat, even though the former be a
scamp of the first water, and the latter a most worthy member of society. They run the risk of the Signor coming
among them after his performance, and picking their pockets.
If my barber performs the duties of his profession better
than any other tonsorial artist of my acquaintance, I patron-
ize him without stopping to inquire into his moral character.
He may, some morning, cut my throat for my purse. I take
my chance of that rather than have my face scarred by the
most Christian bungler that ever lived. Such is the way of
the world, and in the long run it works well.

The other reason was that Severne thoroughly understood Freeling's character, and took an interest in studying its depths, and guarding against its little eccentricities. It was both a source of amusement and of profit to him to watch the current of his agent's thoughts. He thus learned many a practical lesson in psychology, which otherwise would have been lost to him.

Severne had already perceived that Freeling was anxiously looking forward to the period of his departure from New York, and was evidently trying to induce his principal to leave him in entire charge of his interests. When Severne had informed him of his contemplated tour, and had given him· directions relative to any demands the supposed Mrs. Severne might make, he noticed how eagerly the attorney took in the scanty information which he thought it necessary to give him. He did not previously know that Freeling, during his stay in England, had possessed himself of many details, both false and true, relative to that lady and her husband, but the extreme interest the agent evinced when Severne mentioned her name, and his suspicion that she was still alive, betrayed him to the watchful mind of his employer, and put him on his guard.

It was not Severne's intention, however, to vest any great authority in Freeling during his absence. The bulk of his property he was having arranged in such a manner as to require no interference from the agent during the six months' tour which he contemplated. There were a few matters, however, which necessarily required attention, but most of these he intended to hedge about in such a way as to make it almost impossible for Freeling to act a roguish part in regard to them. The rest he was obliged to leave in his attorney's power, but it was not of sufficient value to induce him to decamp with it, and any dishonest mismanagement was sure to be detected when Severne returned.

Severne had made an appointment with Freeling for this morning, in order to perfect details already partly considered, and to give some special instructions relative to property situated in the city. The agent at the last interview between them had very clearly determined in his own mind that Severne was about leaving New York to avoid living with his wife.` The meeting, however, had confused the clear mind which Mr. Freeling ordinarily possessed. He had asked several questions, to which Severne paid no attention whatever, merely telling him such matters as it was essential should be told for the furtherance of his instructions. That Mrs. Severne should be alive was a fact for which the attorney was not prepared, and that his employer should go so far as to offer her the bulk of his fortune, under condition of her ceasing to trouble him with her presence, was marvelous. He had therefore not lacked food for reflection, and he had already conceived several plans for the future, either of which, if carried out, would redound greatly to his advantage. One of these, which struck him with great force, was to induce Mrs. Severne to apply for a divorce from her husband, and when this was secured, to pay court to the lady with the view of making her Mrs. Freeling. He knew that two-thirds of Severne's estate would be a fortune such as he never expected to have under his control; and with Severne absent and his wife thrown into intimate association with him—as would necessarily be the case—he had little doubt of being able so to adapt the means to the end as to insure the success of his scheme. He had accordingly looked forward to this interview with both anxiety and satisfaction. He had a difficult part to play, but he had confidence in his powers of management, and therefore when Wilson came to announce that his master was now disengaged, he ascended to the library without any foreboding as to the result. He had a bundle of papers in his hand, and appeared to be looking at the indorsements as he entered the room.

"Sit down, Mr. Freeling," said Severne. "I will be at your service as soon as I finish this note. Is it warm out this morning?"

"Very warm, sir. As I came up Broadway I felt the heat exceedingly. You are not going out of New York a day too soon. The city is unendurable in hot weather."

Mr. Freeling had been closely observing the condition of affairs while making these indifferent remarks. He had at once perceived that Severne's manner and appearance were very much changed compared to what they had been at the last interview. Before he could altogether get the drift of matters as they now stood, Severne closed and directed his note; and then giving his attention to the business before him, said :

"It will not be necessary to make any estimate upon which to base a settlement on Mrs. Severne."

Freeling concealed his surprise as well as he could, and remarked in a very respectful manner :

"I have not only made the estimate, sir, but I have written out an opinion as to what property it will be best to sell in order to make the settlement, which I understood you to say you preferred should be in cash."

"You are very prompt as usual, Mr. Freeling, but I have ascertained since yesterday that the supposed Mrs. Severne was an unconscious impostor."

"An impostor!" exclaimed Freeling. "I hope, sir, you will have her at once arrested."

"No, I shall not take that trouble, particularly as the deceit was not successful. The resemblance, however, was very great, and for a time led me into error."

"Then I presume, sir, that Mrs. Severne is not in existence?"

"And your presumption is perfectly correct. Mrs. Severne has, as I have always believed till a few days past, been dead several years."

Mr. Freeling saw that one of his cherished schemes had fallen at a blow; still he did not lose all courage yet. He was confident there was a mystery somewhere, and did not for a moment credit the version Severne had given him.

"I scarcely know, sir," he said after a little reflection, "whether to congratulate you or not on the termination of the arrangements commenced at our last meeting."

"It is not at all necessary that you should express an opinion one way or the other about it," replied Severne, coldly. "I would like to hear your views, however, relative to selling some stocks. I wish about fifteen thousand dollars immediately, and I do not think I have over six or seven thousand at my banker's."

"There will be more than that sum due within a month from rents and dividends. And then there are the proceeds of the sale of those Chicago lots which you authorized me to make at the prices offered."

"Yes, I recollect," said Severne. "Eight thousand dollars, I think."

"Eight thousand two hundred and forty-five dollars," replied Freeling, looking at his memorandum book. "The money is to be paid to-morrow. They only cost us four thousand a year ago."

"It will still be necessary to sell some stock," observed Severne, "for I wish to purchase that property in Fifth Avenue above Thirty-fourth Street that you mentioned a short time since. I suppose it is worth forty thousand dollars."

"Yes, sir, every cent of it. In regard to the stocks, I think it would be best to sell Governments; they are up now."

"Very well, then, sell ten thousand to-morrow. I am going to travel for about six months."

"I am sure it will do you good, sir. You have not looked well for several months. Do you go immediately?"

"In the course of a fortnight. The preparations which you recommend, therefore, will be carried out in part—that is, so far as is necessary for a six months' absence."

"The powers of attorney are all prepared, and only await your signature. Will you look them over now, sir?"

Severne took the papers and read them carefully through; several he signed, others he disapproved, and others he laid aside for further consideration. The authority conferred upon Mr. Freeling was not therefore as extensive as this worthy wished it to be. He was disappointed, but he had too much shrewdness to manifest his emotions to any great degree. He understood that Severne did not intend to leave him master even for the short period of six months, and thus several schemes which he had formed for exercising his power would not probably be realized.

"I think it my duty, sir, again to call your attention to the propriety of raising the rent of the houses in Lexington Avenue. They are only yielding about half what they should."

This subject of the rent of the houses in Lexington Avenue was one which Freeling had frequently brought to Severne's attention. The latter had hitherto refused to entertain his agent's proposition, for the houses in question were occupied by a lady not in very good circumstances; but the idea now occurred to him that Freeling was actuated by some more powerful motive than a mere business one, and he determined to ascertain, if possible, what it was. He knew the agent's character too well to endeavor to find it out by any direct process, and he therefore gave his consent to the increase of the rent, having a very strong conviction that some of the occupants would appeal to him directly in the matter, and that he should thus, in all probability, gain the information he was desirous of obtaining. If nothing should be heard from them in the course of a few days, it would be very easy to rescind the order.

Freeling manifested more satisfaction at Severne's consent to his proposal than at any other circumstance which had occurred during their interview; and soon afterward took his leave for the purpose of putting the order into instant execution. As he pursued his way from the Fifth Avenue to Lexington Avenue, his thoughts were not altogether of a pleasant character. He had lost all chance of getting any portion of his employer's fortune into his hands by marrying that employer's divorced wife, and he had plainly perceived that during Severne's absence his authority would even be less than it was at present. The loss of the smallest iota of his power always made Freeling unhappy; but there was one event which had caused him pleasure,—the permission to raise the rent of the houses in Lexington Avenue— and another which had set him thinking—the sudden change which had taken place in Severne's ideas relative to the existence of his wife. There was a mystery here, he was very certain, and it was all the more exciting to him because he saw no possible way of unraveling it to his satisfaction. If he could only, he thought, obtain a meeting with the supposed Mrs. Severne, he would be able to make himself acquainted with many circumstances which were now concealed from his knowledge; but he saw no possible way of effecting this object except through some of Severne's servants, and he was afraid to make the attempt through them while their master was still in town. After his departure, the effort could be made with greater safety.

The houses in Lexington Avenue belonging to Severne were three small but comfortable buildings which he had erected for the use of persons of moderate means, and which were now rented by a widow, who sublet the rooms to lodgers. Mrs. Langley's history was very similar to that of many other women who have been forced to take lodgers or boarders. Originally well to do in the world, her husband dying, left her almost penniless, and she was forced to support herself and two daughters, one of whom was in bad health, by her own exertions. Mr. Freeling had been for several years a lodger in Mrs. Langley's establishment, occupying two rooms in the same building with her and her daughters. For awhile, Mr. Freeling did all in his power to render himself agreeable to Mrs. Langley and the young ladies, and to ingratiate himself into their good graces. He brought them little presents when he came home after business hours, and generally spent his evenings in their small parlor, conversing with them relative to their prospects of success, and giving them advice of a character that would have done credit to the most devout and practical father of a family. No one, therefore, had more influence with Mrs. Langley than Mr. Freeling. One evening, however, her kind lodger came home looking very melancholy and sorrowful. He took his accustomed seat on the sofa with a sigh which expressed his sincere appreciation of the great fall from grace which, in his estimation, the human race had experienced since he left home that morning.

"Has anything occurred to annoy you, Mr. Freeling?" said Mrs. Langley in her most persuasive tone.

"Much, my dear madam," replied Mr. Freeling, with another sigh. "There is scarcely a day that I am not reminded of the frailty and degeneracy of mankind. We hear individuals talk about their organizations to insure the accomplishment of their ends, forgetting that all the power lies with God. We live in godless times, Mrs. Langley. We trust too much to ourselves, and forget that we are but worms in the dust, and that unless the Lord is with us, we can do nothing."

"We certainly ought to put our trust in our Father," said Mrs. Langley, quietly.

"You don't state it strongly enough, Mrs. Langley. What do we see in business, in politics, in war,—yes, and even in religion? Men seem to think they are the arbiters of their own fate. I would teach them differently if I had the power. I am afraid we will never again see the time when those in high places will need only to tell the people, as did Cromwell, ' to put their trust in God !' "

"Did he not also tell them to keep their powder dry ?" said Grace Langley, without looking up from the pattern she was braiding. -

"Perhaps he did, Miss Grace," replied Mr. Freeling, with some indignation. "I don't see, however, what that has to do with the matter, and I would be obliged to you if you would not add to my distress by needlessly interrupting me."

Grace made no reply, and Mr. Freeling continued :

"It is our duty, Mrs. Langley, to forgive our enemies. I always do, and trust I have had an opportunity of exercising that virtue to-day. Oh, it is worth while to be injured in order to experience the pleasure that results from pardoning those who try to do us harm. I place my enemies in the hands of the Lord, Mrs. Langley. He will reward them according to their deserts."

"I am very sorry if any one has wronged you, Mr. Freeling," said Mrs. Langley, feelingly.

"It is very well for you to feel regret, Mrs. Langley. I am rejoiced. Yes, I have been deeply injured,—and by whom ? By a man whom I took to my bosom as a brother, for whom I have prayed these many times, and to whom I would even have loaned money. [" On good security," said Grace to herself.] I am disappointed in human nature. I know not upon whom to rely as a friend. And to think that this man who has wronged me should be an inmate of this house."

"Of this house ?"

"Yes, my dear madam, of this house. One whom you little suspect. Why should I conceal his name from you ? Charles I. Thompson is the man who has tried to lower me in the estimation of my fellow-men. He has been asserting for several days that I owed him five hundred dollars, and that he had lost the note which he says I gave him. I could not recollect owing him any sum at all, but told him that of course when he produced my promissory note I would pay all I had engaged to pay. He was not satisfied with this, but this morning he came to my office, and in presence of

several gentlemen called me a liar and a scoundrel. I may
not fulfill my entire duty to my Maker, but I am not a liar
and a scoundrel.   Oh, no!"   Mr. Freeling shook his head
sorrowfully with these last words, and let his chin drop on
his breast.

"Of course you do not owe him the money, Mr. Freeling?" said Mrs. Langley.

"How can I tell?   Let him produce the note and I will
pay it."

"But it seems to me you ought to recollect such things."

"Perhaps I ought.   But, Mrs. Langley, my thoughts are
occupied in a great measure with matters which are not of
this world."

"I don't think Mr. Thompson should have insulted you."

"And is this all you have to say in my defense, Mrs.
Langley?   I thought you, at least, would be my friend."

"What can I do, Mr. Freeling, other than express my
disapproval of Mr. Thompson's conduct?"

"Is it possible you will allow him to live in the same
house with me, after the unchristian spirit he has manifested?
Do you still regard him as a fit associate for yourself and
daughters?   Perhaps, too, he is guilty of attempting to ex-
tort money from me under false pretenses."

"I do not believe Mr. Thompson would be guilty of any
deliberate wrong.   He is impetuous, and therefore apt to
act rashly sometimes; but he is too good and conscientious
a man to attempt a fraud."

"Does he go to church, Mrs. Langley?"

"Indeed, I do not know; I never asked him."

"Then I can tell you he does not.   Why, it was only last
Sunday that he went fishing.   A man who would fish on
Sunday, Mrs. Langley, would commit a fraud.   He must
leave the house."

"I do not see my way clear, Mr. Freeling, to dismissing
him from the house.   Besides, recollect that I have not
heard what he has to say in his defense."

"Do you want to hear a defense when I make a charge,
Mrs. Langley?   Is it possible you would put Charles I.
Thompson's word on a parallel with mine?"

"Yes, Mr. Freeling, I think I would give as much credit
to Mr. Thompson's word as to that of any one I know."

"Madam, he must leave the house, or I do. See, here is a note which Miss Grace will copy and you can sign. I will read it.

"'Sir:—In consequence of the ungentlemanly conduct you were guilty of this morning toward my estimable friend, Mr. Freeling, I must insist on your vacating the rooms now occupied by you at the end of the coming week. Mr. Freeling is too generous to consider himself your enemy, but I cannot consent that you should, any longer than is possible, live in the same house with him.'"

"I cannot send any such note," said Mrs. Langley with firmness. "Mr. Thompson has always behaved like a gentleman since I have known him."

"Then I shall have to leave your house, madam," said Mr. Freeling, with difficulty smothering his rage, "and I warn you of the consequences of your persisting to refuse. You know I am the agent of Mr. Severne, the owner of these houses. A word from me would double your rent."

"I cannot help it, Mr. Freeling. I must do what I think is right."

"And you will not dismiss Thompson?"

"Certainly not, without hearing what he has to say; and, so far as I can now determine, not even then."

"Then I shall leave your house when my week is out, and I shall feel it to be my duty to discourage any one who has a regard for his reputation from coming here. The rent of the houses should be raised, in justice to Mr. Severne's interests, and I will consult with him on the subject."

"You will of course do what you please, Mr. Freeling; and, in the mean time, I have to request that you will leave us."

Mr. Freeling retired to his own apartments, and Mrs. Langley, sending for Mr. Thompson, heard from him a true account of the difficulty. Freeling had borrowed five hundred dollars, only five days previously, from Thompson, in order to make up a large sum he was about investing, and had given his note, payable at sight. He had subsequently gone to Thompson to pay the money, but the latter was unable to find the note. The loss was at once advertised and the negotiation of the note stopped; but finding that there

11

was no evidence of the debt to be found, Freeling had refused to acknowledge it, and, after repeated attempts to make him do what was right, Thompson had publicly insulted him.

Mr. Freeling left Mrs. Langley's house, and his rooms were immediately taken by a more worthy occupant. He did not, however, forget his threats. He had said all he dared to say against Mrs. Langley in his endeavors to prevent her apartments being taken, and had used every effort to induce Severne to raise the rent. Hitherto he had not been successful in his attempts, but finally his end had been attained; and, as he walked along Twenty-fifth Street, he congratulated himself that at last he was able to make the Langleys feel his power. He particularly disliked Grace, who had always appeared to understand his true character. Mary was almost constantly in bed, suffering, as she did, from a chronic malady which there was but little hope could ever be cured, and he had seen but little of her. Still he disliked her, as he did all persons whom he had injured or was about to injure.

He rang the bell, and was shown into the parlor by the servant, who informed him that Mrs. Langley was not at home, but that Miss Grace would see him.

Grace entered the room in a few minutes, during which interval Mr. Freeling amused himself by looking through a photograph album which lay on the table. As soon as she opened the door he rose from his seat and half held out his hand to her, but she did not appear to notice the gesture, and motioning him to a seat, inquired his business. It may be mentioned, in parenthesis, that Grace Langley was a very pretty, high-spirited, and good girl, well educated, and possessed of a sufficient amount of common sense and decision of character to make her quite a formidable antagonist even to Mr. Freeling. She was in her twentieth year, and though her health had been bad, owing to the combined effects of mental anxiety and confinement to the house, through the necessity of attending on her sister Mary, it had been much improved recently, and bid fair to be entirely restored.

"My business is with your mother," said Mr. Freeling, who was a little afraid of Grace.

"Mamma has no business which I am not perfectly competent to transact for her," said Grace.

"Oh, very well, Miss Grace; it is of rather a disagreeable nature, and I dislike to mention it before you, knowing the delicate state of your health."

"You need not refrain from stating it on that account," said Grace. "My health is sufficiently good to enable me to hear, without danger to it, any intelligence you may have to communicate."

"I am very sorry to have to inform you that I felt it to be my duty to Mr. Severne to represent to him that these houses were worth one thousand dollars a year each instead of five hundred, which your mother now pays for them. From the first of next month, therefore, you will pay three thousand dollars a year, Mr. Severne having this morning acceded to my proposition."

Grace felt a sickening feeling come over her as she listened to Mr. Freeling and understood what he said. She knew how utterly impossible it would be for her mother, even with all her rooms occupied throughout the whole year, to pay such a rent. Yet she was too proud to let her distress become known to Mr. Freeling; she therefore bowed her head coldly and said:

"Is that all your business, Mr. Freeling? I will tell my mother when she returns, and she will doubtless communicate with Mr. Severne on the subject."

"With me, if you please, Miss Grace. Mr. Severne does not care to be annoyed with complaints or demands from his tenants. You will therefore tell your mother that I will call here on Monday for her answer."

"And I repeat to you, Mr. Freeling, that mamma will communicate with Mr. Severne directly. I do not believe, when he hears all the circumstances, that he will allow your schemes to succeed."

"Your mother, and you too, Miss Grace, may make fifty attempts and you will not see him. You were pleased to allude to my schemes; there is no one present but ourselves, Miss Grace, and therefore I can speak plainly. I intend to make you Langleys feel my power. I intend to send you to the alms-house before you die. You thought you could resist me, and you perhaps think so still. We will see, however. You are a proud, stuck-up set, but I intend to bring you to your marrow-bones. I'll bring you to the alms-house or worse.   You especially.   I don't forget how you always treated me.   Out of these houses you go on the first of next month unless you agree to give three thousand a year for them and put up good security for the rent.   I know you can't do it.   You are ruined, root and branch, and I have done it."

Grace had risen from her chair while Freeling was speaking.   Her eyes flashed with anger and insulted dignity, but she heard him through without for a moment forgetting that she was a lady.

"I have never had the least doubt in regard to the character of your machinations," she said, with composure; "and now, having fully revealed them, have the goodness to leave the house."

"Not till I have told you something more, which will probably give you as much delight as that which you have already heard.   You must know, Miss Grace——"

But before he could say anything further, Grace rang the bell and left the room.   She met the servant in the hall, and directing him to show Mr. Freeling to the door, went to her own chamber, and throwing herself on the bed, burst into a flood of tears.   When her mother returned, Grace told her all that had happened.   "I will go myself and see Mr. Severne," she said.   "I do not believe, from all I have heard of him, that he is an unjust man.   So, dear mamma, do not give up, all may yet be well."

In spite of Grace's assurances and predictions, she and her mother experienced many forebodings in regard to the future.   Just as they were beginning to see their way clear, and were passing out of the depths of utter poverty, to have all their hopes dashed to the ground through the influence of a villain like Freeling, was indeed very hard.   They had both seen enough of life to know that it is not always the right side that wins, and that innocence and truth are often crushed out by the iron heel of oppression, so thoroughly that the world looks on with greater admiration for the one wielding the power than sympathy for those who suffer by its abuse.

As for Freeling, he left the house partially defeated.   He had anticipated that appeals would have been made to his mercy, and he had been looking forward with great satisfac-

tion to the pleasure he would experience in hearing and refusing them. There had been nothing of the sort. On the
contrary, he had been rather defied than otherwise. Still
he felt that he had command of the strings that could make
the puppets dance, and he was determined to pull them
when the time came. Nothing in the world at that moment
would have given him such intense delight as seeing the
Langleys reduced to the most complete destitution. He.
felt sure he could accomplish all his ends so far as they were
concerned, and he was resolved not only to make them taste
the cup of sorrow in all its bitterness, but to drain it to its
dregs.

CHAPTER XI.

IN WHICH THE HERO AND HEROINE MEET FOR THE FIRST TIME, AND IN
WHICH THE FORMER INDULGES HIS BIBLIOMANIACAL PROPENSITY.

SEVERNE remained in the house for a short time after
Freeling's departure, and then putting away the papers
upon which he had been engaged, sallied out for a walk.
It was several weeks since he had visited John Holmes's
book-shop, a place where it had been his habit to spend a
portion of nearly every day. He had scarcely ever gone
there without gaining some knowledge about men or books
which was interesting and useful to him. But besides the
motive for his visits due to this cause, he had acquired a
very warm and sincere friendship for both John Holmes
and Goodall. The former he had known and esteemed for
many years, but the latter he had been intimately acquainted
with for a comparatively short period. There was that in
Goodall, however, which endeared him very much to one of
Severne's thoughtful mind. There was such entire simplicity of character, so much thorough honesty and good
nature, and such a vast fund of common sense in him, that
it was impossible for any one who knew him to keep from
loving him.. Severne had thoroughly studied Goodall, and
had become perfectly conversant with all the points of his dis-

position.   He saw that Goodall had endured trouble of some kind which would never be forgotten while his life lasted, but he also saw that he bore it with that calm strength and self-reliance which would never desert him, because he had developed them out of his sorrow and made them part of his mental being.   And then, when he looked in upon himself, he was forced to admit that in the possession of all the elements which give real strength to character, Goodall was vastly his superior.

He thought of all this and a great deal more, as he pursued his way down Broadway toward John Holmes's shop. The street was crowded with beautiful and well-dressed women and fine-looking men.   Many of them he knew, and a few of them he liked—as men of Severne's stamp like acquaintances.   The morning was warm, but he was exhilarated by the fresh breeze that danced up the street from the sea, and played with the ribbons and draperies of the fair promenaders.   Already he felt that his cure was certain if he followed the directions Lawrence had given him.   He began to experience a little of that elasticity of mind which at one time had been a characteristic feature of his temperament.   There was hope for him yet.   There was no reason why he should not be happy, and he determined that he would.

In this frame of mind he arrived in front of John Holmes's shop.   How familiar, how kind, how scholarly it looked, with its begrimed windows full of treasures which kings might have envied!   He smiled as he stopped and tried to distinguish the titles of some of the books they contained. He found it an undertaking requiring all his efforts, but at length, by moving his position so as to get the light from the most favorable quarter, he was able to make out some of them ; others were altogether beyond his perseverance and skill.

"*De Somniorum Interpretatione*," he said to himself, reading the title of one of the books, "by that excellent but credulous philosopher, Artemidorus.   How vainly, since the creation of the world, have men tried to unravel the mystery of dreams, and how great an influence these fancies of the sleeping mind have exercised over the world !

"*L'Histoire des Imaginations Extravagantes de Mons.*

Oufle, Causées par le Lecture des Livres qui Traitent de la Magie, du Grimoine, des Sorciers, Loups-garoux, Incubes, Succubes, etc. I suppose Lawrence will be dishing me up some day as M. l'Abbé Bordelon has M. Oufle. There is no possibility of satisfying a physician's appetite for wonderful cases of disease. He takes them down as a matter of course, and is ready for more before he has digested the first dose.

"*Tractatus de Origina Animæ*," he continued. "All speculation and humbug. Sandius was an ass, and so are all other men, myself included, who waste their energies upon subjects far above their comprehension, and which they cannot by any possible effort expect to fathom. What do they know of the origin of the soul?

"But what is this? As I live, the *Historia Facultatum Intellectualium* of Ulrich de Hutten! The only copy probably in the world. A book which not one bibliomaniac in a thousand has ever heard of. Where could Holmes have found this book, which is worth its weight in gold? I have never forgotten its existence since I first heard of it years ago in Germany, and now to think that I should stumble on it in this way."

With these words Severne turned away from the window to enter the shop, without noticing Sarah Tompkins, who, as we have seen, rose from her seat on the step and fled rapidly in the opposite direction as he approached her. Just as he crossed the threshold, Margaret passed out. He started, for a moment, surprised that so young and lovely a woman should have visited the old book-shop, where, in the whole course of his experience, none but far less charming individuals of her sex had been seen. He caught but a momentary glimpse of her face, but that was enough to captivate him, and he was not a man to be easily thrown off his balance by female beauty, much as he admired it.

"Who can she be?" he wondered. "What a beautiful creature! Is it possible she buys old books? I'll not believe it! Fancy that fresh and lovely girl, whose thoughts should be young and trustful, hardening herself into a petrifaction before she has begun to enjoy the life God gave her. Yet she had a book in her hand, an old one, too. She has been sent for it by her father, or some old curmudgeon of an uncle or guardian. I must ask about this. I shall be miserable till I ascertain that she is not a bibliophile. Pshaw! a female bibliophile without spectacles, or false teeth, or hair, with beautifully gloved hands, and a bonnet like that, is an impossibility. What eyes! what a mouth! what a complexion! what grace in every movement! By Jove! if Lawrence were to hear me talk he would be satisfied at last!

"How are you, Goodall?" he continued, as he arrived at the location of his friend. "You are surprised to see me again after so long an absence, and are wondering how I have been able to endure life away from the old shop."

"Very glad to see you again, Mr Severne, but not surprised; and as to your time, I know you have spent it profitably," said Goodall, as he shook Severne warmly by the hand.

"I am not so sure of that; but if I thought you had such visitors daily as the one who passed me as I came in, I should be disposed to spend a great portion of my life here. Who is she? Not an authoress, I hope."

"Miss Leslie."

"Who?" exclaimed Severne, in great astonishment.

"Miss Margaret Leslie. Mr. Holmes's orphan granddaughter."

"John Holmes's granddaughter! I am more surprised now than ever. I did not even know he had a granddaughter. I had something to say to you of importance, but I have forgotten it. Is John Holmes in his den?"

"Yes; walk in; he will be glad to see you."

"John Holmes's granddaughter!" thought Severne, as he turned away from Goodall toward the door of the den. "The most beautiful girl I ever saw in my life. How dearly the old fellow must love her! I wish she was my granddaughter instead of his. Pshaw! she is happier far as it is. What in the name of all that is paternal would I do with so lovely a being as she is?"

John Holmes was seated at his table, busily engaged as usual in covering small half sheets of paper with writing, an occupation he had resumed as soon as Margaret left him at liberty. He rose from his chair as Severne entered the room, and greeted him with a warmth of manner which showed how much he liked and respected him. John Holmes admired all persons with literary tastes, but he had conceived an especial regard for Severne, which he never failed to manifest upon all proper occasions. Without being very demonstrative, John Holmes was by nature so frank and open-hearted that it was an impossibility for him altogether to conceal his emotions, even when it was desirable for him to do so. No man ever gets credit from the world for frankness and generosity. The exhibition of such qualities is sure to be misinterpreted to the disadvantage of their possessor, and John Holmes knew that he was often regarded as a far-seeing, and even designing man, because of his inability to refrain from the expression of his real feelings. There was no such danger, however, with Severne, who thoroughly understood and appreciated his friend as he was.

"My dear old fellow," said Severne, taking a seat on the sofa, "you never told me you had a granddaughter."

"Did I not?" replied John Holmes, smiling. "It must have been, then, because she was a mere child. In fact, she is not much more now. Remember you have not been to my house for over a year, and then you never came till it was so late at night that Margaret had gone to bed. How did you discover that I had a granddaughter, may I ask?"

"I met her at the door as I came in, and Goodall told me all I know."

"Yes, she was here for a few moments. By-the-by, that reminds me of what I had almost forgotton," he continued, pulling a bell-cord that hung near him. "My granddaughter had her pocket picked, I suspect by a young woman who asked her for alms at the shop door, and who, in answer to her inquiries, gave her residence. I am going to send there and see if she spoke the truth, though, of course, if she took the money, she has given a false address."

"A very sensible conclusion that of yours. I hope Miss Leslie's loss was not a large one."

"Not so great as to be beyond replacing; some fifty or sixty dollars, I think. My granddaughter is, however, much more distressed at the depravity of so young a girl than at the loss of her pocket-book."

"I should think so," said Severne, musingly.

" 'Thomas,' " said John Holmes to the porter, who made his appearance in answer to the summons, " I wish you would go to Dobbin's Court, Baxter Street, and see if you can find a young woman there by the name of—what is her name? I wrote it down. Ah, yes! here it is,—Sarah Tompkins, who——"

" What is that?" exclaimed Severne, who was reading a pamphlet he had picked up, and who was attracted by the familiar sound. " What name did you say?"

" Sarah Tompkins."

" Why, I know her. I have been looking for her these six months. What do you want with her?"

" She is the young woman whom I suspect of stealing my granddaughter's pocket-book."

" I should not be surprised to find your suspicions turn out correct. She cheated me out of ten dollars." Severne then related his adventure with Sarah, and detailed the objects he had in view concerning her. " I am very certain, however, that you will not find her in Dobbin's Court. I think I shall know this evening where she resides. In the mean time if you succeed in discovering her whereabouts, please inform me immediately."

John Holmes promised to do so, and Thomas departed on his errand.

" I think you are about to do a good action toward this young woman," he resumed. " There may be the germs of virtue in her yet, and we should endeavor to develop them if we can. If I can be of any assistance to you in facilitating your plans, do not fail to call upon me. Remember, I have acquired a claim on her."

" You shall certainly help if you desire to do so," said Severne. " I am going to travel for a few months, and will be glad to leave her under your superintendence while I am absent. That is, provided, of course, she accedes to my wishes."

" Going to travel, are you? I am glad of it. You require relaxation of that kind. I have noticed how badly you have been looking for several months past. You have been too assiduous with your literary labor. No man can stand such constant work as you have performed and retain his health. Which way do you go?"

"Across the continent to San Francisco, thence to India, and back through Europe.   Lawrence goes with me as my governor."

"Lawrence, too ! Why, what will the shop do with both of you away? I shall have to go also. Don't be surprised, therefore, if in three or four months you meet me in Paris."

"I wish you would," said Severne. "It would be of great advantage to Miss Leslie. That is, I mean she would see a great deal to interest and amuse her. But I had almost forgotten the immediate cause of my coming in here this morning. There's a book in the shop-window I want."

"Ah, I know what it is,—Ulrich de Hutten's Historia Facultatum Intellectualium. Goodall had never heard of it. He said it was a forgery at first, but finally admitted it to be genuine. There is a mystery about that copy which I am not without hope of having explained to me."

"I should not be surprised if it is the identical copy mentioned to me several years ago in Germany. Did you get it from a German ?"

"Yes."

"A thin, wiry, intellectual, and determined-looking man, with small black eyes, and a head like that of Hamman's Vesalius ?"

"You have described him exactly."

"The same, undoubtedly. Listen. In the month of January, 1847, as I was sitting in my room at the Hotel de Russie, in Frankfort, a servant came to announce that a stranger wished to see me. I directed him to be shown up. In a few moments a gentleman whom I had never seen before entered the room. He was evidently well bred, and there was an air of superiority and independence about him which, though not in the least offensive, struck me as being somewhat peculiar. He was tall, thin, scrupulously clean and neat, and remarkably handsome. Since then I have seen Hamman's picture of Vesalius in the Louvre, and the moment my eyes lighted on it I was astonished at the resemblance to my visitor. I invited him to be seated, and politely inquired his business with me.

" ' You see before you,' he said, 'a lineal descendant of that great warrior and philosopher, Ulrich de Hutten, Knight.'

"I bowed profoundly, though I had at that time no very definite idea of Ulrich de Hutten, except that like many other philosophers he had dared to meddle with theology, and had been persecuted therefor by the Church.

"'You are a scholar?' he continued.

"Not being very certain about that point, I maintained a discreet silence.

"'My ancestor, Ulrich de Hutten,' resumed my visitor, 'wrote a book, of which there is only one copy in existence. One thousand were printed, but as soon as the volumes were delivered to him by the printer they were seized by the bishop —all but one copy, which he had concealed under his bed— and destroyed. I have that copy in my possession. It is yours if you will pay me my price for it.'

"I was even then a hunter of old books, and though, as I have said, I took no particular interest in Ulrich de Hutten, I burned to be the possessor of a volume of which there was no duplicate in the world.

"'If I should agree to buy this book of you,' I said, 'how will I be assured of its genuineness?'

"'I will take care of that,' he answered. 'I have a complete history of the volume, duly authenticated.'

"'How much do you ask for it?'

"'Two hundred pounds of your money,' he replied.

"'Two hundred pounds! That is a great deal of money for one book,—more in fact than I can well afford to give.'

"'Very well, sir,' he said, with perfect composure. 'You, of course, know your own business better than I do. Should you change your determination, recollect that the book is the Historia Facultatum Intellectualium of Ulrich de Hutten, written at his castle of Steckelberg on the Main in the year 1521, and printed at Frankfort in 1522, and that it is unique. I wish you to have it. I have mentioned it as yet to no purchaser but yourself. I have only to take it to Paris to get my price for it.'

"'Give me till to-morrow to decide,' I answered.

"'With great pleasure,' he rejoined. 'Good morning, sir, till to-morrow at twelve, if that hour will suit you.'

"I expressed my acceptance of the appointment, and our interview terminated. The more I thought about the matter, the more I became possessed with the idea of buying the

book that had been offered to me. To make sure that I
would not be cheated by so doing, I consulted several gentlemen of my acquaintance whom I knew to be thoroughly
conversant with books, and upon whose judgment I could
therefore rely. No one of them had even so much as heard
of it, but all agreed that if the volume was such as the owner
represented it to be, it was well worth the price asked for it.

"I then got the life of Hutten by Wagenseil, and made
myself acquainted with the main details of his short but
brilliant career, as philosopher, soldier, and theologian. I
also, by reference to a collection of his works published as
complete, found that the 'Historia' was altogether unknown
to the compiler. I accordingly resolved to secure it, although so doing would require me to practice a rigid econ-
omy for some time in other matters. With impatience I
awaited the return of the owner.

"Punctual to the minute he came. I saw that he was
somewhat embarrassed, and without waiting for him to repeat his offer, I at once signified my acceptance of it.

"'I was sure you would agree to my proposition,' he
said; 'but will you pardon me if I tell you that I am anxious, with your full consent, to withdraw it.'

"I was surprised at this avowal, and asked the reason for
the change in his intention.

"'The only reason is,' he replied, 'that the cause which
existed yesterday for my parting with the book is no longer
in force. Nothing but the most urgent want would induce
me to think of resigning so great a treasure to another.
Since I last saw you my fortune has changed. If you insist upon it, the book shall be yours. I never broke my
word in my life. I beg you, however, to release me.'

"Of course I acceded again; but though I did so as
graciously as I could, my visitor saw that it was disagreeable to me.

"'I am eternally obliged to you for your great kindness,'
he said, with some emotion. 'I beg, as an evidence of my
appreciation of your generous conduct, that you will accept
this letter, the last my illustrious ancestor wrote.'

"With these words he handed me a letter, dated Island of
Ufnan, August 28, 1523, three days only before the great

man to whom Erasmus refused an asylum quitted this earth forever.

"I was overjoyed to get this memorial of a man for whose character I now began to entertain the utmost veneration and regard, and offered my visitor his own price for it. But no, it was a free gift, nothing would induce him to take money for it, as he had now sufficient for all his wants. I therefore thanked him, and asked him if I could be of any service to him.

"'Not now,' he answered. 'I do not know what may hereafter occur. One thing more; if ever I should be obliged to sell the "Historia," it shall be yours at the price mentioned yesterday. You may rely upon this promise. As I told you before, I never broke my word in my life, and never will. The book will never be sold except to you. Here is my card. Do not trouble yourself to give me yours. I know you now as No. 38, the number of your room. I shall be able to find you when I want you. Good-by. Again accept my thanks.'

"Before I could reply to this last speech, he was gone. I examined the card. There was no address on it; only the name Ulrich de Hutten. I have neither seen nor heard of him or his book since. I have made inquiries in regard to the 'Historia,' and have given orders for it to all the principal booksellers of Europe, but to this day have never received the least information in regard to it."

John Holmes had listened with the greatest attention to Severne's recital. When it was concluded, he said:

"The book is yours, I have no doubt. It was left here yesterday for sale by a gentleman such as you have described, who admitted that it was to be sold for two hundred pounds sterling or its equivalent, to but one person, he who in 1846 occupied room No. 38 at the Hotel de Russie, Frankfort-on-the-Main, and who had a card with the name Ulrich de Hutten inscribed on it. So, my dear Severne, if you have a mind to give a thousand dollars for the Historia Facultatum Intellectualium it is yours. How very singular that you should meet with it again, and what a strange story you have told me!"

"The whole affair is a complete mystery to me. Of course I want the book, and will at once write you a check for the money.   But can you not manage to get me an interview with the present owner ?"

"I am not sure that I can.   He said he would return to learn the result in about a week.   I will, of course, mention to him your wish.   Perhaps he will accede to it; but in regard to so singular a man as M. de Hutten evidently is, it would be unwise to make a prediction as to what he will do."

The book was then brought and carefully examined by Severne.   It was undoubtedly genuine, and on a fly-leaf was the following :

"*Nun ist meine arbeit gethan. Stekelberg, dem* 16 *Marz,* 1521.   *Ulrich von Hutten.*"

Severne immediately recognized the handwriting as that of Ulrich de Hutten by mentally comparing it with the letter in his possession, and with undoubted specimens he had seen in public and private collections.   He handed John Holmes a check for the price of the book, and putting it under his arm took leave of his friends, after again reminding John Holmes to inform him as soon as possible of the result of Thomas's search for Sarah Tompkins.

CHAPTER XII.

"SANS PEUR ET SANS REPROCHE."

OF course Thomas did not find Sarah Tompkins or her residence.   No one of the denizens of Dobbin's Court had ever heard of this young woman, or if they had, they were too sharp to part with any portion of their knowledge. John Holmes therefore went home that evening with the firm conviction that Margaret had undoubtedly been robbed and deceived by the girl to whom she had given alms, and certainly with no exaltation of his idea of human nature—that of beggar girls in particular.

When Margaret told him of her subsequent adventure, and of the recovery of her money, her grandfather began to think that perhaps he had been too hasty in his conclusion,

and he felt more disposed than ever to unite with Severne
in his plans relative to Sarah.   He at once wrote a note to
Severne acquainting him with the main facts of Margaret's
last interview with her, and of the address she had given.
Seeing that Margaret was so much interested in the girl, he
debated in his own mind whether it would not be as well to
tell her of Severne's and his plans, and finally concluded
that no harm could possibly result from so doing.

"You have heard me speak of my friend, Mr. Severne,
have you not ?" he said, addressing Margaret, who sat with
him on the piazza overlooking the garden at the back of the
house.

"Oh, yes, grandpapa; I have heard both you and Mr.
Goodall frequently mention him."

"He knows your friend, Sarah Tompkins, and is anxious
to be of service to her."

John Holmes then related to Margaret the facts which
Severne had that morning communicated to him relative to
Sarah, and his intentions.

Margaret was delighted, and was sure Sarah would gladly
embrace the opportunity of being educated and lifted up
from her present depraved condition.

"I should like very much to know Mr. Severne," she
said, after she and her grandfather had fully discussed Sarah,
her supposed antecedents, and her anticipated future. "He
must be a very good man."

"You have already met him," my dear child; "he passed
you at the door of the shop this morning."

"Was that Mr. Severne ? What a handsome man he is !"

"I should call him a handsome man, too, my dear child;
many people would not.   He is a true gentleman, however,
and that is better than being handsome."

"I think it is," said Margaret, musingly.   "How very
much that word gentleman expresses !"

"It means a great deal more than most persons think. I
never detracted from its full signification, and yet of the few
men I know who come within its pale, Robert Severne stands
among the first."

"I am sure he does, or you and Mr. Goodall would not
like him."

There was a silence then of several minutes, during which

John Holmes smoked his cigar with that quiet dignity and composure which showed how much he enjoyed it. Margaret was the first to speak.

"I have been thinking, dear grandpapa," she said, "how very rare it is that people pass for just what they are, neither more nor less."

"Very rare indeed; our judgment is not by any means the most perfect of our faculties. But what caused the thought, my dear child?"

"The fact that you and Mr. Goodall are the only persons I have ever heard speak well of Mr. Severne. Others say he is haughty, overbearing, vain, misanthropic, and that there is a mystery about him which no one in this country understands."

"And who say all this?"

"Mary Jocelyn and Rosalie Mayo, and Mrs. Sanford, to say nothing of Joshua and Mrs. Markland."

"Joshua and Mrs. Markland had better mind their own business. As to the others, I suspect they are annoyed that Mr. Severne does not visit them. He is going away in a few days."

"Going away?"

"Yes, he intends making the circumference of the earth. He says he will be absent six months, but I should not be surprised if even a year were found insufficient."

"Dear grandpapa, I should like to travel, and above all things, to go to Europe, where there is so much to see that is beautiful and venerable."

"You shall go, my dear Margaret; I have been thinking of it for some time, and next October, if all goes well, we will cross the Atlantic."

"Oh, how delightful it will be! What a pleasure to look forward to! I hope we will visit Germany and Italy."

"Yes, and many other countries besides. But, to return to Mr. Severne. It is probable that ere long you will have an opportunity of judging for yourself how true are the assertions you have heard. Hitherto, my dear Margaret, you have seen little or nothing of gentlemen's society, but the time is approaching, has actually come indeed, when it is desirable, if only for your own sake, that such should no longer be the case. Every good woman is made better by the society of refined, and educated, and intelligent men, and, on the other hand, every such man is improved by association with modest, virtuous, and accomplished women. There is no one I would be more pleased to introduce to you than my friend Mr. Severne, and I am very sure he will ask me to do so."

"I am very certain I shall like him. He must be very good and noble to think of doing so much for poor Sarah Tompkins."

"You will not only like him, my dear Margaret, for his benevolence. It is very rarely the case that any one can meet Robert Severne without learning some new fact or hearing some brilliant thought expressed, and yet he is not in the least pedantic. He does not even seem to think himself better educated and as having more knowledge than the majority of mankind."

Margaret made no reply. She was thinking over all the events of the day, and of what might possibly result from them. Her curiosity, and even a deeper interest, were aroused by what she had heard from her grandfather relative to Severne, and she looked forward with undisguised pleasure to becoming acquainted with him.

As her grandfather had remarked, her associations with gentlemen had hitherto been extremely limited. In fact, beyond Goodall and one or two old friends of her grandfather, of about his own age, who occasionally took a Sunday dinner with him, she only knew the rector and the assistant minister of St. Barbara's Church. The former was the father of two grown-up daughters, and the latter was on the look-out for an opportunity of putting himself into that condition of life which in time might also make him a father. He was a prim, rather shallow-minded young gentleman, with a very long neck, a very small nose, very large, colorless eyes, and a very loud and determined voice. Altogether the Rev. Pusey Porterfield was not such a specimen of the genus *homo* as a young girl like Margaret Leslie would look up to as a superior being.

She felt that what her grandfather had said in regard to the influence exerted upon women by association with good, true, and well-bred men was strictly correct. She knew there were such men. She had read of them in history, and she had seen their portraitures drawn in works of fiction.

She had even—what gentle, warm-hearted, and virtuous girl of her age has not?—formed for herself an ideal, of whom she often thought as she built the castles youth so delights to erect, and who, no matter how difficult and dangerous the positions in which she, in imagination, placed him, always came out of them in the end with his courage unsubdued and his honor unscathed, even though sometimes he suffered death for what he deemed the right. The qualities which she had thus learned to love most in men were truth, constancy, courage, and a love of learning. There were many others which she admired, but these took precedence of all the rest. It was quite natural that it should have been so when the character of her education is considered. The stamp which this had received was given by her grandfather and Goodall. The books they had placed in her hands, since she had been of an age to understand them, were not those which merely related dry matters of fact, but such as were also calculated to make her think, to develop her reason at the same time that they added to her knowledge. She had read the Apology of Socrates, and several others of the works of Plato, and had asked herself at first if it were really possible so noble a man as Socrates could ever have lived, who, rather than do what he knew to be wrong, was willing to suffer death! Then, as she read further, she came to understand that God has given a spark of his divinity to his creatures, and that in some men it kindles into a flame which never dies out. She had read how Fichte, when a boy, had thrown his dearly-valued book, the History of Siegfried the Horned, into the brook because it had been the means of causing him to neglect his lessons; and how, when he had made the sacrifice, he sat on the bank and wept as though his little heart would break, as his beloved treasure floated away out of sight. She had read the lives of Bayard, of Sidney, of Raleigh, and of other noble spirits, and she knew that there must be many like them in her own day, only she had never met any but her grandfather and Goodall.

And then the thought occurred to her that perhaps Mr. Severne was such a one. Margaret was not what might be called romantic. There was no sickly sentimentality in her composition; no disposition to exaggerate the situations of everyday life into monstrous improbabilities. On the contrary, no young girl could have been more natural and simple-minded without being weak, more guileless and straightforward without being coarse, than was Margaret Leslie. But it was very difficult for her to resist the thought that it was just possible there was one man who might be the incarnation of the many ideals she had formed in her mind. She had an undefined idea that she should not think about him at all; why, she could not tell. She had never loved any of her imaginary heroes, nor any of the real ones of whom she had read. She looked upon them as superior beings, quite beyond her sphere; as objects for the adoration of all women and models for all men. And this was just the status she was inclined to award to Severne. True, she had never heard that he had ever done any great or noble acts; that he had ever suffered unjustly, and had continued to bear himself loftily like a true gentleman. She hoped, however, that he was a man who, if occasion required, would act his part as became a gentleman, enduring success with modesty, and even apparent disgrace with honor.

While these thoughts were passing through her mind, the laboratory bell rang, and John Holmes, leaving her on the piazza, proceeded to the room in which he passed so great a portion of the night.

CHAPTER XIII.

THE OLD LOVE AND THE NEW.

DURING a portion of the time that John Holmes and Margaret were talking and thinking, as we have set forth in the last chapter, Joshua and Mrs. Markland were interchanging ideas in another part of the house. The housekeeper was a fine buxom widow of thirty-five, by no means bad looking or bad dispositioned, but possessed of certain

peculiarities of mind which gave her a very striking indi-
viduality, and which was probably one reason why Joshua,
who, while omitting no opportunity of picking a quarrel
with her, was unable to debar himself the pleasure he received from her society. Every evening, therefore, before
he proceeded to his work, it was his custom to spend an
hour or so in Mrs. Markland's sitting-room, which, though
adjoining the laboratory, had no direct communication with
that room. Mrs. Markland had just finished her dinner,
and had seated herself in a large rocking-chair, which she
was causing to oscillate with a degree of vigor and rapidity
quite inconsistent with that repose which the digestive
organs are supposed to require after a full meal. The room
was a very cosy and comfortable apartment. There was a
mat on the floor,· a center-table loaded with annuals,
albums, and other resplendently bound books; an *étagère*
covered with such *objets de vertu* as itinerant Israelites dis-
pose of in exchange for dilapidated garments; a mantle-
piece upon which stood a cup and saucer of Brobdignagian
size, elaborately ornamented with arabesques in all the
colors of the rainbow, and others not found in the celestial
arc, and inscribed in gilt letters, "To my Husband." This
triumph of the·ceramic art was flanked on either side by
a china shepherd, in Highland costume, holding a sheep in
his arms, and looking fearfully at a big dog which crouched
at his feet. On the walls hung numerous photographs of
large size, representing smiling personages of the sterner
sex, dressed in various modifications of a costume consisting in the main of stockinet shirt and nether garments, bedecked with spangles. Close observation revealed the fact
that all these represented one and the same graceful individual. Underneath these portraits were legends setting
forth their several characteristics, in this wise : "As he appeared in his great character of Mazeppa;" "As he appeared in his wonderful four-horse act;" "As he appeared
in the grand equestrian drama of the 'Winged Bucepha-
lus,'" and so on for a dozen others. The windows were
hung with white dimity curtains, and in a corner stood a
guitar, which was evidently in frequent use, as the strings
were complete.

The fair occupant was swaying herself backward and forward with all her propulsive force, when there was a knock on the open door, and, without stopping for an invitation, Joshua emerged into full view, and popped into a chair just within the domain of the widow.

"Well, Mr. Joshua," she exclaimed, "this is an awful hot day, and it's very hard on you and me, who have to spend so much of our time over fires. My poor dear Markland—who was as good a man as ever drew the breath of life, if he was a circus-rider—used to say, 'All things are for the best, Adelina; let us act well our parts, and the dim, mysterious future will no longer have power to terrify us.' Is there any news?"

"Yes, there's plenty of news," replied Joshua, "and bad news at that. If there never had been a woman created in this world, there might have been happiness. 'And now what is it?' I think I hear you say. You shall be answered. All the labor of Mr. Holmes and me is gone. Gone by the interference of one of your sex, Mrs. Markland: 197 is played out, for the next two years, at least. And to think that Miss Margaret should have done it! Now, if it had been you, it would not have been surprising."

At this most unprovoked attack, Mrs. Markland, with a Christian forbearance that was truly admirable, smiled sweetly, disclosing as she did so a very fine set of teeth, but made no reply.

"Oh, you may smile, Mrs. Markland," continued the irate Joshua. "Nero fiddled when Rome was burning; and some women I know of, who don't live very far from New York, nor from this house neither, have no more compunctions than a tiger. How would you like it if I was to smash that cup and saucer there?"

Mrs. Markland smiled again; this time quite incredulously. "Oh, Mr. Joshua," she said, very softly, "that would be impossible. You would not have the heart to destroy the gift which a gushing bride of eighteen summers presented to her husband on the first anniversary of her wedding! I never shall forget what he said. My poor dear Markland—who was as good a man as ever drew the breath of life, if he was a circus-rider—took the cup, and filling it with ale—he never drank anything stronger than ale—looked me in the face with all the tenderness of which he was master, and said :

    ' I fill this cup to one made up of loveliness alone '—

and then drained it· to the dregs. Wasn't it pretty? Wasn't it graceful ? But then, Markland was one of the most graceful men I ever saw. Did you ever see him in his great four-horse act ?"

"I never went to a circus in my life," growled Joshua.

"I never shall forget the first time I went," said Mrs. Markland, with a sigh. "It was there that I saw for the first·time my poor dear Markland, who was as good a man as ever drew the breath of life, if he was a circus-rider. I was but a simple-hearted maiden of seventeen summers; he was an agile and a graceful man. Perhaps I was good-looking, and perhaps I had been well educated at the Martha Washington Female Institute. But that was all. I was a giddy and a joyous girl, with no thought for the morrow. The performance was half over, and nothing had occurred to disturb the even current of my thoughts, when suddenly there was a blast of trumpets, and a gentleman dressed in green velvet and white silk, beautifully embroidered in gold and silver—his hair encircled by a band of gold, a winged rod in his hand, and silver wings on his feet—sprang into the ring. The ring-master said : ' Mr. Markland as Mercury.' Mr. Markland bowed to the audience, and as he raised his head our eyes met. I have only a dim recollection of the rest. I was overwhelmed. I did not see how gracefully he rode round the ring on his fiery courser, but I heard the shouts of the crowd, and when I again became myself,·he was gone. The next day ma, at my request, invited him to tea. We took it early, for he had to act at 7 o'clock. He came every day while the circus remained in our village. Why should I say more ? I married him, and have never regretted it to this day."

"I think I have heard that before," said Joshua, sullenly.

"I dare say you have, Mr. Joshua. Perhaps you have heard it from me ; but then I am sure it always interests you."

"No, it doesn't."

"No!" smiled Mrs. Markland. "Then it's because you are so learned. Your thoughts are lifted up beyond this common life of ours."

"No, it isn't that neither. It's because I'm tired of hearing it."

"Then I'll never tell it to you again. It shall be buried with my poor dear Markland, who was as good a man as ever drew the breath of life, if he was a circus-rider. He's dead," she continued, drawing a white cambric handkerchief from her pocket and holding it to her eyes. "He died, doing his duty in his splendid four-horse act, of a broken back, because two of the horses wouldn't go the right way. Cut off in the bloom of manhood, and I am left alone in this cold world, with no one to protect or care for me."

"That's not true," said Joshua, doggedly.

"Oh yes, Mr. Joshua, it is true,—alas! too true. Who is there to care for me? And I am so trusting, so confiding, so simple-minded yet, even if I have passed the bloom of my youth!"

Joshua rose from his chair and paced the room in an agitated manner, while Mrs. Markland sobbed violently behind her cambric handkerchief.

"My poor dear Markland," sobbed the widow, "who was as good a man as ever drew the breath of life, if he was a circus-rider, said to me the night he died—almost the last words he said—'Adelina, you are too good for this world; you have been a good wife to me, a much better one than a poor circus-rider deserved. Will you make me a promise before I die?' 'Anything, my dear Markland, that you can ask,' I said, through my tears, which were falling thick and fast. 'Then promise me that if you should marry again, you will marry a man of science.' He made such a point of it that I promised. And—and—here I am."

The recollection was too much for Mrs. Markland's strength, for her sobs redoubled in violence, and her face, still covered by her handkerchief, fell till it rested on the arm of her chair.

Joshua stopped in his walk and stood in front of the weeping widow. He had evidently made up his mind to say something very decided, for his brows were knit, his hands were clinched, and his whole appearance was that of a man who had determined upon a certain course, though it might not be a very agreeable one.

"I'll tell you what it is that makes you feel lonely and miserable, if you would like me to," he said, in his spasmodic way.

"Oh, Mr. Joshua, if you only would I could throw myself at your feet and bless you forever."

"I don't want you to do anything of that kind, but I'll tell you, and cure you, too, if you'll let me."

"Say and do what you please, I will be like a lamb in your hands."

"Then you just listen to me," said Joshua, getting almost ferocious in his excitement. "You've got a lot of relics here that make you melancholy. What's the use of that cup and saucer, and all those pictures, except to remind you of him that's dead and gone these ten years and more? Every time I come in here to have a little pleasant talk with you about matters and things in general, you tell me about him, and work yourself up into a fever over a man that never can be anything more to you in this world. Now, you've put yourself in my charge, and I mean to do my duty by you just as sure as my name's Joshua. I've stood this kind of thing long enough, and I don't mean to stand it any longer if I know myself."

"Oh, Mr. Joshua, what do you mean to do?" exclaimed Mrs. Markland, clasping her hands together and looking at him in the most anxious manner. "But I am passive, as my poor dear Markland, who was as good a man——"

"Now you stop," said Joshua, "and let me alone, for I'm going to end this thing; I'm not going to have your peace of mind and mine, too, ruined by your relics."

With these words, Joshua began to remove the photographs of the deceased Markland from the wall, and to make a pile of them in the middle of the floor. He then took the cup and saucer from the mantle-piece and placed them on top. Mrs. Markland watched his proceedings with the greatest interest depicted on her countenance and with her plump hands still clasped together, but she did not utter a word,—she appeared to be stupefied by the enormity of Joshua's proceedings.

"Are those shepherds relics, too?" said Joshua, pointing
to the Highlanders who occupied the ends of the mantle-
piece.

Mrs. Markland could only shake her head negatively.

"No more in this room?"

"Oh, yes," she answered, with a great effort. "There's
a photograph in that albnm, and he gave me those wax
flowers on the *étagère*."

Joshua proceeded with the utmost dignity to add these
to the pile.

"Are you quite sure that's all?"

Mrs. Markland bowed her head in token of affirmation.

"Then here goes to make an end of the whole lot," exclaimed Joshua, seizing a flat-iron that stood on the hearth,
and with savage energy dashing it repeatedly with all his
force upon the fragile pile, till he had thoroughly demolished
the materials of which it was composed, and left nothing
but a scattered mass of fragments of broken china and glass
and torn paper. "There's an end of the relics, anyhow,
and I hope I may be blessed forever and ever!"

So intense was his abstraction that he had not noticed
that Mrs. Markland, apparently unable to endure the sight
of the sacrifice which was being offered, had lost consciousness and slipped from her chair to the floor, where she lay
with no sign of life perceptible.

Joshua was not a cruel man, and now that his excitement
had reached its height, he began to experience the feeling
of depression which invariably follows on all exaggerated
emotions. He saw stretched before him on the floor, in an
apparently lifeless condition, a woman for whom he had long
felt a tender regard, which only her constant reference to
her deceased husband had prevented him from manifesting
in an unmistakable manner. He knew that Mrs. Markland
had only fainted, but he thought he ought to do something
to restore her. What, he scarcely knew. In default of any
better proceeding suggesting itself, he sat down on the floor
beside her, took her hands in his, and began to rub them
vigorously. He continued this exercise for several minutes
before the effects began to be manifested. Then his patient
gave a deep-drawn sigh, moved herself a little, and opened
her eyes. She did not look at all displeased; on the con-

trary, there was a melancholy smile playing about her mouth, which seemed to express his pardon, and she did not attempt to withdraw her hands from his.

"I know I've been very weak, and that what you have done is all for the best," she said at last, in a voice scarcely above a whisper, and with a most forgiving expression of countenance. "I'll never talk any more as I used to, and perhaps in time you will get to like me just a little."

"I like you a good deal now," said Joshua, frankly.

"I think I feel strong enough to get up now," she remarked, in a weak voice.

Joshua assisted her to rise, and placed her in her chair again.

"Do you want me to go away?" he said, after he had performed these little offices.

"Oh no, do not leave me. You have no idea how great a comfort your presence is to me."

"Adelina," said Joshua, taking one of her hands, "would you like me to stay with you always?"

"Oh, yes," she murmured.

"Then I'll do it. I'll take the place of him that's gone, and I'll get you a lot of pictures, and another cup and saucer to-morrow."

"Oh, Joshua," said the widow, "how happy I am! Let the cup be inscribed in letters of living gold,—'From Joshua to Adelina;' and you'll take care of your little woman, won't you?"

"Yes, I will!"

"And you'll soon get used to her light heart and thoughtless ways, so unlike your own, which are so weighty and serious."

"I don't want to get used to them. I want to be surprised by them every day. I am used to too many things. There's all that work in the laboratory; I've been used to that for years, and what am I? I should like to have that question answered. What am I?"

"You are my own dear Joshua, forever and ever," said the widow, throwing her arms around his neck.

"Now all my work is to be gone over," resumed Joshua, without seeming to notice the interruption. "Miss Margaret has ruined it. I'm sure now we will never get 197."

"Dear Joshua, what is 197, and why do you spend all your nights in that hot room over a furnace?"

Joshua was now in his element once more.

"Oh, that's science, you see; a vain and a perverse science. Shall I tell you what my worthy friend, Henry Cornelius Agrippa, Knight, says of it?"

"Oh, yes, dear Joshua, whatever your friends say will always be welcome to my ears."

Joshua took a small book out of his pocket and read:

> "'An art which good men hate and most men blame,
> Which her admirers practice to their shame;
> Whose plain impostures, easier to perceive,
> Not only others but themselves deceive.'"

"What beautiful poetry! Blame, shame; perceive, deceive. Did you know Mr. Knight very well, and is he a very good friend of yours? I don't believe you would deceive anybody. You would not deceive me, would you, Joshua?"

"No, I would not. The best and the worst person I ever deceived is myself. I don't know Mr. Knight. This book was written by the great, the immortal Henry Cornelius Agrippa. He was a knight, a doctor of both laws, a judge, and a counselor. The amount of consolation I've got out of this book is wonderful. It's been a great comfort to me. It says, ' Chemists are the most perverse men that live,' and I know that's true; and it says, ' They will sell their souls for three farthings,' and that was true half an hour ago."

"But it's not true now, dear Joshua, is it,—even if you are a chemist?"

"I'm not even a chemist. I am what my guide and my friend, Henry Cornelius Agrippa, calls a cacochemist, and that's worse than a chemist."

"How learned you are! What beautiful names you know! You must teach me some of them, and in return I'll read you some of my poetry."

"Do you write poetry?"

"Oh, yes, I write, and sing my verses to the tunes they used to play at the circus, as my poor dear——"

Mrs. Markland was proceeding with her usual panegyric on her deceased lord, when, happening to cast her eyes on

the floor, she saw the remains of Joshua's act of demolition.
With scarcely a pause of a second, she continued :

"Mother said to me once, 'Adelina, you are a bird of
song as sweet as a nightingale. There's more music in one
verse of your poetry than in the whole village band.'"

"I wish you would say just one verse now," said Joshua,
looking very loving and sheepish at the same time.

"Yes, dear Joshua, I will recite a little waif I wrote not
long since. It is a heart story of a maiden who had been
misunderstood by her lover, and who, rather than exist in a
world that had lost all charm for her, resolved to drown
herself in the raging sea. It is a touching little thing. I
call it—

"THE SHADE AND SUNSHINE OF A MAIDEN'S HEART.

"The moon was rising from the troubled sea,
  The clouds rushed wildly, madly through the sky,
The stars shed forth their twinkling light on me,
  As sadly, mournfully, I came to die.

"I sat upon the cold and clammy beach,
  Prepared to plunge into the roaring foam,
When suddenly I heard a deafening screech,
  And Henry came to bear me to my home.

"He bore me to my humble cottage door,
  Holding me to his true and manly heart;
'At last! at last!' he cried, 'our grief is o'er,
  And Jane and Henry never more shall part.'

"Unto the village church we hied next day,
  And in the silence of that sacred spot
We took the vows that lovers like to say,
  And ever since have gloried in our lot.

"I sing it," she continued, "to the tune the band used to
play when Herr Otto Motty was balancing plates on a long
stick and catching cannon balls on the back of his neck."

"It's beautiful! too beautiful for a cacochemist like me!"
said Joshua, with a shake of his head. "I never liked
poetry before ; for, as my worthy friend, Henry Cornelius
Agrippa, Knight, says, so I thought, that it is 'An art invented to no other purpose, but with lascivious rhymes,

measure of syllables, and the gurgling noise of fine words, to allure and charm the ears of men addicted to folly.' But a man who is right on so many other points must be wrong on a few, and this is one of them. I don't like to lose confidence in my friend and guide though—I don't like it."

"We won't talk about him any longer. Dear Joshua, what will be my name when we are married? My maiden name was so pretty,—Adelina Alderly,—and the one I used to sign to my little waifs was beautiful—Vinie Violet."

Joshua had always been known as Joshua, neither more nor less. The one name was sufficient, and he would not have tolerated Josh. Still, he had a surname, and of course it was a laudable instance of female curiosity that his future wife should wish to know the cognomen she was to bear. It was not, however, at all euphonious; not to be compared to that of Adelina Alderly, or even Markland, and Joshua therefore felt that his affianced bride would experience some disappointment when she heard it. However, there was nothing to do but tell it.

"My name is Joshua," he at length answered.

"Oh, yes, I shall always know you as Joshua, and call you so, too, if you will let me; but what will the world call me?"

"Why, it will call you Mrs. Joshua, of course."

Mrs. Markland smiled at what she regarded as a good joke on the part of her lover.

"Ah, my dear Joshua," she said, laying her hand on his shoulder, "you are making fun of your little woman! Naughty man!" she continued, patting his cheek lightly.

Joshua appeared to like the imputation and the consequent situation of affairs, for he took the rebuke and the chastisement with a grim sort of smile. He had a duty to do, however.

"My name is Joshua Joshua," he said, with a spasmodic desperation.

"Joshua Joshua! two Joshuas?" inquired Mrs. Markland, with a blank expression of countenance.

"Yes, but they both begin with a J, and Adelina Alderly has two A's, and Vinie Violet two V's."

"It's not a pretty name, though, is it, dear?"

"No, it's not pretty."

" We might change the last Joshua," she said, timidly.

" What would you change it to ?"

" We might make an anagram of it, as great men did in years gone by. Let me see ; suppose we change it to Hujaso. That is really beautiful ; *so* expressive, *so* aristocratic ! Adelina Hujaso is sweet, and Joshua Hujaso, Esquire, is dignified and grand."

" I have no objection whatever," said Joshua, resignedly. "Let it be Hujaso. I think myself it is better than Joshua."

" I am sure it is," exclaimed the widow, triumphantly. " You will not regret the change ?"

"No, not a bit. I must leave you now, Adelina. There's plenty of things to get ready in the laboratory to-night, and Mr. Holmes always likes to be called at ten o'clock."

"Must you go ? And so soon, too ! Can I help you ?"

" No, I don't think you can. We have got the whole analytical process to go over again since Miss Margaret made the solution crystallize before it was time. Good night, Adelina."

"Good night, dear Joshua. Won't you kiss me ?"

Joshua kissed her cheek, then her lips, and without another word stalked determinedly out of the room.

When he had fairly closed the door behind him, Mrs. Markland rose from her chair and took a glance at herself in the mirror which hung in the pier. She was apparently well satisfied with the inspection, for a smile passed over her features. She then took a survey of the ruins Joshua had left of her household gods. She regarded the scattered fragments on the floor very attentively and reflectively for several minutes. Then she walked up to the largest pile which still remained and stamped upon it with both feet till she had reduced it to a mass of still smaller pieces, which she kicked with great energy about the room. She then proceeded to a like work of destruction with all the bits sufficiently large to require further demolition.

"There !" she exclaimed, when her labor, which she viewed with intense but savage gratification, was completed. " That's the end of you, you vile, miserable, disgusting brute ! To think that I should have been tied to such a villain. Why didn't you break your back before I saw you, you beggarly mountebank ?" she continued, with increased fierceness, as she perceived a piece of one of the photographs, which she picked up and tore to atoms. "Oh, you scoundrel!"

Exhausted with her exertions, the fair widow dropped into a chair and fanned herself till her heat of mind and body had somewhat subsided. Then she took a broom and swept up the bits of china, glass, and paper quite clean and put them into a coal-scuttle.

"I feel tired," she exclaimed, as she again sat down. "I think I'll go to bed as soon as I feel refreshed enough to mount those stairs. Altogether it has not been a bad day's work. Talk of the sense of men! Why, one woman's worth fifty of them. I'd like to see the one that could fool me. I'll pay him up some day for all his insults; and I'll twist him round my little finger in the mean time, too. I'll not have any of this fool's work going on all night after I'm married,—not I indeed. Joshua!. As if I, a born Alderly, was going to take such a name!"

Apparently overcome with fatigue and the force of her emotions, Mrs. Markland's head fell forward on her breast, and in a few moments she was sound asleep in her chair.

CHAPTER XIV.

"GO AND SIN NO MORE."

AFTER parting with the acquaintance who had given her the information relative to the proposed burglary, Sal Tompkins quickened her pace, and soon reached a section of the city the character of which was easily to be inferred from a very superficial inspection of the residents and of the dwellings in which they lived. There were gaudily-dressed and brazen-faced women leaning out of the open windows and calling to the passers-by, and others who, with scarcely clothes enough on them to hide their nakedness, flitted in their bare feet from house to house, quarreling and cursing, or laughing uproariously, as the feeling of the moment dictated. There were coarse, brutal-looking men, clothed in fine broadcloth, and sporting enormous watch-chains and finger-rings, and others who sat at the doors in their shirt-sleeves, ready to drive a bargain for second-hand clothes or sham jewelry with any one verdant or poor enough to enter their dens; and there were children witnesses of crime and shame, and approaching with rapid strides the stage of wickedness to which their elders had attained.

Sal hurried along, not stopping to reply to the saluta-tions with which she was constantly greeted by men and women, and ere long arrived at a house very similar in gen-eral appearance to those by which it was surrounded, except that it was somewhat larger and in better condition. She ascended the three or four stone steps which led to the en-trance and tried to open the door. It was locked, so she gave the bell a violent pull, and probably knowing by ex-perience that it would not be answered very promptly, sat down on the upper step and waited as patiently as she could for admission. A window was first cautiously opened, and then she heard steps in the hall. It took some little time to unbar and unlock the door, but finally this work was ac-complished, and Sal crossed the threshold.

The woman who opened the door looked sharply at the girl as she admitted her. She had a very piercing dark pair of eyes to use for this purpose, and had evidently once been handsome. Her hair, which was of an intensely black hue, streamed over her bare shoulders unconfined by band or comb, and her frock clung close to her limbs, allowing her naked feet to be seen as she preceded Sal along the pas-sage-way. And yet the woman had an appearance of neat-ness about her not quite in accordance with her surround-ings. Her hair was not at all tangled, but was parted smoothly and brushed back from her forehead, her frock was clean, and her face and hands gave evidence of no very remote application of soap and water.

"You don't seem as if you were in a very good humor to-night, Betsey," said Sal, after they had ascended the first flight of stairs, and the latter stood in the hall with her hand on the door-knob of the front room. "Come in and let's have a talk while I dress."

Thus accosted, Betsey's face assumed a more pleasant expression, and she followed Sal into the room.

The apartment was very comfortably, and in some respects luxuriously, furnished. It extended the whole width of the house, was well lighted, had plenty of chairs and tables in it, a large, neat-looking bed, a good carpet, and many little ornaments scattered about it. Betsey sat down, and Sal at once began to make her toilet.

"No, Sal," said the former, "I'm not in a good humor, and what's more, I don't expect to be while things go on as they do."

"What's the matter, Betsey?" inquired Sal, who had already divested herself of her outside garments and was busy at the wash-basin.

"It's well enough for you to ask what's the matter when you're out of the house all day. But I should think that even you could see what's the matter; and perhaps you ain't so ignorant as you seem."

"Is it me, Betsey? Have I done anything?"

"I don't say you have, Sal Tompkins, and it's well for you I don't know you have."

"Then it is me, is it, Betsey?"

"I don't say yes or no."

"Look here, Betsey," said Sal, stopping in her ablutions and speaking very earnestly. "Don't let there be any bad blood between you and me. If you think I've done you any harm, say so at once."

Betsey was silent, and Sal continued:

"I've told you a great many things in my time, and I never told you a lie. I may have lied to others, but I never lied to any one in this house. If you've got anything to ask me, do it, and I'll tell you the truth; but don't get in a bad humor with me till you know you've cause, and don't you threaten me, Betsey, for I won't stand that from anybody."

"Where's Jack?" said Betsey, angrily.

"I don't know."

"Weren't you with him this morning?"

"No."

"Nor last night?"

"I wasn't out of this room last night, and Jack wasn't in it. If you think I know anything of Jack Duggan, you're mistaken, Betsey."

"Well, I believe you Sal, and I ask your pardon. I

never knew you to tell any of us a lie. Somehow, Jack doesn't seem to care for me any more, and I thought may be he had taken up with you. He was here this afternoon with Jim and Bill, and he hardly spoke to me. Perhaps it was because he was busy."

"Yes," said Sal, not appearing to evince much interest in the matter. "I met Bill, and he told me Jack had got up a party for to-night."

"Yes, they are going on a big lay to-night; but still I think, for all that, Jack might have spoken to me more than he did."

"It must have been because he was very busy, Betsey. I know Jack is a good friend of yours. Do you know who is to be cracked to-night?"

"An old fellow named Holmes, who is very rich, and has plenty of silver in his house."

"Has Jim been here to-day?"

"Yes, he went out about half an hour ago. He told me to tell you he'd be in to supper by nine o'clock. They don't start till late."

"Have you been in the house all day?"

"Yes, and that's another thing I don't like. I'm left at home here to open the door and keep things in order, while you are out all day."

"Don't I always share fairly with you, Betsey?"

"Yes, I believe you do; but I don't care so much about that; I'm tired, Sal, of staying shut up in this house all day and all night, too. I hate the sight of everything in it. I'm weary, weary of this sort of life, and you'll be weary of it, too, when you get to my age."

"You don't look well, Betsey. Is there anything the matter with you?"

"No, Sal, I'm only heartsick."

Sal, who had now finished dressing, and whose metamorphosis from a beggar-girl into a pretty young woman was complete, turned to the speaker, and saw that tears were running swiftly down her cheeks. She went to her and put one arm around her neck and drew her head to her breast. Neither of them spoke for several minutes, the silence only being broken by Betsey's sobs. How vain would be the attempt to probe to the bottom the weariness, the despondency, the despair which filled the heart of this poor, erring girl, who had at last been brought to feel the loneliness of her lot, the bitterness of disappointed hopes, and perhaps even the remorse due to a life spent in sin and shame ! Only heartsick ! We all know what this means; but few of us, perhaps, have felt the pangs of the disease as this girl felt them, as she wept upon the breast of the only one to whom she could pour out her grief with any hope of receiving the sympathy for which she longed. Only heartsick ! The consequence of a life misspent, the apprehension of guilt, the loss of self-respect, the perception of a joyless future,— these are the things which make the heart sick ; which force the mind to look in upon itself and view with horror the ghastly ruins of its own decay.

"I've always liked you, Betsey," said Sal, her own tears beginning to flow. "You've always been kind to me, and sometimes, I know, I've worried you. But I won't do it any more, and if you'll tell me what I can do now I'll do it."

"I want to get away from here, I'm worn out with this life. I loved Jack, but he doesn't care for me any longer. Why should he ? I'm not good looking now; I'm very miserable, and I've tried liquor and laudanum, but they won't do. I thought, last night, I would just take a big dose of laudanum and be done with it. I think I will, for there's nothing to keep me in this world."

"No, no, Betsey," said Sal; "you must not talk in that way. I've been thinking this afternoon, and maybe I'll see my way clear to help you and myself, too. Don't be cast down, and don't cry any more. I'll be your friend and you'll be mine. I want you to help me now, Betsey, by telling me just what you think about what I am going to say.

"Suppose," continued Sal, "you were out prospecting, and you came across a young lady as beautiful as an angel, and you asked her for a little ready, and told your chant; and suppose, when she gave you money, you were to draw her pocket-book, and then feel sorry about it; and then suppose you watched for her, and when you found her you gave her back all her chink, and then instead of abusing you and calling you a thief, or crying out for the police and having you nabbed, she talked to you kindly and said you didn't look like a bad girl, and she'd like to help you, and who was not ashamed to be seen walking with you, if she was dressed finely and you looked like a beggar, and who wanted to come to your house, and do anything she could to make you better, and who was as beautiful and as gentle, mind, Betsey, as any angel ever was,—suppose all this,—what would you do for her in return?"

"I would do all I could to serve her in any way. I don't suppose I would ever have the chance though."

"Would you let her house be cracked?"

"Not if I could help it, Sal."

"Well, Betsey, I don't intend to allow it either. What I've told you is all as true as Gospel, and it's her house that's to be cracked to-night. I must stop it somehow, and I can't think of any other way than to go and tell her what's going on. And if you'll just keep them from suspecting me I'll run round there while they're at supper."

"I'll do it, Sal. She must be very good and beautiful to take your fancy so. I'll stay here with the boys while you go and tell. They would kill us though if they find us out, and I would not like to get them into any trouble."

"I don't think there'll be any danger of that, but if there should be, I can't help it. I'm not going to have her house cracked."

"Very well, Sal. I've made up my mind to leave here, and I wish you would go, too. You are younger than I am by five years at least, and you could make your living without any trouble, for you've got more sense than I have. Perhaps the young lady will put us both in the way of doing something, and I wish you would ask her. If I can't do better, I can kill myself, and I'll do it too, if the worst comes to the worst. And now I'll go up stairs and dress, but I don't feel much like it, except that I think I ought to look nice when Jack comes in."

"Betsey," said Sal, taking her companion's hand, "I never knew what a good heart you had till to-night. Don't you feel glum any more, and you'll be all right before very long. You're a good deal better than Jack Duggan, and you need not mind what he does. I never felt ashamed of myself till to-day, and then when I saw her sweet face, and heard her kind words, I thought to myself I would be will-

ing to die to be like her.   I know that's impossible, Betsey.
I know that while my life has been a bad one, hers has been
like an angel's.   She is just about my age, too.   Perhaps,
Betsey, she'll tell us what we can do when we leave here.   I
suppose I shall have to go too, for I wouldn't like to live
with Jim after blabbing on him."

CHAPTER XV.

IN WHICH SOME PLANS ARE FORMED AND OTHERS ARE BROUGHT TO
AN END.

AFTER Betsey had gone to her own room, Sal busied herself in getting supper ready for Jim Terry and his friends
when they should come in at nine o'clock.   Out of a cup-
board she took a cloth, some plates, cups, and knives and
forks, which she proceeded to arrange on a large table which
stood against the wall.   On a small gas-stove she next
began to make some coffee.   A box of sardines, a jar of
pickles, bread and butter, made up the rest of the meal.   It
did not take long to complete these preparations; and before the coffee was quite made, Jim Terry and his companions
entered the room.

"How are you, my gal?" said he, holding out his hand in
great good humor to Sal.   "What a blessed thing it is to
have a lady-bird like you to see after a fellow's grub!   Give
us a kiss, you little baggage."

With these words, Jim Terry took Sal's face between his
big hands and kissed it.

"There, Jim, let me go now till I get this coffee made.
You and Jack and Bill sit down at the table and help your-
selves.   I'll soon be ready.   Won't you call Betsey, Jack?
She's up stairs in her room."

Jack Duggan, who was the gentleman in whose company
Sal was found by Severne when he walked behind her up
the Fifth Avenue six months since, did not appear to relish

this proposition. He had thrown himself on a lounge, and had assumed a position so comfortable that he was loth to change it, even for the sake of having the pleasure of Betsey's society.

"I guess she knows we are all here without my going up stairs after her," he said. "And if she doesn't, what's the odds? I don't see as her presence is necessary to the success of this princely entertainment."

"Then I'll call her myself," said Sal, and immediately left the room for this purpose.

"I don't think you treat Betsey exactly right, Jack," said Jim Terry. "She's a good girl, and thinks a good deal of you."

"I know she's a good girl, Jim, but she's got to be such a blasted melancholy one that she gives me the blues whenever I come near her. If she'd only be a little lively, she and me would get along first rate. I really don't know what's got into Betsey these last two or three months. She says I don't care for her. She wants me to talk to her and keep with her all the time, which is very unreasonable, to say the least."

"Some women is very worrying," said Bill, who, had hitherto been silently watching the steaming coffee. "I once knew a gal who never would let her cove have his breakfast till he got down on his knees and said his prayers. They do take the strangest notions sometimes. Now there's a sister of mine as went to California when the gold fever broke out. She might have married a white man worth his weight in nuggets, but what do you think she did? Why, as sure as my name is Bill Smithers, she married a Chinese nigger named Hang Foo. Now if all women was like your Sal, Jim, things would be different. She's the girl for my money."

"Yes, and for mine too," said Jim, exultingly. "I can just leave her to look after things alone, and she does it without the need of me watching her all the time. She makes her own living, too, which is a great thing for a woman to do in these times, when men are pushed hard to get enough together to make both ends meet. Here she comes, and Betsey, too," he continued, as the two women entered the room. "Come in, Betsey, don't be bashful;

take a seat here alongside of me.   Sal won't be jealous, will you, Sal ?"

Sal expressed her concurrence, but Betsey passed round to the other side of the table and sat down next to Jack, who, however, took no notice of her except to ask her to hand him the pickles.

"Now, boys and gals," said Jim Terry, after the party had arranged themselves to their satisfaction, "let's go to business at once.   This is a big thing that we've got on hand to-night.   There's lots of hard cole, and soft, too, with a chest full of white wool.   I've been round there all day, more or less, and I think I know how the land lies.   There's a big garden behind the house with three doors opening into it.   Besides, there's seven or eight windows on that side, by which we can get in or out.   My plan is to scale the wall of the garden and get in by one of the windows, which are almost on a level with the ground.   I am pretty sure we can do this without waking the old codger or any of his crew.   If they should get troublesome, however, we have a way to hush them, and we'll use it.   There are two men in the house, the old one and another, and half a dozen women, more or less, and there are two men sleeping over the stable and coach-house.   We needn't be afraid of them if we look sharp.   The best thing will be for Jack and me to go in and gather up the plunder while Bill stays around outside and watches.   What do you say to it ?"

"Well, I've got this to say, Jim," said Jack Duggan. "You know there's a wing to the house on the north end, and that this wing makes a part of the garden-wall on that side.   Now, I've been watching that house night and day, and I've found out that there's a light in that wing till two or three o'clock in the morning, and sometimes later.   It strikes me that our best plan would be to get into that wing, nab the coves that are in there and stop their gab, while we do our work at our ease.   I listened at the window last night, and I'm pretty sure old hunks and his man were in there.   As to the women, we need not go near them.   There's enough for us in the house without our taking their traps. Bill can stay around outside, as Jim says, to look out for the Philistines, and Sal and Betsey will be all ready to help us plant the lurries when we get home besides giving us bene prog.   We'll be awful peckish, I guess."

"You're always thinking of your stomach, Jack," said Bill. "I'd rather have something nice to swill about four o'clock than all the prog in New York. I rather guess your plan is the best, though. What do you say, Jim? I ain't particular myself. I'm mighty good at watching for the crushers, who ain't likely to be about, anyhow."

"I don't know, when I come to think about it," replied Jim, "but that Jack's plan is the best; so we'll consider the thing fixed. There are two rooms in that wing, I think, and a passage leading from it to the main building. There's a window in this passage which opens toward the garden, and it's only closed by inside shutters, which can easily be opened. We'll get in by this window and fix the two old codgers before they know what's up, if they're in the room. If not, we'll have things all our own way. What do you think about it, Sal? Bless my soul! the gals hain't opened their mouths, except to fill them with prog, since they came into the room! Come, Sal, speak up, you always give good advice, because you've got more sense than most men, and there never was a woman born—present company excepted, Betsey—who could come up to you."

Thus addressed, Sal, who had hitherto remained silent, though she had been attentively listening to every word that had been uttered, laid her knife and fork down in her plate, and throwing herself back in her chair, gave expression to some of her thoughts.

"You know, Jim, I never was in favor of this sort of work, though I've always done my best for you when you wanted my services, and I don't like this lay any better than the others. It's dangerous business; and there are plenty of crushers about in that part of the town, too. But I know you ain't going to give it up on my account, and I haven't much time to talk it over with you, because, you see, I've got a little job of my own on hand to-night, and I must be going pretty soon. I think I've got a chance to make a hundred at least."

"What is it, Sal?" said Jim, smiling with great glee at the talent of his female friend.

"Never you mind, Jim, just now; you'll find out before to-morrow morning. I'll be home in time to get things ready for you when you get back, and Betsey will stay here and look after matters,—won't you, Betsey ?"

" Yes, Sal, I'll do my best till you return."

" Then good night, Jim," said Sal. " Take care of yourself. I'm in a hurry, for I wouldn't like to miss the good chance I've got."

" Good luck to you, Sal ! never you fear for me. I'll make you rich with this night's work, and then we'll go off and live quietly somewhere."

The girl laughed aloud at this promise. " That's what you always say, Jim, but you've never done it yet," she said, putting on her bonnet. " Your intentions are good, Jim, I don't deny that, but you ain't strong on the virtuous lay. Good-by," and making a sign to Betsey to follow her, she left the room.

Betsey came into the hall and accompanied her down stairs.

"Betsey," said Sal, earnestly, when they had got beyond the hearing of the men above, " I'm not coming back again. I could not do it. I could not look Jim in the face after what I'm going to do. I don't know how it will end, but I ain't afraid. Meet me to-morrow at eleven o'clock, at the corner of Wooster and Bleecker Streets. Then I'll tell you all. Don't get low-spirited, Betsey," continued Sal, putting her arm around her companion's neck, and kissing her. " You are a good girl, and I'll stand by you as long as I live. I've no time to lose; good-by !" And with these words, Sal darted out of the door. Betsey looked after her anxiously for a few moments, and then, with a sigh, returned to the room in which she had left the burglars.

" Betsey," said Jack, as she entered the room, " why don't you pattern after Sal, instead of moping about as if you had lost all your friends, and making a man feel just like you? I'd like to know what's the use of women if they don't keep in good spirits, and help to cheer a fellow up. Damn you !" he continued, pounding his fist upon the table, " I've stood it long enough, and I'm going to stop it. Sit down here and laugh."

Betsey took the seat pointed out to her, and tried to smile. The attempt, however, was unsuccessful, and far from being satisfactory to her lord and master.

"It won't do," he cried, with a tremendous oath. "I want a good, hearty laugh."

"I can't laugh, Jack; I don't feel like it," said the woman, quietly.

"But I say you shall laugh. Do you think I'm going to be bullied by such a sickly drab as you ?"

"Let her alone, Jack," said Jim Terry. "She's a good enough gal in her way. She ain't lively much, but she can't help that. We can't make our own dispositions, so she ain't to blame if she's melancholy and down in the mouth more than is agreeable. Come here, Betsey, and take a drink; it will do you good."

"She's a damned fool, that's what she is!" said Jack Duggan, sullenly. "But if she won't laugh of her own free will, I'll give her something that will make her grin for a week, and I won't be balked at it either. Here," he continued, as he poured out a glass half full of whisky, "drink this and it will make you lively enough."

Betsey looked imploringly at Jim, who laughed kindly, as he said :

"Drink it, Betsey, it will brighten up your heart. Come, here's your good health."

With these words he emptied his own glass, and Betsey, finding there was no escape, drank hers also.

"Very well," said Jack; "so far so good. Now you've got to drink my health in a bumper. Hand me that nipperkin."

Betsey passed the tumbler to him, and he filled it almost to the brim with the fiery liquor.

"Now down with it straight," he resumed, as he put the glass on the table before her.

"I don't want any more now, Jack," said the girl; "I'll drink it after awhile."

"No," exclaimed the man, with an oath, "you shall drink it now, or I'll pour it down your cursed throat."

"Oh, let her alone, Jack!" said Jim. "Let her alone. What's the use of deviling her any more ?"

"Shut up, Jim Terry, and mind your own business. She's my gal, and I'll do what I please with her."

"So you may, Jack; I don't want to interfere with any of your affairs; but this is my room, I believe, and, damme if the girl don't want to drink her liquor, you shan't force her to do it here."

Without appearing to notice Jim's remark, Jack took the tumbler from the table and held it to Betsey's lips.

" Drink it, I say !" he roared out, with a terrible oath.

" No, Jack, I won't drink it," she said, firmly but quietly.

" Then I'll make you," exclaimed the man, rising from his chair and seizing her by the throat with one hand, while he held the tumbler of whisky in the other. "Open your mouth, you damned slut, or I'll strangle you !"

" Help me, Jim ; he'll murder me !" gasped Betsey, while the ruffian's fingers tightened around her throat.

Jim jumped up from his seat even before Betsey's appeal was uttered, and seizing Duggan by the collar of his coat with one hand, he dealt him a tremendous blow on the side of the head with the closed fist of the other. The man's grasp relaxed, and, partly stunned by the concussion, he staggered up against the wall, a distance of several feet, where, panting with rage, he stood, apparently gathering his forces to return the onslaught.

" I'll teach you, Jack Duggan," said Jim, with the utmost coolness ; " I'll teach you to kick up a rumpus in my room when I've warned you not to do it. This is not the first time I've had to jerk you up with a round turn, and you ought to know that I don't speak twice. Now sit down, and behave yourself, for, so help me God ! if you dare to lay the weight of your finger on this girl again, I'll let a little blood out of your carcass."

Jack stood glaring savagely at Jim Terry for a few moments, and then, seeing that the latter was determined to be as good as his word, he sullenly sat down.

" I was only joking with her," he said, at last. " I only wanted to put a little life into her, instead of the down-in-the-mouth way she's got into."

" No, you weren't joking a bit ; so that's a lie. You're too hard on the gal, Jack. It's not decent nor kind. But it's all over now, so we won't say anything more about it."

Betsey had listened in silence to the altercation, tears were starting into her eyes, when she took up the tumbler from the floor, filled it again with whisky, and going over to where Jack sat brooding over his defeat, she placed herself on his knee, and putting one arm around his neck, said :

"I'm very sorry, Jack. I'll drink it if you want me to."

"I don't care whether you drink it or not," growled Jack. "I wish you would go away from me."

"Won't you make up with me, Jack?" continued the girl.

"No; I don't want anything more to do with you."

"You oughtn't to talk that way to me, Jack. I've always been true to you. I've done you a great many favors, and perhaps I can do you more if you'd only let me, and be kind to me. There's no one I care for but you, Jack."

"It's more than I do for you, anyhow, and I don't ask any favors of you. You can go your way, and I'll go mine. If you prefer Jim Terry to me, I've no objections."

"But I don't. I care for nobody but you. Oh, Jack," she continued, in a whisper, hiding her face on his shoulder, "if you only knew how miserable I am, I'm sure you'd have pity on me !"

"Then don't tell me, for I don't want to know anything about your misery, or to have any pity on you, either. It's no use, Betsey," he continued, as the girl got up from his knee, and stood before him, looking the picture of despair. "It's no use trying to come that game over me any more. It's played out with me. You'll have to try it on with a fellow that's greener than I am."

"Is that so, Jack?"

"Yes, it is."

The girl made no further remark, but putting the whisky on the table, left the room.

The bad feeling which had arisen between Jim Terry and his subordinate was not of long duration. Jim's strength of character was such that he had very little difficulty in causing his authority to be respected by all the members of the gang, and though outbreaks would occasionally take place, they had never, thus far, amounted to anything serious. Bill offered his services as a peace-maker, and thus the breach was healed sooner than would otherwise have been the case. After having further discussed their plans, and arranged all the necessary details of the expedition, the three men, as the clock in St. John's Church struck two, sallied forth on their iniquitous errand, Jim Terry walking several paces in front, Bill being next, with the tools, and Jack bringing up the rear.

And Betsey—Betsey, upon leaving the apartment, went to her own room, and throwing herself on her bed, cried the bitterest tears she had shed for many a day. At last she knew for a certainty that Jack no longer cared for her, and strange as it may seem, the thought almost drove her mad. She lay upon the bed, weeping violently for several minutes, and then getting up she opened a trunk and took from it a photograph of an old man, which she pressed repeatedly to her lips, looking at it in the intervals as though her whole soul were in her eyes.

"My poor, poor old father!" she sobbed; "what would you think if you were alive, and knew of the wretched life your little Bess, as you used to call her, has been leading these ten years past? Oh, my God!" she continued, wildly, "is there no mercy for me? Have pity on me!" she cried, as she dropped on her knees. "*He* would not; I asked his pardon, but he would not give it. Oh, my Saviour, will you give me yours for what I have done through my sinful life, and for what I am going to do now?"

She sat upon the floor, her hands clasped around her knees, and her head bent upon her breast. Suddenly she started to her feet, took a bottle of laudanum from the mantle-piece, and putting it to her lips, drained it to the dregs. Then she lay down upon the bed, and closed her eyes as if wishing to go to sleep. Her thoughts wandered over events in her life which had not for many years been brought to her mind. She saw, as if in a vision, a little white cottage, surrounded by trees, and before which a brook murmured melodiously as it flowed on to the sea. An old man sat at the door reading, and playing by turns with a little girl who was building houses with blocks of wood, and peopling them with tiny paper dolls. Finally, the old man, unable to divide his attention longer, laid aside his book, and gave his whole time to the child. He took her on his lap and kissed her, and told her such wonderful stories of fairies and dragons and ogres, that she either clapped her hands and laughed with childish glee, or else opened wide her eyes with half fear, half amazement, at the marvelous pictures presented to her mind.

And then she saw, but less clearly than before, another scene. It was in a room, from which the full light of day was excluded. An old man, the same she had beheld by the cottage door, lay upon a bed gasping for breath, and apparently unconscious of what was passing around him, for his eyes were staring vacantly at the ceiling, and he took no notice of the young girl who was sobbing on his breast. A clergyman was kneeling by his side, praying that God would receive the soul of him who was about to leave this world forever, and would look with pity upon her whose only earthly friend would soon be numbered with the dead. Gradually the scene faded from her sight; she tried to recall it, but in vain: "I am sure he blessed me before he died," she said, softly. "What did he say? How did he look? I cannot bring it back. How strangely I feel! How my head throbs, and how dark everything looks!"

She sat up in the bed, and pushed back the hair from her face. Her lips were already of a purple hue, and her countenance was dark with the black blood which surged in sluggish torrents through her swollen veins. Her thoughts wandered, and she could no longer weave them into a connected train.

"You loved me once, Jack; but,—yes, yes, Sal, you are kind—no angel for me.—Why did you curse me so?—Blacker! blacker!—How long will this last?—Yes, I will go.—It was different once—long, long ago!—How could you, Jack? I have lost all for you! Oh, my God! what have I done? Am I mad? No, no.—Then you have come? I thought you would.—I will drink it, Jack.—Don't strike him, Jim.—Sal, will you never come back?—So beautiful, Sal! so young!—Bless me, father,—kiss your little Bess!"

She fell back on the pillow, and a slight convulsion passed through her limbs. Her weary eyelids closed, never again to be lifted till the trump of God should raise her body from the dust; her breath came slower and slower, and her heart scarcely stirred the poisoned blood which stagnated in the vessels where once, full of health, it had bounded swiftly with the strength and hopes of youth. Death was very near, and with rapid strides he came to clutch his victim. Already his hard and merciless hand bears heavily on her heart. But not yet, oh, King of Terrors! not yet! Her lips move, and though it is but a feeble whisper that passes through them, it is wafted to the recording angel's ears, and ere he writes the last line of her earthly record, and closes her book of life forever, he hears the words: "Father, pardon, and receive my sinful soul," and knows that one more weak and helpless spirit has obtained the seal of forgiveness, and rests upon the bosom of Him who made it.

CHAPTER XVI.

IN WHICH THE UNCERTAINTY OF HUMAN EXPECTATIONS IS THOROUGHLY DEMONSTRATED IN MORE THAN ONE INSTANCE.

SAL hurried rapidly toward John Holmes's house. The sky was overcast with thick, black clouds, the sharp outlines of which were occasionally brought into view by flashes of lightning, which for an instant lit up the vault of heaven, and then left all as dark as before. The low shops of that section of the city through which she passed were all closed except those in which liquor and other refreshments were sold. The night was very warm; and the doors of these were open. Men and women stood around the counters, drinking, laughing, singing, and cursing, without fear of interruption from the quiet policemen who patroled the neighborhood, so long as they kept within the rather extended limits of propriety fixed by these guardians of the peace. Occasionally half-drunken men would call out to her from their dens, but she hastened on, regardless of their invitations to come in and eat or drink with them.

It was growing late, and she was fearful the house might be closed and all have gone to bed before she reached it. She had not made up her mind what to do in that contingency, preferring to let her future plans be dictated by the occasion as it presented itself. To save the property, and perhaps the life of her who had become so dear to her, was her first object; to avoid bringing Jim and his companions into danger was her second. She was resolved to secure the first at all hazards, and she hoped to provide for the other also. Of this, however, she was doubtful, and the uncertainty gave her a good deal of anxiety. Jim had always treated her with kindness; in fact, as the reader has already had an opportunity of discovering, he was possessed of a good-hearted disposition in some things at least. He had a high respect for Sal's abilities, and had conceived a sincere affection for the girl, which she returned in no small degree. Sal felt badly at the idea of betraying his confidence, and several times lessened her speed, as though she thought of turning back. But she did not. She kept on in her course, firm in her determination of doing an act which would save her ideal from injury.

As she reached a more respectable part of the city she was in less danger of molestation. The sky was still black, and rain had commenced to fall in large, pattering drops, but the lamps were more numerous, and the shops were, many of them, still open, so that she saw her way more clearly than at first. Policemen looked at her suspiciously, and appeared to deliberate whether or not it would be advisable to inquire into her intentions, but they made no attempt to stop her; and so at last she arrived in front of John Holmes's house. Just as she put her foot on the lowest step a neighboring clock struck eleven. She had therefore fully three hours to spare.

Before she ascended to the door she took a rapid survey of the premises. A light was burning in the hall, and she could look into the open windows and see that the inmates had not yet retired for the night. She rang the bell, and in a few moments the door was opened by a man-servant, whose principal duty it was to drive the sleek, rotund, and sedate horses which pulled the old-fashioned carriage in which Margaret's grandmother and mother had ridden, and of which she occasionally made use.

"Does Mr. John Holmes live here?" inquired Sal.

"Yes."

"Can I see his daughter?"

"He has no daughter."

"Has no daughter?" exclaimed Sal, with astonishment. "Does not Miss Holmes live here?"

"There's no Miss Holmes, to my knowledge, in this house or anywhere else," replied the man.

"I saw a young lady go in here this afternoon. I know her, and have some very important business with her."

"Perhaps you mean Miss Margaret, Mr. Holmes's granddaughter?"

"Yes, it must be so. Will you please tell her Sarah Tompkins would like to see her?"

"Sit down here in the hall and I'll tell her."

Margaret was not in the parlor nor in the library. At last she was found sitting on the piazza, where she had remained after her grandfather had gone to his laboratory. For an hour she had been watching the gathering clouds, thinking over the events of the day, and building castles in the air with an architectural skill which only youth possesses in the highest degree.

"There's a young woman in the hall wants to speak with you, Miss Margaret," said the servant.

"A young woman wants to speak with me?" exclaimed Margaret.

"Yes, Miss, she says her name is Sarah Tompkins."

Margaret started at the name, and hurried to the hall, where Sal awaited her. She felt sure it was no trifling matter that had brought the girl to her at that hour of the night, and the moment her eyes met those of her morning's acquaintance her anticipations were fully realized.

"I am very glad to see you, Sarah," she said, as she held out her hand. "Come into the library, where we can talk better than here. Did you come all alone on such a dark night, too?"

"Yes, I came alone. I am used to being out late at night, and I can find my way all over New York, no matter how dark it may be."

"Now, Sarah," said Margaret, when she and the girl had got seated at the library table, "can I do anything for you? You must not forget what I told you this morning, and how anxious I am to help you in any way that is right and in my power."

"I have not forgotten it; but I have come to do you a service, not to ask one."

In as few words as possible, Sarah related to Margaret all she knew of the contemplated burglary.

Margaret listened, with a mixture of fear and astonishment, to the account given her. When it was finished, she took one of Sarah's hands in both of hers and said, with much feeling :

"I told you this morning I did not believe you were a bad girl, and my opinion is already verified. I cannot thank you enough now for what you have done. I can understand how great the struggle in your mind must have been, but it only makes your act a more noble one. Of course you wish me to tell my grandfather ?"

"Yes, I came to prevent the robbery, but I don't want the men harmed if it can be helped. They have always been good friends to me."

Requesting Sarah to remain in the library till her return, Margaret went to the laboratory in search of her grandfather. There he was, with Joshua, busy over his solutions, precipitates, crucibles, and retorts, commencing anew the labor, the fruits of which she, in a moment of thoughtlessness, had destroyed. The occasion was one, however, of too much importance for delay, and so she at once called him aside and related what Sarah had told her.

"I think you had better come into the library and see her for yourself, dear grandpapa. I am sure she has told the truth."

"I have no doubt of it, my darling. There can be no object in telling such a story if it were false. She evidently wishes to do you a service."

John Holmes accompanied Margaret to the library, where Sarah again related the particulars of the proposed burglary.

"There will be three of them," she said. "They will be here between two and three o'clock, and will try to enter by the garden windows, of a passage which they say connects a wing with the main building. I hope it will not be necessary to do them any injury. Can they not be scared away before they succeed in breaking into the house ?"

"You have rendered us so great a service, Sarah," said John Holmes, "that I shall do all in my power, short of compounding a felony, to meet your wishes in this matter. It is very natural you should feel kindly toward those who, as you say, have always treated you with kindness. I think it can be arranged as you wish without difficulty. At the same time, however, we must manage to give them such a fright that they will not be likely to repeat the visit, and afterward we can start so keen a pursuit that they will certainly be forced to leave the country, and perhaps even to change their profession for others more honest. I think I am bound in honor to do this much on your account. As to our plans, we have four men available here, and I think I will send round for Mr. Severne, as much for the purpose of getting his advice as for his assistance. Besides, Sarah, he is very anxious to see you. He takes a deep interest in you."

"I do not know him," said Sarah.

"He knows you, I believe; but I will let him explain his business in his own way."

"I don't think I can wait any longer," said the girl. "I have done all I came to do. I will come and see you to-morrow," she continued, turning to Margaret, "and ask you to help another girl and me to get some honest work. I cannot live any longer as I have lived, much less with those I have betrayed."

Tears started to her eyes as she said these last words. Margaret looked at her grandfather, and, meeting no look but one of kindness and approval, she said :

"No, Sarah, you must not go to-night. Stay with me, and to-morrow we will talk about the future. I shall never forget what you have done for us, and neither will grand-papa. I hope you will never return to the house you have left to-night."

It did not require much persuasion to induce Sal to accede to Margaret's proposal, for besides the fact that she had no definite plan as to where she should pass the night, she could not resist the inducement it held out of further association with the one she had begun to love so warmly. She therefore took off her bonnet, and Margaret rang for the chambermaid, to give the necessary orders relative to providing for her comfort.

While the two girls were engaged in conversation, John Holmes had dispatched a messenger with a note for Severne, requesting his presence immediately, and in a few minutes the latter arrived at the house. John Holmes met him in the hall, and, taking him into the parlor, related all that had occurred, and requested his advice and assistance.

"We must manage the matter ourselves, I suppose," said Severne. "If we call in the police, they will of course take entire charge of the affair, and the enterprising gentlemen who are longing for the contents of your safe and plate chest will come to grief. I should think that, with your chemical knowledge, you could readily devise means for making them regard burglary for the future as a very hazardous profession—and especially so when attempted on your house. I am clearly of your opinion, that you owe it to Sarah to see that these men are not seriously injured nor arrested, unless you are compelled to do one or the other through their persistency. I am at your service for anything, but I am certain you can think out a system of defense and offense better than I can. In the mean time, while you are doing that, I will be making the further acquaintance of Miss Sarah. Is she in the library?"

"Yes, she and my granddaughter are both there."

"Miss Leslie, too! That will be a double pleasure. Will you be kind enough to introduce me to her?"

"Certainly, my dear Severne—with the greatest pleasure. I scarcely think either of them will care to go to bed till this affair is over, and Margaret, I am sure, will be glad to have your society. What a singular thing it is that you should become acquainted with her at such an hour and under such circumstances!"

John Holmes then led the way to the library, and, introducing Severne in due form to Margaret, left the room to make preparations for the burglars' reception.

"I did not think, Miss Leslie, when I saw you this morning," said Severne, "that I was so soon to have the pleasure of knowing you. I presume I must thank my young friend here for this early opportunity?"

With these last words he turned to Sarah, and holding out his hand to her, said: "Do you not recollect me?"

She shrank from taking his outstretched hand, and averted her face in shame.

"Will you not speak to me, Sarah?" he resumed, with a kind smile, "and let me thank you for what you have done to-night?"

"I deceived you once," she at last said, "and I might do it again."

"No, I do not think that of you. On the contrary, I am very sure you would not. The fact that you are here to-night on such an errand as brought you assures me that even I am safe."

"Everybody is too kind to me," said the girl, covering her face with her hands, and weeping. "I do not deserve it. I do not understand it. I have injured you all, and you all wish to be good to me."

"My dear child," said Severne, "when I first saw you last winter I said to my friend—who was with me you will recollect—that I was sure you were a good girl. I have not changed my opinion since then, except for about five minutes, when my better judgment was clouded by a little wounded self-love. I know the power of evil associations, but I know also, as well as I know anything, that they cannot entirely blot out the good traits which God has put into our hearts, and therefore I was certain that if you were removed from their influences, and subjected to others more favorable to the growth of virtue, the effort would not be made in vain. Since then, I have been trying to find you, in order that I might offer you the opportunity of changing your mode of life; but it is only within the last few days that I have received any information as to your whereabouts. I will not say anything further on the subject now, as there are other matters which require our immediate attention. I only ask that you will regard me as a friend who wishes to aid you as a brother would wish to aid a sister. Shall it be so, Sarah?"

"You do not know how bad I am," sobbed Sarah, the tears streaming through her fingers. "I am not fit to be here; not fit to speak to her. If you knew all you would put me out into the street. There is not a girl in New York worse than I am."

Margaret came to Sarah, and putting her arms around her neck, tried to soothe her; but the girl sprang away from her touch, and throwing herself on the floor, gave unrestrained expression to her grief, which the newly awakened sense of her guilty and shameful life had aroused.

Severne and Margaret looked at her silently, but with

intense interest. He knew that Sarah was already experiencing the effect of association with one of Margaret's gentleness and goodness, and he saw in the circumstance additional confirmation of the opinions he had expressed.

"I think it will be better for me to leave her to your care, Miss Leslie," he said, in a low voice. "It is a good sign, and when the violence of her grief has subsided she will be better prepared to hear what we have to say to her. I think all our plans in regard to her will succeed, especially with your aid given to them. Do you know, I think she looks like you? When I passed you to-day, as I was paying a visit to your grandfather, I was struck with the impression that I had seen a face like yours before."

"She is about my own age, I should think," said Margaret. "Her hair is much darker, however, than mine, and her eyes are of a different color. You know, though, we are never ourselves judges of resemblances of others to us."

"She is very much like you, nevertheless; more, perhaps, in expression than in features, though even there I can perceive the resemblance. She seems to have formed a very warm feeling of regard for you."

"Yes; and yet I have done nothing for her except to speak as kindly to her as I knew how."

"Ah, that is it, Miss Leslie. Kind words are the weapons which gain us the most enduring victories over our erring and perverse fellow-creatures, and women know so much better how to use them than men. We either overdo the attempt, or else fail to touch the heart at all. We lack the delicacy of expression, the power to modulate our tones, which belong to your sex, and without which no language, however well meant, will have a full effect. You will do more with a few words to this poor child than I could with all my powers of oratory." He took Margaret's hand as he said these words, and pressing it gently for a moment, let it go, and without another word left the room.

"What a sweet, lovely child she is!" he said to himself, as he passed through the hall in search of John Holmes. Scarcely over eighteen, I should think. I have never seen so beautiful a girl in all my life before. John Holmes's granddaughter! To think that the old fellow should have had such an angel as that in his house for eighteen years, and I not know it! I must see more of her. The mere sight of so much loveliness seems to renew my lease of life. Pshaw! I am almost old enough to be her father! Still, that is no reason why I should not take pleasure in being with her. No man, no matter how old he may be, can be thrown into association with a girl like that, and not be bettered by the contact. Ah, here are Holmes and his factotum!"

John Holmes and Joshua were busy arranging the window through which the robbers designed effecting their entrance, in such a way as to give them a rather astonishing reception. Joshua, who was an excellent pyrotechnist, had brought his skill into requisition, and had devised a system of detonating compounds, and other explosive and illuminating contrivances, which he had no doubt would strike terror into the hearts of the individnals who contemplated a violation of the Eighth Commandment.

"Good night, Mr. Severne," he said. "You see how this thing is fixed. As soon as they open this window to the extent of half an inch, this lever is sprung, that sets off this friction tube, and that sets the fuse on fire, and away goes the whole thing. It's like a row of bricks; start one, and all the rest fall, too. I can't find anything that my worthy friend, Henry Cornelius Agrippa, says against fire-works."

"Yes, I see you have made arrangements which will certainly deter them from entering by this window," said Severne. "They will think that they have run against the lower regions, instead of the residence of a venerable citizen. But this is not enough," he continued, addressing John Holmes, who was regarding Joshua's work with looks of approval; "we must let them understand that we know who they are. We must, therefore, call out their names, and put our other two men in the garden to do the same thing when they are retreating. And, besides this, we must have arms, so as to resist them effectually should they persist in endeavoring to get in. I think that when the rascals find out that we know who they are, they will not remain in New York till morning. Do you know their names?"

"No, I do not," replied John Holmes, "but I can very soon ascertain them. I think your plan is admirable. I suppose the young woman will have no objection to telling me the names of our visitors." And with these words, he proceeded to the library to get the desired information.

"So there's a woman in this affair too, Mr. Severne!" said Joshua. "They can't keep out of mischief if they try ever so hard, and most times they don't try. They like it. They can't live without what they call excitement. I wonder if *she* knows what's going on?" he continued, in a low tone. "I think I'll go and tell her."

"There is a woman in it, as you say, Joshua," replied Severne, smiling, "and it is well for us that there is. You seem to be something of a misogynist."

"I don't exactly know what a misogynist is, but if it means a man who don't like the generality of women, then I'm one. I must say, after having studied the subject for twenty years and more, that in my humble opinion women are very much overrated."

"Then you have never been in love?"

"I don't say I have and I don't say I haven't. That's neither here nor there."

"And you think all women are overrated?"

"I didn't say that either. I didn't make use of the word all. But there's something I've got to see to before these fellows come, and I'll do it now while there's time if you'll excuse me, Mr. Severne, for a few minutes."

"If she has not gone to bed," continued Joshua, as he walked away, "I'll find her probably just where I left her. How she'll be frightened, she's so timid and helpless. She's like the ivy; she can't live without a stronger being to cling to and to shield her from the storms of life. There's one of those storms coming on now, and I'll protect her through it as sure as my name's Joshua. I'd like to see anybody hurt a hair of her head!" he exclaimed, shaking his fist at an imaginary enemy of his Adelina. "If I didn't make mincemeat of him, then may I never be blessed forever and ever!"

Arriving at the door of Mrs. Markland's sitting-room, Joshua tapped on it lightly, and awaited the invitation to enter. Receiving no summons, he knocked again a little louder than before. Still no response. With great quietness and caution—for Joshua felt that he was trespassing on holy ground—he opened the door and peeped in. A solitary candle was burning on the mantle-piece, and by its

dim light he perceived his dear Adelina asleep in her chair.
Mrs. Markland was really quite a pretty woman, and Joshua
thought he had never seen her look so beautiful.   There
was a repose about her features, a soft, confiding expression, which seemed to say, "I have put my trust in him and
have no longer any fear of the world," which caused Joshua's
heart to swell with love and courage.

He approached nearer, and stooped, as if to imprint a
kiss upon the lips which, only partly closed, allowed her
beautiful teeth to be seen through the rosy opening; but, ere
he could bend his head low enough, she moved uneasily in
her chair, and spoke a few words which Joshua did not
clearly hear.   He withdrew a step and waited till she should
be more composed.   Again she spoke, and this time every
word came through her lips with the emphasis which only
comes from strong feeling.

"So my time has come at last, has it?" she said.   "I
knew I could teach you a lesson if I tried.   You haven't
insulted me all these years for no purpose, and now I'll get
even with you.   You thought I loved you?   Who said I
didn't?   Am I to let you do as you please because you
thought I loved you?   Man of science!   Yes, a pretty man
of science you are.   That's what I took you to be and you've
deceived me.   Me, your lawful wife.   Oh, what a life I've
had!   First a clown and then a fool; one was a sham and the
other's the real thing.   I've gone farther and fared worse.
Serves me right, does it?   And you dare to tell me that!
You'll break my heart with your cruelty and oppression.
I'll not endure it!   I'll appeal to the law!   I'll see if there
isn't a way to make you treat me with respect at least, even
if you do hate me.   Markland!   How dare you mention
that name to me, you miserable quack!   You'll do as you
please!   Murder!   murder!   murder!"

Fearful that some of the other inmates of the house would
be aroused by Mrs. Markland's exclamations, which were
given with quite a loud voice, and having heard enough to
destroy his peace of mind for some time, Joshua took his
departure as quietly as he had entered, and closed the door
tightly after him.

When he got fairly into the hall, he stopped and drew a
long breath.

"It's bad enough," he said, "to find out that she's such
a Jezebel, but to think that she should have humbugged
me that way is what I don't think I ever can get over. It's
too bad, it really is.   It gives me a poor opinion of human
nature in general, and much worse of women in particular.
What an escape I've had ! But I'm safe. I've heard enough
to fix that business; and I hope I may be blessed forever
and ever !"

"Come, Joshua," said John Holmes, who at that moment
came into the hall, "I have been looking for you.   It is
nearly two o'clock, and it is time you made the connection
between the window and your infernal machines.   Here is
a pistol for you ; take care, it is loaded !"

Everything was in readiness for the burglars' reception.
The coachman and gardener were posted in the garden concealed from view—but in a place whence they could observe
the approaches to the window—well armed, and with instructions to call out the names of the robbers, and discharge
their pistols in the air as they retreated.

John Holmes, Severne, and Joshua stood in the passage-
way between the wing and the main building, also armed,
and prepared to contest with vigor any attempt the robbers
might make to enter, should they not be frightened by the
pyrotechnic arrangements.   Joshua had placed all his apparatus above and on each side of the window exteriorly to
the house, but in such positions as that the several pieces
were not likely to attract the attention of the burglars.
The lights about the house were all lowered except those
in the laboratory, which were kept burning so as not to induce any change in the programme of operations which had
been agreed upon by the robbers.

They had waited quietly for about half an hour when
Severne's watchful ear heard footsteps on the gravel-walk
of the garden ; looking through an opening which had been
left in the shutters, he saw the men stealthily making their
way toward the house.   The clouds had broken away, and
the moon occasionally permitted him to see them with great
distinctness without any risk of being seen in return, as the
passage was entirely dark.   To reach the window the robbers were obliged to ascend the steps of the piazza, and
walk some twenty or thirty feet on the flooring of the porch.

On they came, the boards creaking under their footsteps so as to be heard by all in the passage, and presently both of them stood in front of the window. Severne still continued to look at them through the shutters, one hand resting on the window-sill and the other firmly grasping his revolver. For a second or two the men were silent, and then one of them spoke.

"Is Bill outside or inside the garden ?"

"He's inside. I told him to walk quietly about the grounds within hail, so as to give us a chance to show our heels if the crushers came about. There's no fears of them, though. They can't keep their eyes open after one o'clock."

"All right there, Jack. Come, open the bag and get the tools out."

"I don't believe we'll have much trouble with this window, Jim. I'll just saw around this fixing, and then the jimmy will do the rest."

With great dexterity, but with very little noise, Jack Duggau used his saw, and in a few moments the piece of woodwork, upon which the fastening of the window was placed, was in his hands.

"Now, Jim, here's the lock; hand me the pig's foot, and I'll make short work of it."

He took the short but strong lever, inserted it into the hole he had made, and began to exert his strength upon it. The window was fastened both above and below by small brass bolts, which, too weak to resist the force brought to bear upon them, were slowly but steadily giving way. Suddenly, with a light crash, the window flew wide open, and at the same instant there was a dreadful explosion, followed by a rattling of smaller reports, a series of hissing sounds, and a burst of red, white, and blue lights, which illuminated the garden. Perfectly taken by surprise, it was some seconds before the burglars could sufficiently collect their senses to form the slightest conception of what had occurred. They had both been knocked down by the force of the first explosion, but were not seriously hurt. Before they could rise, the three defenders of the house were upon them, pistol in hand. Bill, who had been watching in the garden, hearing the terrific noise and seeing the lights, had rushed up to ascertain what was the matter, but perceiving that there were other actors in the scene, he had commenced a precipitate retreat. At the same time, the two robbers, having at last obtained a dim idea of the situation of affairs, jumped off the porch, followed closely by Severne and Joshua, discharging their revolvers as rapidly as they could fire them off, and shouting the names of the three baffled burglars at the top of their voices. In the garden they were joined by the two men, who added to the din, and who took after the intruders with a speed that gave promise of the most satisfactory results. To get over the garden wall, which was of brick, and fully six feet high, would have been no easy task under the most favorable circumstances. To do so with four men at their heels, armed with revolvers, and apparently bent on their capture, was a still more difficult undertaking. Nevertheless, they made at it with all the desperation inspired by fear, and were fairly on top by the most superhuman exertions without the loss of much time, when three men rose up suddenly, as if out of the earth, and each seizing a fugitive, dragged him back into the garden, and held him in a grasp of iron.

"It's no use, Jim, we know you, and have got you this time," said he who appeared to be the leader of the new party. "Hand out those handcuffs, sergeant." In an instant the three burglars were manacled, and by the time Severne and his men reached the scene of action, the contest was over.

"What's all this?" said Severne to the officer in command, surprised at the unexpected termination of the adventure.

"Why, you see, sir," said the captain of police, "I've had one of my men watching these fellows' crib for several days and nights, and this morning I received a report that there was a burglary in contemplation. I detailed three of my sharpest men to lay around and follow them, and they succeeded in finding out where it was to be, just in time to let me know. I came on the ground with a strong force almost as soon as they got here, and so you see we've nabbed them. You seem to have been prepared for them too, sir, judging by the warm reception you've given them. We shall want you and your party to appear to-morrow morning at ten o'clock, at the Tombs Police Court, to testify."

"You have managed the matter very well indeed, captain. I suppose you do not need any further assistance from us ?" said Severne, who was not at all sorry that the burglars had been captured.

"No, sir, we can manage them, I think. I hope you have received no damage. By-the-by," he said, in a whisper to Severne, "was that a cannon you fired at them ?"

"Not so bad as that," replied Severne, with a smile.

"Well, you made an awful racket, anyhow. They have scarcely yet recovered from their fright. Here, men," he continued, addressing some eight or ten officers who had collected around the defeated burglars, "move these fellows off."

"I say, captain," said Jim Terry, "you need not use any violence with us, we'll go along like lambs. This is the worst scrape I ever got in. Lord! what a devil of a rumpus it was,—just as if all hell had broke loose!"

At this point, John Holmes, who, on account of his advanced age, had not joined in the pursuit, appeared on the ground with the bag containing the burglars' tools. Severne, in a few words, explained what had occurred, and handed the bag to the captain.

"Captain," said Jim, "I wish you'd send one of your men to my crib for some duds. There's a gal there, too, who will wonder what has become of me."

"Don't give yourself any uneasiness, Jim," replied the captain. "The girl's all safe, and I'll see about your duds. Of course," he continued, addressing John Holmes, "I know where she is. One of my men followed her here; I rather guess she got scared, and gave you warning. Look out for her. She's a sharp one! There are very few in this city who can beat Sal Tompkins, young as she is. Come, men, move on !"

The gardener had by this time unlocked and opened the gate that led into the street, and the policemen, escorting the handcuffed burglars, passed out on their way to the station-house.

"It's all right," said the captain, who had lingered behind, "I understand the matter, I think. Keep a sharp eye on that girl, though."

A policeman came up and whispered a few words in the captain's ear.

"I'm afraid there's been foul play," he continued, "at those fellows' house. I have just heard that a girl who belongs to their party has been found dead in her room. I should not be surprised if Jack Duggan, one of those rascals there, has murdered her. He's been heard to threaten her, and was quarreling with her to-night. Unless I can be of any further assistance to you, I must say good night."

"Well," said Severne, "I have had my ideas relative to the efficiency of the New York police very materially enlarged within the last half hour. Captain, allow me to bear witness to your skill and courage in this whole matter,— good night!"

"It's a very satisfactory termination to a very unpleasant affair," he continued, addressing John Holmes, as they walked toward the house. "The rascals have been captured without our assistance, so that we have no reproaches to make of ourselves for any breach of faith to our informant. In fact, if we had kept perfectly quiet, and done nothing, they would have been much more quickly secured, and we should have been spared a terrible infliction on our acoustic organs, and a villainous smell of saltpetre and other diabolical substances. They might have made a disagreeable complication too in my future plans relative to Sarah. The probability now is that they will not have much opportunity during the next twenty years for interfering in any matters which may transpire in the City of New York. I hope Miss Leslie has not been alarmed at the disturbance."

"I went to the library to explain the true state of affairs before I left the house, and told Margaret and Sarah they had better both go to bed," replied John Holmes. "I think with you, that the end of the matter is very proper. I did not, I must confess, feel easy at the idea of letting those fellows escape, and yet I could not bring myself to do an act which might have made Sarah repent the part she had performed. Society is well rid of such ruffians. I hope they have not added murder to their other crimes!"

As they entered the house, Margaret met them.

"I have seen Sarah in bed, dear grandpapa. She was very much fatigued, and is already asleep. I put her into the room adjoining mine, where I am sure she will be very comfortable."

"Yes, my dear child, and you must be very much overcome also. I think you had better take some of the medicine you have so successfully administered." In a few words John Holmes then told Margaret how the attempted burglary had ended.

"And now good night," he resumed, as he kissed her. "We must leave something to be talked over to-morrow, and I am sure Mr. Severne will excuse you if you take your leave of him till then."

"Not till I have thanked him, dear grandpapa, for all his kindness," she said, as she put her little hand in Severne's. "Sarah has told me all," she continued, addressing him. "You have been very good to her, and I am sure she will find her best friend in you. And for what you have done for us all here to-night, grandpapa will thank you much better than I can."

Severne's self-possession deserted him for a moment, and before he could regain it she was gone. And then, after making arrangements for a conference in which to discuss future plans, Severne took leave of John Holmes and walked slowly toward his own house.

The dawn was just beginning to break in the east as he reached the door. He turned and looked toward the dim, gray light which overspread the horizon. "God grant," he said, "that it is a harbinger of a day that ere long will break over my soul."

CHAPTER XVII.

IN WHICH THERE IS A LITTLE COMFORTING PHILOSOPHY.

JIM TERRY, Jack Duggan, and Bill Smithers were the next day committed for trial. It may save further anxiety on their account for the reader to be informed that they were subsequently duly convicted, and were sentenced each to Sing Sing for fifteen years. It was also satisfactorily shown at the coroner's inquest that Betsey had committed suicide, and that Jack Duggan was not therefore directly chargeable with her death. The empty laudanum bottle was found still tightly grasped in her hand, and a portion of the contents was discovered in her stomach upon *post-mortem* examination. Sarah Tompkins being called among other witnesses, testified that Betsey had frequently threatened to take her own life. Whether or not Jack Duggan was morally guilty of murder, is a question not admitting of much doubt.

If anything additional were needed to convince Sarah of the depravity of the life she had hitherto led and to cause her to form resolutions for future amendment, it was furnished by the untimely death of Betsey. The event shocked and grieved her, and Severne, in his conference with her in which he unfolded his plans, did not fail to make a proper use of the lesson to' be learned from the sad fate of her friend.

At the meeting to which allusion is made, which took place the day after the attempted burglary, between Severne, John Holmes, Margaret, and Sarah, the former stated in detail the views which, after much consideration, struck him as being most advantageous to the object of them, and most wise in all other respects. Stripped of many details into which Severne entered with fullness, and which showed that he had forgotten no material point, they embraced the following provisions:

1st. That Sarah should acknowledge him as her guardian, and should at once take up her residence at his house as his ward.

2d. That he should provide suitable means for her moral and intellectual instruction.

3d. That John Holmes and Margaret should act as his collaborators, giving him the benefit of their advice and assistance in the thousand ways in which he should need both.

The meeting was in the library of John Holmes's house. Sarah had, in a measure, recovered from her depression of the previous night. Her manner was calm and thoughtful, and she brought the good common sense with which she was so highly endowed to bear upon the subject of her present condition and the prospects which appeared to be open to her. She saw with that intuitive perception, however, which so many women possess, that she was altogether unfitted in every respect for association with Margaret Leslie upon a common ground of equality. She felt that if she appeared as she really was, unrefined, illiterate, reeking, as it were, with the contaminations of crime, vulgarity, and ignorance, she would be acting ungenerously and unjustly to one who had been both generous and just to her. She feared to expose Margaret to the possible danger of such an association, and she dreaded also lest her friend might, little by little, come to understand how desperately wicked and low her life had been, and perhaps even to despair of effecting any permanent improvement in her character. To keep herself as much as possible from Margaret's society, till by dint of courage, and perseverance, and good counsels, she had rendered herself fit for it, was a duty she imposed upon herself, and which she resolved should be honestly performed so far as God should give her strength.

All she wanted was opportunity, and such assistance as she felt sure her newly-found friends would give her. In what form these were to come she did not know. When, therefore, Severne stated his propositions in the clear and simple manner peculiar to him, and Sarah understood that he was offering her home, education, everything in fact which a father could give to a loved daughter, she was so bewildered that she could scarcely credit the evidence of her senses. She asked herself what she had done for him that he should take so deep an interest in her? And she found it utterly impossible to answer the question in a satisfactory manner. She was lost in thought, vainly trying to comprehend the matter, when she was aroused by Severne, who had taken a seat by her side, speaking to her. She looked up from the floor. Her eyes were filled with tears, and her lips quivered with emotion. She tried to speak—to say just one word of thanks, but the attempt was altogether in vain.

"Never mind now, Sarah," said Severne, "I understand you as well as if you spoke volumes of words. We will therefore consider the matter as an *affaire accompli*, and I will leave Miss Leslie to explain to you what that is, for I do not believe you know."

Margaret also came to Sarah. She saw at once that it would be better for her to be alone for a short time, and therefore, after speaking a few comforting and reassuring words to her, she left the room in company with Severne and her grandfather. The latter did not remain long with them, as he had important business to transact in the lower part of the city, and thus for the first time Severne and Margaret were left alone.

"How kind you are!" she said, as she stood by his side in the large bay-window that overlooked the garden from the parlor. "I can scarcely conceive of an action more unselfish than that you contemplate."

"Do you think so?" he remarked. "I am afraid, Miss Leslie, you do not see very deeply into my motives. I do not recollect that I ever devised a scheme in my life more thoroughly selfish in its character than the one you commend. Do not misunderstand me," he continued, as he observed her surprised look. "I do not think I should have thought of it unless I had seen that it would certainly result in benefit to this poor girl; but the prime, the governing motive was and is selfish in the extreme."

"I do not understand you," she said, looking full into his face, with an expression of the utmost frankness.

"It is very simple. I am desirous of gratifying myself, of seeing the pleasure which will arise from the consciousness that I have been instrumental in removing her from low and criminal associations, and from educating her according to my own ideas. Is not that selfishness?"

"Perhaps so," she replied; "but I look upon it as a very noble and worthy kind of selfishness. We are all entitled to the reward of an approving conscience."

"Yes, when we have been actuated to the performance of a good act because it is good, and for no less worthy a motive. I feel myself in the position of a policeman who joins in the hue and cry after a criminal, not because it is his duty to do so, but for the sake of the reward offered for the apprehension."

"I am sure you are unjust to yourself," said Margaret, "and that you have the happiness of Sarah more at heart than your own gratification. Indeed," she continued, "I am very confident that you would not hesitate to sacrifice your own happiness to secure hers."

"I am not sure that I would not," he answered, smiling;

"but even that would be because I should experience more pleasure in being miserable than in seeing her so."

"Then, Mr. Severne, if that is what you call selfishness, I hope I may be selfish all my life. We are always, I think, justified in doing those good acts which will make us happy. I presume very few of us are virtuous from motives of abstract goodness alone. God teaches us to be upright in all our thoughts and deeds, in the hope of happiness here and hereafter. I should not care to inquire into any one's motives for a good action. Let him or her reap all the rewards which belong to it, and one of the best and most valuable of these is our own self-consciousness of a duty well done. When we have that, we can dispense with all others, or can be willing to incur the obloquy and reproach of those who refuse to understand us aright, or else pretend, for their own base purposes, to see wrong where there is none."

Margaret spoke earnestly. Her face glowed with enthusiasm, and her manner showed in each detail that every word was dictated by a spirit of truth and sincerity. Severne looked at her admiringly, more so perhaps than was strictly proper, but it was impossible for him to resist the temptation of studying a face which was more in accordance with his ideas of female beauty than any he had ever seen. He watched with intense interest and pleasure the varying expression of her soft, dark-blue eyes, and the graceful motions of her exquisitely moulded lips, which, as her voice passed from them, gave to her utterance an impress of guilelessness and candor which mere words would never have conveyed with all the powers and subtleties of language brought to bear upon them.

She had finished speaking, and yet Severne did not take his eyes from her face. Her color was heightened a little, and she looked modestly down at the floor, as she said:

"I have merely told you what I believe, Mr. Severne. I confess that my idea of our incentives to virtue is not so high as yours, yet I think it is more real and more generous. I am speaking only of human nature as we find it. Not as philosophers would have it, but as God made it. I do not think the heart of man is altogether depraved, and that good actions are always done for mercenary motives. But though it may be a lamentable confession for me to make, I feel very sure that if virtue was not in some way its own reward, there would be very little virtue in the world. I cannot, however, argue the matter. I am conscious that I have not made myself understood, and am fearful you will attach more meaning to my language than I intend."

"No, Miss Leslie," said Severne, with a gravity of tone which startled her, "I do not misunderstand you. You are telling me what I know to be true, that if the practice of virtue made us unhappy, we would not trouble ourselves to be virtuous, and that we may fairly claim all the rewards which accrue from our good actions. I wish you could make me believe that our conduct is not altogether influenced by the selfish considerations I have mentioned. I might then have a better opinion of myself than I have at present."

"I should not wish to do so, Mr. Severne. I believe it is perfectly right that we should do our duty, because in the full performance of it we add to our happiness. God has held out the hope of reward, both in this world and in that which is to come, as the chief inducement for us to love him and obey his commandments. I do not call it selfishness when we act according to the highest principles of morality for the sake of experiencing the consciousness of having done right. A selfish person is one who, to gratify his desires, does not stop to perform mean, unkind, or criminal deeds. And I do not wish to be understood as saying that there are not noble men and women, who perform deeds of the most pure and self-denying character, and which apparently plunge them into utter wretchedness; but even in these cases there is doubtless always experienced the sweet pleasure, though it may be a melancholy one, which arises from the consciousness of having done right, and which is more than a recompense for any material misfortunes."

"You do not know how much consolation your words afford me," said Severne, "even though I cannot entirely shake off the idea that I am much more of a selfish than a benevolent individual. Ah, Miss Leslie, those who are gifted as you are, with youth and gentleness and purity, cannot take the hard, cold view of their duties which is forced upon those others who have experienced the hollowness and weakness of their own hearts. I can remember when I thought as you do ; when I was impelled to do what I conceived to be right, because my heart approved it. Now I must reason about it and satisfy my mind, and when, as in this instance of Sarah Tompkins, I act mainly for my own gratification, my intellect declares that I am moved by the lowest of all motives—self-love ! When you tell me that the inducement is not a base one, you give me, as it were, your approval, and this is very dear to me. Do not be surprised or offended at what I say. I have not for many years conversed with any woman so frankly as I have with you this morning, nor have I encountered one who has spoken to me so honestly, and at the same time with so much sound judgment. The good opinion of such as you are is worth to me more than all the encomiums I can give myself."

"You overrate the importance of what I have said. I do not pretend to understand the subject as you do, and spoke solely from the dictates of my own heart. You know we cannot always trust ourselves that they are right, because we very rarely get them without their having been more or less influenced by extraneous causes. I can only speak for myself, and I know there is no pleasure to me like that which proceeds from the knowledge that I have done right; and it is the certainty that I will experience this pleasure, and the hope of happiness hereafter, which are my greatest incentives to try to do my best in the life to which God has called me. As to my approval of your motives, Mr. Severne, I am afraid you place a higher value upon it than is just. I am sure, however, I should be doing you great injustice if I did not appreciate, as they deserve, your generous intentions toward Sarah."

"And this assurance that you are pleased is a greater gratification to me than any I have yet experienced. Do you never regulate your actions in accordance with the wishes of your friends, and do such things as you know will cause them pleasure or save them pain ?"

"Often—constantly. To see the happiness of those who are dear to me is one of the most fruitful sources of my own enjoyment. But I do not think I would act in such a manner as to give them pleasure at the expense of my sense of what is right. I could make myself miserable for their sake, and feel the delight of self-sacrifice, but I could not render myself criminal for them. The consciousness that I had been wicked would always be present in my mind."

"You are right, Miss Leslie. You have recognized a distinction which I am afraid is often overlooked. We always experience pleasure when we sacrifice our own happiness for that of our friends; but we cannot obtain this consolation if we commit acts which are essentially wrong to gratify them."

"I think," said Margaret, musingly, "that we should love our friends better than ourselves. It is only when we do this that self-sacrifice is possible; with most of us that god-like faculty which prompts to the disregard of self for the benefit of our enemies is possessed by very few, and even when we exercise it we are perhaps often urged to do so for the purpose of heaping coals of fire on their heads. I think it is somewhat contrary to the nature of our humanity to love those who hate us, better than we do ourselves."

As Margaret ceased speaking, Severne held out his hand to her and said : "I am sorry that it is necessary for me to go, but I have an appointment I must keep. Your grand-father and I have been friends for many years, and I trust the fact will have some weight with you in determining whether or not you will count me among the number of those you like. I am a good deal older than you are, my dear Miss Leslie, and have seen many more phases of life than I trust you will ever experience. I have witnessed false-hood, and deceit, and wickedness of all kinds triumph over the right. I have been misled by the hypocrisy of those who called themselves my friends, and have suffered from their treacherous and time-serving acts. I was once as trustful as you are now, and if I have lost much of my faith in human nature, I have not done so without ample cause. But you have instilled into me to-day hopes and feelings which have long been strangers to me. I cannot tell why this is so. It is not so much on account of what you have said, for I have gone over the same ground with a great deal more thoroughness than I should like you to give to it. Perhaps it is because I have perceived that you were speak-ing your real opinions, undisguised by any fear of what might be thought of them. I am going away in a short time, but I trust you will give me many opportunities before my departure for renewing the most pleasing association of my life."

This was a great deal for Severne to say on so very short an acquaintance; but why should he not express his real thoughts to the granddaughter of his old friend? It *was* the most pleasing association of his life. He had never before met with man or woman who had so impressed him as had Margaret Leslie, and he felt that every day and hour would add to the emotion she had aroused. Why, then, should he attempt to conceal now what sooner or later she would discover for herself, if she had not already done so? Did he love her? Not yet; Robert Severne was not a man to fall in love at first sight. Such was not therefore the emotion he experienced, but it was that dreamy, unpassionate, yet rapturous feeling, full of vague apprehension and ill-defined hope, which creeps into the heart, and making it tremulous with its swelling transports, heralds the approach of that more radiant and sacred passion before which all others fade into insignificance.

Margaret blushed as she listened to Severne's words, because she was pleased with them; and conscious that she was unable to conceal her feeling, she gave him her hand and said, while a sweet smile played over her countenance:

"It would be very strange if my grandfather's house were not always open to one whom he esteems so highly, and I did not do all in my power to make his visits pleasant. And if," she added, with a grave manner, "I have been able in any way to lighten the sad memories of other days and to cause you to take renewed hope for the future, the joy is not all yours. It is not much I can do to increase the happiness of others, but I have never willfully withheld that little when it was right to give it."

He let her hand drop and said, while he looked steadily into her face: "You are very kind, and I shall not forget what you have said. There are times when more than at others I feel the want of some one who will not be wearied with my presence and conversation; and then, if you will let me, I will come to you. And in regard to Sarah, may I not rely upon you for that aid which will not only insure

the success of my plans, but add to her happiness? I agree
with her entirely in the opinion which I think she enter-
tains, that for the present you should not be much with her.
She knows her failings, and that knowledge makes their
cure all the more easy. After awhile I shall ask your advice on many points, and with that and the advantage of
association with you, I am sure all will go well with her.
For a day or two I must ask you to take care of her, as my
bachelor home is not yet prepared to receive her."

Margaret promised him all he asked relative to Sarah,
and Severne, plucking a rose-bud, unperceived by her, from
a flower-stand which stood in the window, left the room.

"I am not very strong on romance," he said to himself,
as he put the flower into his pocket and emerged from the
house into the street, "but I will keep this as long as I live
in memory of the happiest day I have passed for many
years."

And Margaret, after he had gone, continued to stand in
the bay-window for several minutes, thinking of what he
had said. Then she bent over the flowers and tried to
imagine that they required immediate care. She busied
herself for a few moments in arranging the tendrils, and with
a little silver trowel loosening the earth around the roots,
but her mind was too much preoccupied for her to continue
to deceive herself.

"I wonder why he is unhappy?" she thought, as a
tear fell upon her hand. "He is so noble, and kind, and
generous, that I cannot conceive why he should have any
enemies such as he spoke of. They must be very wicked.
I wish I could make him happy. But what can I do? He
knows so much more than I do, that doubtless he has tried
every means already. And yet he said I had given him
some consolation!

"He is very different from any man I ever met before.
I am sure I shall like him very much. I do like him now.
He is grandpapa's friend, and that is sufficient reason why I
should like him. And then he is so kind to poor Sarah,
and then—and then there are a good many other reasons.

"I am sorry he is going away so soon. I should like to
see a great deal of him. Perhaps, however, travel will

make him happier by bringing before him new scenes and new associations, and then I shall be very glad.

"I do not think it can be wrong for me to think of him so much. If he was not thoroughly good, grandpapa would not like him, or let him visit at the house. Grandpapa left him here with me, and that is sufficient, and last night he said that Robert Severne was a true gentleman, one of the first among all he had ever known. I have never heard him say as much of any one before, except Mr. Goodall.

"I am glad he likes me. It is very pleasant to be liked by one whom you can respect and like in return. I do not know why he should think of me as a friend, when there must be so many others who are more worthy of his appreciation. It cannot be merely because I spoke as I thought. He seemed to think that so strange. How much falsehood and insincerity he must have encountered to imagine for a moment that I would try to deceive him!

"I hope Sarah will like him. Poor girl! what a life she must have led! I would rather have the consciousness of having done for her what Mr. Severne is doing than wear the crown of a queen."

Margaret raised herself to her full height as she spoke these words; her face was flushed, and her eyes sparkled with the emotion the idea excited. It was only for a moment, however, but in that moment the beauty which every noble thought excites in proportion to the intensity with which it is experienced, flashed over her countenance, and gave additional life to a loveliness which never wanted vitality, even in her most quiet periods.

"I think," she said, as she left the bay-window and passed through the parlor to the hall, "that Sarah must feel lonely. I have been away from her more than an hour. By this time she has doubtless fully comprehended Mr. Severne's propositions, and it is not well to leave her too much alone when everything about her is so novel. How very ladylike and modest her demeanor has been since she came here!"

CHAPTER XVIII.

SEVERNE had scarcely entered his library, and begun to look over some papers, when Mrs. Wiggins was announced. He directed her to be shown up, and in a few moments that lady entered the room. She was evidently in a condition of great excitement, her face, never very pale, was now preternaturally red; her hair was in disorder, and her breath came and went with a rapidity and a force which, while they argued well for the integrity of her respiratory muscles, showed at the same time how great had been her recent physical exertion, and how intense was now the mental excitement under which she labored.

The state of her toilet was evidence either of great haste in leaving her domicile, or of a contest with some energetic person who had disputed with her for the possession of several of the articles of which it was composed. Her bonnet occupied but one side of her head, her frock was open behind, one of her stockings had settled from its usual elevated position into a mere ring, which encircled her not very delicate ankle, and she had put her feet into shoes belonging to two different pairs.

But Mrs. Wiggins was not alone. A tall, very thin, and dyspeptic-looking man accompanied her, whom she immediately introduced to Severne as Brother Jenkins. Brother Jenkins crossed his large, bony hands behind his back, and inclined the upper part of his lank body toward Severne, in what he intended to be a bow, while at the same time his arms fell into a sort of paralytic condition, assuming a line, which, if carried out, would have connected his shoulders with a point situated about twelve inches in front of his feet, and his eyes, which bore no very indistinct resemblance to two balls of pipe-clay, described an arc of a circle, of which the center of the ceiling and the extremity of his boots were the limiting points. Brother Jenkins then ran his hands throngh his hair, which was very black, very long, and worn behind his ears, and without waiting to be invited, dropped into the most convenient seat he could perceive.

"I've come, sir, as I said I would, to tell you all about Sal Tompkins," she began, as soon as in compliance with Severne's request she had seated herself. "This mornin', my old man, John Wiggins, as used to be in the shoemakin' business, says, 'Mary,' says he, 'I had a dream last night of a white rat, and whenever I dreams of a white rat, there's always somethin' goes wrong. Once I dreamt about a white rat, and Jim Johnson's wife got drowned, and once more, Marthy fell down stairs and sprained her wrist, and once more, the Baptist Church in Hightsville burnt down, and once more, the price of leather went up twenty-five cents on the pound, and once more, Mrs. McAlpine's baby was born with a club-foot, so I'm certain,' says he, 'things is not right.' I took the *Sun*, and I looked all through it, and says I, 'Wiggins,' says I, 'there was a fire last night in Nassau Street, and a man was knocked down in Broadway, and a house was struck by lightnin' in Boston, and the Philadelphy train didn't get in till twelve o'clock, and there was a murder in Wayne Street at Number 110, and a burglary at——' 'You need not read any more, Mary,' says Wiggins, 'for I guess that murder is the particular thing that's gone wrong.' And then I bethought me of Sal, for I had found out that she lived in Wayne Street, and says I, 'I'll go round there right away after breakfast,' and then as I was thinkin', for I hadn't got out of bed yet, it struck me that mayhaps Sal was a welterin' in her gore, and says I, 'Wiggins,' says I, 'I can't stand this no longer; I'm goin' round to Wayne Street now.' So I jumped out of bed, and hurried on my clothes, and round I started.

"Well, sir, you see," continued Mrs. Wiggins, stopping for a moment to recruit her almost exhausted breath, "just as I turned our corner, who should I see but Brother Jenkins, as is sittin' in that chair, and says I, 'Brother Jenkins, there's been a awful murder.' 'Where, sister?' says he. 'Murders is of this world, worldly, and we are told that there shall be wars and rumors of wars, before the final comin' of the King of Glory, and murders is wars on a small scale.' Wasn't that just what you said, Brother Jenkins?"

Thus addressed, Brother Jenkins again ran his long fingers through his hair, and rolling his eyes up to the ceiling, said, with a strong nasal twang:

"Sister Mary, and you, sir, that was it. I always try to adapt my language to the particular circumstances of the case. I believe in spiritual gifts more than in human learning, because one comes from God, and the other is the offspring of man's sinful devices. I have always had a natural gift of interpretation of Scripture, and I do it through the signs of the times, which are full of awful import to those Christians who stand in the white robes of righteousness waiting for the coming of the Lord."

Severne was intensely amused, but preserving as grave a countenance as possible, he turned to Mrs. Wiggins, and requested her to resume her narrative.

"Well, sir," continued that lady, "Brother Jenkins said he would go with me, 'For,' says he, 'perhaps the poor creature's not quite dead yet, and may want a little religious consolation;' and says I, 'True,' says I, and we went together.

"And when we got to the house, Brother Jenkins says, says he to the policeman at the door, 'Can we go up? this lady is a friend of the murdered woman, and I'm a minister of the Gospel.' And says he nothing, but only nodded his head. And then we went up stairs, and says I to another policeman, says I, 'Where's the murdered Sarah?' and says he, 'There's no murdered Sarah here, nor has been.' And says I, 'Who is murdered?' And says he, 'A woman, named Betsey, and the coroner's a sittin' on her now with a jury.' I didn't know nothin' about no Betsey, but we went in, and there she laid on a bed, a bottle of pizen in her hands, and the jury had just found as it was no murder but a suicide. And says Brother Jenkins, says he, 'My friends, this is a awful occasion, and perhaps a few remarks will not be out of place.'"

"I think, Sister Mary," said Brother Jenkins, clearing his throat and wiping his face with a scriptural pocket-handkerchief, upon which were printed various scenes described in the Book of Revelations,—"I think it will be more to the edification of our friend, if I should in a few brief words repeat the discourse which I commenced, but through the wicked interference of the minions of Satan was not allowed to complete.   Would you like to hear it, my brother?   It is short and may prove comforting."

Thus addressed, Severne, who was enjoying the adventure with a zest he had not given to anything amusing for many a day, replied in the affirmative; and Brother Jenkins, again adjusting his hair with his fingers, rose from his chair, stuck his hands under the tail of his coat, and thus spoke:

"My friends, we find it said in the Book of Revelations, in the ninth chapter and sixth verse, as follows:

"'And in those days shall men seek death, and shall not find it; and shall. desire to die, and death shall flee from them.'

"Many of you, my brethren, might take this in a too literal sense, and imagine that because this our sister has found death, it was a proof that the coming of our Lord was not at hand.   I do not blame you for such an opinion, for all are not endowed with the gift of interpreting prophecy.   For it is written, 'Many are called but few chosen.' But what is this our text, my brethren?   Is it not 'For in those days *men* shall seek death, and shall not find it.'   It does not say *women*, my brethren,—oh, no! and in that fact we have a most remarkable coincidence between prophecy and the facts of the case before us. A woman has found death after seeking for it. How did she seek for it?—with a sword? Oh, no!   With a rifle?   Oh, no!   With a Colt's revolver? Oh, no!   With a club?   Oh, no!   With water or with fire? Oh, no!   Many poor brothers and sisters have sought death by all these means; and one of the best of them is a Colt's revolver with all the barrels loaded, because if one fails, there are five more chances left.   And charcoal is a good means, and I have known it to be used with great power and case; but this our sister, for reasons known to herself, as our brethren, the coroner's jury, have just told us, chose to seek death with a bottle of laudanum.

"A bottle of laudanum!   What is laudanum? I hear some of you say.   It is a medicine, my brethren, which is not without its virtues.   It is good for the colic and the cholera and the bowel complaint, and divers other of the diseases with which it pleases God to afflict us for our sins. I have tried it in many disorders, my friends, and I speak

what I do know, and testify what I have seen.   My friend,
Dr. Snaffle, puts it into his compound cure-all, which is
an excellent remedy for all diseases, and which you can get
for only fifty cents a bottle.   I recommend it to all my flock;
and Dr. Snaffle offered me twenty per cent. on all the sales
he made through me, but I did not say I would take it.

"But laudanum is a sleep-producing article, and here it
has caused the sleep of death.   A small quantity is good,
but a large quantity is bad, and causes the separation of the
soul from this mass of corruption which we call our body.

"And where does the soul go?   Ah, my brethren!—
where does it go?   Where has the soul of our sister gone?
Let us look around us a little before we answer that question.   Was our sister a sister of the Lord?   Alas, my brethren, I fear not!   Was she brought up in our Zion?   Alas,
no!   Did she believe in the speedy coming of our Lord?
Alas, no!   Did she aid in spreading the Gospel?   Alas, no!
Did she put her trust in God?   Alas, no!   Then, my brethren, where is her soul?   Alas, it is with the devil and his
angels, where it will remain forever and ever swimming in
a lake of melted sulphur!

"I had got this far, my brother and sister," said Brother
Jenkins, lowering his voice, "and was about to describe in
detail the bottomless pit, when one of the servants of Satan,
clothed as a policeman, came up to me and said :

"'Come, there's been enough of this.'

"'Enough of the Gospel?   Do you not know, my brother,'
I replied, 'that if I was to speak here till doomsday, I could
not give you enough of the Gospel?'

"'I know this,' said he, 'that you've got to clear out.'

"'I will let you know who I am,' I answered; 'I shall
mention this next Sunday to my flock.'

"'Who are you, anyhow?' he said.

"'I am a servant of the Lord my Master,' I replied, 'and
my name is Jenkins.'

"'Well, Mr. Jenkins,' he said, 'if you don't leave this
room at once, I'll take you to the station-house.'

"I declined to do so, and then he, with three others, laid
violent hands on me, and with many sinful exclamations
took me to the place they called the station-house, when I
was fined five dollars for obstructing the officers in the dis-

charge of their duty—so the son of Belial said who sat upon the bench. I gave him my views about his ungodly conduct, and then he fined me ten dollars more, and said that if I should open my mouth again, he would send me to Blackwell's Island for thirty days. I saw I was in the hands of the Philistines, and so I paid the fifteen dollars and came away."

"A very satisfactory termination I should say of the whole affair," said Severne, whose amusement, as the reverend brother proceeded with his discourse, had changed to disgust. "Why could you not refrain from such conduct at the death-bed of the poor woman who, for all you know, died with her sins forgiven?"

"Ah, my brother, you little know the ways of this wicked world, if you think she was of the kind that humble themselves before their Maker! Besides, it was my duty to do my Master's work, and to improve the opportunity to the advantage of the godless people who were assembled there. I did not finish my discourse; for besides pointing out the terrors in store for the damned, I had to make the application of my text to the most important point, the coming of the King of Glory. Now, my brother, I do not believe you see the nature of my argument."

"No; nor do I wish to. I think it more than probable, from all I have heard, that Betsey, as she was called, will meet with more favor from her God than will such persons as you."

"My brother, I know it is my duty to forgive you, and I do. I hope God will pardon you, too, for insulting one of his servants. I would like to explain to you that as it is said in the text *men* shall seek death and shall not find it, we are justified, by all the rules of exegetical reasoning, in assuming that when *women* seek it, about the time of the coming of our Lord, they shall find it. But I refrain, my brother, 'Cast not your pearls before swine.' I mean nothing insulting. I have been well brought up and educated, and though I despise all gifts that do not come from on high——"

"If you will be silent, and allow Mrs. Wiggins to go on with what she has to say, I will be much obliged to you," said Severne, who was getting tired of the man and his cant.

"Yes, my brother, I will be silent, and pray to God to change your heart." And thus again obtaining a hearing, Mrs. Wiggins resumed :

"Well, sir, you see while Brother Jenkins was a preachin' I was lookin' around, not but what I was listenin', too, and learnin' every blessed word; and I looked in the poor thing's trunks and closets, because, you know, sir, says I to myself, 'Maybe there might be somethin' as would tell who she was,' but I only found a few pictures and two or three books, and such like. And I was beginnin' to despair, when all at once it struck me all of a heap-like that I knew that room; and when I came to think about it I remembered that it was the very one Julia Tompkins, Sal's mother, used to live in. And then I recollected that one day when I went there to talk to Julia about Sal, who was to come to us, I opened the door all of a sudden-like, and there was Julia puttin' some things under a brick of the hearth. And I went home, and says I, 'John,' says I, 'do honest women hide letters and such like under the hearth?' And says he, 'Mary,' says he, 'they does whatever they wants to, be they honest or be they not.' And then says I, 'I saw Julia Tompkins a hidin' letters and things under a brick.' And says he, 'Mary,' says he, 'I guess you'd better mind your own business.' Which I did—rememberin' my marriage promises, which is always harder on women than on men—and never thought no more about it till this mornin'."

Severne's interest was aroused by this new revelation of Mrs. Wiggins, but he knew from experience how useless it would be to attempt to cut short her circumlocutory method of telling her story, so he waited patiently for the expected *denouement*. It was all evidently new to Brother Jenkins also, for that worthy gentleman opened his eyes wider, elevated his eyebrows, and contorted his face in a manner that was frightful to behold. He was about to give utterance to his feelings, but a look and a gesture from Severne restrained him, and Mrs. Wiggins, having drunk off a tumbler of water which stood by her on the table, resumed her narrative.

"Well, sir, you see I looked for that brick. There it was just as Julia had left it, I guessed; I pressed my foot against it and I found it was loose. It was just at the time Brother

Jenkins was bein' persecuted by the policemen; I stooped down, coverin' it with my frock, and lifted it up without no sort of trouble, and there was a little tin box, which I put into my pocket right off. I thought I had seen that box before, sir, and I thinks so still, much to my sorrow, too, but that's neither here nor there. Them as God has joined together let no man put asunder; and when Brother Jenkins married me and John Wiggins, nigh on to twenty year ago, I promised to do my duty by him, and whether he has done his towards me will be known in the great day when the sea shall give up its dead and the dry land likewise. That is supposin', of course, sir, my suspicions is correct, for you see, sir, John always had a hankerin' after Julia Tompkins, and me, his lawful wife, always doin' my duty by him a mendin' of his clothes and a cookin' of his victuals, night and day, and all because her feet was small, as if I made my feet, which I didn't, God knows."

The subject was so heart-rending that Mrs. Wiggins burst into a flood of tears, and sobbed in the most despairing manner.

Severne endeavored to comfort her, but without success; and turning to Brother Jenkins, who, since his recent snubbing, had preserved a discreet silence, he asked him to endeavor to restore Mrs. Wiggins to a condition of equanimity.

Brother Jenkins received the proposal with every mark of pleasure, and going to the disconsolate female, knelt by her side, and taking her by the hand said, in his sepulchral though nasal voice:

"Sister Wiggins, do you love the Lord?"

"Yes, Brother Jenkins, I hope I do," she sobbed.

"And do you believe that the hour draweth nigh?"

"Yes, Brother, I hope I do."

"Then why should you weep over the sorrows of this wicked world when you have laid up treasures in the world to come, where there is neither marriage nor giving in marriage?"

Mrs. Wiggins being unable to give a satisfactory response to this question, or in fact any answer at all, suddenly dried her tears and prepared to continue the description of her adventures, while Brother Jenkins, looking triumphantly at

Severne, walked majestically back to his chair, which he resumed with—as the novels would say—a dignity and grace peculiarly his own.

"I put the box in my pocket, sir, as I said; and while Brother Jenkins and the policemen was a wranglin'——"

"Oh, Sister Wiggins, me wrangling!" said Brother Jenkins, in a deprecatory tone.

"Leastwise they was wranglin', and you was a bearin' of it all, like a lamb as has lost his shepherd and has got among wolves. But, as I was sayin', I went down stairs with my box to look for Sal, and I went into her room, which was empty, and a policeman, as was very civil, Brother Jenkins, and quite contrariwise to them as was wranglin' up stairs, told me, says he, 'Sal went away last night and hasn't come back to her room, and it wouldn't be at all surprisin' if she didn't come back at all, for she was up stairs this mornin' a givin' of her evidence, and there was folks with her as will look out for her hereafter.' And says I, 'What's their names?' And says he, 'One's named Mr. Holmes and the other's named Mr. Severne, and they came in a carriage with a big S on it, and a coachman in uniform.' And says I, 'Is that so?' and says he, 'As sure as my name's Miller,' which it was, seein' as how he used to keep a cigar store in Broome Street. And says I, 'I knows one of them.' And says he, 'Which one?' says he. And says I, 'Mr. Severne.' And says he, 'He's the one as offered me ten dollars to stay here and look after things to-day.' And so, sir, I just held on to my box, and here it is, sir, at your service, seein' as how I suppose you knows all about Sal."

With these last words, Mrs. Wiggins plunged her hand into a capacious pocket in her frock, and drew forth a tin box about the size of those formerly used for Seidlitz powders, but much more neatly made.

The sight of it appeared about to call up the feelings which had been so effectually subdued by Brother Jenkins, but with an effort she restrained herself and handed it to Severne, merely remarking as she did so :

"I knows it too well, sir, by the letters as is painted on the top—J. W. He used to keep buttons in it."

Severne took the box, and untied the cord which was wrapped tightly around it. He opened it, and finding it

,contained nothing but letters, he placed it on his table, intending to look them over when more at leisure.

"And now, Mrs. Wiggins," he said, "I must express to you my thanks for all your trouble, and must beg of you to accept this note, as an evidence of my appreciation of your good offices. I think, too, you need give yourself no un-easiness in regard to Mr. Wiggins and Julia Tompkins. Doubtless your husband merely admired her through an artistic feeling very creditable to him, and it is not at all probable he will ever have another opportunity of being fascinated by her. Besides, I am very sure that he has long since found that a good wife, like you, is a man's best friend !"

"I am very much obliged to you, sir," said Mrs. Wiggins, as she took the hundred dollar note which Severne handed to her. "I've not seen as much money as this, sir, for many a long year. We was a gettin' hard up for money, for you see our rent was due last week, and there ain't much sewin' to be done now, and Marthy doesn't get much, and as to John, he can't work, as you knows, and the Society for the Relief of Destitute Families ain't a doin' much in that way, 'cause you see, sir, they ain't got no money when you goes to them, notwithstandin' all they gets. And I ain't ashamed or afraid to work, for that's what I expect to do, and if you ever wants any shirts made, or drawers either, or for the matter of that, any gentlemen of your acquaintance, I hope, sir, you'll not forget as Mary Wiggins has worked for the firm of Goggle and Sharp, as keeps the big shirt emporium in Broadway; and as to Julia Tompkins, I don't care for her, and I can't say as John mistreats me, for you see, sir, he has a hard time of it, not able to work, as was his great pleasure, and now only able to go about on crutches, which is not comfortable for him or for me. And is Sal all right, sir ?"

"Yes. I intend to educate her, and if I find her to be as good a girl as I think she will prove to be, I shall adopt her as my daughter. She will be glad to see you, Mrs. Wiggins, and she says you were always very kind to her. As to the future, so far as you are concerned, give yourself no uneasiness. I will see that you are in want of nothing necessary for your comfort, and that of your husband. I shall come and see you in a few days, and bring Sarah with me."

"Sal was always a good girl while she lived with me, sir, and I don't understand why she went away. She's been gone close on to four year, and I'm glad things is to be well with her in the future."

"Ah, my brother," sighed Brother Jenkins, who had been listening and looking on with undisguised astonishment and chagrin, "be careful how you cast your pearls before swine. There are many virtuous and godly young women in New York who would be glad of a chance such as that you are about to give to this wanton and dissolute girl, who knows nothing about the anticipated coming of the King of Glory. And as to myself, my brother, I try to do my duty to my people like a good shepherd, and I think—I humbly think I have succeeded in bringing many of them into the true fold. I expect to be rewarded hereafter, my brother; for in this life there is not much to be had, notwithstanding we are told that those who preach the Gospel shall live by the Gospel. You gave a hundred dollars for a little box of old letters,—I think it was a hundred, for I saw a C on the note, but if I am mistaken, my brother, you will correct me. Have you nothing to give toward instructing the Apaches in the doctrines of the New Light Millennium? Oh, my brother, forget not the heathen in thy prosperity."

"No," replied Severne, "I have nothing to give for any such purpose; but as you accompanied Mrs. Wiggins, and may have been of some service to her in gaining admittance to the room where these letters were found, I will give you this for yourself. You may give it to the Apaches if you choose." So saying, Severne handed the reverend gentleman a twenty dollar note.

Brother Jenkins's eyes glistened with pleasure as he stretched out his hand for the money, which he at once proceeded to put into his pocket-book.

" It is well, my brother, and I thank you sincerely. Some other time, perhaps, you will give for the spread of our religion to the poor Apaches. Them you will have always with you, while, as for me, a few short and wearisome years, at most, will see me laid in my grave, where the wicked cease from troubling and the weary are at rest.   Farewell, my brother," he continued, seeing that Mrs. Wiggins had risen and was ready to go, "farewell.   If you should ever wish for religious instruction or advice in matters of faith or doctrine, I shall be glad to serve you and the Lord by expounding the true principles of prophetical interpretation.   I wish you well, my brother, I wish you well."   And Brother Jenkins inclined the upper moiety of his body so as to form with the lower half, an angle, a little more than a right angle, and, with Mrs. Wiggins, took his departure. The last thing that met his eyes was the little tin box which Severne was about to place in his desk.

After Mrs. Wiggins and her spiritual adviser had got into the street, the latter turned to his companion, and said:

"Sister Mary, it may be that the Lord has endowed you with more sense than he ordinarily gives to women, but you do not make it very manifest, my sister.   No, by no means. You might as well have had five hundred dollars for that box of letters as one, and then you would have been able to help. the poor Apaches and the friends who are feeding you with righteousness.   You may do it yet, my sister, and if my feeble words have no influence with you, pray for advice, and you will get it, as a dream or a vision, which I will interpret for you.   I should not be surprised, my sister, if those letters were of great value.   You ought to have told me of them before you took them to that scoffer and unbeliever. It was not right.   There should always be unlimited confidence between the shepherd and his flock.   For without the shepherd the flock would go astray into the wilderness of sin.   Think of this, my sister, think of this!"

CHAPTER XIX.

IN WHICH CERTAIN MATTERS OF IMPORTANCE ARE SETTLED TO THE
SATISFACTION OF ALL CONCERNED.

As we have seen, in the last chapter, Severne put the tin box of letters which Mrs. Wiggins had given him into his desk, intending to look over the papers that evening. He had glanced at the directions of some of them, and had ascertained that they were addressed to Miss Julia Tompkins, the former possessor of them, and he had no doubt but that they would clear up many points of which he now had either very imperfect information or none at all.

His thoughts had recurred to Margaret, and he was engaged in the pleasing occupation of bringing her features back to his mind, when Wilson came into the room and handed him a card on a salver.

Severne took it and read the name.

"Miss Grace Langley," he said; "verily I am in luck this morning as regards lady visitors. I do not know this one, but she has a very pretty name. Ask Miss Langley to walk up, Wilson—or stop. Is she in the parlor?"

"No, sir, she is in the reception-room."

"Well, then, show her into the parlor, and I will join her in a moment. I don't think this is a very inviting place into which to ask a lady to come," he continued to himself. "There is too much of the shop about it."

The step which Grace had resolved upon, in order, if possible, to prevent the success of Mr. Freeling's schemes, was one in regard to the success of which she felt more and more apprehension as she came to think it over. She had never seen Severne, and had imbibed the idea that he was of a harsh and repulsive disposition. If such were the case, there was little to be hoped for, as such persons always sustain their agents. Her mother, too, had endeavored to dissuade her from making any attempt to change the situation of affairs.

But Grace had very wisely considered that at the worst things could not be rendered more unfavorable for them than they were. "Mr. Severne," she had said to her mother, "if he does not think proper to allow us to retain the houses at their present rent, can do no more than refuse, and so, dear mamma, I am determined to see him. He has not heard our side of the story yet, and he never will hear it from Mr. Freeling."

She had only waited in the parlor a few moments when Severne entered the room. Grace was a very pretty and a very sweet-looking girl. She was dressed very plainly, for her means did not admit of any display in this direction, but everything was made and worn with that unmistakably good taste which bespeaks the lady more than anything else which a casual inspection places at our disposal when we are forming an opinion as to the status of one of the softer sex. Severne at once made up his mind in regard to the position in life which his visitor ought to occupy. Female beauty always exercised a great influence over him, and he took every opportunity of which good breeding admitted to look at Grace's face. He thought it very lovely, but nothing like so lovely as Margaret's.

On the other hand, Grace was agreeably surprised to find that Severne was far from being the haughty and disagreeable individual she had conceived him to be. She gained courage as she perceived that he was gentlemanly and considerate in his manner. She saw that he was handsome, too, but she was afraid to inspect his features very closely.

"I have come, Mr. Severne," she said, with a very soft and musical voice, "to see you in regard to the houses in Lexington Avenue belonging to you, and which are occupied by my mother. We have lived in them for several years at what has been considered a fair rent, and now, Mr. Freeling informs us, it is to be doubled after this month. It is impossible for my mother to pay this great addition, and we shall consequently be obliged to leave them, to our very great inconvenience and regret."

"May I ask what rent your mother pays now, Miss Langley? I have really forgotten, and I neglected to ask Mr. Freeling when I authorized him to increase the rent," said

Severne, who now remembered that the houses were occupied by a widow lady named Langley.

"Five hundred dollars a year each. It is to be increased
to a thousand."

"That is a very large increase, I should say, Miss Langley. Do you think, or does your mother think, they are
worth so much a year?"

"They are very comfortable houses, Mr. Severne, and are
in excellent order, but we do not think they are worth so
high a rent as Mr. Freeling demands. If we thought differently I do not think mamma would have allowed me to
call on you about the matter. They may be worth more
than the sum we now pay, but they are not worth double
that amount."

"Do you know Mr. Freeling, Miss Langley?" ·

"Oh yes, sir, he used to occupy rooms in one of the
houses."

"Is there any reason why Mr. Freeling should wish to
raise your mother's rent?"

Grace hesitated for a moment. Though she despised
Freeling, she did not—now that she was called upon to do
so—like to say anything that would injure him with his employer. She reflected, however, that she might answer that
question without entering into any particulars.

"I think there is," she said.

"I will not question you further, Miss Langley," said
Severne. "Please give my compliments to your mother, and
say to her that the rent shall not be raised. Why did not
she come?"

"Mamma is very timid. She has had so much to trouble
her that I took the duty off her hands. I cannot thank you
enough, Mr. Severne, for your kindness. I am sure mamma
will be very glad to call and see you now, and thank you in
person."

"She could not have had a more acceptable ambassa-
dress," said Severne, smiling. "But, Miss Langley," he
continued, with an excited manner, as if a new and brilliant
idea had occurred to him, "will you allow me to accompany
you home? I would like to have a little conversation with
your mother."

Grace signified her acquiescence, though she wondered what the business could be which had so suddenly arisen.

As they walked toward Lexington Avenue, Severne entered into conversation with Grace, and discovered that she was possessed of both good sense and good education. Here, then, within twenty-four hours, he had met with two women who had compelled him to acknowledge their beauty and worth, two things which Severne had hitherto been half disposed to think rarely went together in women.

The conversation was more on Grace's part, however, than on his. She had had a great load lifted from her mind, and therefore felt in the vein for making herself agreeable to him who by a word had raised it. He was engrossed with the new idea which had flashed across his mind, and which he was still considering. He said enough, however, to keep Grace's tongue in action, and he was not so busy but that he heard and understood the greater portion of what she said.

And what was the thought which had struck Severne with so much force that he must rush off at once to put it in action if possible? Simply this:

He had been reflecting more or less since his interview with Sarah, at which he had stated his views in regard to her, that there would be several practical difficulties in the way of carrying them out with entire success. These would all certainly be increased by his absence at the very time that Sarah would most require support and advice. He could not take her into his own house without getting a lady of refinement, education, and intelligence to enter it in the capacity of Sarah's governess, and he did not consider that it would be altogether right, even if he found such a one, to leave her and Sarah alone in his house during his tour.

To place his ward in a boarding-school would be, he thought, under the peculiar circumstances of the case, altogether inadmissible. John Holmes and his granddaughter were also going to travel in a few weeks, so that he could not obtain much assistance from them. While they remained in town there would be no difficulty, but as they were to leave in so short a time, it was of course expedient to make arrangements now that would at least last till his own return.

He had thus been led to think that if he could find some quiet, respectable, and refined family, who wonld be willing to receive Sarah as one of their members for the few months during which he contemplated being absent, he should be able to place the matter in the best possible position for all concerned. While Grace was in his parlor, he had been struck with her ladylike appearance and manuers, and had consequently formed the idea that Grace's mother must also be a very superior woman. The transition from this thought to Sarah was very natural. What if Mrs. Langley were just the person to take charge of her? How very convenient and desirable such an arrangement would be. And hence his sudden wish to make that lady's acquaintance, and to escort Grace to her home.

Mrs. Langley was seated in her little parlor, anxiously awaiting Grace's return, when this young lady bounded into the room, and throwing her arms around her mother's neck, exclaimed in a whisper:

"Oh, mamma, Mr. Severne was so kind! All is right. He is in the hall, and will be here in a second."

And before she had finished speaking, Severne had entered the room.

Grace immediately presented him to her mother, who began to thank him for his consideration.

"I beg, madam," he said, "that you will say nothing more on the subject. The houses are really not worth more than five hundred a year, and I should feel like a swindler if I exacted more than that sum for them. In justice to myself, however, even at the risk of appearing to lessen the efficacy of Miss Langley's mission, I must say that I intended to rescind the order given to Mr. Freeling before it should go into effect. I am extremely sorry it has caused even a moment's uneasiness, and I must ask your forgiveness for my want of consideration."

"I am very sure, Mr. Severne," replied Mrs. Langley, "that the idea would never have occurred to you but for Mr. Freeling. As it is, instead of offering you forgiveness, we must never cease to remember your kindness."

"I did not press Miss Langley for information in regard to Mr. Freeling's motives, but I shall be very much obliged to you if you will tell me what you may know of the matter."

In compliance, therefore, with Severne's request, Mrs. Langley entered into a detailed account of the agent's conduct.

"I was very sure," said Severne, when she had concluded, "that he had an object other than the false one he alleged, and it was in the hope of discovering it that I consented to his proposition. I must request, however, that you will not inform him that I have been enlightened. When he comes for the rent, hand him the paper I will give you in a moment, but enter into no explanations." With these words, Severne went to a writing-desk which occupied a corner of the room, and wrote a certificate to the effect that the three houses in Lexington Avenue had been continued to Mrs. Langley for three years, should she require them so long, at the rent of five hundred dollars each.

"I will see," he continued, "that your lease is made out in accordance with this certificate before I leave the country. In the mean time, this will be sufficient."

Mrs. Langley was again about to break out in the expression of her thanks, when Severne again interrupted her.

"You have given me an evidence of your confidence, madam," he said. "I have now to ask your consideration of what I have to say. I am very sorry," he continued, "that it will be necessary for Miss Langley to leave us for a short time. I can safely state, however, that what I have to say to her mother is not of a character to cause her any uneasiness, but, on the contrary, will, I trust, in the end, give her a great deal of pleasure."

"I think, mamma," said Grace, laughingly, as she quitted the room, "you can safely trust yourself with the lion in our den after I have bearded him so successfully in his own."

After her departure, Severne gave Mrs. Langley a detailed account of Sarah so far as his relations with her had extended, and of his intentions in regard to her.

"I am very sure," he said, in conclusion, "that she has many excellent points of character, which only need opportunity and the care you will be able to exercise over her for their full development. I would not ask you to assume so great a responsibility were I not perfectly satisfied of her disposition to receive the instruction which will qualify her for a more elevated position in life than that she has heretofore occupied, and also of your fitness for the duty of educating her in accordance with my ideas. I cannot ask you to decide the question immediately, but I trust you will allow me to hope that you will bestow upon it your full consideration, and give me an answer of as favorable a character as possible at your earliest convenience."

" I will not conceal from you, Mr. Severne," replied Mrs. Langley, "that while I am fully sensible of this mark of your confidence in one whom you scarcely know, I am also deeply impressed with the feeling of responsibility your proposition excites. You will, I am sure, also excuse me, when, as a mother, I tell you that I am not free from apprehension in regard to introducing one whose whole life has been so thoroughly dissolute and low to the companionship of my daughters. Before deciding, I would like to see Sarah, and ascertain for myself, so far as I can, her present disposition. If I should find that she is not radically depraved, but is anxious and determined to avail herself to the fullest extent of your generous and Christian purposes, I will be the last one to thwart them by any act of mine. I would also like, if you have no objection, to mention to my daughters so much of what you have told me as may be necessary to enable them to give me the benefit of their advice. My oldest daughter, Elizabeth, has been an invalid for many years, but she has a great deal of her father's strength of character and good sense, and her opinion would be valuable to me. And Grace, though she would probably look at the matter from a different point of view, would give a decision based upon honorable and just motives."

"I should be very glad if you would mention it to your daughters, my dear madam, in such terms as you may see fit to employ, and to any extent you may deem proper. Though I have not the pleasure of knowing your eldest daughter, I am very certain you do not overstate the value of her judgment, for I know you have said no more than is strictly true in regard to Miss Grace Langley. I am very apt, as you have doubtless perceived, to form my opinions of individuals from first impressions, and though I am sometimes deceived, this is very rarely the case, not perhaps so frequently as if I waited for more thorough acquaintance. I have seen sufficient of you and Miss Grace to convince myself that I am not wrong in giving you my confidence. As to an interview with Sarah, I recognize fully the propriety of your request, and will be very happy if you will meet her at my house to-morrow morning, at such an hour as may suit your convenience."

Mrs. Langley appointed a time for the interview, and Severne took his leave, with the confidence that there would be no further difficulty in the case.

There were still, however, many preparations to make. He commissioned Margaret to supply Sarah's wardrobe with suitable clothing, and to purchase such other articles as might be necessary. And by the next morning the millinery, mantua-making, and other arrangements essential to a presentable *parure* were so far completed, that when Severne drove round in his carriage to John Holmes's house at ten o'clock, Sarah was as tastefully attired a young woman, and looked as pretty as he had any right to expect.

She came toward him and held out her hand, as he entered the room.

"I was not able to thank you yesterday for all your goodness," she said, "and I cannot do so now in proper terms. I will show you, however, by my actions how much I appreciate it, and I hope and believe you will never have cause to repent of your kindness."

"No more of that, my dear child," said Severne, smiling, and looking admiringly at her. "I am very sure you will do your best; but I have come now to take you to your home. You will not be there long, however, for I trust matters will be so shaped as to give you, till my return, a much more cheerful residence and more agreeable society than you would meet with in my bachelor establishment. I suppose Miss Leslie has told you of the contemplated arrangements, which I mentioned to her yesterday."

"Yes. I am very sorry you are going away."

"I am almost sorry now, myself," said Severne, smiling; "but I am under a solemn promise to my physician, and he is a great tyrant, and might poison me if I broke my agreement."

"I see you are joking," said Sarah, as she noticed his smile, though she was for a moment disposed to give full credit to his words. "The best man I ever knew but you

was a physician. He was very kind to a woman and her
child who lived in our house, and who had the cholera. He
gave them both food and medicine, and nursed them himself,
with a little assistance from me, till they recovered. There
is nothing now that Ann Simmons would not do for him.
I think," she continued, while her face became crimson with
shame, "that he was with you that night in Fifth Avenue."

"Lawrence!" exclaimed Severne.

"That was his name," said Sarah. "He did not recognize me that night."

"You will see him this morning. Do not be afraid, my
dear child," he continued, observing Sarah's look of con-
sternation. "He is still as kind as he ever was. He is one
of my dearest friends, and will meet you with all the sympathy and consideration he knows so well how to show."

"Everything seems like a dream to me," said Sarah, with
emotion. "Is it possible it will all last? I am so happy,
and all around me are so good, that I can scarcely believe
it to be real. Do not be angry with me," she continued, as
the tears came into her eyes. "I try my best to be quiet,
but I cannot. I am so unlike Miss Leslie that I am afraid
to speak to her, or even to come near her. Oh, do you
think I can ever be like her?"

"My dear Sarah," said Severne, leading her to a sofa and
seating himself by her side, "God has so ordered things in
this world that we are, to a great extent, the arbiters of our
own destiny. For a time he may allow us to suffer wrongs
and indignities, even when we have conscientiously endeavored to do our duty. I cannot say, therefore, what he has
in store for you, but I believe that if you earnestly strive to
do your part with faithfulness, and trust in him, you will not
labor in vain. Do you ever read your Bible, Sarah?"

"I used to read it when I lived with Mrs. Wiggins, but
I got out of the habit, as I saw that many people who came
there and read it a great deal were really worse than those
who did not."

"That may have been so, Sarah. Many persons pretend to be religious, in order to effect their evil purposes
with greater certainty. You will learn, however, to discrim-
inate between those who are guided by the Word of God,
and those who, while pretending to heed it, are really more

depraved than those who openly practice all manner of wickedness."

"Last night," said Sarah, softly, "Miss Leslie—she told
me to call her Margaret, but I do not feel as if I ought to
yet—came into my room before I went to bed, and asked
me if I ever prayed. I was obliged to tell her no. And
then she got her prayer-book, and asked me to kneel down
with her and say the Lord's Prayer. She put her arm around
my neck, and we knelt down together and prayed. And
then she told me that God was ready to forgive all my sins
if I came to him with a contrite heart. I told her she did
not know, and that I could not tell her how wicked my life
had been. And she said she did not want to know, that
God knew, and that was enough. And then she kissed me,
and bid me good night, and said that God would take care
of me."

"He will take care of you, my dear child," said Severne.
"When we have brought ourselves to confess our sins, they
are already more than half forgiven. Let me relate to you
the particulars of an incident which happened to me in
Spain several years since, and which, I am sure, will interest you."

While Severne was speaking, Margaret entered the room.
She would have at once retreated, as she saw he was earnestly talking to Sarah, and that neither had perceived her,
but a strange fascination she could not resist compelled her
to remain. She sat down on a chair near the door and
listened.

"I was crossing the Pyrenees, and had reached a défile in
the mountains," continued Severne, "which led out to the
open country, when our party was stopped by a man, who
inquired if there was a physician in it. There was none,
but as I had spent a good deal of time in the society of
physicians, and had studied medicine to some slight extent,
I offered him my services. He accepted them with many
thanks, and led me to a squalid hut, built among the rocks,
at a short distance from the main road, but in so retired and
secluded a spot that no one would have been likely to find
it unless guided by a person perfectly acquainted with its
location. I entered the wretched cabin after my conductor.
Its interior was even more forbidding than the outside;

there was no floor, and, though the weather was cold, there was no fire either. On a pile of wolf skins, in a corner of the only room the hut contained, lay a tall, fine-looking man, apparently in great pain, judging from the expression of his features, though he uttered neither groans nor complaints. I approached him, and inquired as to the nature of his illness. He made no answer, but with one hand threw down the rug that covered the lower portion of his body, and I saw that both his legs had been mashed, and were in a state of mortification. At the same time he held up the stump of his left arm, showing me that he had also lost his hand.

"In answer to my questions, I ascertained from him and my guide that he had been injured by the fall of a large piece of rock, four days previously, and that they were afraid to appeal to the local authorities for aid, as they were both robbers, and would certainly be shot immediately without even the form of a trial.

"I examined him according to the best of my ability, and told him, what was indeed perfectly true, that death was inevitable. Even then he was almost pulseless, and life could not by any possibility have been prolonged over a few hours.

"'I was certain of it, señor,' he said. 'I have been a very bad man, but since I have been on this bed I have thought a great deal of my wickedness, and I have asked God to forgive me. I am not, therefore, afraid of death. You may think it is very late for me to ask pardon, but I am perfectly sincere in it. If I was to live I should try to do my duty my life through.'

"I saw he was exhausted by talking. I gave him a drink of brandy from my flask, and begged him not to exert himself, but he seemed desirous of conversing with me.

"'Do you believe in dreams?' he asked me, with an anxious manner.

"I told him I did not, but that dreams oftentimes were serviceable to us in bringing matters before our minds which in our waking moments would have escaped us.

"'That is it,' he replied. 'I have frequently thought things out in my dreams which I could not succeed in making clear when I was awake. Last night I had a dream which has impressed me very forcibly, and which I would like to relate to you.'

"I signified my willingness to hear it, and raising himself in bed as far as he could, he said:

"'Last night, señor, after I had spent the day in trying to satisfy my mind in regard to God's favor to me, I had a dream which has given me great comfort, and which has convinced me that He has heard my prayer. I dreamed that I was at an inn, and that in the room with me was a company composed of many high and noble persons. There were princes, and bishops, and doctors, and dignitaries of all kinds, who seemed to be good men. In a corner, however, sat a man who did not appear to belong to the rest, and whom they all looked upon with disgust and suspicion. Some said he was a heretic, others a robber, and several declared they were certain he had committed murder. All shunned him, and one of the bishops said he ought to be given up to the police at once.

"'The man, although he evidently saw how he was avoided, said nothing, but ate his supper in silence, and prepared to sleep in his chair, as all the beds were taken by the others.

"'I stood in the midst of the assembly without apparently being seen by any of them, when suddenly my eyes were dazzled at the sight of a bright being who approached me. Do not be afraid, he said, I am an angel of God. Mark well what you shall see and hear.

"'He then rendered himself visible to the assembled company, and all fell on their knees with terror except the poor man in the corner, who alone looked at him without fear.

"'I am sent, said the angel, to announce to you that before twelve o'clock this night your souls will all be required of you, and to hear what you may have to say.

"'All began to speak, but the angel stopped them, and approaching one of the bishops said:

"'Are you ready?

"'I am ready, he replied; I have done my duty.

"'Not so, said the angel to me. He has made himself rich from the gifts of the poor laid upon the altar of God.

"'Are you ready? he said to another.

"'I am, was the answer. I have repented of all my sins, and have been righteous these many years.

"'That is not true, said the angel, addressing me. His life has been iniquitous from the time he could judge right from wrong to this hour.

"'Are you ready? he said to one of the princes.

"'Yes, I have always been at peace with God; I go to mass every day of my life.

"'For thirty years he has oppressed the widow and orphan, said the angel.

"'And thus he went to each one. Each was ready, each was righteous in his own sight, but of each one the angel had something to say in condemnation.

"'Then he went to the man who sat in the corner, and who looked piteously up at his approach.

"'Are you ready? said the angel.

"'I am not ready; my sins are so great that I dare not stand in the presence of my God.

"'Have you not tried to do God's will?

"'I have not, replied the man, bowing his head. I have disregarded his word every hour of my life.

"'And have you no hope? said the angel. ·

"'No hope, replied the man, clasping his hands and weeping. No hope but in the mercy of my Father.

"'The angel regarded him sorrowfully, but with a gleam of joy shining over his countenance, and then putting his hands on his head said: Fear not, God will take care of thee. And then coming to me said: Behold the only one who is not afraid to confess his own unworthiness. Now watch.

"'He had hardly said these words before the clock began to strike twelve. All looked anxious, as the sound of each stroke rang on their ears, except the man who sat in the corner of the room; his face was calm, but lit up with hope and trust. The hour had passed, and all were dead. I saw the spirits rise from the bodies of the great people who were certain of eternal life and then suddenly disappear from my sight, as if dragged down by an invisible hand. I looked toward the poor man in the corner. He had fallen back in his chair dead, and his soul was rising into the arms of an angel who stood ready to receive it. He clasped it to his breast, with a radiant smile upon his features, and swiftly ascended with it beyond my sight.'

"The man suddenly stopped," continued Severne, after a moment's pause. "I looked at him and saw that his eyes were closed and that his breath was almost gone. I felt his pulse; it was still. He was dead. A smile was on his cold, pallid face, and he had entered upon an eternal life, conscious of his failings, but trusting in the forgiveness of the Father who made him. Can we doubt, my dear child, that God was merciful to him, or that He will have equal compassion on you if you acknowledge your transgressions and strive to do His will? And therefore it is that I say fear not,—God will take care of you."

Sarah was unable to speak from excess of emotion, but she took Severne's hand and raised it to her lips, and Margaret coming forward, knelt by her side.

"I have heard all," she said to Severne, looking up into his face through the tears which filled her eyes. "You need not fear for her, and she need have none that you will not be to her a good, a wise, and a just guardian."

Severne was surprised, but he was always pleased now when he saw Margaret. He did not know exactly what to say, so he rose, and walking to a distant part of the room busied himself in studying a picture the details of which he knew by heart. After he had left the two girls sufficiently long together, he returned, with his watch in his hand, and reminded them that it was time to keep the appointment that had been made with Mrs. Langley. They went to get their bonnets, and in a few moments were on their way to Severne's house.

"I am anxious," said Margaret, smiling, "to see what sort of a place a bachelor's house is. I suppose you have very little in it," she continued, archly, "to conduce to your comfort?"

"I have not a very great deal, I must confess, but books and a few pictures," replied Severne.

"I shall look at both," said Margaret. "I have a natural right to be fond of both, for my grandfather is a bookseller and my great-grandfather was a painter."

"I have a very fine work of the latter which I must show you," said Severne. I picked it up in this country several years ago, though of course it was painted in Germany. I have no idea how it got here. I value it very highly."

"I have heard grandpapa speak of it, and I should like to see it very much."

When they entered Severne's parlor, they found Mrs. Langley already there, though Lawrence had not yet arrived. It was a very informal meeting. Mrs. Langley talked a great deal, and tried to make Sarah talk also, but with indifferent success. The latter of course did not know that she was being studied with a critical eye, but such was nevertheless the case, and, in the course of half an hour, Mrs. Langley announced in a side whisper to Severne that she was satisfied she had no cause for fear, and that she had no doubt Sarah would fulfill his best anticipations. She then stated that she had two nice rooms in the house adjoining the one she herself lived in, upon the same floor as her own and her daughters' rooms, and that by cutting a door through the party wall direct communication could be established between them. Nothing could have been more satisfactory than this arrangement, and Severne gave Mrs. Langley *carte blanche* as to the fitting up and furnishing of the apartments. It was settled that as soon as the rooms were ready, Sarah should take possession of them, and in the mean time, as several days would be necessary to get them in order, he decided, in accordance with John Holmes's and Margaret's requests, to leave her with them.

Mrs. Langley then took her leave, after a few words to Sarah, expressive of the pleasure she and her daughters would take in seeing her with them, which language Sarah warmly reciprocated, and Severne and the two young ladies proceeded to the picture gallery to look at the painting which Margaret's great-grandfather had made. While they were examining it, and the other fine pictures which hung on the walls, Lawrence entered the room. Severne presented him to the ladies. He started as he looked at Sarah, and then went up to her frankly and held out his hand.

"I know you now," he said, with a smile. "You are the little nurse who was of so much assistance to me when Ann Simmons and her baby were sick, grown into a tall young lady. Severne," he continued, aside to his friend, "she was one of the most faithful little creatures I ever saw at a bedside. I wish you joy of your bargain. I have great hopes of it. What a lovely being John Holmes's granddaughter is!"

"Hush !" said Severne, half annoyed at Lawrence's un-disguised admiration.   "She will hear you."

"I will never say it again to you," said Lawrence, smiling.

"Now, Mr. Severne," exclaimed Margaret, "I have suf-ficiently studied my ancestor's picture to get a tolerable idea of it.   Some other time I shall ask you to let me see it again, as well as your other paintings.   I will not express an opinion about it now, except to say that I am very favor-ably impressed with it.   It is so large, and there is so much detail in it that several inspections will be necessary in order for me to form a correct judgment in regard to its position, when compared with his other pictures which I have seen. What I want now is just to have a glance at your library. I think I like books even better than pictures."

"And in that I fully agree with you, Miss Leslie," said Severne, as he led the way to his library.   "We could live without paintings, but what would we do without books? We should go mad some of us, I think."

"Some of us are more likely to go mad through our books than without them," said Lawrence.   "Do not, Miss Leslie, I beg of you, say or do anything to encourage his love for books.   He is infatuated enough already."

Margaret could not refrain from an exclamation of de-lighted surprise when she entered the library and witnessed the completeness and beauty of all its arrangements; and when she came to examine the volumes with which the shelves were loaded, her pleasure was still greater.   "What a funny book this must be !" she exclaimed, taking one of the volumes into her hand: "'A Discourse on Artificial Beauty.   Espe-cially against Painting the Face.'   Pray, Mr. Severne, do you read this frequently, and do you form your opinions from it, 'A Censure on the Epidemical Practice of Re-proaching Red-Haired Men'?"

"I cannot say," replied Severne, laughing, "that I have formed my opinions from reading the very conclusive book you have in your hand.   I certainly, however, am willing to go as far, or even farther, than the learned author in praise of the red-haired of both sexes."

"I will never laugh at them again," continued Margaret, in great glee.   "The author says here, that 'they that laugh

at red-haired men are tickled by the Devil.'   I shall always
think of that when I see one hereafter."

"I hope, Miss Leslie," said Severne, as he escorted her
and Sarah to the carriage, "that after my departure you
will do me the favor to make use of my library as if it were
your own.   I will leave the key of it in your hands, so that
you will always be able to obtain access to it."

"Oh, I am very much obliged to you," said Margaret,
while her face lighted up with pleasure.   "There is nothing
I would like better, and I am sure grandpapa will be glad,
too."

"Well, Severne," said Lawrence, as the former returned
to the library and proceeded to light a cigar, "you have
certainly had a remarkable 'streak of luck,' as they say in
the West.   Your ward, as I suppose I must call her, is a
very pretty, and already quite a *distingue* looking girl.   A
few months will do wonders for her.   It is really wonderful
to me to see how rapidly some women adapt themselves to
new conditions of life.   Their tact is marvelous.   And how
much fine clothes do for them, too!   How well she wore them!
No one could have suspected that she was the same dirty
little beggar girl, who, last New Year's night, fleeced me
out of twenty-five cents and you out of ten dollars, and
who, a year ago, helped to nurse a woman and her child as
poor as herself.   What nice little hands and feet she has,
and how well her boots and gloves fitted her!   Seriously,
my dear fellow, I congratulate you.   You have done a good
thing, and I render you my homage.   You will make a good
woman out of her, I am sure.   As to Miss Leslie,—I beg
your pardon, I forgot that I was treading on forbidden
ground, I will say it though, in spite of my promise,—she is
the most beautiful creature I ever saw in my life.   My dear
fellow, if she is as good as she is beautiful, and I can already form an opinion on that point, you have drawn a
prize, for which I can thank God with as much sincerity as
you can."   With these words, Lawrence jumped up and
shook his friend by the hand with an energy which made
Severne wince.

"I am not in love with her, Lawrence," said Severne,
gravely, "though she is everything you say of her, and a
thousandfold more."

"I know that as well as you do," replied Lawrence; "but twenty-four hours will not elapse before you will love her more dearly than you ever did or ever will love anything else which has been or ever will be in the world."

CHAPTER XX.

NEGOTIATIONS.

Two weeks had elapsed. Sarah had become established in her new home. Teachers had been found for her, and through their instruction, and the kindness and care of Mrs. Langley and her daughters, she gave every promise of becoming a credit to her sex, and worthy the love of those who had rescued her from a degraded and a wicked life. Severne's preparations for the journey across the plains and mountains of the continent were nearly completed, and in two days he and Lawrence were to leave for St. Louis, where they were to make their final arrangements. His health had scarcely ever been better, for the cessation of the sedentary habits into which he had fallen, and the change in the character of his mental occupation, had of themselves nearly effected his cure, as Lawrence had predicted would be the result. Still, his friend was of the opinion that travel would very materially improve his mental and physical condition, and therefore the idea had not been abandoned.

Severne had met Margaret Leslie daily in all that time, and loved her—loved her as only those of strong passions and strong minds can love. He had not tried to resist the spell which he felt each moment of his life was binding him more closely in its thraldom, but he had brought up for the fair and full consideration of his mind all the circumstances of his life and condition which could in any way affect the subject, and he was able to lift up his face before God and say, with a clear and an honest heart, that there was no reason why he should not love Margaret Leslie and ask her to be his wife. Whether she loved him or not, he could not yet tell. That she liked his society, that she looked up to him as a teacher, that she regarded him as one worthy to be her friend, he knew full well. But he was twelve years older than she was, had seen more of the world than most educated persons of his age, had mingled in society under all its different phases, had read and studied till his mind was full of subjects which interested her, had been her grandfather's friend for many years, and had been brought into association with her under circumstances which could scarcely fail to impress her with a favorable idea of his character. It would have been strange therefore if she did not like him. He felt sure of her friendship and esteem, and sometimes, as he watched for those little signs which may mean a great deal or nothing at all, he thought he was beloved in return.

To be loved by Margaret Leslie! He who had hoped for the love of a virtuous woman and had passed his life in disappointment and regret; he who less than a month ago had looked upon his future as almost without hope, was now daring to dream of happiness such as in the wildest visions of his youth he had never imagined possible. Was it possible now? A few short hours would answer the question.

He sat in his library wreathing clouds of smoke from a fragrant Cabaña, thinking deeply, as was his wont when thus engaged; forming plans, abandoning others, and providing in his mind for all possible contingencies attendant on success or failure. Sarah was safely provided for, the details of his journey were settled upon, his business affairs were in order. Two things were still to be arranged. He had not yet determined in regard to the advisability of retaining Mr. Freeling as his agent, and he had not yet told Margaret Leslie in words how much he loved her.

Relative to the first he found it difficult to decide. Everything connected with his property was arranged. To dismiss Freeling would necessitate a change in many matters, and might delay his departure two or three weeks. He had become fully convinced of the agent's lack of principle, and could scarcely bear the thought of continuing the association. There had been no open quarrel, but when Freeling came for an explanation relative to Mrs. Langley's rent, Severne had given him very clearly to understand that he was acquainted with all the particulars of his scheme.

Freeling's disappointment and chagrin had been complete. He had failed in a measure of revenge upon which he had set his heart, but he was not subdued. He had reflected upon the matter of his relations with Severne, and he had confirmed himself in the determination to retain the agency if possible. To humble himself before his employer and at the same time entertain feelings of the bitterest hostility toward him, was so entirely consonant with his nature that he resolved to see what could be done by this means. He owed a great deal to Severne, but he was one of those monstrosities of human nature, whom God for some wise purpose beyond our ken occasionally creates, who take a fiendish delight in injuring those to whom they are most indebted, and in mounting to power through their destruction. He waited, therefore, for an opportunity of injuring Severne, and it was almost essential to his success to retain his present position. With every affectation of regret he had accordingly begged Severne to overlook his conduct relative to Mrs. Langley. He had confessed that he had been actuated by a feeling of revenge, but had offered in excuse the fact that he was a man liable, like all other men, to err, and that his anger against Mrs. Langley had been but of short duration, and had now entirely disappeared. He had even been to this lady to acknowledge his wrong, and had succeeded in inducing her to intercede with Severne for him.

Severne had listened to all that Mr. Freeling had to allege in his behalf, and had given due consideration to Mrs. Langley's request. Upon a full consideration of all the circumstances of the case, he could find nothing to extenuate the agent's misconduct, and he was entirely convinced that it would be highly proper to dispense with his services for the future. Still there was a strange fascination for him in the study of Freeling's character, of which he now began to comprehend the salient points, and he reflected that his own affairs were in such a condition now that it would be almost impossible for the agent to do him any injury in that direction. "I will let him alone," he said to himself, as he reclined in his comfortable chair studying the gyrations of a revolving ring of smoke he had succeeded, after several failures, in constructing. "If he does not succeed in hanging me or himself, it shall not be for want of rope. I think I understand him completely. He hates me with a most satanic fervor. It will be interesting to keep *au courant* with his machinations. To be forewarned is to be forearmed, however.

"One thing more remains to be done, and this night will witness its accomplishment. If she loves me, my happiness in this world will be complete, and I can return to my adopted country with a heart full of trust and hope. I must see her grandfather though first, and get his consent. I have no fear as to what my old friend will say. Three o'clock," he continued, looking at his watch. "I must hurry off if I mean to catch him before he leaves the shop. Where could there be a better place in the world for such a conference than 'the den' where he and I have passed so many pleasant hours ?"

John Holmes was in his den, engaged, as usual, in writing. He was always glad to see Severne, however, and immediately ceased his labor, and turning to his friend began to converse upon certain topics of the day which were attracting a good deal of attention from literary and scientific persons.

"My dear old friend," said Severne, "do you think I would ride all the way down here in a crowded omnibus, on such a hot day as this, too, to talk about such matters? I have come on an affair that concerns us both personally, and which is intimately connected with my happiness."

John Holmes looked at Severne for a moment, as if trying to divine, from a study of his countenance, what the subject was, but apparently not succeeding, he said:

"I need not, I am sure, tell you that you have only to mention in what way I can be of service to you in order to insure my co-operation in anything that you may think desirable for your welfare. We have not been friends these ten years for nothing."

"I shall not take an unfair advantage of your promise. I believe you have confidence enough in me to know that I would not ask you to do anything which was not right. But I am not going to make any long prelude to my application. I have become convinced that I love your granddaughter, and I have come to request your permission to ask her for her hand."

There was no hesitation in John Holmes's manner. He rose from his seat, and grasping Severne's hand, said, while his eyes become moist with pleasurable emotion :

"My dear friend, there is no man in the world I would rather give her to than you. I have thought within the last two weeks that I might be called upon to resign her to you, but I had no idea matters had proceeded so far. Her happiness is very dear to me," he continued. "I love her above all earthly things, and I would rather die than do an act which would give her a single pang of sorrow. You have said nothing to her yet, and do not know how she regards you ?"

"Not a word," replied Severne. "I have sometimes thought there was a stronger feeling for me than friendship, but I am uncertain. I think, however, that I have reasonable grounds for hope, and I propose, with your approval, to ascertain my fate this evening."

"I see, of course, more of her than you do," said John Holmes. "Perhaps, however, that assertion is not correct as regards the last two weeks," he continued, smiling; "but, at any rate, I know her better than you do. You will not object, I am sure, if I tell you that I have formed the opinion that she has become strongly attached to you. She is so truthful and so honest that even her modesty cannot altogether prevent my watchful eye detecting little evidences of her regard for you."

"You have made me very happy, my dear friend, by what you have said, and I do not believe you will ever regret the consent you have given. If Margaret does not love me, that is, of course, the end of the whole affair. Much as I love her, I love her too well to think of trying to induce her to marry me unless she is sure her happiness would be secured by the union."

"Perhaps, before you definitely decide on so important a step as asking her to marry you, you ought to know something of her father and mother, and of her pecuniary prospects."

"I know she is the daughter of your daughter," said Severne, "that her father's name was Leslie, and that he has been dead for many years.   As to her pecuniary prospects, it will not affect my intention one way or the other whether you tell me she is to receive ten millions of dollars or ten cents at your death, which I hope will never take place during her or my lifetime."

"There is something more than that which you ought to know," said John Holmes, gravely.   "Her father, Richard Leslie, was a very bad man, and caused the death of her poor mother by his ill treatment.   He was a gambler, a drunkard, and a forger; Margaret never saw him, nor has he, so far as I know, been in this country since her birth. He disappeared then, and I have never heard of him since."

John Holmes persevered till he had given an outline of Richard Leslie's misdoings, notwithstanding Severne's repeated attempts to interrupt him.   He was resolved, with an honest determination, that the latter should not act blindly in a matter which it was so important he should thoroughly understand.

"I am very sorry for your sake and that of Margaret's mother," said Severne, "that Mr. Leslie should have been so bad a character and have accomplished such wickedness. I do not see, however, what relation it has to my marriage with your granddaughter.   I know that she is as good as God ever made woman, and that is enough for me."

"Of course," replied John Holmes, "I think you are right. I thought it my duty, however, to tell you this much.   I shall give Margaret fifty thousand dollars on her wedding-day, and she will have two hundred thousand more when I die."

"That is all very well," said Severne.   "I should have no sort of objection to your endowing your granddaughter with all the riches of the earth, if you possessed them. Personally, as far as I am concerned, it is a matter of the most perfect indifference; she will appreciate your kindness, and I will also, as I would any other act of good will to her.   If she becomes my wife, I will take care that she never has a wish ungratified that a moderate degree of wealth can give her.   So, my dear friend, as far as we are concerned, the matter is settled.   You have acted just as I thought you would, and I can never say all I want to say in the way of thanks."

"You owe me no thanks, Severne," replied John Holmes. "I know you will make her a good husband, and I am sufficiently rewarded in being able to look forward with confidence to the realization of that anticipation."

"By-the-by," said Severne, as he was about to take his departure, "there is another matter I had almost forgotten. Have you heard or seen anything of my friend de Hutten?"

"Yes, he was here yesterday, and was rejoiced that you had got his ancestor's book. There is a mystery about him which I do not understand yet. He took his money and hurried off with it, saying that he might possibly be back in New York before the year was out. He requested me to say to you that he regretted the impossibility of meeting with you now, but that when he returned he hoped to have that pleasure. He went to St. Louis."

"Perhaps I shall meet with him there. I shall never regret having purchased his book, for besides being an unique specimen, it is—what is seldom the case with bibliographical rarities—a literary treasure. I have never read a work on the faculties of the mind which was more philosophical in its plan and in its treatment of the subject. Good-by, my dear old friend," he continued, as he shook John Holmes's hand; "you will know my fate soon after I learn it. Why, what has become of Goodall?" he exclaimed, as he passed into the shop. "That reminds me that I did not see him when I came in."

"He has gone into the country for a few days. He left good-by for you. He always takes an excursion to the trout region every summer. Fishing in the mountain streams is the only one of the so-called sports he cares for."

Severne expressed his regret at not seeing him, and jumping into an empty hack which stood near the door, was driven to his own home.

"There's a man in the reception-room waiting for you, sir," said Wilson. "I informed him that you would not be home till dinner-time, but he said he would wait, as he had business of importance. I told him to wait in the reception-room because he said he knew you very well, sir."

"Why, Joshua, how are you?" exclaimed Severne, as that individual came out into the hall. "Nothing wrong at home, I hope?"

"Yes, sir, there's an awful lot of wrong a going on there. Not about anybody you care for," he continued, observing Severne's look of alarm. "She's well enough. I want to talk to you about it, if you please, sir. I know you are a learned man, and though, with my worthy friend, Henry Cornelius Agrippa, Knight, I despise all the arts and sciences without exception, the force of the habit into which I've got is too strong for my feeble sense of what is right."

"Very well, Joshua," replied Severne, amused at the harangue, "come up into the library and tell me all about your troubles at your ease. I have an hour which shall be at your service."

They proceeded, therefore, to the library. Joshua took a calm survey of the room and its contents, and then began.

"I suppose, sir, you know all about my worthy friend, Henry Cornelius Agrippa, Knight?"

"I know something about him. I think I have all his works."

"If it is not being too exacting," said Joshua, modestly, "I would like you to give me your opinion of that great man."

"You want my candid opinion, Joshua?"

"Oh, yes, sir, certainly!"

"Well then, Joshua, I have no hesitation in expressing it as my deliberate conviction, that of all the silly, shallow, and bombastic mountebanks that ever put pen to paper, Henry Cornelius Agrippa, Knight, etc., stands in the front rank."

"You think he was a fool, then?"

"He was both fool and knave."

"I am very sorry to hear you say so, sir. He has been a great consolation to me, and if I had followed his advice and kept away from chemistry and poetry and such like vanities, I might have been a better and a wiser man. But I will not detain you, sir, with any criticisms on him. I'm very sorry, though, you don't like him. He always had his enemies, poor man!

"There's a woman at our house," continued Joshua, plunging at once *in medias res*, "and she's at the bottom of all my troubles, as there is always a woman at the bottom of all troubles. Her name is Markland, and for these two years and more I've loved that woman in a way that men

don't often love women. I saw that she had her little failings of one kind and another, and I set myself to work,
after my own fashion, to cure her of them. Well, sir, gradually I got her rid of all of them, which would not be becoming in the wife of a man of science, except one, and that
was the worst of all. She would talk to me about her late
husband, telling me how much he loved her, and what a fine
man he was, and repeating all the ridiculous things he ever
said in his life. He was a circus-rider, and every time I
went into her sitting-room, I was told about his elegant per-
formances, and made to look at his photographs hanging on
the wall, and a lot of other relics she had of him. Strong
diseases require strong medicines, you know, sir, so I determined to use them too. So the night the robbery was
attempted, I went into her room, and, after a little talk in
the old way, I told her I was going to cure her, and—she
making no objection whatever—I took all the pictures and
other relics and made a pile of them, and then I smashed
them with a flat-iron.

"It was a little too much for her, so she fainted, or, as I
believe now, she pretended to faint. Of course, sir, I, being
a human being, and not by any means a cruel one, either,
felt as if I had, may be, gone a little too far, and, besides,
I really did like her, too. So I asked her to be my wife in
my own way, and she said she would, and we went along as
easy together as quicksilver and gold. I thought we were
going to make a perfect amalgam; but it's all changed now,
and it's as bad a piece of business as any I ever had in my
life."

"I am very sorry, Joshua," said Severne, "that the matter should have had so unfortunate a termination; perhaps
it is not yet past remedy."

"Yes, sir, it's clean past all cure now, and this is why.
Of course I couldn't spend all my evening with her, having,
as you know, to attend to Mr. Holmes's laboratory, so I left
her, everything being as smooth between us as if we were a
mixture of oil and alkali. When we had got through fixing
things for the robbers, I thought I would just go and see
how she was getting along, and to comfort her a little about
the burglary that was to come off. I went to her room
again, and there she was sound asleep. She was talking,

and I thought I would listen a little, expecting, as I had a right to, that she would be saying things appropriate to the circumstances. Well, sir, I was astounded to hear her speaking of me in a way that almost made my blood boil. She was congratulating herself on having got me at last, and threatening what she would do when she had me completely in her power, and then she seemed to be having a quarrel with me in a dream, and she called me a fool. Now, sir, I may not be a Berzelius, or even a Sir Humphrey Davy, but I am not a fool. And I ask you, sir, whether that wasn't more than flesh and blood could bear ?"

"It was not exactly suitable to the occasion, I must say," said Severne. "But perhaps Mrs. Markland's dreams go by contraries, like those of the Irishman in the song."

"No, sir, not a bit of it. There was too much heart in her words for that. So I went away and shut the door after me, and the robbers came,—and, would you believe it, sir ?— she never heard the explosion, nor knew anything about it till next day, when she heard it from the servants. Of course my feelings were such that I kept away from her, and then she came up to me, and asked me why I had not told my dear Adelina all about the robbers, and I told her she was no dear Adelina of mine. And then she looked as if she was going to faint again, but I told her it was no use, and that I had heard her talk of me in a way no woman should talk of the man who was to be her husband, and that she must get the doctor to give her some medicine to stop her talking in her sleep. Well, she colored up as red as blood could make her, but she saw I had the advantage of her, and she walked off without saying a word. I thought that was the end of it; but yesterday she sent me a bill for ten photographs, twenty dollars each; a bunch of wax flowers, twenty-five dollars; and a cup and saucer, fifty dollars,—two hundred and seventy-five dollars in all. Of course I refused to pay it, but wrote her word I would get other photographs that would do as well as those I had mashed, and other wax flowers, and cup and saucer. But she won't take them, and writes me again that if I don't pay her bill, she will put it in the hands of a lawyer, and have me indicted, besides, for malicious mischief. I tell you, sir, if ever there was a she-devil, Mrs. Markland's one, as sure as my name's Joshua !"

"I am very much surprised by what you tell me," said Severne, scarcely able to restrain his features from relaxing into a broad smile at the ludicrous termination of Joshua's matrimonial adventure. "She has always appeared to me to be a very respectable and well-behaved woman."

"Oh, she's respectable enough, I suppose, and well-behaved enough, too, to Mr. Holmes and Miss Margaret; she knows her place, as far as they are concerned. But I am not free to speak my mind about her in public, for she said if ever I dared to open my mouth against her, she'd sue me for libel, too."

"Have you mentioned the matter to Mr. Holmes?"

"Oh no, sir, I didn't like to speak about it to him, because, you see, sir, I've always told him she was a fool and a humbug, and I know he would laugh at me and tell me I was another."

"You have not told me yet how I can help you," said Severne.

"You are going away, sir, I hear, in a few days, and I would like to go with you. I am not above doing honest work of any kind for my living. I was born in Swatara Township, Dauphin County, Pennsylvania, and was brought up on a farm. I can take care of horses, black boots, or do anything in that line you might want. I got a good education at the Middletown Academy, and then went to Philadelphia, where I was janitor, and took care of the chemical room in the University. Then I came to Mr. Holmes, and I've learned an awful amount of valuable matter from him. I'll tell you, sir, though I've never told mortal man before, that I've invented a new kind of gunpowder that beats the old all to pieces, and I'm going to apply for a patent."

"Your application requires consideration, Joshua, and before deciding upon it, you must give me permission to state the matter to Mr. Holmes and obtain his consent, in case I should conclude to take you with me."

"That is all right, sir; I've no manner of objection to your mentioning it, only I would not like to do it myself. You see, he is going away himself in two or three months, and will not return before you do, if then."

"Do you think Mrs. Markland seriously contemplates suing you?"

"I don't know about that for certain. Perhaps she only wants to frighten me into marrying her, but that I don't intend to do, and I won't pay that bill either," said Joshua, in his most dogmatic and spasmodic manner.

"I have no idea that she will proceed to extremities," continued Severne. "I would advise you, however, to replace the cup and saucer, and the flowers, and as it is perhaps impossible to get copies of the photographs, give her something else in their place. As to the application you have made, I will see Mr. Holmes about it, and if you come to me some time to-morrow I will give you an answer."

"I'm very much obliged to you, sir. There's a good deal I might say to you from the great work of my worthy friend Henry Cornelius Agrippa, Knight, but as you don't believe in him, perhaps I had better not allude to him further. I wish you good evening, sir."

CHAPTER XXI.

IN WHICH SEVERNE, MARGARET, AND JOHN HOLMES ARE SHOWN TO BE ON THE HIGH ROAD TO HAPPINESS.

THE night was much cooler than those which ordinarily belong to the month of July in New York. A thunderstorm had occurred late in the afternoon, laying the dust, freshening the atmosphere, and giving a delicious perfume to the trees and flowers with which John Holmes's garden was filled. Severne and Margaret sat upon the piazza at the back of the house. The parlor windows were open, and the light which streamed through enabled them to see each other's faces, and thus to converse with more pleasure than they could have done in the dark. If we are unable to observe the play of the features of those we talk with, the most tender words or brilliant sayings lose half their effect.

John Holmes had, as usual, gone to his laboratory. He had never been afraid to leave Margaret alone with his friend, and on this night he had excused himself earlier than was his custom, on the plea of important operations requiring his personal superintendence. On his return from the shop after his conversation with Severne, he had said nothing to his granddaughter relative to the matter in which he felt so great an interest. There was, however, perhaps a little more gravity in his manner than was usual with him, and he kissed her forehead with more fervor, and looked into her face more anxiously, as if endeavoring to read in the light of her violet eyes the fate which might be in store for her.

"I was thinking, Miss Leslie," said Severne, after a short pause in the conversation, "that, looking back upon my past life, the last two weeks have comprised more happiness for me than all the years of my existence put together. I can now recall without regret events which have hitherto always awakened the most painful recollections. It *is* true that the temper of the moment influences our judgment in regard to incidents of our lives, so as to give us pleasure or pain, as the case may be, at the remembrance of great misfortunes or great joys."

"We never know," said Margaret, "to what our troubles will lead us. We think when they occur that they have no redeeming features about them, but it rarely happens, I think, that they do not, at some time or other of our lives, open up in our hearts joys which are all the more pleasurable because they are unexpected."

"Two weeks ago," continued Severne, "I was one of the most miserable of men. There was scarcely a memory of the past that was not gall and wormwood. I had been deceived where I ought to have met with confidence and truth. I had been hated where I ought to have been loved. I had been treated with coldness and disdain by those who owed everything to my favor; and worse than all, my home had been dishonored by a wife I would have loved even now had she possessed one noble womanly quality. I had seen, with but little exception, only the worst side of human nature. In fact, there were only your grandfather, Mr. Goodall, and my friend Lawrence for whom I entertained the least regard. I loved them, but I believe I despised all the world beside. Now I feel in charity with all men. They have not changed. It is I who have been metamorphosed from a misanthrope into a rational being, and you, Miss Leslie, have caused the transformation."

"I ?" said Margaret, with an accent in which surprise and pleasure were mingled, while her heart throbbed wildly in her breast.

"Yes, Miss Leslie, you; but for you I should be as wretched to-night as I was two weeks since. Do you care enough for me to be glad ?"

"I am very glad if I have been able to make you happier."

"Two weeks ago, Margaret," said Severne, taking her little hand in his, while he looked fearlessly, fondly, and truthfully into her dark blue eyes,—"two weeks ago I would not have dared to say to you what I am going to say now. I would not have been so dishonest as to ask you to love a man with a heart so full of bitterness as was mine. It is different now. I have parted with, I trust forever, the distrust and the cynicism which pervaded my nature. To you I owe it all. And when I tell you, as I do now, Margaret, that I love you as I never have loved and never hoped to love human being, you will believe me, will you not ?"

Margaret was silent, but the tears—tears of joyous emotion—welled up into her eyes, and she let her hand lay trustingly in the loving grasp of him who had opened his heart to her.

"Dear Margaret," continued Severne, "do you love me ?"

Still she was silent; but if Severne needed any more eloquent language than that of her loving eyes, he was hard to please.

He put his arm around her waist and drew her to his heart.

"My darling," he said, with all the fervor of his great love, "will you trust me? will you give me the right to love you, and to secure my own happiness by laboring for yours ?"

"So long as God shall give me life," she said, softly, as she hid her face in his breast.

"And you do love me, dear Margaret ?" he whispered.

"With my whole heart and soul," she replied, raising her eyes, and looking into his. "You are everything in this world to me. Oh, Robert, can I make you happy ?"

"I am happy now, dearest. Happy in the knowledge that I possess the love of a true, virtuous, and noble woman. Do I not look so? Is there a single vestige of sorrow in my face? My darling, if there is a happy man in the world I am that man!" As he said these words, he bent down toward her and kissed her sweet, rosy lips.

"I am very happy," said Margaret, all her fresh, gushing frankness returning to her. "I have wondered whether you really loved me or not. Sometimes I was sure you did, and then I was fearful that what I took for love was only the interest which you felt in me, such as a man of your great kindness of heart would feel for a child. And then I thought it would be truly selfish in me to wish for your love, unless you felt confident that in giving it, you would be adding to your own happiness. Now, I am sure. All my doubts and fears are gone forever."

"You will never again have cause for fear on that score, my darling. There never was cause, for I loved you almost from the first moment of our meeting."

"I am sure grandpapa will be pleased. He has always looked upon you as one of his dearest and best friends. Even before I knew you, he told me you were one of the truest men he had ever known."

"He knows it already. I told him this afternoon, and he gave me his consent to ask you to be my wife."

"Did he tell you I would say yes?" said Margaret, with an arch smile.

"He said he had formed the opinion that you had become strongly attached to me," replied Severne, smiling in return.

"Why, what sharp eyes he must have!" said Margaret, laughing. "How glad he will be when he finds how correct his opinion was!"

"You will not forget me, dearest, while I am absent?"

"Forget you!—absent!" exclaimed Margaret. "Oh, I had forgotten that you are going away. Must you go? And so soon, too?"

"I am afraid I must. It would disappoint Lawrence if I refused after all the preparations are made. And yet I never in all my life felt less like traveling than I do now. He is very certain that it is necessary for my health, which was very bad a few weeks ago."

"Then, of course, you will go," said Margaret. "And I shall be very happy during your absence—not so happy, of course, as if you were with me. But I shall think of you constantly, and I shall know that you will be ever thinking of me."

"Perhaps we shall meet in Europe and come home together."

"How delightful that would be! We could not possibly have a better guide than you to the art collections and other sights of Europe. You have traveled all over it, have you not?"

"Very nearly. I believe I have been in every country of Europe. But now my journeying will be mainly in regions of which I know nothing but what I have picked up from other persons or their books."

"How much Sarah will miss you!" said Margaret, after a little pause, during which the lovers were deep in thought. "She seems to be very fond of you."

"I think she is," replied Severne. "I am very certain she has a great deal of love for all those who have befriended her. She improves very rapidly in everything essential to her changed position in life, and I have no doubt but that when I return I shall find her fit to associate on equal terms with all my friends."

"I am very sure of it," said Margaret. "I love her very dearly, and I love her more because you have been kind to her. Dear Robert," she continued, looking into his face with an expression of thorough frankness and truth, "I began to love you from the moment I knew of all your goodness to her. I felt then that your love was the one thing in all the world which I should always prize the most."

"I believe I told you once before," said Severne, smiling, "that I was moved by the most thorough selfishness in all that I did relative to Sarah."

"Yes, you did, and it is the same sort of selfishness which makes you love me, which prompts you to seek your happiness by securing mine. And I suppose you will be telling me next that your love for me is a very selfish feeling. I hope it is. It is the kind of love I want from you, and it is the kind I give you in return."

It is very probable the two lovers would have sat on the

piazza till broad daylight, without thinking of the passing hours, had not Severne heard sounds which convinced him that portions of the house were being closed for the night. Looking at his watch, he found that it was past twelve o'clock.

"Good night, my darling!" he said, as he again pressed her to his heart and kissed her. "God forever bless and keep you!"

"Oh, my love! my love!" said Margaret, passionately, as she nestled her head on his breast, "He has been very good to us. What can I do to deserve His continued favor?"

"My dear Margaret, if we trust each other, God will trust us. The time may come when you will be asked to doubt me. I may not be present to defend myself, and my good name may be aspersed by vile calumnies, which can only be disproved by a lengthened investigation. If this should happen, you will remember this night, and you will continue to have faith in my honor and my love?"

"Can you doubt it for an instant, dear Robert? Henceforth my life is bound up with yours. Whatever others may say I will always know you to be good. You have been unhappy. You have suffered wrong, I am sure, but I love you all the more for that, and I almost wish my love could be put to the test, as you seem to fear. You would then see how strong and fervent is the trust I repose in you."

"I have been wronged, deeply wronged, as I will tell you some day, and further trouble may be in store for me. I do not know why I should think so, but I cannot get rid of the presentiment that lying assertions will be made against me, which you will be asked to believe. I ask you to trust me, even should everything appear to be adverse; to remember that I stood here with your hand in mine, and in the presence of God told you that there was no reason why a pure woman should not give me her love. You will remember this, will you not, my darling?"

"I will remember it, Robert. I will never lose the faith in you which I now have."

"Then I shall go, sure that there is one who, at the worst, will have confidence in me. That thought alone will make me happy. And now, dear Margaret, again good night!"

And their lips met in the parting kiss of their first meeting
as lovers who had pledged their faith to each other for the
weal or woe of their lives.

Margaret sat on the piazza after he was gone, thinking of
this, the greatest joy of her existence.

"He loves me," she said to herself; "and oh, how I love
him! He has suffered, and may suffer again. He will then
see how firm is my love. Let them slander him! I will
take his word before that of all the world. If he himself
were to come here now and tell me he had spoken falsely, I
would not believe him. Nothing could make me doubt
him!" And then she went into the house, and going to the
laboratory door knocked at it softly, and then opening it a
little, said:

"May I come in, grandpapa?"

"Certainly, my dear child," said John Holmes, looking
up at her with an inquiring expression on his face, from a
little agate mortar in which he was triturating a deep, yel-
low-colored powder.

Margaret entered the room, and standing by his side, laid
her hand on his shoulder, and said:

"Dear grandpapa, I am going to be Robert Severne's
wife."

"God bless you and him, my darling!" said John Holmes,
putting his arm around her waist, and drawing her to him
till her cheek rested against his. "He is worthy of you,
my dear child, and you are worthy of him. I have hoped
for this, Margaret, and when I see you Robert Severne's
wife I shall be ready to leave the world, confident that he
will love and protect you better than ever I have done."

"I shall never forget all you have done for me, dear
grandpapa," said Margaret. "All I have in the world I
owe to you. Your care has made me what I am. And if
I am worthy of Robert Severne's love, it is you who have
made me so."

"My dear child, I could have done nothing without your
constant aid. Your virtues are all your own. If I have
assisted you to develop the germs which God planted in
your heart, I am content. You will become still more perfect with such a guide as Robert Severne."

"Yes, dear grandpapa, I feel that I will.   He is so true and noble, so generous and self-denying."

"He is, and you will be happy.   My darling, you look very beautiful to-night," he continued, with a smile of infinite pleasure.   "Did he tell you how beautiful you are?"

"No," replied Margaret, with a blush; "he said nothing about it.   But you must not ask me what he said."

"I do not intend to, my dear child, but I am so proud of your beauty that I want every one to see it too.   He does see it, I am sure."

"If I please him in this, and in all other things, dear grandpapa, I am very glad.   Good night!"

"Good night, my darling!   What you have told me has made me very happy."

Margaret was gone, but John Holmes continued to work in his laboratory.   "Everything in the world seems to go well with me now," he said, as he kept on triturating the yellow powder in the agate mortar.   "My darling to be the wife of the man in all the world I would have chosen as her husband, and my labor here rapidly coming to a successful termination.   Strange, too, that I should owe this last result to her, as I believe I do.   If she had not shaken the test-tube that day, and crystallized the solution in it, I might have worked on for years without getting to the end.   How glad she will be when I tell her, as I will as soon as I am absolutely sure!   Yes, my work is almost done.   Lead 104, silicium 22, sulphur 16, nitrogen 14, oxygen 8, hydrogen 1, nickel 30, and the new form of matter which my dear Margaret separated by crystallization 2, and here is the grand total, 197.   What a singular substance this new form of matter is!" he continued, looking at the mass in the mortar.   "It must be to this that gold owes its color.   Exactly twice the combining equivalent of hydrogen!   What a pretty story the account of its discovery will make!   I have only now to recombine my materials and make gold, when my work is ended, and I rest from my labors with the consciousness that my life has not been in vain.   My God," he continued, covering his face with his hands, "when I look back upon what I have done already, I am almost mad with amazement!   Gold, a compound substance of eight different phases of matter!   One of them, too, hitherto unknown, and the heaviest ever discovered.   What name shall I give it ?   I ought to call it after my dear Margaret, but she will like it better if I name it after one she loves better than herself—Severne.   I'll call it Severnium.   He deserves the honor, for while I am but a hewer of wood and a drawer of water in one science, he is a thinker and a generalizer in all. Yes, that shall be its name.   What will the world say when I publish the results of my researches ?   What they do in regard to other discoveries I suppose.   First, that they are false ; second, that they are valueless ; third, that there's nothing new in them.   That is the general course of men's thoughts relative to everything of the kind.   What do I care ? Nothing. I am not working for fame, but for science, and there's a very great difference between the two.   As a rule, they bear an inverse ratio to each other.   However, I am not going to abuse the world to-night.   I am too happy for that, and upon the whole it is not a bad world.   I am very sure I could not have made as good a one.   It has not used me badly.   The most of the trouble I have derived from it has been the result of my own action.   The death of my poor dear child was primarily my fault.   I should have guarded her better and kept that scoundrel out of my house. Well, well, I must not think of that now, when I am made so happy by what has happened to-night.   How she will miss him after he leaves us ! I must prepare a pleasant surprise for her and him, by arranging matters so that they will meet in Europe.   I was quite certain she loved him, although she was so modest and coy about it all.   There is not a woman in the world who when she loves a man can hide it from every one's eye.   And I would not give a cent for love that could be entirely concealed.   Such a passion cannot be very strong.   But the love that fills the heart, that worships its object, that stirs up the mind continually to thoughts of the loved one, cannot be smothered ; a look, a tone, a blush will some time or other reveal it to those who are watching for it.   It's a strange thing.   I loved once myself, and only once, years and years ago.   Pshaw !" he continued, getting up suddenly and going into his bed-room, "why can I not stop this continual recurrence to events that have forever passed away, and which it is better for me to forget ?"

CHAPTER XXII.

IN WHICH SEVERNE DISCOVERS SARAH'S PARENTAGE.

When Severne received the tin box of Julia Tompkins's letters from Mrs. Wiggins, he put it into a drawer of his table, intending to look the contents over that evening. One thing and another, however, had interfered with the execution of this purpose, and thus the day previous to that fixed for his departure had arrived, and the letters had not been examined.

That evening he was to see Margaret for the last time in many months. He had parted with Sarah an hour before, and now sat in the room, where the reader has so often seen him, surrounded with piles of papers, which he had arranged in order, and which he was putting away, till his return, in the drawers of his writing-table. In opening one of these he came across the box of letters just as he had placed it, and he was thus reminded of a duty which he ought to have performed several days since, and which he had been in danger of forgetting altogether. He took the box out of the drawer and opened it. There were ten letters, all directed in a firm, business-like hand, to Julia Tompkins, and arranged in accordance with their dates, which were indorsed, in a female hand, on the backs. Severne had no doubt in regard to the propriety of his proceeding to make himself acquainted with their contents. As far as it was possible for him to know, Julia Tompkins was dead long ago, and his ward, her daughter, was entitled to the benefit of any information which these letters might contain. That they were important there could be very little doubt.

The first one was very short, and was word for word as follows :

State Street, New York,
January 16th, 1841.

My dear Julia,—

I will certainly see you to-morrow; do not be distressed at the idea of my marriage. It was absolutely necessary to

save me from ruin, and when I tell you this, you will be satisfied, I know.   I never can love any one but you if I married a thousand times.   Good night, my darling.

Ever yours,   R. L.

The next was dated in February.   It was quite long, filling four sides of a sheet of quarto letter paper.   The last
paragraph was as follows :
"I find I have married a smooth-faced doll, who has no
more life or strength of character in her than a white mouse.
I shall not stand it long, my dearest.   A few more months
and I shall have got matters arranged to my liking, and
then we will go off together to a home of our own that I
know of."
It was signed, as the other, with the initials R. L.
The next, which, with the two preceding, was directed to
Albany, was more important.   Severne had, as yet, read
nothing to give him a clew to the mystery which the reader,
with his or her superior information, has already divined.
This one, however, enlightened him fully.   It was as follows :

STATE STREET, NEW YORK,
June 10th, 1841.

MY DARLING JULIA,—

Things are going on well.   I have already succeeded beyond my expectations in getting the better of old Holmes,
my respected father-in-law.   I am trying to disgust my wife
—as I suppose I must call her—with her liege lord, and, I
flatter myself, I am succeeding admirably.   She seems to
be pretty fond of me yet (confound her!), but I am quite sure
I will knock all the sentimentality out of her before long.
You know that I am a pretty good fellow when I have taken
a little drop too much, but this fine lady of mine cries over
me like a sick kitten if I come home later than ten o'clock,
or with an extra glass of toddy in me.   I am devilish sorry
to receive the information you gave me in your last.   What
will we do with the brat?   I suppose, too, my lady will be
making me a present also before long.   I shall not give
myself much anxiety about its future welfare, however.   I
will try and see you, as usual, every two or three weeks,

21*

though old Holmes watches me now pretty closely. I get off, however, on the plea of business for my father. That's good, isn't it? I think, however, you had better move a little nearer to this city. How would you like Yonkers? It's a nice, quiet sort of place, and I can reach you in a half hour or so without exciting the suspicions of my she dragon or her stern parent. You ought to be there by the autumn at any rate.

Do not imagine for a moment that I will ever forget you. I mean to take care of you as long as I live, and I hope before very long I shall be free to cut loose from the strait-laced party I have been obliged to make use of. Good-by, my little Julie.

Yours, as ever,   R. L.

When Severne had finished reading this precious epistle he laid it down upon the table, and for several moments was lost in deep thought. The whole matter was perfectly clear to him now. Richard Leslie was Sarah's father as well as Margaret's, and consequently the two girls were half-sisters. The resemblance which had already attracted his attention, but which no one else appeared to have noticed, was thus explained. And who can deny that the instinctive feeling of regard which the two had manifested for each other from the first, was not due to the yearning of one kindred soul for another?

Though this letter made him sick at heart when he thought of the consummate depravity of the writer, and the miserable life which the mother of his dear Margaret must have endured with this monster, there was nothing in the discovery of the relationship between the girls which gave him any uneasiness. On the contrary, he was rather pleased than otherwise that it existed, for it could not but tend to strengthen the bond of friendship between Margaret and Sarah when they learned that the blood of one father flowed in their veins, vile and brutal though he was, and his own regard for the one could not but become stronger through the tie which he now knew bound her to the woman he loved best in all the world.

As he read further, he became certain that the impression he had formed relative to Richard Leslie's relationship to

Sarah was correct. All the subsequent letters were addressed to Yonkers except the last, which was directed to 110 Wayne Street, New York. As this contained information of importance, Severne read it over several times. It confirmed him in the opinion he had conceived, and, moreover, indicated the place to which Leslie had gone when he left New York the night of his wife's death.

STATE STREET, NEW YORK,
December 30th, 1841.

MY DEAR JULIA,—

I expected to see you this evening, but I find it to be impossible, and therefore I am forced to write. I think we have made the best possible disposition of our little Sarah. The shoemaker is evidently in love with you, and will take good care of her for your sake. I never expect to see my *legal* encumbrance at all, so you see my little *illegal* embarrassment has had the advantage of having known her illustrious progenitor.

I hope, as I told you yesterday, to have everything ready by to-morrow night for our departure. I shall then finish my plans on my respected father-in-law with a *coup de main* which will astonish him, I think. Be ready therefore to leave early on New-year's Day. I have already received enough to make us comfortable in Santa Fé during the remainder of our lives. We must be in St. Louis by the 10th of January, and at Independence by the 18th. There will be a good deal for me to do in both places. The wagon train starts from the latter town on the 20th. A winter trip across the plains is no very pleasant matter. Mrs. Leslie will be rather astonished when she wakes up New-year's morning and finds herself minus her "dear Richard," who will then be on his way to a happy home with the only woman he has ever loved.

I send this by a friend who will give it to you promptly. Good-by, then, till to-morrow night.

Yours ever,   R. L.

This letter, of course, settled the matter conclusively in Severne's mind; but there were several particulars he was desirous of obtaining, if possible, so he rang the bell and directed Wilson to go immediately and bring Mrs. Wiggins to him. In the course of an hour that lady made her appearance.

"I find, Mrs. Wiggins," said Severne, "that the letters you left with me when you were here last are very important, and I am anxious you should answer as concisely as possible a few questions which I shall ask you.

"Do you recollect the precise day that Julia Tompkins left Sarah with you?"

"Of course I do, sir, I knows it by this, that on that day I went to a love-feast, and my old man went with me, and says he, 'Moll,' says he, he always called me Moll when he wanted——"

"I have really no time to spare, Mrs. Wiggins," said Severne, impatiently, "and I must insist on your answering my questions with as few words as possible. What day of the month was it?"

"Well, sir, I was just goin' to tell you that it was the very last day of the year, about three o'clock in the afternoon, and its just eighteen years ago next last of December."

"Very well, Mrs. Wiggins. Was there any one with her when she came?"

"Not as I knows on. No, there was not; I remember now, she came by herself; but there was a gentleman with her once before when she came, as John said was Sal's father, and as Julia said was very rich."

"Do you remember his name?"

"I never heard his whole name, sir. I remember though as Julia called him Dick. He was a very handsome man, sir, and I recollect, as John said, when I said, 'What a handsome man that was as was here with Jule Tompkins,' John says, says he, 'Mary, you'll make me jealous,' and says I——"

"And Julia disappeared the next day?"

"Certainly. We never saw anything of her after she brought her baby to our house. And the next day was New-year's Day."

"Did you ever hear that Dick, as Julia Tompkins called him, was married?"

"As to that, sir, I really don't know for certain. I think he was, sir, but it wasn't to Julia. One day Jule said to Wiggins, as Wiggins told me, 'Wiggins,' says she, 'if it wasn't for one thing I'd be livin' in splendor and ridin' in my carriage, but my day will come yet, for there's only a sick woman in the way.'"

"Very well, Mrs. Wiggins, I don't think there is anything else I wish to ask you. Does anybody know that you brought those letters to me ?"

"Why, sir, Brother Jenkins knows it of course, for he was with me, as you know. And he said as I ought to have kept them, for they was very valuable letters. And he asked me last night whether I couldn't get them again, and I told him no, as you had given me more money for them than they was worth to me."

"They are worth nothing whatever either to you or Brother Jenkins," said Severne.

"That's just what I told him, sir, but he said as how he'd like to have them letters, and he'd soon see what they were worth."

"He never will have them, depend upon it. Good-by, Mrs. Wiggins; take this for the trouble I have given you to-night," he continued, handing her a bank note, "and don't let Brother Jenkins or any one else fill your head with foolish notions."

After Mrs. Wiggins had gone, Severne reflected still further upon the information he had received, and though doubtful as to the expediency of informing Margaret and Sarah of their relationship, he had none in regard to the propriety of putting John Holmes in possession of all the facts which had so singularly come to his knowledge. He therefore took the tin box with its contents and proceeded to John Holmes's house. He inquired for his old friend at the door, and was shown into the library, where he sat with Margaret, who was reading the last novel to him while he was enjoying a cigar, the fragrance of which perfumed the room.

"I am very sorry," said Severne, after a few minutes, during which he had, in compliance with John Holmes's request, lighted a cigar. [Listen, all ye wives and *fiancés*. Margaret never objected to the odor of a good cigar, and John Holmes and Severne smoked no others.] "I am very sorry to break up this *tête-à-tête*, but for once in your life, mademoiselle, you are *de trop*. I never put so many French words into an English speech before," he continued; "but if one is obliged to say a disagreeable thing, a word or two from what some people call the 'language of the politest nation on earth,' helps one along amazingly."

"I suppose you intend to intimate that my presence can be dispensed with," said Margaret, smiling.

"The acuteness of your perception is not the least of your good qualities, mademoiselle," said Severne, bowing with mock gravity. "I do not know which most to admire, the wonderful depth of your intuition or the marvelous knowledge you possess of the French language."

"There, sir," resumed Margaret in the same vein, as she prepared to leave the room, "you need not say another word; first, you tell me I am in the way, and then you make fun of me. I wish you good evening, gentlemen," she continued, making a stately courtesy; "when you have mended your manners, and evinced a sufficient degree of repentance, I may be induced to return."

"My dear old friend," said Severne, taking a seat at the table by John Holmes's side, "I have just become possessed of information which, apart from the insight it has given me into a character of almost inconceivable depravity, has afforded me a great deal of pleasure. Are you acquainted with Richard Leslie's handwriting?"

"As well as with my own," replied John Holmes. "It was a very singular handwriting. He always wrote with a soft quill pen."

"I shall not say a word till you have read these letters," said Severne, putting the package into John Holmes's hands.

While his friend read the letters, Severne took up the evening paper, and hiding himself behind it, smoked and read in silence, without appearing to be aware of the emotions which their perusal excited, and which was evidenced by many exclamations of anger and pity.

"There can be no doubt, my dear Severne," said John Holmes, when he had read the letters through, "in regard to the true state of affairs. Sarah Tompkins and my dear Margaret are half-sisters. And it was for the woman to whom these letters are addressed that my shameless and depraved son-in-law deserted my poor child and broke her heart! You will not blame me when I tell you that I find it diffi-

cult now to regard the offspring of this wicked union with
the same favor as before I knew of her parentage?"

"I should blame you a good deal," replied Severne, "if
you were to persist in telling me so after you have had
sufficient time to reflect upon the matter I can make allowance for all the feelings which must necessarily be excited in
your breast when you think of the contents of those letters;
but God alone has the right to visit the sins of the fathers
upon the children, and he has already punished this poor
child sufficiently for the iniquities of her father and mother.
Is she not now expiating their crimes in the consciousness
that she is not worthy of the favor of those who have been
kind to her? Ask her if her life has been a happy one, and
see what her answer will be. To whom is she indebted for
all the degradation and sin which have hitherto marked her
youthful existence, if not to those who gave her life? My
dear friend," continued Severne, walking up to John Holmes
and putting his hand on his shoulder, "you must not forget
that our dear Margaret is his child too."

"Margaret is my daughter's child. I never think of her
as the offspring of Richard Leslie."

"Have it so, if you will," said Severne, gently; "but as
you love Margaret, give a portion of your love to Margaret's
sister."

"I will try," said John Holmes, with emotion, grasping
Severne's hand. "I will try honestly and fairly to love her
as I ought. She is a good girl, I think."

"She will become better every day of her life, and you
will soon come to regard her with the affection which is her
due. Do you think I love her any less because she is Margaret's sister? If I had hated her before I knew of the relationship, I would love her now."

"You are right. Poor child! how different has been her
life from that of my darling! Yes, yes, she has been punished enough for the sins of her parents. We must be kind
to her; we must strive with redoubled efforts to make her
forget the past. My dear friend, you must allow me to take
the charge of her off your hands, in view of my relationship."

"Indeed I shall do nothing of the kind," said Severne,
smiling. "You forget that I am one of the family now.

You may go up and look at her occasionally, and she may spend a day or two now and then with you; but you must remember that I found her, and claim her by right of discovery and possession."

"Well, well, I dare say you will not object to my doing all I can for her. Does she know of her relationship to us ?"

"Of course not, nor do I intend to tell her ; I shall leave you to do that when you are entirely satisfied the time has come for it. No one knows of the connection but you and I."

"Do you think she ought to be told now ?"

"Not perhaps now, but certainly very soon. I bade her good-by this afternoon, and though it was only three days since I saw her, I was astonished at her improvement in every way. She could not have been more affected at my approaching departure if I had been her father; and Mrs. Langley tells me she is as affectionate, high-toned, and lady-like in her demeanor as a girl need be. However, I leave the matter to you, confident that you will know when to act."

"I am going to take Margaret to Lake George next week," said John Holmes, "and, if you have no objection, would like to have Sarah accompany us. I will tell her all then."

"I should be very glad to have you do so. Ah, my dear old friend, I was sure that your kind heart would not long stand out against our poor Sarah. I leave her to you until you go to Europe. Mrs. Langley will then take good care of her till we return."

"Severne," said John Holmes, getting up from his chair under the excitement of the idea which had occurred to him, "why cannot Sarah go with Margaret and me to Europe? Let us arrange matters so that we shall meet, say in Paris."

"Why, there's no such thing as stopping you, now you have got started," said Severne, laughing. "Take her with you by all means ; she will be delighted, and so will I. As to meeting you all in Paris, I will try what can be done toward it. Let me see," he continued, reflectively. "In this age of steam I ought to be able to get to Paris, by way of San Francisco, India, and Egypt, by the first of

March. Yes, I will engage to meet you all on the first of next March. God grant it may be a happy meeting."

And then, after a little further conversation relative to plans for the future, Severne bid John Holmes good-by, and went in search of Margaret.

Long and sweet was the interview, and it was at a late hour that the lovers spoke their final adieus. "May God forever bless and keep you, my love, my love!" said Margaret, as their lips met in the last kiss.

"He will, my darling," said Severne; "whatever may happen in the mean time I feel sure that in his own good season he will make us happy in a union which death alone will end in this world. Till then, dearest, let us live in trust and hope."

The next morning, Severne, Lawrence, and Joshua, who had obtained John Holmes's and Severne's consent to his making one of the party, took their departure at an early hour for the boat. Two experienced men-servants accompanied them, and others acquainted with prairie life were to be obtained at St. Louis. In every other respect the party was well supplied with all the paraphernalia requisite for the peculiar character of a journey across the vast plains of the United States.

Joshua left in exceedingly good spirits. He had been told of John Holmes's great success in his alchemical operations, and had been consistent enough to be disgusted at the fact that Margaret's visit to the laboratory, and its consequences, which he had used ever since as a text for many orations against women, should have resulted so very different from what had at first been apprehended. "It's no fault of hers," he grumbled, "if Miss Margaret's meddling with things she did not understand helped to get 197 after all. What business had she to touch test-tubes and shake them up? If it *had* been something else, she would have ruined it, so it's all the same thing so far as she's concerned."

As to Mrs. Markland, no change had taken place in his relations with that injured lady. He had persistently refused to pay the bill she had presented to him, and the indignant widow had kicked into the back yard all the offerings he had brought in the way of atonement for his iconoclastic operations. She did not sue him as she had threatened to do, preferring, apparently, to hold the rod *in terrorem* over him for another occasion. It had lost its power to frighten him, however, like many other menaces frequently employed, but never carried into actual effect. The fact was that Joshua had threatened that if she sued him, he would make a full *exposé* of the whole of his love affair in open court, and this had terrified the widow into a wholesome fear of resorting to the law for redress.

Severne had left the key of his library with Margaret, in order that, as he had promised, she might make use of his books at her convenience; he had given the keys of his writing-table to John Holmes, so that the latter might get the letters of his son-in-law, when he would have occasion to use them for Sarah's enlightenment. Nothing had been omitted by Severne which a far-reaching prudence and foresight could dictate. Time will show whether the results were such as he anticipated.

CHAPTER XXIII.

MR. FREELING SHOWS HIMSELF TO BE MASTER OF THE SITUATION.

A MONTH had elapsed since the occurrence of the events detailed in the last chapter. Severne and his party were far out on the prairies, the last letters which had been received from him being dated at Fort Kearney. The purport of them to Sarah and Margaret can readily be imagined by the reader, and need not therefore be quoted. In the one, however, to John Holmes, he said:

"You will be surprised when I tell you that my former acquaintance, Ulrich de Hutten, forms one of our party. He joined us at Fort Leavenworth, and begged hard to be allowed to accompany us. He is exceedingly entertaining, and is altogether a most remarkable man. He is certainly a lineal descendant of the great de Hutten, but there is a deep mystery in regard to his purposes which I cannot fathom. He appears to be on the look-out for some person whom he expects to meet, and whom he evidently intends to injure bodily to the extent of his ability. Last night he told me, as we sat round our camp-fire smoking our pipes (I have come to a meerschaum, cigars are not adapted to a prairie life), that if he succeeded in the object of his journey, he intended to give up the nomadic life he had led for many years, and make his home in New York. Lawrence and he have become very intimate. In fact, every one likes him."

John Holmes, Margaret, Sarah, and Grace Langley had gone to Lake George. Mr. Freeling still remained in the city. He had business to look after which required his closest attention, and schemes to carry out which would not admit of delay in their execution.

The day was oppressively hot, and Mr. Freeling sat in his shirt sleeves in his office with a clerk in similar *dishabille*. Being endowed with a superfluity of adipose substance, Mr. Freeling felt the heat very severely, and as his office was on the sunny side of the street, and the ceiling was low, it was by no means the coolest place of the kind in the city. He sat at a large table, covered with coarse green baize, which, however, could scarcely be seen for the multitude of papers which were on it He seemed to be annoyed at some circumstance or other, and the state of his mind evidently added to the heat of his body, for he wiped the perspiration continually from his face and head with a linen handkerchief, which, when it came from the laundry, was probably white, but which was now of a dirty yellow color from saturation with cutaneous exhalations, and which also, from this circumstance, had very little effect now in drying his skin.

The clerk, a thin, hatchet-faced individual, with a pimply skin, weak eyes, ash colored hair, and very dirty hands, sat at a high desk, copying, but occasionally looking round furtively at Mr. Freeling with a terrified expression of countenance.

"Have you got that work done yet, Collins ?" said Mr. Freeling, without raising his eyes from a document before him.

"Almost, sir," replied the clerk, with a frightened manner.

"Almost ! That's the same answer you gave me half an

hour ago. Damn you, sir, what do you mean? Do you take me for a fool that you try to impose on me?"

The clerk made no answer, but his look of fright became more decided in its expression, and he wrote as fast as he could on the paper before him.

"Do you hear me, sir?" roared Freeling, turning his pivot chair around·so that he faced the clerk. "Do you take me for a fool?"

"No, sir," answered the man, submissively, while he trembled with apprehension.

"No, sir!" said Freeling, sneeringly, "that's a lie. You know it's a lie. I'll make you tell the truth, you lazy vagabond! To-morrow's Sunday, and you'll be wanting to go to Newark to see your mother, I suppose. Now, sir, tell me the truth instantly, or I'll keep you writing here all day. Do you take me for a fool?"

"I'll say anything, sir, to be allowed to go," exclaimed the clerk, while his weak eyes became still more watery; "I'm afraid she's dying."

"Then say it," said Freeling, with a smile of savage pleasure.

"Yes, sir, I do."

"Oh, you do!" exclaimed the lawyer, malignantly. "I'll let you see whether I am or not. You'll stay here all day to-morrow for your want of respect, and if you dare to leave the room,—you know the consequences!"

"I beg your pardon, sir," said the clerk, humbly; "I thought you wished me to say it."

"Lying again, are you?" exclaimed his master. "I'll teach you! Here you'll stay to-morrow, and if you leave this room you'll get into a worse difficulty. Don't forget that you robbed me of ten dollars once, and that I've got your confession of it. Leave this room, and you'll stay out of it for five years in Sing Sing."

"I did not take it for myself. My mother was starving," said the clerk, covering his face with his hands.

"What do I care about your mother? She's always starving or dying or something of the kind. You stole my money, and I've got you in my power, and I'll do what I please with you. Do you understand that? I'll do as I please with you! What time did Mr. Jenkins say he would call here?"

"At twelve o'clock, sir."

"And it's half-past twelve now.   Why isn't he here ?"

"I don't know, sir.   He didn't say anything to me about it."

"You don't know, you infernal idiot !   Now, sir, is that copying done ?"

"Yes, sir, it's done," replied the clerk, as he wrote the last word, and handed the sheets to the attorney.

"And well for you that it is, or I would have starved you to-morrow, you beggarly, thieving, lantern-jawed fool ! Next week, if you behave as you have done this, I'll cut your wages down.   Now, sir, write an answer to Mr. Gordon in Boston, and tell him I'll take the property at the price asked by his principal, if he'll pay me five hundred dollars."

"I've already written and mailed a letter to him as you ordered me to do yesterday, in which I informed him you would not take it."

"Why, hell's furies ! do you mean to say I told you to do that ?"

"You did, sir; here's the rough draft of your letter," said the clerk, with a little firmness, as he handed Mr. Freeling a half sheet of paper, folded and indorsed, "Rough draft of letter to Gordon."

Freeling looked at it a moment, then his face colored a little, and he tore the paper to pieces, throwing the fragments in the clerk's face.   "Do as I tell you," he shouted, "or I'll kill you, you impudent scoundrel !   I'll——"

What further punishment Mr. Freeling contemplated inflicting on his slave was not disclosed, for as he was about enunciating his kind intentions, the long, lank body of our reverend friend, Brother Jenkins, appeared at the door.

"You're more than a half hour after your time, Mr. Jenkins," he continued, in a changed, but sullen tone.   "You spiritual gentlemen seem to think that men of business have nothing to do but wait your convenience.   You will have to be more punctual, sir, if you expect to transact any business with me.   Leave the room, Collins."

"Now, sir," he continued, after the clerk had disappeared, "sit down and tell me what you know of this matter."

"All I know," said Brother Jenkins, "is that I saw Sister Wiggins give Mr. Severne a tin box of letters, and that he

22*

gave her a hundred dollars for it.   He refused to give me
anything toward supporting our mission to the Apaches,
who are in total ignorance of the expected coming of the
King of Glory."

"Damn the Apaches!   I don't want to hear any cant or
humbug, Mr. Jenkins.   I have promised to give you two
hundred dollars if you will put me in possession of such information as will enable me to get that box into my hands.
Sister Wiggins, as you call her, won't open her mouth, as
you know.   You offered to tell me as much as she could for
two hundred dollars.   Now do it without any circumlocu-
tion.   You say she gave him a tin box, and that he gave
her a hundred dollars," continued Mr. Freeling, sealing a
note.   "Now what do you suppose is the character of those
letters ?"

"I have no doubt they concern the girl, Sarah Tompkins,
and her mother, Julia Tompkins."   Brother Jenkins then
told Mr. Freeling how Mrs. Wiggins had got possession of
them, and related the main points of her conversation with
Severne, all of which Mr. Freeling noted down.

"Do you know exactly where Mr. Severne put the box ?"

"Certainly, sir.   He put it in the upper left-hand drawer
of his writing-table."

"Very well, Mr. Jenkins, I shall attend to the business
to-day, and if I find the letters, will give you the money I
promised.   It is all perfectly right.   It is necessary for me,
as Mr. Severne's agent, to see those letters.   His business
requires it, and it is of course impossible for me to communicate with him and ascertain where they are.   Still, you
need say nothing about it.   And now, as I am very busy, I
must ask you to excuse me.   Call here to-morrow for your
money."

"I'll see what there is in this affair," said Freeling to
himself, after Brother Jenkins's departure.   "I don't think
there will be much difficulty in getting into the library.
There is a mystery which Severne wishes to keep close, that's
certain.   Good heavens, if I can only get him into my power,
how I'll grind him to powder!"   Mr. Freeling grit his
teeth together savagely in anticipation of the fate to which
he desired to subject Severne, and then continued: "It's
lucky I happened to see this fool Jenkins and the woman

coming out of his house, and that I took it into my head to follow them. I might have waited for months without knowing what I do now. He takes a thieving prostitute and adopts her. Is making a fine lady out of her. Keeps her at Mrs. Langley's, too. Well, it's not difficult to see through his object thus far. He passes for a very moral man. A sort of Sir Philip Sidney. Ha! ha! I comprehend his morality thoroughly. I know now why he wouldn't raise the rent on that infernal virago. The Jezebel! I'll settle with her before long, too. Collins!"

"Yes, sir," said the clerk, making his appearance from a distant part of the hall, where he had apparently been waiting till he was summoned.

"Perhaps I was a little hard on you, Collins, this morning; I was out of spirits and cross. Here's five dollars for you. You shall go to Newark to-morrow, and in the mean time I want you to do me a favor, Collins."

The clerk took the money and muttered out his thanks. He was more fearful, however, of Mr. Freeling's kindness than of his rage, much as the latter always frightened him.

"Never mind the thanks, Collins. I know you are grateful. I've no great fault to find with you since I've had you. You know, though, I could send you to Sing Sing if I pleased ; but don't be afraid, as long as you suit me and do your duty I'll keep you out of that institution. Now I want you, as I said, to do me a little favor."

Collins listened, with an expression of intense terror depicted on his countenance, but said nothing.

"I want you, Collins," continued Mr. Freeling, "to go to Mr. Severne's house and tell the housekeeper you are sent by me for some papers which were left on Mr. Severne's table, and which it is very important should be attended to at once. When you get into the library, as you probably will without being watched, open the upper left-hand drawer of the table which stands in the center of the room, and bring me a small tin box which is in it. There are some papers in this box which I shall want you to copy. You need not, of course, say anything about this to any one, for though it's all right, there are reasons, growing out of Mr. Severne's interest, which make it desirable the matter should not be talked about at present. In case the drawer should be locked, here is a key which will probably open it." With these words Mr. Freeling handed Collins a small skeleton-key, which looked as if it would, as he said, open any ordinary drawer-lock.

Collins took the key, and though he seemed relieved when he found that the task required of him was not so bad as he had expected, he did not betray much anxiety to enter upon its execution. He knew very well that it was a rascally piece of business, and that he was the tool who would get into difficulty if detection followed.

"You don't appear very anxious to oblige me, Collins," said Mr. Freeling, with a menacing mien. "Perhaps you are becoming conscientious; I am sorry you did not form virtuous habits before you opened my safe, Collins. They might have kept you from all danger of Sing Sing. By-the-by, that reminds me that the confession you wrote is at my room; I must bring it down here, so as to have it convenient in case I should have to make use of it."

"I'll go, sir," exclaimed the clerk, quickly.

"That is right, I like to see you obliging and considerate toward one who has done you as many favors as I have. It is now two o'clock. Jump into an omnibus and you can be back here by half-past three."

Within the time specified by Mr. Freeling, Collins returned, but without the box.

"I went, sir, as you directed," he said, "and asked to be allowed to go to the library for some papers which were left by you on the table, and which were of great importance. Mr. Severne had left the key of the library with a friend of his, the housekeeper said, and the door was locked. She had a pass-key, however, and she opened the door and let me in; I had to make a show of getting some papers from the table, but I could not get a chance to try the key in the lock of the drawer, as she stayed in the room with me all the time. The drawer was locked; that I ascertained for a certainty. The housekeeper seemed to think I was a suspicious character, and I saw she was doubtful as to my being your clerk. She asked me why you did not come yourself. Here's the key you gave me."

"Very well, Collins, it's all right; I'll go there myself this evening; she knows me, and perhaps will not watch me as closely as she did you. You can go now, I shall not want you till Monday morning."

That evening Mr. Freeling set out from his lodgings for Severne's house with the purpose of attempting to obtain possession of the tin box which Mrs. Wiggins had found. He had endeavored to get it through his clerk, so that in case the theft should be discovered, the crime might in some way or other be laid to his charge. As it was, it would not be a difficult matter to cast enough suspicion around Collins whenever it should become necessary for his own safety to do so. As Mr. Freeling had said, the house-keeper knew him, and he had no difficulty in getting an entrance to the library.

"There was a man here this morning," she said to him, "who came for some papers for which he declared you had sent him; I did not like his looks, and so I watched him closely. He said you had sent him, and that he was your clerk."

"Said I sent him!" exclaimed Mr. Freeling. "Why, who could it have been? I sent no one here."

"He was a thin, tall man, with light hair, and a face all covered with freckles."

"That's my clerk, to be sure!" said Mr. Freeling with an air of surprise. "He is a great rascal, I am afraid. I did not send him. Are you sure he took nothing from the room?"

"He took some loose papers from the table, which I saw were not written on at all, and I saw him try to open one of the drawers."

"There's something wrong here, Mrs. Smith, something wrong," said Mr. Freeling, musingly. "I must see to this, and am very glad you watched him so closely. I hope he did not succeed in carrying anything off of value. I shall be here a few minutes, as I have some notes to make," he continued, as they entered the library. "You need not wait, unless you choose."

"Very well, sir," said Mrs. Smith, as she finished lighting the gas. "When you have got through, please ring the bell, and I'll come up and lock the door again. Mr. Severne was very particular in his orders to me to keep the library locked."

As soon as Mr. Freeling found himself alone, he inserted the key he had given to Collins into the lock of the drawer which he had reason to believe contained the letters of which he was in search. It opened without difficulty. The box was there as Severne had left it. Mr. Freeling removed it, took out the letters, and proceeded to make himself master of their contents. He read them over hastily but without missing a word.

"Well," he exclaimed, "this is news, truly, but I must say it is not of very great importance to me. Very well to know it, though. So his *protegé* is sister to old Holmes's grand-daughter! I recollect Leslie. A sharp fellow, very! Not perhaps overrighteous (who is, when righteousness would be in his way?), but a remarkably shrewd man. I don't want these letters," he continued, as he put them back into the box. "I know what's in them, and that's enough. No one will know I've seen them till I choose to tell them."

After replacing the box and locking the drawer, Mr. Free-ling looked over the papers which lay on the table. He next opened the port-folio, and took from it several loose sheets of paper, containing memoranda. As he put them back, he discovered a folded sheet, which he had not seen at first. He opened it, and as he read it his face lightened up into an expression of fiendish pleasure, mingled with one of intense astonishment. He threw himself back in his chair with the open letter in his hand.

"Good God!" he exclaimed; "can it be possible? Am I dreaming? Let me read it again, it seems too great a piece of good fortune to be real. Confesses to the murder of his wife! It's his own handwriting throughout, and signed by him, too," he continued, as he folded up the letter Severne had written to Lawrence, and which the latter thought he had destroyed. "I'll keep this, at any rate! but I don't understand it at all. I heard of this thing in England, but I thought I had ascertained positively that there was nothing in it. He must have killed her though. There's no getting over this confession! At last I've got him in my power, and he shall hang, yes, he shall hang as sure as my name's Freeling! This is the happiest moment of my life. I would not take any money for this letter. Money is sweet, but power and revenge are sweeter. I'll think this whole thing over, and arrange my plans. It will require caution, but if I fail, with evidence like this in my possession, it will be my own fault. I'll hang him first, and get a good slice of his funds afterward.

"So, Mr. Robert Severne, my Sir Philip Sidney, my Chevalier Bayard, my admirable Crichton, you murdered your wife, did you? I am very glad of it, for otherwise I would not have had the pleasure, which I shall enjoy hugely, of seeing you hang. What a disappointment it will be to his reformed female thief, and to old Holmes and his grand-daughter, who, I verily believe, would be glad to make him a member of their precious family! A fine family it is, with two girls in it whose father was a drunken gambler, and the mother of one a strumpet. It would be adding greatly to its already illustrious character to let a murderer into it. As to this Dr. Lawrence, he is evidently an accessory after the fact. I hate him, too!"

Mr. Freeling put the letter into his pocket-book, rear-ranged everything on the table, and then rang the bell for Mrs. Smith. Thanking her for her kindness, he left the house, and proceeded to his own lodgings to meditate further over the plans which, if he succeeded in them, would bring un-happiness to many, and consign one to the gallows.

He had not noticed that a sharp pair of eyes were looking at him through one of the library windows while he was busily engaged in his disreputable work.

CHAPTER XXIV.

PRAIRIE LIFE.

SEVERNE's party comprised, besides those already known to the reader, six men to take care of the horses and mules, and do such other work as might be required of them; two hunters, whose chief duty it was to provide fresh meat; two cooks, two servants, and an individual of very considerable importance, who, having spent nearly all his life on the prairies, was well qualified to act as guide and adviser to Severne, and to attend to all the practical details connected with the journey. There were thus fifteen in all, and as each was well armed, and as several of them were old prairie men, they were strong enough to make any attack upon them by hostile Indians, sufficiently dangerous to the assailants.

Severne had provided for all possible wants, and had organized the expedition on the most liberal scale. Two light spring wagons, each drawn by four large mules, contained the baggage and stores, and a still lighter wagon was loaded with the surplus arms and ammunition, and with stores which it was advisable to transport in such a manner as to admit of easy access to them at all times. There was, besides, a wagon which contained nothing but forage. Exclusive of the four drivers, each of the party was well mounted, and there were, besides, several extra horses and mules available in case of emergency.

The route, which had been decided upon after a good deal of consideration, was one which led them by Fort Kearney, and Bridger's Pass in the Rocky Mountains, to Salt Lake City, and thence across the Great Basin and the Sierra Nevada to San Francisco. They had passed Fort Kearney, and were moving up the broad valley of the Platte River, when the thread of our story again returns to Severne. Thus far everything had been favorable. He had felt the genial influence of the pure air of the prairies, and had already experienced the greatest benefit from the simple though rugged life he was forced to lead, and of which he partook with a zest he had not thought possible. Accustomed in early life to a great deal of out-door exercise, he had in later years almost entirely abandoned the amusements of hunting and fishing for the intellectual labors in which he had learned to take more interest. At first, therefore, he was apprehensive that he would not be able to acquire a taste for them again. But the moment he obtained his first sight of a herd of buffaloes he was undeceived. There they were, about two miles distant, looking like an immense drove of black oxen, grazing in fancied security against danger. The rolling nature of the ground, and the fact that the wind was blowing from the herd toward the party, allowed the latter to approach to within a quarter of a mile without apparently exciting any alarm. Here they halted, and Severne, Lawrence, and de Hutten prepared to make a dash upon the unsuspecting animals. Each was superbly mounted; and armed only with their revolvers and hunting-knives, they rode from the defile to the crest of a ridge, from which there was a gradual descent to the herd, which was scarcely three hundred yards distant. The moment they came in sight, several old but sharp-sighted bulls on the flanks of the herd, whose duty appeared to be that of sentinels, lifted up their shaggy heads, snorted loudly, and galloping to the main body, gave the alarm. "Now's your time!" shouted Tim Ormsby, the guide. "Go it with all your might!" Away went the herd in a dense body, as if mad, and away went our embryo buffalo hunters as fast as good horseflesh, urged by sharp spurs, could carry them. Severne soon distanced his companions. It was not a time to stand on ceremony. Holding his rein lightly in his left hand, he singled out a fine, fat cow, and made for her. Waiting till he came to within about twenty feet of her, he drew his revolver from the holster, and urging his horse to still greater speed, delivered his first shot at the fore-shoulder of the animal. His aim was good, and the trigger was pulled with a steady hand, but his horse, which seemed to be instinctively aware of what was coming, gave a slight but unexpected spring just as the pistol was discharged, and the ball took effect at a point at least a foot to the rear of that at which he had aimed. The cow lunged heavily forward, but instantly regained her footing, and rushed on as wildly and as rapidly as before. It was the first time Severne's horse had ever seen a buffalo, and his behavior, under the circumstances, was admirable. He could not, however, altogether prevent the exhibition of a little nervousness, and for a moment Severne lost ground in consequence. It was only for a moment, however, for again putting spurs to his horse he soon approached near enough to renew the attack. On he went. This time he reserved his fire till he had got half a length ahead of his victim, and then turning suddenly, fired with the muzzle of his pistol scarcely a yard from her body. A gush of bright crimson blood from the mouth and nostrils convinced him that the wound was mortal. The poor beast staggered onward for a half a dozen yards or so, and then falling heavily to the earth, in a few minutes was dead. Severne dismounted, drew his hunting-knife from his belt, and cutting of the tail of the huge animal, waved it in the air toward the main body of the party, several of whom were now galloping up. A short halt was ordered, and in less than half an hour the tongue, the hump, and others of the most esteemed parts, were in the wagons, ready for the cooks when camp should be reached. Severne had killed the first buffalo.

But where were Lawrence and de Hutten. The first was out of sight, still probably in pursuit of the herd. The last that was seen of him was by Tim Ormsby, who, with a glass, had made him out in the dim distance firing away at an old bull, which appeared to be endowed with a wonderful tenacity of life. As to de Hutten, there he was coming to answer for himself. His story was not a long one. He had picked out his cow, and was riding at full speed (he had served in the Russian cavalry, and knew how to ride), when his horse, putting his foot into a gopher hole, stumbled, throwing his rider fully twenty feet forward. Before de Hutten could gather himself up and remount, the herd had gained a quarter of a mile. There was still a chance, however, and on he rode like a madman. He had lost sight of his first selection, but where there were so many to choose from, it was not difficult to make another. A fine young heifer was the favored animal this time, when just as he was about to make his onslaught, down went his horse again !

"I am a little superstitious. Perhaps some day I will tell you why," he said to Severne. "Two falls constituted a warning which I dared not resist; I was really afraid of what might accompany the third; besides, I had some difficulty in catching my horse, and when I succeeded, the herd was so distant as to render any attempt to regain my lost ground rather doubtful. So I remounted, and turning my horse's head in this direction, returned a wiser but not a sadder man than when I started, for what I had of the hunt was splendid, and perhaps would not have been more pleasurable if I had been more successful."

"There's nothing like putting a good face on it, de Hutten," said Severne, laughing ; "but you will never know what buffalo hunting is till you kill your animal. I have hunted a great deal in my lifetime, from a hare in England to a wild boar in Hungary, but this has certainly been the most exhilarating sport I ever indulged in. And yet I felt sorry for the poor thing. I have had a pang, therefore, de Hutten, which you have escaped. As she received my second shot, and as the blood came in a torrent from her mouth and nose, she turned her head and gave me a reproachful glance which really went to my heart, and stayed there, too," he continued, smiling, "for fully a second. I suppose to-morrow I should try it again without the least compunction. Man is surely the most cruel animal in the world. He is probably the only one who destroys life merely for amusement. I dare say if I were to analyze my emotions I should find that the shade of regret I experienced was due to the fact that the victim was so large. I have never killed so big an animal before."

"Not exactly," said de Hutten; "I have killed a great many animals in all parts of the world. The higher they are in the scale of development—that is, the nearer they approach to man—the greater the remorse which is experienced. Monkeys always excited it in me at first. I soon got used to it, however," he continued, with a shrug of his shoulders. "In fact, after a little while I believe I preferred killing them to other animals, for the reason that they possessed so many features assimilating them to mankind. I don't know that I have quite reached to such a point that I could kill a white man in cold blood without being sorry for it afterward, but I am sure I should not be rendered at all miserable after sending an Indian out of the world."

"You appear to be especially severe on the red men," said Severne, smiling. "Did you ever see one?"

"Never; but I expect to see one at least before I finish this journey, and I intend to kill him."

Severne smiled. He did not give de Hutten credit for being very bloody-minded, or he would have argued the matter with him, and have attempted to convince him that all Indians were not worthy of being murdered. He therefore changed the conversation by asking Tim Ormsby if it would not be better to send some one in search of Lawrence.

"I'll go myself," said Ormsby. "Both the hunters are out, and I guess if he's met with any accident I can be of more service to him than anybody here."

"I think I'll go with you," said Joshua, who had been listening to the conversation between Severne and de Hutten, and who, having formed a strong attachment for Lawrence, was getting uneasy at his long absence; "I think I'll go with you, Mr. Ormsby."

"Indeed and you won't, Mr. Joshua," said Ormsby, very decidedly. "I don't want a man with me when I go on an expedition who can't ride ten yards without getting off his horse to pick up a rock or a weed or a bug, or some other darned thing that ain't no use to nobody. No, sir, just you stay where you are. There's plenty of 'specimens' about here."

"Then you go your way and I'll go mine," exclaimed Joshua, indignantly; "I don't want your company, Mr. Ormsby. I never heard you make a sensible observation in my life, and I suppose I've heard you make no less than twenty thousand observations since we left Fort Leavenworth. Where there's so much smoke there might be a little fire, one would think. But there's nothing but carbonic acid gas and vapor of water comes out of your mouth. Perhaps the sense is all frozen up since that voyage of yours to the north pole that you told us of last night."

"You darned dictionary!" muttered Ormsby, as he rode away, "I'd like to pound your head! I'll do it, too, some day, if you don't look out."

Joshua set off in almost the opposite direction. He had seen what Ormsby had not discovered, that the herd had made a circuit, so as to get to leeward of their pursuers, and were then probably several miles to the eastward. Taking out his compass, without which he never traveled, he took the bearings, and pushing his horse into a fast trot was soon out of sight. Severne ordered the wagons to move on to the river, about half a mile distant, and the party went into camp for the day.

The sun was just sinking behind the belt of hills that formed the valley of the Platte, when one of the men reported that a party was approaching. Severne took his glass, and made out Joshua and another man, both mounted,

leading what appeared to be a horse with an empty saddle.
Full of apprehension, he ordered his own horse to be sad-
dled, and mounting him, rode off rapidly toward the men,
who were still more than a mile distant. As he neared them,
he perceived that the horse which was led dragged a litter
behind him, made, after the manner of the prairie Indians, of
two poles, fastened each to the saddle by one end, while the
other dragged on the ground. A buffalo skin or a blanket
being stretched between the poles, a very comfortable means
of conveyance for a sick or wounded person is provided.
There was no room for doubt as to who was the person
Joshua and one of the hunters were transporting. The
horse drawing the litter was Lawrence's. Severne could
only, therefore, while suffering the most painful apprehensions, hope for the best.

"Don't make yourself uneasy, sir," said Joshua, who advanced to meet him. "He'll be all right in an hour or two.
He's only had the breath squeezed out of him by a buffalo,
and José (who, for a Mexican, is as good a fellow as one
would want to see) and me have got him fixed up pretty
well."

"Thank God, it's no worse," exclaimed Severne, dashing
up to the litter. "Lawrence, my dear fellow, how are you?"
he continued, as he sprang from his horse and approached
his friend. "I hope to Heaven you are not seriously hurt."

"I think not," said Lawrence, in a weak voice. "I'm
bruised a good deal, but I think no bones are broken. I
should have been dead, though, if it had not been for José
and Joshua. I'll tell you all about it after awhile."

Severne hurried the party on to the camp, and in a short
time Lawrence was undressed, and laid on a comfortable
cot in the shade of his tent. Severne examined him carefully, and ascertained that beyond some pretty severe bruises,
and a cut on the scalp, which extended across the top of his
head, he had received no serious injuries. The bruises were
bathed, and the cut dressed, and after the administration of
a little whisky, Lawrence felt sufficiently strong to relate
his adventure.

"The animal that I selected as my prey," said Lawrence,
"was a large and powerful bull. He ran very fast, and before I knew it I was in the midst of the herd. I kept my

eye on him, however, and pushed my horse forward to his utmost speed. If I had stopped, or attempted to get out, I should have been trampled to death by the furious animals who rushed blindly onward, and who would have upset my horse and his rider without knowing what they were doing. At last I reached my victim, and as I rode up alongside of him I gave him my first shot. I struck him somewhere in the body, and though the wound was not a fatal one, it reduced his speed, so that I had no difficulty in keeping up with him. Again and again I fired, but without giving him a mortal wound. When I took time to look around me, I found that the herd had gradually been getting over the ground more rapidly than I had, and that the bull and myself had the field all to ourselves. A fourth shot brought him to bay. He wheeled round suddenly, and stood stamping the ground with his fore-feet, tossing his head, and bellowing, not loudly, but with an emphasis which convinced me that he meditated mischief. I rode up to within a few feet of him, and gave him another shot. He lowered his head as if about to come at me, but I fired again—it was my last shot—and brought him to the ground. I immediately jumped from my horse, drew my knife, and prepared to finish him with that weapon. As soon, however, as I came within reach of him, he rose to his feet, and made at me. I am ashamed to say I retreated, still however facing him. Backward I went, and on came the bull. Suddenly I felt my foot stepping on nothing, and before I could turn I fell down a bluff, the buffalo following. I saw that he would strike me as I went down, and when I reached the ground again I rolled myself a little out of the way, not enough, however, to prevent him falling partly on me and cutting my head with his horns. I was completely stunned by the blow, and knew nothing more till I found José and Joshua standing over me."

"He was pretty far gone, sir," said Joshua, who was busily engaged in making himself useful, "when José and I found him. After I left here I met José over the hills there, and told him what was the matter, and we started off together toward where he had heard firing. About three miles from the hills we struck the trail of the buffaloes, and soon came to where the doctor had fallen down. It must

have been at least fifteen feet; but the ground was very soft,
else he would have been killed outright. There he lay at
the bottom of the ravine, looking as if he was dead, and a
dead buffalo almost covering him up entirely. José and I
crawled down and dragged the beast off, when we found
that the doctor was only stunned. We threw water in his
face and gave him a little whisky, and after awhile he opened
his eyes. He could not stand, however, but José said he'd
get him home. So while he went to a spring near by where
there was a cottonwood-tree growing, to cut a couple of
strong poles, I hunted for the doctor's horse, which I found
grazing about half a mile off.

"Well, sir, José rigged up the litter and we put the doctor on it, and moved off with him as comfortably as you
please, and to-morrow or next day at furthest, he'll be as
well as he ever was. And here's the tongue and the tail
of his buffalo, too," he continued, untying them from his
saddle-bow as he spoke. "I cut them off as his trophies."

At this moment Ormsby made his appearance, having, of
course, been unsuccessful in his search. The enmity between him and Joshua had existed ever since they left Fort
Leavenworth. There was no very strong feeling of hate,
however. Joshua laughed at Ormsby, and the latter despised
what he regarded as Joshua's affectation of superior knowledge.

"I'm sorry you would not allow me to persuade you to
go my way, Mr. Ormsby," said Joshua, maliciously. "Your
superior knowledge would have been of great service to us.
However, José—who is one of the best guides and hunters
I ever saw, and I would recommend all travelers who can
get his services to do so without fail—did all that was actually necessary. He didn't talk much, Mr. Ormsby, and
there's where we missed you. José doesn't understand
much English; and the doctor was stunned, so that I would
have had you all to myself."

Ormsby walked away, muttering something expressive of
his intense desire to do Joshua a bodily injury.

It was several days before Lawrence was able to ride on
horseback, and in the mean time he was transported in one
of the wagons which was arranged for the purpose. All
went on well with the party, and nothing of importance oc-

curred till after they crossed the Black Hills. The events which then took place are of sufficient importance to deserve a separate chapter.

CHAPTER XXV.

IN WHICH ULRICH DE HUTTEN TELLS HIS WONDERFUL STORY.

SEVERNE's party had crossed the Black Hills and were passing through the broad valley which separates this ridge from the Medicine Bow Mountains. As yet they had seen no Indians either friendly or hostile, and Severne frequently bantered de Hutten on his warlike intentions having been thus far frustrated. The latter, however, would smile confidently and declare that his opportunity would come ere long.

The sun was down behind the long black range of mountains, which stretched like a great dark wall before them, when the party went into camp on the west fork of the Laramie River, a clear, swift stream which flowed from the mountains through the plain they were traversing. The sun had disappeared, and the shadow of the high hills darkened the prairie verdure—though the sky was still bright and beautiful with the sunlight which illumined it. The tents were pitched, and Severne, Lawrence, and de Hutten sat before them smoking their pipes and enjoying the delicious coolness of the atmosphere, which always prevails on the plains, even during the hottest weather, as soon as the sun has set, and which at their elevation and at that season of the year —September—was particularly bracing and agreeable.

"I think I shall meet my Indians before long now," said de Hutten. "This is a very fine place for them, and to-day, as I was off there to the right, I saw signs which assured me they are about."

"They are in our vicinity," said Severne. "I have just had a talk with Ormsby, and he tells me he saw undoubted evidences of their presence in this valley. He thinks they are Cheyennes."

"I don't suppose we shall have any difficulty with them," said Lawrence. "They have nothing to gain by attacking us, unless they can take us by surprise. We should certainly kill more of them than they could of us, and they value a life very highly."

"They will attack us," said de Hutten, quietly, "and that before to-morrow morning."

"How do you know?" said Severne. "My dear de Hutten, you must be a sorcerer, for if I am not mistaken, there are a dozen or so coming over the plain to the left there."

All sprang to their feet, and in a moment the camp was aroused and prepared. The cooking which had been going on was interrupted, and each man, armed with his rifle and revolver, was ready in case an attack should be made.

The Indians came to within a hundred yards and made signs of peace. There were sixteen of them, and the party of whites was more than a match for them in a fair fight. Ormsby recommended Severne to allow them to come into camp, but on no account to relax in vigilance. Each man was ordered to keep his arms in his hands, and to be prepared to repel any attack that might be made. The signal was given, therefore, and the Indians rode single file into the camp. They did not dismount, and appeared to be actuated more by curiosity than any other motive. Ormsby carried on the conversation with them. They were Cheyennes, and the chief declared that it was the main object of his existence to preserve peace between his people and the whites.

"You may take that, sir, for what it is worth," said Ormsby to Severne, "which is just nothing at all. I don't know this chief at all, though I've seen most of the head men of this tribe."

"Ask him," said de Hutten, in a low voice, "if his name is not Long Knife."

Ormsby did so, and reported that the chief replied in the affirmative.

"I thought so," said de Hutten, in a strongly agitated voice to Severne—at the same time looking at the caps on his revolver to see that they were in order. "My dear friend, I cannot allow that man to escape me,—I am going to kill him."

"No, no, de Hutten," said Severne; "I cannot permit that."

Scarcely were the words out of his mouth, when Ormsby gave an exclamation of alarm, and an arrow from Long Knife's bow whizzed between Severne and de Hutten, grazing the latter's hair. In an instant all was confusion. The Indians discharged their arrows, and putting spurs to their horses endeavored to escape. They were not all quick enough, however; a general volley was discharged by Severne's party, and six of them fell either dead or mortally wounded. One of his own men was killed, and four were badly wounded. But this was not all. As soon as de Hutten felt the arrow brush his cheek, he turned round and fired at Long Knife. The ball struck his horse in the breast and the animal fell dead. Long Knife, with surprising agility, disentangled himself from his saddle, and, plunging into the tall grass, endeavored to escape. But de Hutten was at his back, and another shot brought his flying antagonist to the ground. In an instant de Hutten was on him. "Foltz," he shouted, frantically, "double-damned villain! have I found you at last? Die! die! die!" he repeated, firing a shot into the prostrate body of his foe with each exclamation. "At last I am avenged," he continued. "Do you know me? I am Ulrich de Hutten, and the prophecy has been fulfilled!"

"I know you," said the dying man, in German; "I knew you the moment I saw you, and understood that it was your life or mine. I hate you. I do not repent. If I could kill you now I would."

"What is this, de Hutten?" said Severne, as he approached the group. "Do you know this Indian?"

"Indian!" shrieked de Hutten. "Indian! look at his skin." As he spoke, he stooped down, and tearing open the dying man's shirt, showed Severne the white skin under it. "This is Rudolph Foltz, the enemy of my race, whom I have spent the best part of my life in seeking, and who at last has paid the penalty of his crimes."

"Yes," said the dying man, "I am Rudolph Foltz. I have the advantage of him. I killed four of his family and he has killed me. I am satisfied. I will meet him hereafter. Our score is not yet settled. No, no. You were avenged, Frederica. I curse you," he continued, raising himself on one arm, and fixing his eyes on de Hutten; "I curse you!" and then, falling back on the grass, he expired with a scowl on his face.

It was some time before everything was quiet again. Six of the Indians were killed, and several more were certainly wounded, as spots of blood were found on the grass over which they had fled. The men wounded in Severne's party were severely but not dangerously hurt, and through Lawrence's assistance gave promise of doing well. The one killed was a teamster, whose loss it would be difficult to supply. He was shot through the heart.

De Hutten became more composed after the death of his enemy, and an expression of satisfaction took the place of the anxious and expectant one which had been present since he had been with Severne.

"De Hutten," said Severne to him as they sat round the camp-fire that night, "you promised me once that you would tell me some portions of your history. I can understand from what has occurred to-day that your life has been an eventful one. If you can relate those parts now without giving yourself pain, I should be much obliged to you. I am sure we shall be edified by what you will say."

"Yes, my life has been, as you say, an eventful one. For fifteen years I have been in search of that man, and though for nearly all that time I have been on his track, I never met him till to-day. But, my dear Severne, and you, my dear Lawrence, I am afraid that what I would say would not be very diverting. My life has not been a joyous one, and though, perhaps, there are some passages in it which are not without interest, and which might even be instructive, I doubt if they are of the kind which would add to your cheerfulness."

"I don't particularly care about being made cheerful to-night," said Severne. "The day has been a solemn one, and I would rather have the impression which now prevails in my mind kept up. There is sometimes a happiness experienced in being made miserable. You know, my dear fellow, that both Lawrence and myself are your friends. We have the most thorough confidence in you, and whether you tell us anything of the past or not, we shall not lose an iota of faith in you."

"Yes," said Lawrence, "we are only anxious to hear your story if you can tell it without recalling events to mind which may cause you distress. We don't want to be satisfied in regard to anything. We believe in you fully. But whatever concerns you, interests us for that reason."

"Very well," said de Hutten, "I feel that I ought to give you my confidence. You have been very kind to me, and but for you I should never have been made happy by the death of my foe. I warn you, however, that there are some frightful scenes to be depicted. I can look back on them now without much pain. Years have elapsed since they happened, and I have expiated them all in the death of that monster who lies there. Listen, therefore."

One of the men came up with an armful of wood which he threw on the fire, and amid the solemn silence of the vast plains, only broken by an occasional groan from one of the wounded men, or by the tread of the sentinel as he approached the place where they sat, Ulrich de Hutten thus told his history.

ULRICH DE HUTTEN'S STORY.

"I was born on the family estate in Bohemia. My father was a baron of the Austrian Empire, and had derived his title from his ancestors, in whose possession it had been for several centuries. We were direct descendants of the great de Hutten, and I was named after him. I was a younger son, and as such received from my father but little consideration, for he was a stern man, and rarely exhibited tenderness even toward those he most loved. He appeared to regard me as a superfluity, as a kind of inconvenience which must be tolerated, out of a certain regard for external propriety. As to loving me, the idea never seemed to enter his head. My mother, however, treated me with all the more kindness, and more than repaid me for my father's neglect. I loved her with all my soul. She was so sweet and gentle in her manners, that even my father's gloomy nature was at times softened by her influence.

"I was educated with all those anti-republican ideas which the nobles of Austria entertain, and was accustomed to regard the peasantry of the country as beings created expressly for the use of the higher classes. It is perhaps scarcely necessary to say that I have long since abandoned all feelings of that nature. I am a republican, not from necessity, but from choice. I have seen enough of mankind to know that they are able to govern themselves.

"My brother was a high-spirited and noble boy, and possessed none of the overbearing spirit which elder brothers in Europe are so apt to assume. I rarely saw him, however. He departed for the University at Vienna when I was scarcely ten years old, and only visited the castle during the vacations.

"My sister was a wonder to me. She was strikingly beautiful, but there gradually came over her disposition a melancholy and a reserve toward me for which I could not account. Once we used to play together, and she was as blithesome as the lark. But by degrees she changed entirely, and became thoughtful and sedate. She seemed to shun my company, and when I, with childlike obstinacy, would force my presence upon her, she would steal away, and retire to some unfrequented corner of the castle or grounds, where I would find her weeping as though her heart would break. She was a year my senior by birth, but far older in acquirements and intellect.

"I was afraid to press her to tell me the cause of this strange demeanor, for whenever I mentioned the subject she would fix her large blue eyes upon me and gaze so earnestly into my face that I trembled with an indefinable fear, whether of evil to her or myself I could not tell.

"There was also the chaplain. Father Rudolph was not a man whose appearance pleased me. I dreaded him, and yet he was kind to me, and seemingly devoted to the services of the Church. He was a small, well-formed man. His piercing black eyes and his thin and compressed lips indicated him to be a person of energy and decision of character. He never, however, seemed to do anything from impulse or feeling; all his acts were done calmly and deliberately, and apparently because he was fully satisfied of their expediency after due reflection. He was a peasant's son, and was born on the estate. Exhibiting talent of no ordinary kind, my father had sent him to Rome to be educated for the Church; and since his admission to

24

orders and return to Bohemia he had filled the post of domestic chaplain. He stood high in the estimation of both my father and mother, who respected him as much for his seeming piety as for his learning and zeal.

"I was about fourteen years old when the events occurred which I am about to relate. They made an impression upon me which has not been diminished with time, and determined, in a great measure, the then budding traits of my character. Even now, after the lapse of many years, I recall them shudderingly; but now that I have made the wretch who caused them atone for his treachery and crimes, I can think of them without experiencing the anguish which once filled my heart at their recollection.

"One morning while sitting in the garden with my sister reading Virgil (she sometimes read with me, but always with a seriousness which made what was formerly a pleasure appear like a task), she stopped suddenly in the midst of a sentence, let the book fall, and turning as pale as death, darted into the house with a rapidity which defied my efforts to overtake her. Adlerfels was a large, old baronial castle, and like all buildings of the kind possessed numerous long, narrow, and dark passages in almost every part of it. I ran after her at the top of my speed, hardly knowing why; but she reached a door at the end of one of the passages I have mentioned, which she hastily opened, and entering, closed it behind her. When I arrived there it was securely locked. I placed my eye to the key-hole, but saw nothing; then my ear, but all was still.

"I was resolved to unravel the mystery. I walked away from the door, making as much noise as possible, and after proceeding a few yards, hid myself against one of the buttresses which supported the archway. In a few moments the door was cautiously unlocked, and I heard some one come out and walk about the passage, as though looking to see if there were any listeners. The steps approached close to me. I trembled with fear. I was but a child, and though brave enough as far as known dangers were concerned, I was easily terrified by one which was attended with mystery. It is so with us all, even after we reach maturity. We fear most those perils which we do not understand or to which we are not accustomed. The physician walks calmly amid

all kinds of pestilence, but would tremble if obliged to face
a battery for the first time; and the soldier cares nothing for
bullets, but shudders if he is told the cholera is in the camp.
In this as in other things 'familiarity breeds contempt.'

"Apparently satisfied with the scrutiny, the person who
had come out into the passage slowly retraced his steps, and
I heard the door closed and bolted; I removed my shoes and
noiselessly approached. I again listened attentively. This
time I heard a voice, which I recognized as that of Father
Rudolph, speaking in a language I did not understand.
My sister replied; she also spoke in an unknown tongue.
Again the first voice spoke, and now in German.

"'Bertha,' it said, 'you have sinned not only against me
but against the order of which you have become a member.
You were told when admitted to its mysteries that the first
duty you had to accustom yourself to perform was obedience. You have failed so frequently in this as to deserve
the most severe punishment at my hands. If you are not
more attentive, how do you expect to perform properly that
great act which will soon be required of you? Am I constantly to overlook your derelictions? Have you forgotten
your vows and the penalties to which you render yourself
liable by your misconduct?'

"'Oh, pardon me!' exclaimed Bertha, piteously. 'I
forgot the hour. I came the moment I remembered. I
would not disobey you for the world.'

"'It is well, Bertha,' replied the priest; 'you are forgiven;
see that you offend not again, for the next time pardon will
be more difficult. And now tell me, does your mind increase
in power over your earthly feelings, and are you yet prepared to execute the task assigned you?'

"'Not yet, oh, not yet!' answered Bertha. 'I still love
them all, though not so dearly as I once did. I wept last
night when my mother came to my bed, and bending over
me, kissed my cheek. And my brother Ulrich! He seems
so troubled that I do not laugh and jest with him! Must
I cease to love him also?'

"'Yes, you must not only cease to love him, but you must
hate him, Bertha—him and all others of this accursed house.
Think you I have toiled for nothing, that I have spent a lifetime in the service of my foe, that I have dissembled, and

bowed, and cringed before him, that for these many years I have had my wrongs constantly before me, ever looking forward to the vengeance for which alone I have lived, and then in the end to yield one jot or tittle of that, the contemplation of which has alone made life endurable? Not so, Bertha, not so. None can be spared. All are necessary ; and even then I will not have repaid one-tenth of what I owe. Although you are the daughter of him who has injured me, I love you, and the angels have chosen you as the instrument of my vengeance.'

" 'What was this great wrong my father did you? Oh, is it not possible to wash it out by other means than by blood?'

" 'I cannot tell you now, Bertha, what it was. In time you shall know all. But as I have told you before, and as I tell you now for the last time, nothing but blood can atone for my injuries. Ay, oceans of it would scarcely suffice. You cannot see my heart, Bertha, and you do not understand these things. It is now nearly four years since you became a member of our most sacred order. You have not made rapid progress. You must strive harder, my child. What is the body compared to the soul? What are the affections of this life compared to those which await us in heaven? Are not the few short years of trouble here sufficiently atoned for by the eternity of happiness which awaits us in the world to come? You will soon be called upon to show yourself a fit companion for the angels of heaven. In the mean time exercise yourself well in the course I have pointed out to you.'

" 'And are the angels pleased with me now?' said Bertha.

" 'Yes, but they will love you more as you become more and more zealous in our cause. To deserve the perfect love of spiritual beings you must shake off all that clings to you of earth. Earthly love is all corrupt, and based on selfishness and sin. We must hate the world and all that is in it. God hates it. He has told us so. The saints and other glorious men and women of the Church hate it, and hence they shut themselves up away from all its allurements and passions, and meditate upon the glories of the New Jerusalem. Neither father, nor mother, nor brothers, nor sisters, are aught to them.   It must be so with you, Bertha.   And now you can go; reflect upon what I have said, and be careful and discreet.'

"At these words I hastily retreated, and hid myself in a dark and narrow recess which led from the passage, and terminated at a door opening I knew not whither.   In a few moments Bertha passed by me, as pale as marble, and the tears still standing in her eyes, and shortly afterward Father Rudolph strode past.   He peered into the darkness which sheltered me, and I had a good look at his face.   There was a smile of triumph on it, and he muttered some words as he went by, of which 'Frederica' was the only one I could distinguish.   When the sound of his footsteps had entirely died away, I came out from my hiding-place, and going to my own room, sat down to think over what I had heard.

" What was the object of the mysterious conversation I had heard ?   I understood enough of it to know that some scheme of vengeance was on hand against our family, and that Bertha was to execute it.   But I was superstitious, and the words of Father Rudolph about 'our sacred order,' and the agency of the angels in the matter, somewhat staggered me.   I was young, too young to understand the whole tenor of Father Rudolph's words.   At one time I resolved to reveal all to my father, but upon reflection I changed my mind ; for what would my unsustained story avail against any version Father Rudolph might give?   I felt assured from what I had heard that Bertha would die rather than betray her secret.   I could not, therefore, appeal to her.

"I had but one course open to me, and that was to play the game of dissimulation, and this I resolved to do.   Though no match for Father Rudolph in duplicity and cunning, I had one great advantage.   I knew of his scheme, and he was ignorant of my knowledge.

"I therefore noticed particularly the demeanor of the priest.   It was always the same, no matter under what circumstances I regarded it.   He still performed the services of the Church regularly, still blessed us all when we parted for the night, and in the morning thanked God that we were all allowed to meet once more.   There was not the least evidence that there was any secret understanding between

him and Bertha.   He took no more notice of her than of
me, and I never discovered even a look of intelligence pass
from one to the other.   I did not confine my observations
to him.   Often would I cautiously approach the door I have
mentioned, but it was always securely locked, and all within
was perfectly silent.

"Bertha acted as usual.   I never gave her reason, either
by word or action, to suspect that I was wiser than she
thought me.   I was, however, greatly changed.   New feelings had taken possession of my heart.   I felt more manly,
more determined, more crafty than before.   My mother was
the only one to notice the alteration, for I could not conceal
from her watchful eye that which others failed to perceive.
Several times I was on the point of disclosing to her all
that I had discovered, but I dreaded the influence of the
priest, and therefore refrained from an act which might have
thwarted all his schemes.

"Time rolled on.   I had not diminished in vigilance, but
all my watching had led to nothing.   Preparations were
being made at the castle for my brother's return.   He had
completed the course of education at Vienna, and was daily
expected to arrive.   At last he came.   All the peasantry
of the estate had assembled on the lawn to greet him, and
when he leaped from the carriage they raised a shout of
welcome which brought a blush of pleasure to his cheek.
He was in truth a noble-looking youth, and as my father
gazed upon him, his eyes glistened with pride and satisfaction that one so handsome was his son and heir.

"Fritz (so my brother was named) seemed pleased with
me.   He joked with me on my rapid growth, and said I
would be a worthy successor to him at the University.
Bertha was not present when he arrived.   No one but myself appeared to notice her absence, for all were too much
engrossed with my brother.   Father Rudolph welcomed
him with every manifestation of pleasure, and entered
heartily into the spirit of the occasion.

"Seeing his attention occupied, I resolved to attempt an
entrance into the room I have mentioned, and where I had
no doubt of finding Bertha.   I left the parlor unobserved,
and bent my steps toward the part of the house in which the
apartment in question was situated.   I quietly approached

the door and looked through the key-hole. My suspicion was correct. Bertha was seated at a table opposite. A large book lay open before her, which she was attentively reading. She betrayed no signs of emotion; on the contrary, her countenance wore an expression of repose and contentment I had never before observed. There was a lifelessness about it, however, which pained me, for she seemed to have lost the soul which once shone so brightly through her eyes. I had heard of magic arts by which the spirit could be removed from the body. and with the superstition common at that time throughout Germany, a suspicion crossed my mind that Father Rudolph had taken away her soul.

"As I leaned forward to observe her more closely, my right hand was pressed with increased force against the wall beside the pillar which supported the doorway. I was astonished to feel it yield before the pressure, and as I continued to bear against it, it slowly turned upon a pivot and left a small recess open before me. The aperture was not more than two feet square. I crawled through it, and found the closet much larger than I had at first sight considered it. A small window, scarcely as large as my hand, cut into the thick wall, afforded light enough for me to see that the recess was empty. I closed the opening behind me, the panel shutting with a sharp click which somewhat startled me. I then turned toward the window. What was my surprise to find that it opened into the room upon which my thoughts had so long been placed! There before me sat Bertha, so much engrossed with the subject which engaged her attention that she had not been disturbed by the noise I had made. I took a hurried survey of the room. It contained a table, two chairs, and an open wardrobe, in which latter hung a singular-looking dress of black silk and a red mask. Upon the dress was painted a large red hand grasping a skull transfixed by a dagger, underneath which were some words which I did not understand. On the table at which Bertha sat were a retort, a spirit-lamp, several glass flasks, and three small phials, each of the latter containing a colored liquid. There were also several old books bound in vellum and closed with silver clasps. The one from which Bertha was reading was printed in Latin. It was so close to me that I could read the title, and I have never since forgotten it.   It was DE ALCHIMIA OPUSCULA COMPLURA VETERUM PHILOSOPHORUM.

"On the wall opposite me was written : HE WHO GAINS A VICTORY OVER ANOTHER IS HUMAN, BUT HE WHO CONQUERS HIMSELF IS DIVINE.   And over the door : SEEK NOT TO RETRACE THY STEPS, FOR BETWEEN THEE AND THE WORLD THERE CAN HENCEFORTH BE NO COMMUNION.

"While I was wondering at the strange sight before me I heard the sound of approaching footsteps in the passage, and ere I had time to be greatly frightened, the door of the room opened and Father Rudolph entered.

"Bertha raised her eyes from the book before her and looked at him steadfastly.   'Has my brother arrived?' she at last said, calmly.

"'He has,' replied the priest.

"'And is all prepared for the great act which seals my covenant with Heaven?'

"'All is ready, Bertha.   The hour approaches.   Nerve your heart for this solemn duty; falter not in the execution, and you may DEMAND the reward of your fidelity.'

"'I am firm,' answered Bertha.   'I have conquered all earthly feelings.   I love no one.   See, Father, do I tremble? Am I not calm?   There is not one tie that binds me to this earth; and when I have convinced you of it, we will go, and, shutting ourselves out from the world, wait with patience for our departure to Paradise.'

"'True, Bertha, true,' said the priest.   'I see you are prepared, and that there is no sign of wavering; but before the final step is taken, I wish to let you hear the last revelations the spirit will make to you.   You will then be if possible more fully assured of the righteousness of your course, and of the benefits you and I will derive from it.'

"Father Rudolph then opened a drawer in the table and took from it a brass ring about two feet in diameter.   He touched a spring and an opening was disclosed, and I saw that the ring was hollow.   Into the opening he poured a quantity of a pale, thin fluid from a large bottle which he took from a shelf, and then, as he placed the ring on the table, I saw that the upper surface was pierced by numerous small holes.

"On the table with the ring he next placed a silver plate, which he took from a pocket in the breast of his coat. Upon this plate were traced in black and red enamel several letters and figures surrounding two interlaced triangles, called, as I have since ascertained, a pentagramme. But why should I stop to describe this plate as I have it here, and you can inspect it for yourselves?"

De Hutten here drew from an inner pocket of his coat a silver plate about four inches in diameter, which was attached to a gold chain passing around his neck. Removing the chain, he handed it to Severne and Lawrence for their examination. The plate was round; the figures were marked upon it in black enamel and the letters in red.

"I know it," said Severne, smiling. "It is the pentagramme, and by it the mind controls the elements, and subdues the demons of the air, the spirits of fire, the specters of water, and the phantoms of the earth. It is fully described by Paracelsus in his Occult Philosophy."

"What a wonderful figure!" said Lawrence. "One is almost lost in the attempt to trace and comprehend its interlacings. But go on, de Hutten. You were correct in calling your history a sorrowful one. What a monster of iniquity that priest was!"

De Hutten took the plate, and putting the chain again around his neck, placed his treasure in his pocket and resumed his narrative.

"You will ascertain presently how this came into my possession. Without it I could have done nothing, for so long as any one else had it, that one was my superior. But I must not anticipate.

"The plate having been carefully laid in the middle of the space inclosed by the brass ring, the priest said a few words over it, and sprinkled a small quantity of a blue powder within the circle. He next opened a recess in the wall and took from it a small silver lamp, which was burning with a pale-green flame when he removed it. For a moment he appeared to be confused, as if he had forgotten his part, for he stood looking at the arrangement without apparently knowing what to do. Bertha, however, came to him and whispered a word which I did not understand. It was enough for him, as he immediately passed the flame rapidly around the ring, and in an instant it was surmounted with a sheet of flame throughout its whole extent. The color of the blaze changed from red to yellow, and from yellow to green, and back again, continually.

"Father Rudolph then fixing his eyes on the plate, crossing his hands over his breast, and bending his head forward in a reverential manner, commenced to speak. At first his voice was very low, and I could not distinguish a word; but by degrees he spoke louder, and I found that he was invoking the spirits in the French language, which I understood tolerably well. Suddenly he raised his hands aloft and called aloud in a language I did not understand. Occasionally I heard the words ADONAI and SADDAI, and the conjuration concluded with AMEN. I looked at the table while he was speaking. The figures on the silver plate had assumed a deep-red color, and the flame from the ring was as black as pitch. Bertha stood erect, her arms crossed on her breast, and her eyes gazing vacantly at the priest.

"As the latter concluded his address, the flame went out with a slight explosion, and the figures on the silver plate resumed their black color. The priest now went to the wardrobe and put on the mask and gown which hung there. Returning to the table, he passed his hands through the air over the plate, and called aloud three times in a language unknown to me. The skull and red hand stood out in bold relief upon his breast, and the red mask, through which shone his jet-black eyes, appeared to sparkle with a more than earthly crimson. As he said the last word, a tall figure, clothed entirely in white, became indistinctly visible. At first it looked like a mist, but gradually it assumed a more solid form, and at last was clearly recognizable as that of an aged man, who might have been, from his appearance, several hundred years old. I was half dead with terror, and strove to withdraw from the window. I found I could not stir. I think I should have fainted from fear; but the voice of the priest recalled my sinking strength.

"Speaking now in German, and bending his head low before the old man, the priest said :

"'It is well, and I thank you. This is the last time I shall call you, for your work and mine will soon be over. And now, by the sacred star which has evoked you from your retreat, and which I now raise before you, I adjure you to answer the questions I shall propound.'

"As he uttered these last words, Father Rudolph took the silver plate from the table and held it aloft.

"As he did so, the figure bowed low, and said : 'Speak !'

"' Tell me,' said the priest, 'what shall be the end of the work I am now engaged in.'

"' Peace !' replied the spirit.

"'And for the child ?' continued Father Rudolph.

"' Forgetfulness and rest,' said the spirit.

"' For whom will there be peace ?' asked the priest.

"' For those who will leave this earth,' answered the spirit.

"'And will there not be peace for me ?' asked the priest.

"' No ! You will satisfy your vengeance; you will fulfill their destiny, and one of their blood will accomplish yours.'

"'And what will be my destiny ?'

"' I am not permitted to reveal it,' replied the spirit.

"Bertha now approached the priest and whispered a few words to him.

"Turning again to the spirit, he said : 'The child wishes

to know whether or not in eternity she will be united to those she once loved in this world.'

"'She will,' replied the spirit.

"'Then,' said the priest, taking the plate again into his hands and elevating it above his head, 'depart and tell your master I will take care of my own destiny, and of that blood which has wronged me.'

"The spirit smiled contemptuously, and bowing low before the emblems on the silver plate, faded gradually from my sight.

"'I am satisfied,' said Bertha, 'and ready to execute my task. Prepare me for it. Every moment's delay is so much lost from the store of happiness prepared for us.'

"'All is ready, Bertha,' replied Father Rudolph. 'And now hear what I have to say, for we have yet a few moments to spare.' He then removed the gown and mask, and, taking Bertha's hand, spoke as follows:

"'Over four years ago I found you a worldly-minded child. You loved earth more than heaven, and your thoughts were more of your father, mother, and brothers, than of the saints and angels of a better world. It was painful to me that one so beautiful and so richly gifted in intellect, should remain in ignorance of the happiness of a more than mortal life.

"'I interested myself in you, for I had another object to attain most dear to my heart. I found that with patience I could mould your mind to such a form as to fit it for a higher sphere of existence. I labored hard to impress my ideas upon you. I conversed with you and gave you learned books to read. Ere long you were initiated into the mysteries of that secret but mighty order, the members of which are able to hold communication with the spirits of the dead and the ever living. You still, however, clung to the beings of this world; but now you have shaken off the fetters of humanity, and in obedience to the orders of angels, communicated through me, are about to execute the deed for which my soul is athirst. Much as I desire its performance, if your heart goes not with the act, refrain. I wish no feeling of fear to govern you. Look upon it as a righteous duty, and perform it because you deem it just. Your father wronged me in my youth so deeply, that I dare not dwell upon it now, lest I forget that you are no longer of his kin. I have sworn to destroy all of his name but one, who should be the instrument of my vengeance. You are that instrument, and you are reserved for a state of happiness far beyond all you have ever conceived as possible in your wildest dreams.

"'And now listen to the directions I am about to give you' and follow them implicitly. This phial contains the essence by which the duty assigned to you is to be accomplished.'

"He took one of the small phials from the table and placed it in Bertha's hand.

"'The dinner hour has nearly arrived,' he continued. 'Before the meal, all will, as is customary on the occasion of a friend's arrival, drink to his health and prosperity. One drop of the contents of that phial placed in each wineglass will produce the desired effect. Before you go, I wish you to sign this paper. I will read it.

"'I, Bertha de Hutten, do declare, of my own free will, that I have ceased to love my father and mother, and all others who are related to me; that I have this day poisoned all of my name within reach, and this because of the wrong done by my father to Rudolph Foltz on the twenty-third day of October, 1824.'

"Bertha took a pen and wrote upon the paper. 'Well done!' exclaimed the priest, looking at what she had written. 'BERTHA DE HUTTEN!' 'Boldly signed! No one can deny the authenticity of that signature!'

"He then folded the paper and gave it to Bertha.

"'This you will put under your father's plate,' he resumed, 'immediately after having complied with my directions regarding the wineglasses. Be quick, cautious, and certain in the execution. The family has not yet assembled in the dining-room, and you will have time to act without being suspected till success is attained. Rejoin me here. I will await you. They will seek for us in this room, but I have prepared for our flight, and the moment you return, we will depart together for a home of happiness ready for you. Now go. I see you are firm and determined.'

"Bertha silently left the room. No flush of excitement mantled her cheeks; no gleam of enthusiasm sparkled in

her eyes.   Calm and passionless she went forth on her mur-
derous errand.

"I had heard and witnessed enough.   God only knows
how I had been sustained through the terrible scenes and
conversation which had transpired.   But I took no time to
think of them.   It was for me to prevent the atrocious
schemes of the priest from being successful.   I hurried
toward the door through which I had entered, careless
whether heard by the priest or not.   I forced myself against
it with all the strength I was master of, but it resisted my
efforts.   I sought for the spring, but in vain.   I called
aloud for assistance, but no one answered me.   If the priest
heard my cries, he paid no attention to them.   I prayed to
God for aid, and even he was deaf to my supplications.   In
the frenzy of despair I dashed myself violently against the
panel, till at length, utterly worn out, I fell upon the floor
in an unconscious state.

"I must have remained in this condition for several hours,
for when I regained my consciousness there was no longer
any light admitted through the little window which opened
into the adjoining room.   I staggered toward it, and looked
through.   In one corner of the room burned a dim taper,
by the flickering light of which I discovered a figure
crouching close to the wall, and on the floor three irregular
dark masses, the character of which I could not distinguish.

"By degrees my eyes became accustomed to the darkness,
and I saw that the figure against the wall was Bertha.   I
called her by name.   She started, and sprang toward me.
'Who are you?' she exclaimed.

"'I am your brother Ulrich, Bertha,' I answered.

"'Oh, I am so glad, Ulrich, dear Ulrich!' she replied.
'Then you are with me in heaven?   I thought the spirit
would not have spoken falsely to me.   But where are my
father and mother and Fritz?   See! here are their bodies;
but their spirits, Ulrich, their spirits,—where are they?   Did
you not pass them on your way here?'

"'Their bodies!   Oh, Bertha, what have you done?' I
exclaimed, bursting into tears.

"'Why, Ulrich, are you not happy?   Come to me, dear
brother!   Come and I will tell you how I pleased the angels, and how I am now a spirit.   Oh, I have acted so

nobly, and they tell me so every moment! I was fearful you were never coming, and I felt lonely even here. But now I am so happy. Hark! Here come our dear friends. No! They would not tread so loudly. The demons are coming again to try and drag me away. They were here a little while ago, but I would not go with them, and the angels sent them away without me.'

"I heard the tread of many feet near the door. It was opened suddenly, and a number of persons bearing lights entered. I recognized among them several old retainers of the estate. I quickly made myself known, and with axes and crow-bars they soon burst in the panel and released me from my prison. As I entered the room, Bertha rushed toward me, but I heeded her not. I prostrated myself beside the dead body of my mother, and gave way to the anguish of my heart. No one disturbed me. All respected my grief, and stood in solemn silence around me. Among the number assembled were several officers of justice, who were commencing preparations for an inquiry into the horrible events which had taken place. After I had become more calm, one of them approached me, and addressing me as baron, desired me to relate what I knew of the awful murders which had been perpetrated. I did so, concealing nothing. I told all from the moment I first became aware of the priest's influence over Bertha. The latter, during the recital, remained silent. When I had finished, she stooped down and took a paper from my father's hand, which till now no one had noticed. She handed it to one of the officers. 'Read it,' she said; 'it is his passport to heaven.' He took it, and having glanced over it, desired silence, and read aloud, as follows:

"'Paulus de Hutten, nineteen years have passed since you injured me. Nineteen long and weary years, during which I have suffered every moment more anguish than you could feel in a century. Do you remember Frederica Giesler? You start, and well you may, for though she lived in your memory but for a few short days, now that the icy hand of death has grasped your heart, you do not find it difficult to recollect her and the wrong she endured at your hands.

"'I loved her. She was my betrothed. You knew this, and yet with a base exercise of the power you possessed,

you robbed her of her purity, and left her a blighted and a
wretched being. She died in my arms broken-hearted. You
smiled when you heard of it, while my mind became so
much deranged, that for months my reason was considered
lost.

"'I recovered, and then I vowed never to forgive your
wickedness. I had my own wrongs to redress and Frederica's memory to avenge. I entered the church, for I had
no other earthly object in view than the vengeance I had
sworn, and as your chaplain I would possess unbounded
opportunity for its accomplishment.

"'For nineteen years the sword has been suspended over
your head, and now it has fallen.

"'In a happy moment I conceived the plan which has
now been carried out. I induced you to consent that Bertha
should be educated by me. By the agency of means she
could not resist, I obtained a complete ascendancy over her
mind. I changed her whole nature, poisoned her heart
against all her family, told her you had injured me,-and at
length brought her to glory in the idea of your destruction.
She has poisoned you, your wife and sons. Yes, your own
daughter, Baron de Hutten, is my avenger! And she!
Think you I could allow her to escape? Ere twelve hours
have elapsed, she will be a raving maniac. All this I have
done. You have now had an exhibition of my power. Is
it equal to yours?

"'Paulus de Hutten, I speak to you for the last time.
You are dying, no human power can save you. Take one
more look at your wife and children, and in the hell to which
you are going, remember

"'RUDOLPH FOLTZ!'

"His prophecy was fulfilled. Bertha was that night removed to a mad-house, where she died, after the lapse of a
few months, unsconscious to the last that she had been deceived. For her there was the forgetfulness and rest which
the spirit promised.

"I became Baron de Hutten. The estate belonging to
the title was held in trust for me by a guardian appointed
by the Emperor, and soon after the sad occurrences I have
related, I went to the University at Vienna. Now comes
the second great episode in my life.

"Time, that great assuager of sorrow, at last softened my grief, and I tried to draw the veil of forgetfulness over events by which I had been deprived of my natural guides and protectors. In this I succeeded to a very great extent. Young in years and ardent in disposition, I sought the companionship of the joyous and light-hearted, and with them plunged into the dissipations which so frequently attend upon a student's life. Being plentifully supplied with money, I had little trouble in finding amusements or in getting associates for any wild excesses into which I launched. I neglected my studies, was rarely present in the lecture-rooms, and, in fact, almost entirely lost sight of the duty I owed to perfect my·understanding and make myself fit for the responsible position which ere long would devolve upon me.

"But one thing I never forgot. In the midst of all my dissipation, I remembered the language which had been addressed to Father Rudolph by the spirit he had evoked. 'You will satisfy your vengeance; you will fulfill their destiny, and one of their blood will fulfill yours;' and I waited as patiently as I could for the opportunity which was to satisfy my desire for vengeance, and at the same time rid the world of a monster too vile to incumber it with his presence.

"In the course of time I became of age, and returned to my home as its master. Here, quitting my wild associates, I gave myself up to study, and rarely saw persons of any class of life other than those who lived on the estate. There was a fine library in the castle, and the many searches which I instituted, resulted in my finding numbers of old and valuable books concealed in the closets and great oaken chests with which the castle abounded. It was thus that I became possessed of many of the books of my illustrious ancestor, the great Ulrich de Hutten, and of several very valuable manuscripts, 'written with his own hand,' as the colophon invariably said.

"It was two days before I first saw you, Severne, in Frankfort, that I was sitting in my library deeply engaged upon a literary labor I had undertaken. It was a history of heresy in all religions, a work of so vast a character, and requiring so much study and research, that I am astounded now that I should ever have thought of it. I had been working at it all night; for it is a peculiarity of my temperament, that

when once I have entered upon a line of thought, I cannot
stop till I have carried it through to the end.   I felt an un-
wonted activity of mind, my ideas flowed rapidly, and I was
conscious that never before had I done such honor to my
reasoning faculties as in the remarks I had made during the
last twenty-four hours on Lucilio Vanini, who, as you both
well know, suffered a cruel death at the hands of those who
assume to themselves the office of the defenders of the
majesty of God, and whose intolerant spirit is still abroad
in the world.   I did not feel in the slightest degree exhausted with my labors, although I had not slept for nearly
forty-eight hours, nor tasted a morsel of food during that
time.   As I have said, my mind was never clearer or more
active.   I am thus particular, because I know you will form
the opinion that in what I am about to relate, I was the
victim of a hallucination.   The sequel will abundantly show
that such was not the case.

"I was thus deep in the subject I have mentioned, and
had just finished a sentence laudatory of Vanini, when happening to raise my eyes from the paper before me, I saw the
figure of a man, clothed in the garb of a student, standing
immediately in front of me, and regarding me with an expression of intense interest.   He was rather above than
below the medium height, wore a long pointed beard, had
light curly hair, a fair complexion, and large eyes of a dark-
blue color, which were deeply placed in his head, and which
had a most benignant though melancholy expression.

"I would have risen from my seat, but with a gesture my
visitor desired me to be still, and then in a low tone said:

"'Ulrich de Hutten, time flows rapidly on, and in the
midst of the events it brings, you have forgotten the one
great duty you owe your race.'

"I started up with surprise, but I answered him calmly.

"'I have not forgotten it.   I am waiting for the opportunity of performing it.'

"'You are the only one of your blood now on the earth
in the flesh, and I am here to give you the opportunity you
say you long for.   Will you take it?   Will you give up till
the decrees of fate are accomplished, the labors upon which
you are now wearing away your life?'

"'Who are you?' I asked.

"'The spirit of Ulrich de Hutten, returned to earth to guide you in a work which must not be forgotten.'

"'And you, a great portion of whose life was passed in study, ask me to renounce habits and inclinations which have become almost a part of my nature.'

"'To what did similar habits lead me?—Oh, Ulrich, my son, listen to the warning of one whose experience of mankind has rarely been equaled by mortal beings. Why should you labor for them? Why spend your days and nights in striving to improve and enlighten them? They will return you nothing but contempt and insult. Your superiors will deride you; your equals will be jealous of your abilities; and your inferiors will disregard what you may say. Who can estimate the heart-burnings, the injuries, the outrages, the misfortunes I might have been spared, if instead of giving my thoughts and actions for the benefit of my fellow-men, I had turned both to my own profit? Ulrich, have you forgotten Rudolph Foltz? He still lives!'

"'I have not. God knows I have not,' I exclaimed, all my thirst for vengeance returning. 'Tell me where he is, and then you will see whether or not I recollect him.'

"'Not yet, Ulrich,' said my visitor, smiling. 'The time has not yet come. You will never see him till the hour arrives that gives you his life, but you will be near him continually. Will you place yourself under my guidance till the work is done?'

"'I will,' I answered. 'I swear it before God.'

"'Then listen to me, Ulrich. I accept your oath. Henceforth I will lead you. It will be years before the work can be accomplished, but it is only a question of time. It will be done, and though you will do it, others will aid in the fulfillment of the ordinances of fate. And now the game begins.

"'At the Hotel de Russie, in Frankfort-on-the-Main, in room No. 38, is a gentleman without whose aid you cannot succeed.'"

Severne and Lawrence would have spoken, but de Hutten motioned them to be silent. He continued:

"'He is an Englishman, and a lover of books. Without him you can do nothing.'

"'How can I engage his aid?' I exclaimed. 'I do not even know him.'

"'By attending to my directions. The day before I died, at Steckelberg, I placed under my pillow the only copy in the world of my greatest work, De Facultatum Intellectualium. That copy is now in this Castle of Adlerfels in a recess in the wall of the highest room of the north tower. Exactly twelve feet west of the window and five feet above the floor is a stone which can easily be removed   Behind it is the book.   It was placed there by my nephew Maximilian de Hutten, who found it after my death, and who built this castle.   Take this book to Frankfort to-day, and offer it to the occupant of room No. 38 for two hundred pounds, English money.   It will attract his attention, and he will never forget you.   Farewell till we meet again.'   With these words he faded slowly from my sight.

"I started to my feet with all the energy excited by new-born hopes of vengeance.   I tore into fragments the sheets which I had filled with my thoughts, and I swore never to lose sight of this great object of my life till it was attained. I found the book, as I had been told I would, and immediately started with it for Frankfort, where I arrived the next day.   It was very much against my inclination to offer the book to you.   In the first place, I wanted it myself, and in the next, I did not like the idea of being a hawker.   Still, I had sworn obedience, and there was nothing for me to do but to be faithful to my oath.   When I met you I studied your countenance and manner closely, and I was pleased with both.   I was also inwardly delighted when you asked time for consideration before purchasing the book, and still more -so when that night my mentor appeared to me and told me not to sell the book, that the object had been accomplished, and that there would be use for it again.   At the same time he gave me the letter which I brought you the next day, and in disposing of which as I did I followed his directions implicitly.

"I returned to Adlerfels, and soon afterward again received a visit from the spirit of my illustrious ancestor. 'Rudolph Foltz,' he said, 'is now in Vienna.   He still possesses the talisman which is essential to our success, and which, therefore, you must obtain.   He resides on the fifth floor of No. 659, Dorotheergasse.   He keeps the talisman in a tin box, which is hidden under the floor.   As you enter

his room you will observe a spot of ink on one of the
boards of the floor near the hearth. Raise this and you
will find the box. On the seventh of the present month he
will forget to lock his room door, and will go to the theater
at eight o'clock. Then will be your opportunity.'

"It was then the third. The next morning I took my
departure for Vienna. I well knew the value of the talisman I had seen Foltz use, for I had studied the subject
thoroughly since the event which deprived me of every one
of my kin. I knew that while I wore it he could not harm
me, and that through it I could always discover his whereabouts.

"I found everything as had been foretold, and returned to
Adlerfels. I would have remained in Vienna, and there
have ended the matter, but I was told that the time had not
yet arrived.

"Time rolled on, and several years elapsed, during which
I received many visits from my guide. He always told me
that Foltz was suffering great anguish of mind, and was
roaming over the world, fearful of being discovered by me.
This was a part of his punishment which the spirit of my ancestor seemed to take great pleasure in contemplating. 'I
know what it is,' he would say; 'I have fled from my persecutors, suffering in a just cause. Foltz flies, imagining
that he is pursued, and writhing under the reproaches of a
guilty conscience. Now he is in Tartary; now in India;
now in Algiers; now in England. The hour approaches,
Ulrich. Action will soon be required.'

"On the tenth of last June the spirit appeared again.
'Take the talisman,' he said, 'and use it as you saw Foltz
use it. My office is ended; for the future you will have a
higher guide than I am. Farewell for the present. We
will meet once more, and then I shall go to rest.'

"I did as I was directed, and evoked the old man who
had appeared at Foltz's bidding.

"'Your enemy is in America,' he said. 'Take with you
the great book your ancestor wrote and go to New York.
You will there be told what to do.'

"I at once made arrangements for a long absence; and
leaving Europe as soon as possible, arrived in New York
early in July. Here I had another interview with the spirit

of the talisman, and was told to take the book to Mr. Holmes's book-shop and leave it there for the former occupant of room No. 38, Hotel de Russie, Frankfort, who would find it, and buy it at the price previously asked. I did so, and everything resulted as I had been told it would. I was then informed that you, Severne, were going to cross the prairies, and I was told to join your party. I was ordered to go to St. Louis and Fort Leavenworth, and await you at the latter place. Here I had a long conference with the spirit, and was then informed that Rudolph Foltz had joined a band of Indians, and that I would meet him on the prairies. Another interview resulted in my being told that he was with the Cheyennes, that he called himself Long Knife, and that we would meet west of the Black Hills. You know the rest. How he tried to kill me, and that I, protected by the talisman, slew him like a dog. That is all. His destiny is fulfilled, and as to mine—who knows what it will be?"

"My dear de Hutten," said Severne, "yours is a most remarkable story, and I sympathize with you in all the sorrows you have passed through, and admire the fortitude and courage you have shown. I do not know what to think of the supernatural agencies you have dwelt upon. Certain it is that whether they were real or not, their predictions have met with a wonderful amount of fulfillment."

"It is all very astonishing," said Lawrence. "I thought at first you were the victim of a hallucination, but I cannot think so now, and have no explanation to suggest. At any rate, de Hutten, you have triumphed, and I am glad of it. You will now be able to resume your history of heresy."

"Yes, I shall go back to Adlerfels and go to work again. I shall never, however, forget your friendship and the many favors you have both done me. And though Severne has been an unconscious aider and abettor in my designs, I am not the less obliged to him. As to this talisman, I have been directed to throw it into a deep pond situated near Bridger's Pass, not far from a high table-land, and not to use it again. Of course I shall obey, as I have in all other things."

Six days subsequently they approached the break in the Rocky Mountains called Bridger's Pass. A high table-land on the left of the road attracted attention, and thither de

Hutten went in search of the pond. He climbed the steep ridges, covered with pine-trees, and at last reached an eminence from which he could look down into deep gorges and ravines into which the foot of man had probably never entered. Far down at the bottom of one of these he descried a pond, fed by the rills of snow-water which trickled along the steep, rocky sides of quartz and granite. De Hutten descended as far as he could with safety. He stood upon a ledge of rock which overhung the pond and looked down into its depths. It was as clear as crystal, and, judging by the declivity of the sides, perhaps fifty feet deep. Taking the talisman from his breast, he unfastened it from the chain and looked at it fixedly for a few moments; then, pressing it to his lips, he let it drop from his hand, and in an instant it had disappeared from his sight forever.

<hr>

CHAPTER XXVI.

IN WHICH MR. FREELING DISCOVERS THAT HE CANNOT HAVE EVERY-
THING HIS OWN WAY.

AFTER a month spent at Lake George, during which John Holmes, Margaret, and Grace Langley—who was also of the party—became much more warmly attached to Sarah than before, preparations were begun for a return to New York. Sarah was of course delighted with the idea of going to Europe, and she and Margaret promised themselves the most intense gratification in the new life which would then be open to them. The young ladies had gone out boating on the lake with a very pleasant party, and John Holmes sat alone in a corner of the hotel piazza which faced the water, looking out on the lovely prospect before him, and thinking that the time had come for telling Sarah of her relationship to Margaret and himself. He had just arrived at the conclusion that he would do so that evening, when he heard his name called, and turning his head he saw Mr.

Freeling standing near him. John Holmes knew nothing of him except that he was Severne's agent, but having seen him once or twice before, he had conceived a great dislike to him, a thing that John Holmes often did toward disagreeable people at a very early stage of his intercourse with them.

Mr. Freeling was not naturally a polite man. He frequently, however, felt it advisable to affect politeness, as he did other virtues, so he touched his hat to John Holmes and expressed his great pleasure at meeting him again, away from the heat, the dust, and the foul air of a large city.

John Holmes made an indifferent reply, but did not express any delight at seeing Mr. Freeling.

"I have come here," said the latter, "not only for purposes of relaxation, but also to see you on some important business which concerns you. Will you therefore please to allow me a few minutes' conversation with you?"

"I cannot imagine what it can be, but of course I am at your service, Mr. Freeling. Shall we walk along the lake and discuss it?"

"A very admirable suggestion that of yours, Mr. Holmes. I can always talk better when I am walking than under other circumstances.

"I am Mr. Severne's agent, as you may know," said Mr. Freeling, as they reached the road that ran along the shore; "but circumstances which have come to my knowledge make it necessary that I should resign my situation. I shall accordingly do so to-morrow. These circumstances are of such a nature as to prevent any one having a regard for his own character continuing a connection with Mr. Severne. It is out of consideration for you and your granddaughter that I have deemed it my duty to put you on your guard against forming one."

"I do not know to what you can allude, Mr. Freeling. Of course you are at perfect liberty to do as you please; but there is nothing you can say to me that would induce me to change the opinion I have formed of Robert Severne."

"That is all very well, Mr. Holmes. It is just what I expected you to say; exactly what I would have said myself if any one had come to me about a friend as I have to you. We cannot be too cautious how we credit tales to the disadvantage of our friends; but there is such a thing as positive proof, evidence which admits of no doubt, and this is the kind I have to offer you."

"I shall not attempt, Mr. Freeling," said John Holmes, with a contemptuous smile, "to fathom your objects in this matter. I take it for granted, however, that you are not altogether disinterested. As to evidence in any case against Robert Severne, it would have to be of the very strongest character to convince me. I do not think anything less than his own confession of wrong conduct would satisfy me of his guilt."

"Right again, Mr. Holmes," said Mr. Freeling, with animation. "A person whose character has—in this country at least—been as high as Mr. Robert Severne's, should not be liable to the loss of his good name except upon overwhelming evidence. There are cases indeed in which our faith may properly be so strong as not to be shaken by anything short of ocular demonstration or a confession. It is this latter which, among other proofs of Mr. Severne's criminality, I have to submit to you."

"Very well, Mr. Freeling. Here comes my granddaughter, to whom you may also unfold your budget, as you have ascertained, in some way or other best known to yourself, that Mr. Severne's reputation is not a matter of indifference to her. Whatever you have to tell me is therefore of tenfold importance to her."

"Certainly, my dear sir; there is not the least objection to Miss Leslie being also informed in regard to Mr. Severne's real character. On the contrary, as it is with the view of saving her that I am induced to make the communication, it is desirable that the purport of it should reach her through first hands."

Margaret, Sarah, and Grace were coming up the shore in company with several ladies and gentlemen, and John Holmes, leaving Mr. Freeling, went forward to meet them, and returned accompanied by Margaret alone.

"Take my arm, my dear child," he said. "This gentleman, who is Mr. Severne's agent, has some information to communicate which I am anxious you should hear."

"I *am* Mr. Severne's agent," said Mr. Freeling, with a

strong accent on the verb, "but will not be to-morrow. I
have become acquainted with facts which render such a relation between us impossible, and—if I may be allowed to
say so—when a rough man of the world like me finds it im-
proper to act as agent for Mr. Severne, there need be no
difficulty in so upright and refined a lady as Miss Leslie
severing any connection she may have formed with him."

"Grandpapa," said Margaret, her face flushing with
honest anger, "I cannot believe you would ask me here to
listen to such insults. You surely did not know what this
man was going to say?"

"Hush! my dear child," said John Holmes, taking her
hand, which trembled with indignation, and which she was
in the act of withdrawing from his arm. "You know that
Robert Severne's good name cannot suffer in my estimation
by anything his enemies may say. I brought you here, my
darling, to hear and to answer, and thus to end a matter at
once which otherwise might linger on for a long time. Now,
Mr. Freeling, will you proceed with your communication?"

"As rapidly as possible. Several years ago Mr. Severne's
wife died under circumstances which caused him to be suspected of taking her life He was not arrested, for there
was no proof sufficiently strong to fasten the guilt upon him.
That proof is now in my possession, and it is my painful
duty to inform you, Mr. Holmes, and you, Miss Leslie, that
Mr. Robert Severne is a murderer!"

Mr. Freeling communicated the words of his charge in
the most emphatic manner, and with all due solemnity of
tone. John Holmes was prepared for a grave accusation,
not, however, to the extent of murder, but he controlled his
emotion almost perfectly. Margaret's hand started slightly
in his as she heard the words, but she had thought in an instant of her first and last interviews with Severne, and her
boundless faith and love coming to her rescue, she would
have died rather than have willingly betrayed the least excitement or anxiety to the man who was watching her every
look and motion in the hope of detecting some evidence of
agony too great to be concealed. What she felt was anger,
hot, passionate anger, the anger that would have prompted
her to strike the base accuser of Robert Severne dead at her
feet had she been endowed with the physical strength to carry

out her will. She said nothing, but the flashing of her eyes, the crimson hue which overspread her face, the quivering of her lips, and the quick, heavy throbbing of her heart showed what she felt. They were not exactly the feelings which Mr. Freeling had hoped to arouse.

"I perceive," said Mr. Freeling, after a slight pause, during which he had waited in vain for some remark from John Holmes or Margaret, "that like most bearers of unwelcome intelligence, I am in danger of gaining a vast amount of ill will. I shall therefore hurry through the matter as rapidly as possible. It is not at all difficult for me to see that you attach very little importance to what I have said, except to accuse me in your hearts of having perpetrated a vile and malignant slander. You are both acquainted, I presume, with Mr. Severne's handwriting?"

Margaret made no reply; John Holmes answered in the affirmative.

"I presume, then, if I show you Mr. Robert Severne's confession, written and signed with his own hand, you will credit my assertion that he is a murderer?"

"Never!" said Margaret, calmly, but with all the firmness of which she was mistress. "Not even if I saw him write it. I would doubt his intellect rather than I would his honor."

"That's all very pretty, Miss Leslie, and quite romantic. Now——"

"Stop, sir!" said John Holmes, interrupting him. "I did not bring my granddaughter here for you to talk to her. Please, therefore, address your conversation to me."

"Well, Mr. Holmes," rejoined Freeling, "I don't think I have anything more to say. The rest will be best said by Mr. Severne himself. Will you be kind enough to read that letter?" So saying, he handed to John Holmes the letter he had abstracted from Severne's port-folio.

John Holmes, with a steady voice, read aloud as follows:

June 28th.

MY DEAR LAWRENCE:

It is said that an honest confession is good for the soul. I hope my soul will be benefited when I acknowledge to you that I admit myself to be guilty of my wife's death. I

am her murderer. I no longer wish to make a secret of it.
I am now suffering the torments of the damned.

Yours, in utter despair,
ROBERT SEVERNE.

Margaret listened to every word of this note. How to
explain it she did not know, but it had no more effect in
making her believe Robert Severne to be a murderer than
if it had been bnt the empty wind.

John Holmes gave the paper back to Mr. Freeling.

"It is in Mr. Severne's handwriting throughout," he said.
"You have been as good as your word. But I nevertheless
do not believe your accusation to be true."

"And you, Miss Leslie?" said Freeling.

"You have had my answer. I have nothing further to
say."

"Very well, you will probably ere long read of Mr. Robert
Severne's execution at Newgate for murder," said Freeling,
with a disappointed air. "I have tried to warn you. Now
I shall take this to England, and as soon as our friend
reaches civilized society he will be arrested."

Mr. Freeling retraced his steps, and walking rapidly, was
soon out of sight.

John Holmes and Margaret walked on in silence for several minutes. At last he said :

"I was thinking, my dear child, how brave and faithful
you are. There are few persons who would not have yielded
in the face of evidence like that. It almost staggers me, I
must confess, and I cannot attempt to understand it. The
writing is certainly Severne's."

"It makes no difference whether he wrote it or not," said
Margaret. "It bears internal evidence of error, for if Mr.
Severne had been seized with a sudden fit of remorse, he
would never have written a letter like that. But I do not
intend to descend to the point of reasoning on the subject.
I know, as well as I know of my own existence, that Robert
Severne is not a murderer, and but for the annoyance which
I see that wicked man will give him, I should care nothing
for all this."

"But, my dear child," said her grandfather, kindly, "we
ought to reason upon the matter, for I think that by so

doing we will be able to arrive at a satisfactory solution. I shall go immediately and see Wilson, who is still at Severne's house, and make some inquiries. In the mean time, my darling, we will both retain undiminished confidence,—I in my friend, and you in one who is more than a friend."

"I have heard Grace Langley speak of this man," said Margaret. "She has told me how he treated her mother, and how Mr. Severne thwarted him in his villainy. I am sure he has devised this as a scheme of revenge."

"It is very evident that he is actuated by vindictive motives. But that will not prevent the evidence he has in his possession from having great weight. We must endeavor to counteract him, not for our own satisfaction, but for Severne's safety. The letter is addressed to Dr. Lawrence. If it was sent, he understands the whole matter; if it was not, Freeling must have taken it from Severne's house, and in that case Wilson may know something about it."

"Do you think, dear grandpapa, that harm can come to Mr. Severne from anything that man can do?" said Margaret, anxiously. "Ought we not at once to put him on his guard?"

"I will not conceal from you, my dear child, that that letter, unexplained, and supported by suspicious circumstances, would lead to very serious results. I am very sure Severne has had trouble of some kind in England,—what I do not know; but as Dr. Lawrence knew him then, he is probably acquainted with its character. It is almost impossible for us to communicate with him before this man sets his schemes in operation. The last letter you had from him was dated San Francisco, just before he sailed for Calcutta. He said in that to write to him in future at the latter place. This man will take such steps as he contemplates at once, and they will doubtless be of such a character as to interfere with any we might propose. However, Severne will not try to avoid an investigation, I know."

"I will go myself," said Margaret, "as soon as we return to New York, and see what this man has been doing in Mr. Severne's house. Dear grandpapa, we must defeat the scheme of this wicked man."

"Be of good heart, my dear Margaret, we will defeat him. His discomfiture has already begun, for he had high hopes

of being able to poison our minds against Severne, and he
is conscious of failure. Depend upon it, too, that he has
given us all the proof he has in his possession. He imagines
there is more, but he does not know it. There may be evidence in Severne's favor which all the confessions in the
world could not overturn. Such a paper as this man has, unless corroborated, would be utterly worthless. As you say,
the letter is not one that a man like Severne, in full possession of his senses, would have written. It is such a document as I should suspect a person laboring under great excitement would have indited. Do not brood over this sorrow,
my darling, but with a firm, true, and faithful heart, look
forward with confidence to its being cleared up to his honor."

"Oh, my dearest!" said Margaret, as she sat that night
at her bed-room window, looking out upon the calm, but
tremulous lake, which gleamed in the moonlight like molten
silver. "Oh, my dearest, you surely thought of this when
you told me to believe in your truth and honor through all
the evil reports which might come! I do believe. God,
who sees my heart, knows that with unbroken confidence
and undiminished love it is yours as truly and as firmly as
when I gave it to you. My darling! my darling!" she
continued, passionately, "you knew when I pledged my
faith to you that I spoke the truth, and you will see how I
will keep my word!"

She raised her eyes to heaven, as if to implore God's protection for him she loved, and then she laid her head upon
her pillow and closed her eyes, with her heart untouched by
a doubt or a fear, or her soul tarnished by the shadow of a
suspicion.

CHAPTER XXVII.

IN WHICH MARGARET AND SARAH DISCOVER THE REASON WHY THEY HAD FALLEN IN LOVE WITH EACH OTHER AT FIRST SIGHT.

JOHN HOLMES was not in the humor that evening for revealing to Margaret and Sarah the relationship which existed between them. But the next morning, while the two girls sat on a rustic bench in the woods, whence—though in a great measure secluded from the observation of idle loungers—they could see the bright, broad expanse of the lovely lake, with its green banks, and its mountains in the background, he joined them for the purpose of carrying out an intention which he felt had already been too long deferred.

- "I have been looking for you two young ladies this half hour," he said, smiling, as he took the place they made for him between them. "What could have induced you to hide yourselves in this out-of-the-way corner?"

"Grace is busy packing," said Margaret, "and Sarah and I stole off here for a little quiet reading and talking. She is so much interested in her book, however, that I cannot get a word out of her that does not relate to it. I think she's in love with Captain Cuttle," continued Margaret, with an affectation of malice, and in a whisper intended for Sarah to hear. "With Captain Cuttle or Uncle Sol, I am not quite sure which."

Sarah laid aside her book when John Holmes addressed them. Three months had made a great difference in her, and no one would have suspected from her appearance and manners that she had not always been used to refined society. Her figure was tall and graceful, and had lost the angularities which are so characteristic of an irregular life. She was dressed in white Swiss muslin, her dark-brown hair was looped up in curls, and on her head was one of the prettiest little hats that ever bedecked a young lady's *chevelure*. The expression of her features had become more sedate and thoughtful. It was not melancholy or even grave, and so far from detracting from her beauty, harmonized admirably with her dark-brown eyes and clear, rich *brunette* complexion. Nothing could have shown better the impressibility of her character than the fact that in so short a time she had apparently lost all the traits which her former associations had engrafted upon her. If Severne could have seen her then, even he would have been astonished at the progress his ward had made.

The matter which John Holmes had in hand was a delicate one. It was not his intention to spend much time over it, however. Already the relations between the two girls were of the most affectionate character, and what he had to say need not therefore be prolonged by words calculated to develop a feeling which would take good care of itself. During the time they had been at Lake George, he had seen a good deal of Sarah, and had busied himself in studying her disposition and character. He had noticed her great desire to learn everything which could be of advantage to her; with what rapidity she had acquired those little graces of person and mind which give so great a charm to a woman, and how, in all her intercourse with him and with others, her demeanor was always that of a well-bred lady. He had ascertained too from Margaret and Grace Langley many little circumstances relative to her behavior in private, which otherwise would not have come to his knowledge, but which convinced him that she was in no danger of losing the ground she had gained, and had caused him to entertain for her a regard second only to that which he had for Margaret.

"I am sure," he said, in reply to Margaret's remark, "that there are few characters in real life more worthy of love than Captain Cuttle and Uncle Sol. I am glad, Sarah, that such old fellows are favorites of yours, for I am going to ask you to look in future with favor upon another one, who, if not so good, is older than either of them,—and that is myself."

"Why, grandpapa," said Margaret, laughing, "you are so serious about it that Sarah will think you are proposing to her. Don't take him, Sarah. To think of a man pleading his great age when he makes a declaration of love!"

Sarah was about to speak, but John Holmes interrupting her, continued:

"Among the last things that Mr. Severne did before his departure was to make a discovery which gave both him and myself a great deal of pleasure. A number of letters written by your father, my dear Margaret, came into his possession. They were addressed to Sarah's mother, and established the fact beyond the possibility of a doubt, when taken in connection with other circumstances, that you are half-sisters. Richard Leslie was the father of you both."

It would be impossible to describe the surprise which this announcement created in the two girls. There was no boisterous affectation of pleasure. Both understood that such a relationship was not unaccompanied by shame, but both were glad for their own sakes that a nearer tie than any they had dreamed of united them. Margaret was the first to recover her equanimity. She put her arms round Sarah's neck, and, kissing her, said: "I am very glad. Now I know why I have always loved you so dearly." Sarah could only return her embrace in silence, for the feelings excited in her breast were so strong as to overpower her in her attempts to give utterance to the great joy which filled her heart. John Holmes thought it best to leave them alone for a few moments, and so, while they were locked in each other's arms, he quietly slipped off, and did not return till he judged the first ebullition of emotion had subsided. When he rejoined them, he found them with their hands clasped together and their faces full of that sad, sober satisfaction which the intelligence they had received could not but awaken in them. Neither asked for any further explanation. Both were content to know that they were sisters, without wishing to be informed in regard to details which they instinctively felt could but detract from their joy.

John Holmes sat down beside Sarah, and taking her hand, bent over and kissed her forehead. He told her that not only was Margaret her sister, but that he had claims to being regarded as her grandfather which she must not overlook. "You are a dear, sweet girl," he said; "I shall always love you, and though I was not able to induce your guardian to give you up to me, I succeeded in getting him to acknowledge my authority to some extent. We therefore made several arrangements which will interest you, and among them one which will cause you to meet with him sooner than you expected when he left us."

"I am very happy," she replied. "I loved Margaret from the first moment I saw her. It is to her that I owe all I am, and everything I can ever hope to be. There was a feeling excited in me by the first meeting with her which it was impossible for me to resist, and which strengthened with every moment of my life. I can understand it now. It must have been because she was my sister. And now she has just told me that my guardian will some day be her husband, and that we will all live together, never to part."

"And what am I to do," said John Holmes, smiling, "if both my grandchildren leave me?"

"You will come with us, dear grandpapa," replied Sarah.

"I certainly shall, if you'll let me. I am getting old enough now to require the services of all my grandchildren in taking care of me."

"You said I would meet my guardian sooner than I expected. Is he coming home? I wrote to him last night, and told him how happy I was; but I must write again to-day and tell him what I now know."

"We will go to him. It was settled between us that you were to accompany Margaret and me to Europe, where we will meet him."

"I am very glad of that too. I do not wish ever to be separated from you."

Grace Langley was now seen approaching them. As she came nearer they saw that she was laboring under some excitement, for she walked very fast, and her countenance showed anything but a quiet frame of mind.

"I have just parted from Mr. Freeling," she said. "I would have been here an hour ago, but he joined me on my way, and I could not get rid of him, as he threatened to accompany me, and I knew you would not want to meet such a man. If I had known Mr. Holmes was with you, I should not have hesitated. He has been trying to frighten me by telling me a very ridiculous story about Mr. Severne, which I do not for a moment believe, and then he told me what I really hope is true Ah, I see it is true!" she continued, kissing Margaret and Sarah. "I am so glad!"

"I do not know how Mr. Freeling knew it," said John

Holmes. "He seems to have been prying into Mr. Severne's affairs in a most unwarrantable manner. Yes, Miss Grace, Margaret and Sarah are half-sisters."

"Then she is Sarah Leslie?"

"I think she will prefer to be called Sarah Severne, as her guardian desired she should be."

"Oh, yes; I never knew my father nor mother. I owe a thousand times more to him than to them."

"You are right, Sarah," said Margaret, in a whisper. "I will tell you very soon all I know of our father."

"What could Mr. Freeling have had to say against my guardian?" continued Sarah.

"Never mind, my dear child," said John Holmes. "He unburdened his mind to Margaret and me last evening, and you see it has not disturbed us. Don't let us think about him or his stories now. After our return to New York, we will hold a family council over the matter, and set ourselves to work to defeat his schemes."

As they were on their way back to the hotel, a carriage in which sat Mr. Freeling passed them, driven at full speed. He looked out of the window, and recognizing them, bowed with a sort of determined expression on his countenance, which seemed meant to assure them of his unaltered intentions.

"The game is not yet yours," said John Holmes to himself, as he looked at the carriage, without returning Mr. Freeling's salute. "It is perhaps as well that you should understand that war has been declared and accepted. You have undertaken to hang our friend, and we are determined to establish his innocence. May God defend the right!"

It was settled that as the voyage to Europe would be commenced in less than two weeks, Sarah should till then remain nominally with the Langleys, though it was at the same time expected that the greater portion of her time would be passed with her newly-found relations. This, and various other plans growing out of the circumstances of their relative positions, were discussed that evening. Grace informed John Holmes of Mr. Freeling's antecedents as far as she knew of them, and the information she communicated not only touched upon some of the more striking features of this gentleman's character, but likewise indicated a motive for his animosity toward Severne.   John Holmes knew, upon reflection, that the source of Freeling's information in regard to Sarah's parentage must have been the letters which Severne had replaced in the drawer, of which he, John Holmes, had the key.   It was very evident then that Severne's privacy had been invaded, and he looked forward to his return to New York throwing a good deal of light upon the whole subject.   The next morning at an early hour the whole party took their departure from Lake George, and ere nightfall were comfortably settled in their respective homes.

CHAPTER XXVIII.

UT AMERIS AMABILIS ESTO.

THE longer John Holmes reflected upon the charge which Mr. Freeling had made against Severne, the more he was convinced of its absurdity.   Why the latter should have written such a letter as had been shown to him he could not possibly discover, and there was no one in New York who could give him such information in regard to Severne's previous history as might have elucidated the subject.   He had a long conference with Goodall over the affair, and though both agreed that Severne had undergone trouble of some kind, neither for a moment doubted that he had done his whole duty in any trials to which he might have been subjected.

"I cannot imagine, though," said Goodall, "why he should confess to having perpetrated an act from which I am sure his whole soul would revolt. You say the date of the letter was the 28th of June.   Now I know that about that time, and for several months previous, he was deeply engrossed with his studies.   You may recollect that on the occasion of his sending an order here for a number of books, not one of which we had, you were struck with the singular fact that they were nearly all on hallucinations, dreams, visions, and the like. It was just about the time this letter must have been written."

"I remember it well, and the circumstance may be a clew to the solution of what is now a mystery. He may have written that letter in his sleep, for all we know; stranger things than that have been done in that condition. Maury tells us that he knew a gentleman, possessed of a very gentle disposition, who often dreamed that he had killed people. It is very probable that Severne does not even know of the existence of this confession."

"I recollect now," answered Goodall, "that it was on the 1st of July that Severne came here, the first time in many weeks, and got the Ulrich de Hutten. You may remember that it was that night that the attempted burglary took place. I remarked then that he looked as if he had been ill, so very much was his appearance altered. And a few days afterward I met Dr. Lawrence, and he told me, in answer to my inquiries, that Severne had seriously impaired his health by too close application to study, and that he was going to travel with a view to its amendment. Now I know, as the result of my own excessive intellectual exertion, that hallucinations of various kinds occur to me. I fancy that I have done things of the most out-of-the-way character, which never, by any possibility, could have really occurred. I always, however, take those visionary ideas as serious warnings, and for a time suspend all mental labor."

"There may be a good deal in what you say. I am going this evening to Severne's house, where I shall question the servants closely. I think it is important to collect all the evidence I can, have it properly authenticated, and take it with me to Europe. I am very sure Mr. Freeling intends to have Severne arrested, and I know the latter will do all he can to facilitate an investigation. I shall write to him at once and inform him of what has transpired."

Before leaving the shop, John Holmes wrote to Severne, giving him a full account of all that Mr. Freeling had said, and assuring him of the undiminished confidence with which he regarded him. He also told him of Margaret's and Goodall's unchanged feeling—a duty he might have spared himself, as far as she was concerned, for that young lady had written for herself before she left Lake George, and her letter was already far on its way across the ocean—and of the fact that she and Sarah were happy in the knowledge that they were sisters.

"We shall leave here," he wrote, "on the 22d of this month, and will be in Paris by the 20th of November. I shall bring with me such evidence as I can collect and as I think will be useful to you. I do not suppose it will be possible for you, using all dispatch, to reach that city before the 1st of January. Of course you will hurry forward as soon as possible to meet this atrocious charge. Do not forget that thus far your enemy has met with a signal failure. It will require something more than your own confession to make us believe that you have done this wrong."

As soon as he had concluded and mailed his letter, John Holmes went home, where being joined by Margaret, the two proceeded to Severne's house. Margaret had made several visits to the library and picture-gallery since their owner's absence, and therefore was well known to Mrs. Smith, the housekeeper, who had received instructions from Severne both in regard to her and John Holmes. Inquiries being made for Wilson, Mrs. Smith informed them that he had gone out, but would be back in a moment, and John Holmes and Margaret ascended to the library to await his return.

When they reached the room, John Holmes opened the drawer in which Severne had placed the letters relating to Sarah, and found them apparently undisturbed. He was about to close it again, when his eye was attracted by a sleeve-button lying half-concealed by a paper. He picked it up and examined it. It was a small gold button, of odd, rough workmanship, of the kind that several years ago were brought from New Mexico and California. On the top was the letter F, formed of very small garnets. John Holmes at once arrived at the conclusion that Mr. Freeling had dropped this from his sleeve, and had gone away without at the time being aware of his loss. It was therefore important as one link in the chain of evidence he wished to . get together.

While he was showing it to Margaret, Wilson entered the room. John Holmes informed him that it had become important to ascertain in what frame of mind his master had been on and about the 28th of June last, and to obtain information in regard to any occurrences which took place at that time. It was not long before Wilson was enabled to recall the circumstances of that period, and he gave a very clear and satisfactory account of them.

"I recollect," he said, "that it was about that time Mrs. Wiggins came to see Mr. Severne for the first time. He had given me orders to allow a woman whom he had been expecting for some time to come up at once, and as she said her business was important I showed her the way and left her at the door. She went in, but she did not stay long; and when she came down into the hall she told me I had better hurry up stairs, as Mr. Severne was not well. She said he had called her Francisca, and addressed her as his wife. I went up and found him very much agitated. He was just about ringing the bell; and as soon as I entered the door he asked me some questions in regard to her. I saw that he took her for a lady, when in fact she was a very coarse-looking woman in every way. The next day, I think in the evening, he rang the bell, and again I found him a good deal excited. He gave me orders about a lady who he supposed had been up stairs, but no person had gone up that evening, for I sat in the hall, and could not have been mistaken. The next night he consulted Dr. Lawrence, and had a long conversation with him. I was sent for, and the doctor asked me some questions, which showed me they had been talking about these things. I heard the doctor say, as I went out of the room, that they were delusions, all of them, and that Mr. Severne was studying too hard."

John Holmes and Margaret listened to Wilson's recital with the most painful interest. Both were sure that Severne had suffered under a temporary mental aberration, due to intense intellectual labor, and that during one of these attacks he had written the letter which Mr. Freeling had taken from the room.

"I am very certain that Mr. Severne was working very hard," continued Wilson. "Frequently he sat up all night in this room reading and writing. I am sure that for a week at a time he has often gone without sleep, or eating anything of consequence."

Having received from Mrs. Smith a full account of the

visits Collins and Mr. Freeling had made to the library, and requesting Wilson to send Mrs. Wiggins to him the next day, John Holmes called to Margaret—who had gone to the shelves, and was looking through the books—and told her it was time for them to go.

Margaret made no reply, but continued to peruse the volume, a small one, which she held in her hand. She was alone with her grandfather, for Wilson and Mrs. Smith, finding that they were no longer required, had left the room. John Holmes seeing her abstraction, approached her and looked over her shoulder. It was a Spanish book, the poems of Calderon de la Barca, which Margaret held in her hand; but though she understood the beautiful language in which these exquisite verses were written, her attention was concentrated on the marginal notes, written in a delicate hand-writing, with which the book abounded. Her quick, hurried respiration, her parted lips, and the straining of her eyes for each word, which in the dim twilight she could scarcely see, showed how absorbing was the interest which had been excited in her.

It was impossible for John Holmes's old eyes to distinguish enough of the writing to make any sense of it, and he was about to walk quietly away and wait till Margaret had completed her study, when she suddenly turned toward him with a look of most intense pleasure and triumph; and holding out the book to him, said :

"There, grandpapa, read that ! I knew Robert Severne was not a murderer. How wonderful, and yet how simple, are the ways that God takes to make the truth known ! Oh, my love," she resumed, as she sank into a chair,—and John Holmes, taking the open volume, walked with it to the window,—"oh, my love, I have never doubted you : this was not needed for me ; but God has heard my prayer, and will make the world acknowledge your innocence and your untarnished honor !"

"My dear child," said John Holmes, as he laid his hand on her fair young head and drew it to his breast, "we who have never faltered in our faith and love, can read these words without surprise and without receiving a single additional assurance of the justice of our convictions. But we have here evidence which does not admit of a question, if this is, as I am confident it is, the handwriting of his late wife. Wretched woman, what a story of guilt and shame is here unfolded, and how bitter must have been the anguish he has endured!"

"And he has borne it as an honest and a true man should," said Margaret, proudly, "with the resolution to live it down; and with a spirit unbroken and a heart unsubdued, to move on through life till God should give him the victory. Dear grandpapa, I never knew how much I loved Robert Severne till now. We were wrong to think this was not needed. It was needed to make me comprehend the full measure of his noble, heroic, and generous nature, a nature that, rather than allow the shadow of a stain to rest on the name of his wicked wife, prompted him to take upon himself the odium of a crime he abhorred. We will take this book with us to England, and the world shall know how self-devoted, how peerless he is. Oh, grandpapa!——" But the tension upon her nervous system was too great for the strained fibers to bear, and bursting into a flood of tears, Margaret laid her head upon John Holmes's shoulder, and sobbed convulsively with the tumult of emotions which swelled within her.

John Holmes did not attempt to restrain her. He knew that her tears welled up from a soul full of womanly pride and the exalted feeling which sprang from the consciousness that she had given her trustful love to a man whose lofty honor was not only free from guilt or stain, but which had led him to prefer the loss of his own good name rather than bring reproach upon the one in all the world who had wronged him most. It was well that she should feel the full force of the impression which had been produced; so he stood in silence, with his arm around her waist, waiting till the passionate utterance of her joys and her hopes should yield to the calmer but not less earnest glow which would shine upon her while life should last.

Margaret's agitation was not of long duration. In a few minutes she had obtained the self-control natural to her, and she and her grandfather went home, happy in the knowledge which the day had given them.

When she got to her own room, Margaret took the volume which contained the evidence that was to overthrow Mr. Freeling's machinations, and carefully sealed it up without reading another line in it. She had seen enough to know that it contained the record of events which she felt should only come to her knowledge through him whom they so intimately concerned.

The next morning, John Holmes received from Mrs. Wiggins a full account, given in her usual circumlocutory manner, of her first interview with Severne. There was no longer the least doubt in his mind, or in Goodall's, to whom he related the details given by Wilson and Mrs. Wiggins, that their friend had labored under a temporary aberration of mind, due to severe intellectual exertion, and that he had written the note to Lawrence during that period. The statements of the two witnesses were written out, sworn to by them before both the British and French consuls, and such other means taken as would insure a fair investigation of the matter.

On the 22d of October, John Holmes, Margaret, and Sarah took their departure from New York in the Arago for Southampton. Goodall was left in charge of the shop and of John Holmes's house, in which latter he was to reside during the absence of the owner. The night before leaving, John Holmes told him of Margaret's engagement to Severne.

"How different are my feelings in regard to this marriage from those which I experienced when my poor child was about to marry Richard Leslie!" he continued. "Then I was full of apprehensions, which were too fully realized; now I am confident that my dear Margaret will be happy."

"She will be happy, depend upon it," replied Goodall. "I have hoped that what you have told me would come to pass. You have given me your confidence, now listen to mine."

The story that Goodall related greatly moved John Holmes, and when it was ended, with a long and loving grasp of hands, they parted, saddened at the recollections that had been awakened, but hopeful for the future of one who was now first in their hearts.

As to Mr. Freeling, immediately on his return to New York from Lake George, he had begun his preparations for the campaign against Severne. Confident that the latter would be convicted of murder, he had, to the utmost of his power, so deranged Severne's business affairs, that when the desired result should be obtained, nothing would be easier than for him to appropriate a large portion of the property to himself. His previous visit to England in Severne's interest had resulted in his forming an acquaintance with a distant relative of Severne, to whom, in the event of the latter's decease without heirs, the estate would descend as the next of kin. It was Mr. Freeling's purpose to visit this individual, and, if possible, to form an alliance with him which would be to the material advantage of both parties. It was also his intention to trace up all the circumstances connected with the death of Mrs. Severne, so as to get from them such material as would best serve the ends he had in view. Then with this evidence, and with the confession he had taken from Severne's library, he would call upon the proper legal officer, and submit his case. Whether the arrest would take place within the British dominions, or in those of a country from which Severne's extradition could be demanded, was a matter with which he could not interfere. His opinion was, however, that no proceedings should be had till Severne had arrived in Paris.

If Mr. Freeling had been actuated by a due regard for justice and the safety of society, or if, even governed by motives of personal revenge he had believed Severne to be a murderer, we should do wrong to endeavor to cast odium on his proceedings. On his first reading Severne's note addressed to Lawrence, he had for a moment believed it to be a confession of a crime actually committed. But upon a full consideration of all the circumstances connected with the matter, he had arrived at the conclusion that such was not the case. He was too sharp a lawyer not to perceive that the letter had been written under great mental excitement, and had not been sent to its address. He knew also that Lawrence was fully acquainted with many of the particulars attendant on Mrs. Severne's death, and his own idea was that the letter had been dictated by a morbid feeling of self-accusation growing out of the unhappy relations which had existed between Severne and his wife during their marriage. Neither could he believe that if the letter was a genuine confession, the writer would, after repenting having written it, leave it in his library, exposed to the gaze of any inquisitive person who should open his port-folio. This was incredible. Still, he was confident that with proper management and a little perjury, he would be able to accomplish the object he had at heart. It was important to include Lawrence in his scheme, as an accessory, so as to destroy the credibility of his evidence, but he had strong doubts in regard to his ability to do this. Nevertheless, he had taken passage to Liverpool, in a steamer which left New York a week before the Arago, and when John Holmes, Margaret, and Sarah arrived at Southampton, he was in Cornwall, holding his first interview with Severne's heir-presumptive.

CHAPTER XXIX.

THE BEGINNING OF THE END.

As soon as John Holmes arrived in London, he sought out the best legal advice which it was possible for him to obtain. The gentleman to whom he was directed·listened attentively to all he had to say, and then telling his client to give himself no further uneasiness about the matter for the present, promised to look up all the persons who it was probable knew anything of the circumstances attendant on Mrs. Severne's death. "I will send," he continued, "my best clerk to Suez immediately, by the overland route, so as to guard against the possibility of your letter having miscarried. I shall urge Mr. Severne to come as quickly as possible direct to London, and await the issue here. I have all the data now that I wish, except the book which you tell me your granddaughter has in her possession. I should like to have that."

John Holmes replied that he did not believe his granddaughter would feel justified in giving up the book unless it was essential to the success of Severne's cause that she should do so.

"I can't say that such is the case," replied Mr. Wickham.

"If it should become necessary, I will let you know. If you
have any letters to send to your friend, get them ready by to-
night, as Mr. McAlpin will leave early to-morrow morning.
And now, as you can do nothing further to help me," continued Mr. Wickham, "the best thing you can do is to take
your granddaughters over to Paris till I telegraph for you,
which I will do in time for you to meet Mr. Severne here
immediately on his arrival. By-the-by, you are sure this
Mr. Freeling is in the country?"

"Certainly! He left New York a week before I did,
and I was told at Southampton that he had gone to Cornwall."

"Very well, we will take care of him. Go to Paris, and
the Continent generally, enjoy yourselves, and do not entertain any anxiety in regard to Mr. Severne. I may as well
tell you now that I know something of his case, and that
my information is not in the least to his disadvantage. I
say this in order that you may be perfectly easy. You will
probably think I am very anxious to get rid of you. In
truth I am. Your presence here will certainly become
known to Mr. Freeling, and thus, perhaps, lead to the discovery of movements I wish to keep from his knowledge."

Acting upon this suggestion, John Holmes, the following
day, proceeded with Margaret and Sarah to Paris by way of
Folkestone and Boulogne. After spending a week in this
city, they went to Cologne, and thence up the Rhine, stopping at those places on the way which possessed features of
interest to them.

The two girls were delighted with all they saw, and even
John Holmes took pleasure in recalling the scenes which
many years ago were familiar to him. They explored the
famous ruins which stand upon almost every rock, over-
hanging the dark-blue waves of the beautiful river; listened to the many legends that old and young peasants
had to tell of them, and saw more of the life of the people
than most travelers who pass up the Rhine. The weather
was cold, but they did not care for that, they kept themselves warm by long walks through the day, and at nightfall they gathered round the big porcelain stoves to hear
the gossip and wonderful tales which circulated till a late
hour.

Thus they reached Frankfort, and thence they went to Heidelberg, where they found more to interest them than in any other place since they had left Paris. The University, with its museum and splendid library; the cathedral, divided into two nearly equal parts by a wall, so as to give both Protestants and Catholics a share of it; the Philosophen Weg, where the students resort to settle their difficulties by cutting at each other with schlagers; the Church of St. Peter, to which Jerome of Prague affixed his theses; the Tower of the Königstuhl, from which the most magnificent view in all Germany is to be obtained, and whence even the spire of Strasburg, nearly a hundred miles distant, can be perceived; the Wolfsbrunnen, where they dined on trout taken not half an hour previously from the sparkling stream; and above all, the glorious old Schloss, the most magnificent ruin in Europe except the Alhambra, were sources of pleasure which could not fail to make Heidelberg long an object of remembrance with them.

From Heidelberg they went to Basel, where, in the old cathedral, high above the rapid stream at its base, they saw the tomb of Erasmus, the chamber in which the great Council of Basel was held, and the maiden, whose arms and breast, full of concealed knives, gave torture and death to the victim forced into her hideous embrace.

It was almost time now to be expecting Severne's arrival in Paris, and John Holmes judged it best to hurry back to that city. Interfering somewhat with Mr. Wickham's plans, he had, in his letter to Severne from London, stated that he, with his two granddaughters, would be in Paris, and had suggested that, instead of proceeding direct to London, it would add greatly to the pleasure of them all if Severne would join them in the former city, and then all go to London together. They did not, therefore, remain long in Switzerland, but taking Zurich and Geneva on their way, in a few days were back in their lodgings in the Rue de Choiseul.

The next morning, as soon as John Holmes had finished his breakfast, he went to the Place de la Bourse, to inquire of his banker, who was also Severne's, in regard to the last intelligence of his friend. To his great surprise, he was informed that Severne was expected that evening, having telegraphed from Marseilles to that effect. Margaret and Sarah were of course delighted when their grandfather returned and communicated this intelligence to them, and they were in no frame of mind to make the excursion to Marseilles which had been planned. The train from this city was due at six o'clock, and John Holmes, unable to restrain his impatience, went to the station to await Severne's arrival.

Punctually to the minute the train rushed into the station, and John Holmes, on the look-out, soon espied Severne, with Lawrence and de Hutten, emerging from one of the carriages. Greetings were given, inquiries made, and the whole party, getting into a carriage, proceeded to the Grand Hotel du Louvre.

"Of course," said John Holmes, addressing Severne, after they had reached the latter's apartments, "you received my letter written from London?"

"No, indeed; I have received no letters for several months."

"Did not Mr. Wickham's clerk meet yon at Suez?"

"I have not the least idea who Mr. Wickham or his clerk may be, but to my knowledge neither of them met me at Suez or anywhere else."

"Then you do not know what has happened during your absence?"

"I have not the slightest notion of what has happened. You have told me that Margaret and Sarah are well and are expecting me. I propose to see them in the course of an hour. So long as they and you are happy, I don't care a great deal for anything else."

In as few words as possible John Holmes then gave Severne the details of Mr. Freeling's conduct and supposed plans, and of the measures he had taken for their defeat. To say that Severne was astonished, would not express the extent of his emotion; but after the first shock had passed off, his feeling was one of amusement at the absurdity of Freeling's ideas.

"I shall have no difficulty, my dear old friend, in defeating all his infamous schemes. It is as well that the matter should be settled now forever, and I intend to give Mr. Freeling every opportunity to effect his object. If he does

not succeed, it will simply be because my cause is too strong
for him. Of course I shall go at once to London and await
the measures which the officers of justice may see fit to take
on his information. You have acted with very great dis-
cretion; but I never can thank you sufficiently for your continued confidence in the face of what must have struck you
as a most damaging proof of my criminality. And Goodall,
too! You tell me he also did not lose faith. You are true
friends, indeed. And Margaret," continued Severne, his
face lighting up with pride. "I will not say to you what I
think of her. As soon as I can get myself into a presentable shape I will go with you to see her, and will tell her in
person. I do not know what book you can refer to as containing valuable evidence in my favor, and which she found
in my library. I have no recollection of any such volume.
It will not be needed, I think. Mr. Freeling is reckoning
altogether without his host."

"And Sarah," resumed Severne, after a moment's pause;
"of course she did not suspect me of this guilt?"

"No; with the rest of us, she has been perfectly firm in
her confidence. You would scarcely know your ward, my
dear Severne. She is altogether a different being from what
she was when you left her six months ago, and even then
she had very greatly improved, as you know. She is one
of the most gentle, artless, and truly religious girls I ever
knew. Everything she does is dictated by a high sense of
duty and right. You have proven that none are so low as
to be beyond the hope of elevation. Every precept you
gave her is treasured up and acted upon. She fairly seems
to worship you."

"She and you both give me more than my due," replied
Severne. "She is a good girl, however, and that is the
chief point in her favor. I am very proud of her, I assure
you. But come, I am ready now to go with you to the Rue
de Choiseul. Lawrence and de Hutten will take care of
themselves for the evening. To-morrow we will introduce
them to the ladies, and we will all go at once to London.
I must not lose a moment in putting myself within Mr. Freeling's reach."

John Holmes left Severne in the parlor of their suite of
apartments while he went to acquaint Margaret and Sarah

of his arrival. Margaret was the first to enter the room. It is not necessary to describe the meeting. It was ·just what it ought to have been. That is enough to say about it.

"And you have returned in good health, I am sure," she said, smiling with the joy that filled her heart. "Your looks tell me that, although you are almost as brown as an Indian."

"Yes, I am well both in mind and body. I believe Lawrence is perfectly satisfied with my condition, and will not insist upon any more traveling. My darling," he continued, "before I say another word, I must tell you that the confidence you have shown in my honor has not been misplaced. You do not require any such assurance, I know, but it will be a satisfaction for you to hear from my lips the expression of my pride·in you for the constancy you have shown. There is nothing in this world so valuable to me as your love; and now that it has been so severely tried, it is a thousand-fold more precious to me than ever before. I am glad this test has been applied to it, for though I was certain that come what might there would be no danger of your faltering in your affection, it is a pleasure for me to know that you have stood the trial. Such experiences as that you have undergone never pass away without leaving us better than they found us."

"You know I told you you could trust me, dear Robert. But I, too, am glad at what has occurred. I know more of you now than I should have discovered by years of uninterrupted smoothness in our lives. I understand something of what you have endured, can appreciate in some degree the nobility and unselfishness of your nature. You would never have told me of those events in your life, which have given you so much sorrow, in such a way as to reveal the magnanimity·of your actions. I know enough now for you to tell me all."

"My dear Margaret, in a few days I will lay bare my past life to you. I always intended to do so, because it is your due. When you hear my history, you will find some things to give you pleasure, more to pardon, and still more to pity; but you will not find that I have done anything that I knew to be morally wrong. I may have been weak, but I have not been dishonorable."

Before Margaret could reply, Sarah and John Holmes

came in. She held out both hands to her guardian, and greeted him with the most unaffected grace.

"You have not forgotten me?" he said, with a smile of admiration, as he gazed upon her face, which had increased very much in loveliness since he had last seen it.

"Oh, no ; how could I ever forget you ?"

"I should scarcely have known you, my dear child," he continued, as he kissed her forehead. "A few months have made such a difference in you. You are as tall as your sister, and resemble her still more than when I saw you last."

"Do you still think I look like Margaret?" asked Sarah, with manifest pleasure. "Many persons notice it now, though I think you were the only one who deteeted a likeness at first. I have been so happy," she continued, in a low whisper to him, "in the knowledge that she is my sister. And she has told me something else which has given me still more pleasure."

"Has she ?" said Severne, with a smile. "Yes, we will all be together before very long, my. dear child. But come," he continued, addressing them all, "let us hold our first family council, and arrange our programme. In the first place, we must start for London to-morrow; Lawrence and de Hutten will go with us. After we arrive there, our future movements must depend upon circumstances. Of course I shall see Mr. Wickham, and be guided to a great extent by his judgment. My present intention is, however, to go at once and deliver myself up for trial on the charge Mr. Freeling has brought."

"They will imprison you then, will they not?" said Margaret.

"Yes, I shall be imprisoned, for murder is not a bailable offense."

Margaret's and Sarah's eyes filled with tears, but the former succeeded in subduing her emotion in a great degree, and said:

"You are right; bear it through to the end, and your triumph will be all the greater."

"I will tell you nothing now," said Severne, "relative to the character of the defense I shall make, except in regard to the letter to Lawrence which Freeling must have taken from my port-folio.   I thought Lawrence had destroyed it, but of course I gave him another paper by mistake.   There is such a ludicrous side to the history of that document that I can scarcely think of it without laughing, although it has been the means of causing me this annoyance."   Without going into all the particulars, Severne then gave an account of the main circumstances which led to his writing the note to which Mr. Freeling attached so great a degree of importance.   "My dear Margaret," he continued, "I would like very much to have the book to which you all appear to ascribe so much value.   I cannot imagine what it can be."   Margaret left the room, and soon returned with the volume in question.   She handed it to Severne, who, observing that it was carefully sealed, gave her a glance which showed that he understood her delicacy, and then proceeded to open it.

He looked at the title-page first. "Calderon de la Barca," he said, as if endeavoring to recall the volume to his mind. "I have a dim impression that this book has somehow or other been connected with incidents of my life, but I cannot now bring it to mind."   He then looked through the leaves, and at once became intensely interested in their perusal.   His face glowed with anger and shame as he read the guilty record of his wife's dishonored life, and at last he covered his eyes with his hands, and sat for several minutes apparently absorbed in the reflections that had been awakened. No one said a word, but Margaret went quietly to his side and put her little hand on his shoulder, and looked down upon him as if her whole soul were in her eyes.

"My darling," said Severne, in a low tone, which only reached her ears, "I understand this now.   This book was mentioned to me several years ago as being in existence, and a thorough search was instituted for it without success.   I think I know how it came to be in my library.   It is strange, though, that I should never have noticed it.   It contains the record of so much baseness and duplicity that your pure mind could not comprehend it in all its guilt and ignominy and dishonor.   I trust I shall not be obliged to make use of it in my defense, but I shall not sacrifice myself any longer to save her name from disgrace.   I have you to live for, your honor to protect, and I will see to it above all things that no stain rests upon that of your husband."

"I know you will do what is right. I have no fear for you or myself."

Severne put the book into his pocket, and the conversation turned upon his adventures during his long journey. Everything had gone on well, and when the party arrived at San Francisco, and were about to take passage in a sailing vessel for Calcutta, a steamer was advertised to leave the next day for that port, and thus, by taking passage in it, they had been enabled to shorten very materially the voyage across the Pacific. Upon arriving at Calcutta, they were so fortunate as to find another steamer just about to start for Suez. Taking passage in it, they had arrived at this latter place before Mr. McAlpin, but instead of coming direct from there to Paris, they had gone to Constantinople, where they had remained several days. Owing to their rapid movements, Severne had failed to receive the last letters written to him from the United States, or those sent from London.

Joshua had remained in San Francisco, with every prospect of becoming in a short time a very wealthy man. His chemical knowledge was in great demand, and he had, besides, found a capitalist who had bought from him a half-interest in his patent process for making the new explosive compound he had discovered, and which, it was believed by many, would ere long lead to the complete disuse of gunpowder. He had intrusted Severne with two letters, one for John Holmes and the other for Mrs. Markland, and had been profuse in his messages of remembrance to all of the household.

It was late when they separated that night. On his return to his hotel, Severne communicated to Lawrence and de Hutten so much of what had taken place during his absence as was necessary to enable them to form a clear idea of the subject. They both agreed that his plan of going at once to London was a perfectly proper one, and announced their determination to go with him and aid him to the full extent of their ability.

The following morning early, the whole party met at the station of the Northern Railway, and the same night arrived safely in London.

CHAPTER XXX.

IN PRISON.

WHEN Severne and John Holmes called at Mr. Wickham's office the day after their arrival in London, they found this gentleman unprepared to give them an immediate audience. In the course of half an hour, however, he was disengaged, and they were invited into his private office.

"I am very glad to see you," he said to Severne. "I scarcely suppose that you recollect me, but this is not the first time I have been employed in your case. I was on the other side over ten years ago. Your cousin in Cornwall employed me to ascertain the extent of the evidence against you, and I had the satisfaction of telling him that the less he moved in the matter, the better it would be for him. There was not enough evidence against you then to hang a suspicion on. You did not notice that woman who was with me when you were announced, and who just went out? Well, that woman was the late Mrs. Severne's nurse, Ellen Whiting. She is a very valuable witness, as you know. Mr. Freeling and your cousin think she is dead. We'll show them a thing or two on the trial. McAlpin got back last night. You had left Suez two days before he arrived there. He followed you to Constantinople, but missed you again. However, it's all right now. There's a warrant out for your apprehension. They don't know you are here. I think you had better go with me at once to a magistrate and deliver yourself up for trial. There's a good fellow at the Clerkenwell Police Court, who will treat you like a gentleman—Sir James Truman. He is a friend of mine, too. Don't be afraid. I wish I was as certain of living a thousand years as I am that you will not be convicted. Don't ask me any questions. It's all right, though, and I'll call round and see you after your committal, and pump out of you all I want. I have asked Hickling to take the brief.

He's a terrible fellow with a jury, and he'll show off Freeling and your worthy cousin in their true colors."

Severne and John Holmes said little, as it was very evident that Mr. Wickham knew all about the case, and preferred hearing himself talk to listening to them. Severne expressed his readiness to go at once before the magistrate; and Mr. Wickham calling a carriage, went with them to the office, a few squares distant.

"My dear Sir James," said Mr. Wickham, as they were ushered into the magistrate's private office, "allow me to introduce to you my client, Mr. Robert Severne, son of the late Robert Severne, Esq , of Severne Hall, Kent. Mr. Severne arrived in London last night from a circumnavigating tour of the earth, and learns that a warrant has been issued for his apprehension on the charge of having murdered his wife. The warrant has not been served, but he is desirous of being at once committed for trial."

"Ah, yes," said Sir James. "I issued the warrant myself on the affidavit of a Mr. Freeling, an American gentleman. I trust you will be able to clear yourself of the charge, Mr. Severne. I knew your father very well, and I think I must have seen you years ago when you were a boy. As you know, my action was based altogether on *ex parte* evidence. I am glad you are here this morning, it does not look as if you were guilty, and I will say," he continued, with great kindness of manner, "that I don't believe you are guilty. Of course I shall have to commit you. It is just what you wish me to do, if I understand you aright. I will do all I can, however, to render your stay in prison before your trial as comfortable as possible. We don't often hear of persons accused of murder giving themselves up."

Severne thanked him for his kindness, and asked him when the trial would probably take place.

"There's a session of the court, at the Old Bailey, tomorrow week, and I am very sure that Mr. Wickham and myself can get your case put on the calendar for an early day. In the mean time you will be as comfortably situated as possible. I will write a note to the governor of the prison, and request him to allow you every indulgence consistent with the discharge of his duty. Here, Johnson," he continued, addressing an officer who stood just outside the door, "go with this gentleman to the House of Detention and deliver him to the governor, with this note. You can allow these gentlemen to accompany you if they wish to go."

"I presume there is no objection," said Severne, "to his taking me first to my hotel, in order that I may get some clothes and give my servant some necessary directions?"

"None in the least. Let the gentleman go to his hotel first, Johnson. Come here, I wish to speak to you."

Sir James spoke a few words in a whisper to the officer, to which the latter replied, "Yes, Sir James, I understand." And then Severne, again thanking the magistrate for his consideration, proceeded to the carriage, accompanied by John Holmes, Mr. Wickham, and the officer, and was driven rapidly to Morley's Hotel, where the whole party was stopping. After giving his servant the necessary orders relative to his clothes and a few other necessaries, he sought out Lawrence and de Hutten, who were expecting his return. There was no time for more than a few brief words of comfort and assurance, and then, with a cheerful heart and countenance, Severne said good-by to Margaret and Sarah. The latter could not restrain her grief, but Margaret, though grave, was composed.

"I know," she said to him, as he led her aside, "that you will be sustained by the consciousness of innocence. It is sometimes a pleasure for us to suffer for the right, and I do not believe that your days in prison will be altogether sad. Remember, too, how dearly I love you."

"I will never forget that, dear Margaret. You see I am not sad. I would not avoid the trial now for worlds. You and Sarah will come and see me sometimes?"

"As often as they will allow us."

A few more words followed, and then Severne, accompanied as before, was taken to the House of Detention, Clerkenwell.

Johnson delivered Sir James's note to the governor; and the latter, looking closely at Severne for a few seconds, said:

"This seems to be somewhat of a peculiar case. I have never known a stronger letter of the kind to be written by any magistrate. I think I can trust you; and if you will give me your word of honor not to pass beyond certain limits which I will prescribe, you may occupy a vacant room in my part of the prison, and have such food as you choose to pay for. I shall place no restrictions on any persons whose names you give me, visiting you between the hours of nine in the morning and six in the evening."

Severne expressed his thanks for these favors, and gave the required promise.

"Then we will consider the matter settled. You are now therefore an inmate of the prison. You can use the room I mentioned, and walk in the corridor fronting it. You are not, however, to go farther without my special authority. That authority is given you now to make use of my little garden for exercise every day between the hours of six and eight in the evening. Hodkins," he continued, addressing a turnkey who had been listening to his remarks, "you have heard what I have said. Show Mr. Severne to the vacant room in my suite of apartments."

The room allotted to Severne was a large, cheerful one, with a high ceiling and plenty of light. The windows were barred, but they looked out on a side street, and the view, if not a very brilliant one, was far more so than could reasonably have been expected. There was a good bed, three or four chairs, a table, and a carpet in the room. There were two large closets, one of which contained a bath-tub, and the other a large chest of drawers. Severne therefore had every reason to be satisfied, and when the governor came up and told him that if he wanted his servant to remain with him, there was a small room he could occupy at a moderate expense, nothing was wanting to make his condition comfortable.

After Mr. Wickham and John Holmes had gone, Severne thought over the circumstances of his situation with more thoroughness than he had yet given to them. Although he felt strong in the justice of his cause, he was aware that his adversary was utterly unprincipled, and would not hesitate at perjury, if this crime were necessary to secure his conviction. His anticipations in regard to Freeling had been more than realized, for never had he thought him so completely debased as his present conduct showed him to be. As to his cousin, the heir-presumptive to his property, Severne had never seen him; but the facts that he had entered into combination with Freeling, and had been the means of propagating scandalous rumors in regard to him soon after his wife's death, left no room for doubt as to his character. In looking carefully into all the circumstances of the case, and giving full credit to his enemies for their unscrupulousness, Severne could see no cause for the slightest alarm if tried before an unprejudiced court. He knew that a great deal depended upon his judge, but as his trial was to take place before a court constituted by the civil law of England, and as all the safeguards which protect an individual in a free country would be thrown around him, he had no fears as to the result.

That evening Mr. Wickham paid him a visit for the purpose of conferring with him in regard to his defense. Severne referred him to Lawrence for evidence relative to the confession in Freeling's possession, and gave him the book which Margaret had found, telling him to use only such portions of its contents as were absolutely necessary to·clear him from the least suspicion of guilt.

During the ten days that elapsed before his trial, his friends visited him so constantly that it was rarely the case some of them were not with him every hour of those during which he was allowed to receive them. Generally Lawrence and de Hutten spent the morning with him, and John Holmes, Margaret, and Sarah came early in the afternoon and remained till six o'clock. His evenings were passed in looking over the many books brought to him, and in talking with the governor, who either visited him in his room or invited him into his own apartments. The yard in which he was permitted to walk for two hours every day was not of very ample proportions, but it was nevertheless a source of amusement to him to tread its stone pavement and look through its grated gate into the busy street. Altogether, his prison life was not a cheerless one. He had dear friends who sympathized with him, and one to love him, who was far dearer to him than his own life. Never before, however, had he been forcibly restrained of his liberty, and the sensation of being a prisoner, of being unable to go where he wished, even though he might not wish to go anywhere, was inexpressibly peculiar and disagreeable.. Had he been prevented by injury or disease he would not have cared. He had frequently remained longer than a week in his own house, busy with his studies, without desiring to leave it, and there was no particular reason now for wishing to take a walk with the crowd that day after day hurried past his windows, except the inability to do so. Like mankind in general, he sighed for that which was beyond his reach. However, the ten days fled by rapidly enough. Margaret and Sarah had paid their last visit to him, and had left him full of the hope that ere the morrow's sun had set he would be free, with his name untarnished and his honor unscathed. Mr. Wickham had had a long conversation with him, and had announced that all his preparations for a successful defense were made. John Holmes, Lawrence, and de Hutten had spent several hours with him, talking of everything in the world but the trial, with the charitable intention of diverting his thoughts from a disagreeable subject, and Severne had humored their fancy from pure good nature, and had gone over all his prairie experience for John Holmes's benefit. And the governor had wished him good night, paying him the compliment of telling him that never before had there been so true a gentleman in the Clerkenwell House of Detention since he had been governor of it, and expressing the hope that it would be his last night under its roof. All was ready, and Severne went to sleep with as much serenity of mind, and with as thankful a heart to the Father of all things, as if, instead of being about to be tried for his life, he were on the eve of attaining to some great good fortune, for which he had striven in vain for many years.

CHAPTER XXXI.

THE TRIAL.

THE sun was shining brightly, and the air was crisp with frost, when Severne, Mr. Wickham, and an officer got into the carriage that was to take them to the Old Bailey. Mr. Hickling, the celebrated barrister who was to manage the case before the court, and Mr. Seymour, the junior counsel, had already paid him a visit, and obtained from him several facts and leading circumstances of which they intended to avail themselves in the course of the trial. Mr. Hickling was a fine-looking man, with a bald head and a red face, the one indicative, perhaps, of a constant and intense employment of his brain, the other certainly pointing to a liberal use of old port, of which Mr. Hickling's cellar was well filled. Mr. Seymour was calm, thoughtful, and with, perhaps, a better knowledge of the philosophy of law than his senior. Mr. Hickling's experience, however, was immense, and his memory faithful to a fault. He could cite precedent after precedent, telling the volume and page with unerring accuracy, and was consequently looked upon by jurors as a wonderful being, who knew more law than the Lord Mayor, the Lord Chancellor, the Judge of the Admiralty, the Dean of the Arches, or any others of the notable judicial personages whose privilege it is to sit on the bench at the Old Bailey, and before whom criminals and tipstaves stand in awe.

Severne got into the carriage with a light and elastic step, without fear, but with a feeling of joy in his heart that at last the issue was to be made between him and his enemies. A few short hours he was sure would see him at liberty, and then,—well, he would not consent to a very long postponement of his happiness. He would have thought of a good many things besides the trial, but for the fact that Mr. Wickham was one of the most loquacious men in the world, and kept up such a running fire of words that it was impossible for Severne to concentrate his mind a minute on any one subject. At last they reached the Old Bailey. "Now," said Mr. Wickham, "keep your eyes about you. In ten minutes after the jury are sworn, you will not know who is being tried, yourself or your friend, Mr. Freeling. I hate to be hard on a brother, even if he is an unworthy one, but there is no help for it. Ah, here are our friends," he continued, as he perceived John Holmes, Lawrence, and de Hutten about to enter the court-room. "You'll all find seats somewhere. I hope you'll enjoy it as much as I will."

Stopping for a moment under charge of the officer to say a few words to his friends, Severne then passed into the court-room, and took his place in the dock as quietly, and apparently as naturally as if he had been used to doing so all his life. As soon as he was seated, he looked around him and took all the bearings of his position.

The judge had just taken his seat on the bench, and the crier was opening the court in that mixture of bad English and worse French which all Anglo-Saxon criers indulge in. Barristers in their wigs, and with green bags, and bundles of papers in their hands, were getting ready for work. Mr. Hickling was there, the table before him almost bare of documents, while that at which Mr. Seymour sat was covered with papers of all sizes, some of them arranged in bundles and others scattered about as if without order or system. Mr. Wickham was talking, first with one and then with the other, in a low tone about some matter which appeared to give him intense satisfaction.

At a table by themselves sat the law officer for the crown and other counsel for the prosecution, and in close consultation with them were Mr. Freeling and a gentleman whom Severne supposed, from a certain degree of family resemblance, to be his cousin. Mr. Freeling was apparently very calm and confident. Severne's eyes met his two or three times, but neither gave any sign of recognition.

The judge was a burly, gentlemanly-looking personage, who did not seem to take a great deal of interest in the case that was coming off, as he was glancing occasionally at a newspaper before him. As soon, however, as the crier had finished his harangue, his lordship folded up his newspaper, and a few words of audible conversation took place between him and the senior counsel for the crown, the result of which was that a jury was impaneled without much difficulty. The indictment was then read by the clerk of the court. It set forth, with the customary legal verbiage, that Robert Severne did, on the twenty-ninth day of October, 1847, in the City of London, County of Middlesex, feloniously, and with malice aforethought, administer to Francisca Severne, his wife, a large quantity of corrosive sublimate, with intent to deprive the said Francisca Severne of her life, and of the effects of which corrosive sublimate so administered, the said Francisca Severne died. In answer to the usual questions, Severne, in a firm but low voice, pleaded not guilty, and the trial began.

The law officer for the crown, in opening the case for the prosecution, called attention to the fact that the murder for which the prisoner at the bar was about to be tried for his life, had been committed over eleven years ago, and had been brought to light mainly through the exertions of a foreigner, whose sense of what was due to the outraged majesty of the law was so great that he preferred to vindicate it rather than allow the criminal, his friend and employer, to escape the punishment which justice might inflict. The prisoner at the bar, he continued, has lived in fancied security, in the enjoyment of a large property, and would probably never have been called upon to answer for his crime, but for the fact that Providence, in its inscrutable wisdom, had brought him to confess his guilt. The jury would not, therefore, be asked to strain their consciences in finding the prisoner guilty. The written confession of his criminality, written and signed by himself, would be produced, and if they were satisfied that this was the handwriting of the prisoner, it would be their duty to convict him, unless, indeed, it should appear that he was of unsound mind at the time, of which, however, he did not think there was even a pretense.

But this was not all. They would find that the prisoner at the bar had lived unhappily with his wife; that he had been heard repeatedly to utter expressions of hostility to her; and that on the day of, and previous to her death, he had purchased a quantity of corrosive sublimate from a chemist's shop. They would hear, too, from a most respectable witness, that before she died, Mrs. Severne accused her husband of her death, and that he did not deny it.

It might be asked, continued the learned gentleman, if these things are true, why was not the prisoner arrested at the time and brought to trial? He would be obliged to reply that there had been a most lamentable disregard of duty somewhere, and he could only attribute it to the previous high character of the prisoner, and to the position he occupied in society, which prevented an examination on what was then, he must admit, a mere suspicion. Taken alone, these circumstances would scarcely have secured a conviction, especially as at the post-mortem examination no corrosive sublimate had been found in the stomach of the deceased; but when considered in connection with the prisoner's confession, they were of frightful import. As to the absence of the poison from the stomach of the deceased, he would show that no importance was to be attached to that fact, as at the best it was but negative evidence. In conclusion, the learned gentleman implored the jury to do their duty to their country, and not to forget that the higher the rank of an accused person, the more important it was that if guilty he should suffer the punishment the law awards to his crimes.

When the counsel for the crown had finished his speech, a murmur ran through the crowd, and many looked as if they regarded the matter as having only one possible termination. Even his lordship on the bench looked grave, and the faces of the jurymen had become much more solemn in their expressions.

The first witness was a chemist, who swore that on the morning of October 29, 1847, he had sold to Robert Severne one ounce of corrosive sublimate. He had recorded the fact in his book, and recognized the prisoner at the bar as the person who had purchased it. No effort was made to shake his evidence by cross-examination.

Mary Ross next testified that she had lived with Mr. and Mrs. Severne in the capacity of chambermaid. Frequently heard angry words between the deceased and the prisoner at the bar. Mrs. Severne frequently told her, prisoner had threatened her life, and that she was afraid he would murder her. Was present when Mrs. Severne died. Deceased was just recovering from what was said to be typhus fever. Heard Mrs. Severne say to prisoner, "You have killed me."

On cross-examination, it appeared that the angry words were always from Mrs. Severne. Never heard Mr. Severne say anything unkind, except once, when he told Mrs. Severne that her conduct was highly disgraceful. Had frequently found that Mrs. Severne did not speak the truth. Did not at the time attach any importance to what she said of prisoner's threats. When Mrs. Severne told the prisoner that he had killed her, prisoner said he hoped not, that he had tried to do his duty by her. Always liked Mr. Severne, always found him gentlemanly and kind. Mrs. Severne frequently had gentlemen to visit her during Mr. Severne's absence.

Dr. Maxwell testified that he had conducted the post-mortem examination at the request of Mr. Severne. Found the stomach of the deceased inflamed. Such a condition would have been produced by corrosive sublimate. Did not, however, detect this substance, though, at the instance of a relative of Mr. Severne's, he had examined for it.

On cross-examination, the doctor testified that he had attended Mrs. Severne for typhus fever, of which she was recovering from a severe attack, when she suddenly died. Was sent for to see her in her last illness by Mr. Severne. Had found poison in her stomach, strychnia, and the symptoms observed before her death had all indicated that she had died from the effects of this substance. Had never before been called upon to testify in regard to the case, and had said nothing about the matter out of regard to Mr. Severne's request, who believed that his wife had committed suicide. Dr. Lawrence, an American physician, had been present at the post-mortem examination.

Dr. Maxwell's evidence excited a sensation among the members of the court and the audience. The prosecution was very much impressed, they were unprepared for the disclosures of the cross-examination.

Mr. Bagley Freeling next took the stand. As Mr. Freeling was the most important witness for the prosecution, we give his evidence in full, as follows:

"I know the prisoner at the bar, Robert Severne. I have acted as his agent for several years, and have always entertained a high regard for him. I never had cause to suspect him of the crime for which he is now being tried till just previous to his departure from New York last July. Soon after he left the city, I had occasion to send my clerk to his house for some papers it was necessary for me to examine. He could not find them, but brought several others which he thought might be the ones I required. Among them was this letter, in the handwriting of the accused, and with his signature to it." Mr. Freeling here read the letter, and it was handed to the judge and the jurymen for their examination.

Mr. Hickling arose, and said that in order to save time, he admitted the letter to be in the handwriting of the prisoner throughout.

Mr. Freeling resumed :

"I did not notice the paper at the time.   And soon after my clerk's return I went myself to Mr. Severne's house to look for the papers I wanted; I did not find them, however. I then returned to my office, and upon looking among the papers brought by my clerk I found the one the contents of which have just been given in evidence.   I was very much surprised when I read it, and then I recollected what previously had given me a little uneasiness, that Mr. Severne had told me a few days before his departure that he never expected to die a natural death, and that he was haunted with the memory of a great crime.   I also recalled to mind that when I was last in England I heard whispers against him as being suspected of the murder of his wife."

Severne started with surprise as Mr. Freeling gave utterance to the falsehood alleging a verbal confession on his part.   Neither of his counsel, however, looked astonished. They had evidently anticipated that Mr. Freeling would perjure himself, and appeared to be relieved that he had disclosed his whole game.

The cross-examination was conducted by Mr. Hickling, in the most bland and composed manner.   After several questions of no very great importance, the learned counsel asked :

"You say you visited Mr. Severne's house after your clerk returned to your office ?"

"I do."

"Did you make any very thorough search for the papers you say you wanted ?"

"I only looked on the table for them."

"Can you swear that you did not yourself take that letter, which has just been read to the jury, out of a port-folio that was on the table ?"

"I do so swear.   As I have said, the letter was given me by my clerk."

"Did you not, when you went to the house, tell the housekeeper that your clerk had come there without your knowledge, and that he was unreliable ?"

"Never."

"That's a lie," whispered John Holmes to Lawrence. "Mrs. Smith told me he did; and I would believe her before him any day."

"What is your clerk's name?" continued Mr. Hickling.

"James Collins."

"Did he ever see this letter?"

"No; I kept it locked up."

"What is Collins's character for truth?"

"Excellent; he is one of the most reliable young men I ever knew."

"You would believe him on oath?"

"Certainly."

"I object to this kind of cross-examination," said the law officer for the crown. "Mr. Collins's character has not been inquired into, and the questions of my learned friend are altogether irrelevant."

"I differ with my learned friend," replied Mr. Hickling. "The relevancy of my questions will soon appear; however, I have no more to ask relative to Mr. Collins at present.

"Now, then, Mr. Freeling," he continued, "you have sworn that you did not open a port-folio on the table and take that letter from it. Did you open any drawer of that table?"

"I did not."

"You are positive you did not open the upper left-hand drawer of that table?"

"Perfectly. All the drawers were locked, and I could not have opened them if I had tried."

"When you sent your clerk to Mr. Severne's house, did you tell him to open any of the drawers?"

"No."

"Did you give him a key which you said would open the upper left-hand drawer?"

Mr. Freeling looked surprised at this question, and became a little confused. He could not imagine how the knowledge necessary to ask it had been obtained. He trembled a little, but answered "No!" in a loud and indignant voice.

"Was any other person present when, as you have sworn, Mr. Severne told you he never expected to die a natural death, and that he was haunted by the memory of a great crime he had committed?"

"No one else was present."

"Did you never try to induce your clerk, James Collins,
29*

to make an affidavit that he had heard Mr. Severne use these words in your presence ?"

Again Mr. Freeling trembled and turned pale, but again he answered "No!" with an angry voice.

"Very well, Mr. Freeling, that will do. By-the-by," continued Mr. Hickling, in the politest possible tone, and with an affectation of having forgotten a trifling circumstance, "How were you dressed when you visited Mr. Severne's library ?"

"Really, your lordship," said the counsel for the crown, "I hope this style of cross-examination is not going to be allowed. Of what importance is it how the witness was dressed ?"

"I do not see myself of what consequence it is," said his lordship. "I hope the time of the court will not be taken up with irrelevant questions."

"Certainly not, your lordship," said Mr. Hickling. "I have no intention of consuming the valuable time of the court, but the question is important, as I hope to show before I have done."

"Very well," replied his lordship; "I have confidence in what you say. Answer the question, witness," he continued, addressing Mr. Freeling.

"I was dressed very much as I am now," said Mr. Freeling, with some appearance of trepidation, for although he did not perceive the drift of the question, he felt sure there was danger in it.

"In a coat, and trowsers, and shirt, I suppose ?"

"Certainly."

"Did you wear sleeve-buttons in your shirt ?"

A profound silence pervaded the court-room as this question was put. Every one understood that it meant something. Mr. Freeling grew more and more confused. He did not apparently know what reply to make, for he was unaware of the extent of his adversary's knowledge. He took out his handkerchief and wiped the perspiration from his face.

"Did you wear sleeve-buttons that day in your shirt ?"

"I believe I did," he at last answered.

"I observe that those you now have on are not alike."

"I lost one before I left New York, and was unable to match it."

"Ah, yes. Is this the one you lost, Mr. Freeling?"

"Yes, that is the one," he answered. "I do not know, however, what you are doing with it."

"If you will remain in the court-room a few moments you will ascertain. I would like your lordship and the jury to examine that button, and to compare it with the one in the witness's left sleeve," continued Mr. Hickling.

"Remove the button from your left sleeve, witness, and let me see it," said his lordship.

Mr. Freeling tremblingly took out the button, and it, with the other, were carefully examined by the judge and jury.

"Now, Mr. Freeling, I believe I have done with you for the present," said Mr. Hickling.

"The case for the prosecution is closed," said the counsel for the government.

Mr. Hickling opened for the defense. He said that for more than ten years the accused had been content to bear the suspicion of having committed a heinous crime, rather than cast odium upon the name of his late wife. The time had come, however, when it was no longer possible for him to do so without sacrificing other interests besides his own, and he intended to vindicate himself once and forever from the foul aspersion which had been thrown upon him. The counsel for the prosecution had endeavored to make the most of their case. It was their duty to do all, so long as there was reasonable ground for a suspicion of guilt. Their case had, however, utterly broken down. It had been shown by their own witness, Mary Ross, that the accused had been a kind husband; by their own witness, Dr. Maxwell, that the deceased had died from the effects of a large dose of strychnia; and by their own witness, Mr. Freeling,—well, he would not say now what had been shown by this witness, the court and jury would discover for themselves before long. Without taking up the time of the court, he would proceed to examine his witnesses, and first he would call Ellen Whiting.

At this name, Severne's cousin started, and Mr. Freeling smiled incredulously. He whispered a few words to the counsel for the crown.

"I'm afraid," said the latter, "that my learned friend will

call in vain.   The woman has been dead several years, or we should have had her as a witness for the prosecution."

"Call Ellen Whiting again," said his lordship to the crier.

"Ellen Whiting!" roared the crier, at the top of his voice.

There was a slight bustle near the door of the court-room, and a little old woman was perceived making her way through the crowd.   In a few moments she reached the witness stand, and was duly sworn.   ·

"Now, Ellen Whiting," said Mr. Hickling, "tell all you know of the death of Mrs. Severne."

Mrs. Ellen Whiting was a sharp-looking little body.   She took off her spectacles, wiped them on a réd silk handkerchief, put them on again, and glanced complacently around the court-room.

The moment she detected Severne, she made him a very polite curtsy.   "I am glad to see you looking so well, sir," she said, "though God knows it's sorry I am to see you here.   I wish you well out of it, sir, for if ever there was a good gentleman, it's yourself!"

"That will do, Ellen Whiting," said his lordship.   "Tell all you know in regard to the death of Mrs. Severne."

"I know a great deal, your lordship and gentlemen of the jury, and all you that hear me.   I was nurse for Mrs. Severne when she was ill with the fever just before she died. And Dr. Maxwell was the physician.   And on the 29th of October, eleven years ago last 29th of October, Mrs. Severne said to me, 'Ellen, there's a powder in my toilet-case which I wish you would give me.'   I looked in the case and found a little package, which I opened.   It contained a white powder.   I asked her if that was the one she meant, and she said it was.   I tasted it, and, said I, How bitter it is!   And she replied that it was very bitter, but that it was a powder that would make her strong.   I gave it to her in a little currant jelly, and in less than half an hour she had a very bad fit, and then she had another, and she straightened out on the bed quite stiff, and I asked her what it all was, and she told me that Mr. Severne had given her poison. And said I, That can't be, because he has not been here today.   And she said he gave it to her early that morning.

And then I got scared, and I went for Mr. Severne, who was not well himself, because he had been sitting up with her, and I told him what she had said.   He came into the room at once, and knelt down by her bedside, and said she's poisoned with strychnia.   He told us to send for Dr. Maxwell and Dr. Lawrence, who was a friend of his, who lodged close by, and before they came, Mrs. Severne said to him, 'You have killed me !'   And he said, 'I hope not.   I tried to do what was right by you.'   And Mary Ross was there and heard him. .And then he said: 'Francisca, why have you done this?' and she said she was tired of life, and that she hated him, and meant to have him hung for her murder; and then she said again, in a loud voice, 'You've killed me! You've killed me !'   When the doctors came she could not speak any more, and she died in a convulsion soon afterward."

"Did you ever see this book ?" said Mr. Hickling, handing her the volume of Calderon de la Barca's poems, which Margaret had found in Severne's library.

Mrs. Whiting took the book, and examined it very carefully for several minutes.   Then she returned it, and said:

"Yes, sir.   I know that book very well.   It's a Spanish book that Mrs. Severne was very fond of, and when she thought of anything that she wanted to write down, she wrote it in that book.   The morning of her death, just before she took the powder, she told me to throw it into the fire, and I went to do so, and forgot it, and I have not seen it since.   After her death, Mrs. Severne's mother got all her books, and I suppose she got this one too."

"Are you acquainted with the late Mrs. Severne's handwriting ?"

"Oh, yes, sir !   I've seen her write often."

"Are you certain that the writing in this book is hers ?"

"All I see is hers."

"Is this passage hers ?" said Mr. Hickling, pointing to a dozen lines or so on a fly leaf.

"Yes, I'll swear that is her handwriting."

"I will read it, and then submit the book to your lordship and the jury for examination."

" 'I see now that I never will be able to show him the full measure of my hate while I live.   Women have died for

their love, I will die for my hate. Yes, death would be
pleasant to me if I knew that he would die also,—die like a
dog, on the gallows. He has had the better of me in my
life. I will have the better of him in my death. A few
short days and my agony will be over, while he will suffer
in prospective, die in torment, and leave behind him a dishonored name.'"

A death-like silence pervaded the audience while Mr.
Hickling, in a full and impressive voice, read these words.
When he had finished, strong men drew a long breath of
relieved suspense, and shuddered at the thought of the marvelous wickedness of the woman who could entertain such
fiendish ideas. His lordship looked as if he had become
satisfied that he was going to be spared a disagreeable duty,
the jurymen exchanged glances of astonishment and satisfaction, and even the counsel for the crown look pleased.

The cross-examination of Mrs. Whiting was short, and
did not alter the tenor of her evidence. In answer to a
question of the law officer for the government as to where
she had been during the last ten years, she said :

"I suppose there's no harm in my telling all about it now.
When Mr. Severne knew that I was aware of all the facts
about Mrs. Severne's death, he told me that there was no
danger of his being tried for murder, and that he did not
wish it known that Mrs. Severne had killed herself. He
said, too, that a great deal would come out which it would
be cruel to give to the world. That she was dead, and he
wished her faults to be buried with her. He gave me money
then, and told me to go and live where I chose, and that as
I had been a faithful nurse he would support me while I
lived, and begged me not to tell what I knew about the suicide ; and I never have told it, and I would not tell it now
if it wasn't to save his noble life."

As she finished these words, Mrs. Whiting took out her
pocket-handkerchief, and removing her spectacles, applied
it to her eyes. She was not the only one in the court-room
affected to tears ; and one enthusiastic juryman rose to his
feet and said : "My lord, I think we have had enough of
this." And was going on to make an address, when his
lordship, with an affectation of harshness, ordered him per-
emptorily to take his seat. Severne sat in the dock, his

lips quivering with emotion, but giving no other outward
manifestation of the feeling within him. John Holmes had
buried his face in his handkerchief, and de Hutten, though
he tried to be calm, could not restrain the tears that flowed
down his cheeks as he thought of the magnanimity of his
friend. As to Lawrence, he was composed. He had known
all this for years.

Mrs. Ellen Whiting left the stand, and was succeeded by
Lawrence. He gave a full account of the death-bed of Mrs.
Severne, which corroborated the statements of the last witness, and of Dr. Maxwell. He had examined the remains
of the poison left in the spoon, and had detected strychnia;
as to the corrosive sublimate purchased by Severne, it was
bought for some chemical investigations on which they were
both engaged, and was used for that purpose a few minutes
after the purchase. In regard to the supposed confession,
his testimony was minute and to the point. He dwelt at
length upon Severne's severe literary labors, and the state
of mind to which he had brought himself, and then related
the details of a case of similar character occurring in his
practice at the same time. He stated that Severne had
read him the letter, and that he, Lawrence, had supposed
it was destroyed, as he had suggested and attempted. The
cross-examination led to no other result except to strengthen
his evidence. And when Lawrence left the witness-stand,
court and audience had evidently made up their minds that
the last doubt of Severne's innocence was removed.

But Mr. Hickling had not yet completed his case, although
he could have rested it there and then with perfect safety
to his client. There were two more witnesses to call, whose
evidence, if not of much importance to Severne, were of
very great consequence to Mr. Freeling; and first, John
Holmes was placed upon the stand.

His evidence was restricted to the sleeve-button of Mr.
Freeling's shirt which this gentleman had dropped into the
drawer, and which was of course conclusive in regard to
the fact that he had opened it, and to the facts connected
with the finding of the book. The cross-examination was
brief and immaterial; the counsel for the crown were evidently getting tired of their adviser. Mr. Freeling's condition was clearly uncomfortable. All eyes were upon him,

and all waited anxiously for what was to come next. They
were not kept long in suspense. "Call James Collins," said
Mr. Hickling.

If Mr. Freeling's position had been disagreeable before,
it was infinitely more so now; and when the crier called
James Collins, and the clerk walked into the witness-box in
obedience to the summons, he grasped his hat and looked
around, as if meditating escape. It was but the action of a
momentary impulse of self-preservation. He saw Mr. Hickling's eye fixed upon him, and he knew that if he attempted
to put his wish into execution, he would be at once arrested.
He therefore replaced his hat on the floor by his side, and
endeavored to look as friendly at the clerk as his waning
courage would allow.

"Now, Mr. Collins," said Mr. Hickling, after the oath
was administered, "we have brought you a long way to testify in this case. Please be thorough, but as short as possible. I think we shall save time by letting you tell your
story in your own way."

"I am clerk for Mr. Freeling," said Collins, "or rather
was till I left New York two weeks ago. On the 21st of
last August Mr. Freeling told me to go to Mr. Severne's
house and get some papers which he said it was important
for him to obtain. He said they were in the upper left-hand
drawer of the library table. They related to a ward of Mr.
Severne's, as I learned from overhearing a conversation between Mr. Freeling and a man who came to see him that
morning. I heard Mr. Freeling tell him that if they were
found, he would give him two hundred dollars. I afterward
drew a check for that amount in favor of this man, a Mr.
Jenkins, and Mr. Freeling signed it.

"As I was saying, Mr. Freeling told me to go to Mr.
Severne's house and get those papers. He gave me a key
which he said would fit the lock of the drawer. I went
there, but I was so closely watched by the housekeeper that
I could not try the key, and I came away, bringing only
some blank sheets of paper with me, as a show of having
got what I came for, so as to satisfy the housekeeper. There
was no writing on any of these papers.

"When I returned to the office and told Mr. Freeling of
my want of success, he said he would go himself. I followed

him when he left the office, and saw him go to his own lodgings. I waited till he came out, and kept close behind him till he entered Mr. Severne's house. It was now quite dark. I got over the garden-wall at the side of the house, and by climbing up an iron trellis was able to look into the library window. I had scarcely got up when the house-keeper and Mr. Freeling entered the room. She lit the gas, and I could now see him distinctly, without being seen myself. As soon as she was gone, he took the key which I had returned to him, and inserted it into the keyhole of the upper left-hand drawer of the table. He opened the drawer and took out of it a small tin box of letters. He read these through carefully, and then replaced them in the box, put the box back into the drawer, and locked it.

"There was a port-folio on the table; Mr. Freeling opened it and took several papers out of it. One of these he read with great astonishment; and I heard him say 'Good God!' After some time he put this paper into his pocket-book and left the room.

"Two or three days after this, Mr. Freeling asked me if I would swear that I had heard Mr. Severne acknowledge to having committed a great crime, and told me he had mur-dered his wife, and that he had the evidence of it in his pocket. I refused; and then he told me it made no great difference, for that Mr. Severne would hang anyhow, and that whether he was guilty or not, he meant to hang him. He then cursed me, and threatened to turn me into the street."

The cross-examination was exceedingly severe, but Col-lins did not swerve a hair's breadth from his story. Mr. Freeling's appearance was that of a man who had lost all hope. Still, he glanced defiantly at Collins, who evidently, however, was in no fear of him now.

"The man is a thief," said Mr. Freeling at last, unable to contain himself longer. "He stole money out of my safe."

The senior counsel for the crown told him in an audible voice to keep silent, and asked him if he had forgotten that he had sworn to his good character. His lordship informed him that on a repetition of his disrespect to the court, he would fine him heavily and commit him for contempt.

"We have nothing further to say," said Mr. Hickling.

"We are ready to let the case go to the jury as it is, without even summing up."

The law officer for the crown then rose, and said that he had been actuated by a sense of what he considered to be his duty, and that still acting from a regard for what was right, he desired to say that the crown had altogether failed to establish a shadow of a suspicion against the accused, whose honor, in his opinion, was as free from blemish as that of any gentleman in the kingdom. He hoped, therefore, that the court would instruct the jury to bring in a verdict of acquittal. As to the manner in which he had been deceived, he would say nothing about that at present, as doubtless it would become a matter for future judicial proceedings.

His lordship stated to the jury that they had heard all the evidence for the prosecution and defense, and could not avoid being struck by the thoroughness of the vindication which the accused had obtained. There was not a jot or tittle of proof tending to fasten the crime of murder upon him. On the contrary, it had been shown that no murder had been committed, and that the accused had, through the purest and most generous motives, endeavored to shield from the disgrace attaching to the crime of suicide, a wife who had evidently been actuated by the most malicious feelings toward him, and whose life had very clearly not been such as that of the wife of an English gentleman should have been. In regard to the chief witness for the crown, he had a few words to say. This man had, from purely personal considerations, perjured himself to secure the conviction of one who had employed and trusted him. Why he had conceived so horrible an idea was not now very apparent. There was a motive, however, and time would reveal it. For the present he should deem it his duty to arrest him and hold him to bail, to await his trial for perjury. His lordship then instructed the jury in regard to their verdict, and they, without leaving the box, unhesitatingly brought in one of acquittal. The foreman stated that he was authorized to say that the jury had arrived at their present opinion before the evidence for the defense had been finished, and would have returned a verdict of acquittal without instructions.

A low murmur of applause ran through the court-room.

John Holmes, Lawrence, and de Hutten shook Severne by
the hand, as did his counsel, and many other gentlemen with
whom he was not personally acquainted. Even the counsel
for the crown came to offer their congratulations.

"Come," said Severne to John Holmes, "let us drive to
Morley's as rapidly as possible; we must not forget the suspense our friends there are in."

As Severne emerged from the Old Bailey, free, and with
the heartfelt regard of all good men who had witnessed the
trial, his unworthy cousin slunk out of a side door, vainly
endeavoring to escape the indignant glances of the crowd,
and Mr. Freeling was escorted out by a stout officer, who
evidently, if an opinion could be formed from his face, performed his duty with the consciousness that it was a righteous one. It was not long before the perjured witness, unable to find bail, was occupying a cell in the same prison
which Severne had left a few hours previously.

CHAPTER XXXII.

IN WHICH SEVERNE HAS MOST OF THE CONVERSATION TO HIMSELF.

NEVER was there a happier party than that assembled at
Morley's that evening. John Holmes had made preparations for celebrating the event of the day by a dinner,—
a family dinner, as he called it. Everybody was in the best
possible spirits, and when the feast was over, Margaret and
Sarah still lingered at the table, loth to retire from the room,
even though there were evident signs that a combined fumi-
gatory movement was about being begun.

"You don't want us to leave, I am sure?" said Margaret,
imploringly, to Severne. "Neither Sarah nor I mind smoke
in the least. I was brought up to like it, and Sarah has
become thoroughly used to it."

"Want you to leave us? Of course not. I would rather

dispense with the cigars than have you go. Besides, I have something to say, as soon as we can get rid of the servants, which I wish you both to hear."

All objected to the ladies vacating the room. "It was a family gathering, and there was to be no absurd formality," John Holmes said. So Margaret' and Sarah, making it a condition of their stay that the four gentlemen present should smoke as much as they liked, and the four gentlemen inwardly resolving that they would not avail themselves of the privilege to a very great extent, an arrangement highly satisfactory to all parties was arrived at.

Of course all the points of the trial were freely discussed, and none gave more general satisfaction, after that of Severne's acquittal, than the signal discomfiture which Mr. Freeling had met.

The servants had been dismissed. John Holmes continued to occupy the head of the table, Severne sat on his right and de Hutten on his left, Margaret sat next to Severne, and Sarah occupied the seat next to de Hutten, while Lawrence was at the foot of the table.

"We are all together now," said Severne, "and the duty which I owe you cannot be performed on a more suitable occasion than this. You have adhered faithfully to me when appearances were adverse, and when you had nothing to justify your friendship but your knowledge of my general character, and the consciousness springing from the examination of your own hearts that you would not have been guilty of the foul crime laid to my charge. The pure and honest-minded are always slow to suspect those of dishonor whose lives have always, to their knowledge, been above reproach; while the low, the mean, and the false among mankind are the first to raise an outcry against one whose high position they envy, and in rejoicing over whose fall, they hope to convince the world of their own upright and truthful bearing. Through all my troubles you have never asked for an explanation, and I have felt that the attempt to offer one would be an insult to your artless and lofty friendship which I should be the last one to proffer. In the hour of triumph, however, when every vestige of suspicion of my integrity has disappeared, it would be wrong for me to withhold from you a knowledge of the facts which justified me in my course, and in the existence of which, though ignorant of their exact character, you had the most boundless faith. You have a right to know all, and though I am sure it is one that you would never claim, it is none the less my duty to insist on giving it."

"My dear Severne," said John Holmes, "I do but give utterance to the feelings of all of us when I tell you that any such revelation as that you mention can only give you pain, and that we therefore neither desire nor expect it. We need nothing to convince us of your thorough singleness of heart, and fidelity to all that is right."

"What do you say?" said Severne, turning to Margaret, who sat silently by his side.

. "Tell them," she replied, while her face was illumined with the wonderful beauty which swept over it, like the sunlight over a fair landscape, whenever she was moved by a noble emotion. "Tell them. They will never be able otherwise to comprehend the full measure of your honor and unselfishness."

He smiled, as he replied : "I will do so, but not with that expectation. However, if you all like me better after you have heard what I have to say, I shall not complain." He covered his face with his hand for a moment, as if to abstract his thoughts from what was passing around him, and then, amid the unbroken silence of all, thus told the story of his life.

ROBERT SEVERNE'S STORY.

"I pass over the events of my early life, which did not differ materially from those which occur in the career of most young men reared in affluence with no predilection for dissipation and fashionable society, but with a strong bias toward literature and science. I went through Oxford creditably, but as I had no very great liking for mathematics, preferring, instead, the natural sciences, I did not contend for the honors of a double first.

"I was on my way home, with the world before me. I had determined, while I sat in the railway carriage, the course I intended to pursue. I had made up my mind to go to Germany, and spend several years in attendance upon the uni-

versities there, and then returning, live upon the small fortune
which I had inherited from my mother.   My father's house,
I was afraid, would not prove a very pleasant residence for
me.   He had recently married a second time, and from what
I had seen of his wife I was satisfied she would not be a congenial step-mother.   She was a Spanish woman, the widow
of a gentleman who had been in the diplomatic service, and
who had married her at the Spanish Court.   She appeared
to think of nothing but pleasure, and had entirely changed
the character which Severne Hall had borne for so many
years as the residence of a sedate and quiet gentleman.

"I was my father's only child, and was consequently the
heir to his estate, which was quite large.   I was therefore a
person of some consequence in my step-mother's eyes.   We
had seen but little of each other, and I might have liked her
had I not perceived that she was given so thoroughly to her
own selfish pleasures as to neglect all the duties which her
married vows imposed upon her.   I saw that she preferred
the society of every man about her to that of her husband;
and one evening, as I was in the conservatory, I unavoidably
overheard her carrying on an intrigue with a guest who
passed for her husband's friend.   I received all her advances
therefore with a coldness which I did not affect to conceal.
She saw that I did not like her, but she seemed determined
to return good for evil, and made me more than ever before,
the unwilling recipient of her favors.   She overlooked nothing that could conduce to my comfort, and showed me
many graceful instances of apparent kindness, which, if I
had not been convinced were not the offspring of a disinterested heart, would have won me completely to her side.   I
could not forget, however, that I knew her to be false and
depraved, and I continued to avoid her as much as possible.

"She had a daughter by her first husband, whom I had
never seen, but who was spoken of by those who knew her
as a miracle of beauty and cleverness.   When I had paid
my last visit to Severne Hall, she was absent, but her mother
did not fail to tell me of her daughter's perfections at every
opportunity, until her praises, and those of others who had
seen the young lady, my father among them, would have led
me to look forward to meeting her with no small degree of
pleasure had I not been told by my father, and had I not

understood from his wife's conduct, that they had set their hearts upon making a marriage between us.

"I thought of all these things as I sat in the railway carriage on my way home, and therefore it was that I determined to remove myself from associations which I was convinced would be unpleasant.

"It was dark when the train stopped at the station nearest Severne Hall. I alighted, and was looking out for a conveyance to the house, when I was arrested by my father's coachman, who told me that Mrs. Severne had expected me that evening, and had sent the carriage. Here was another instance of her forethought for me. I had not written to say I was coming that day, and she must have calculated the time of my return for herself.

"As the carriage approached the house, I saw that there was a large assemblage of persons present. The drawing-rooms and grounds were brilliantly lighted up, and music and conversation were heard on all sides. In answer to my inquiries, the footman told me that Miss Sefton, Mrs. Severne's daughter, had arrived a few days previously, and that the ball was in her honor. I ordered the carriage to be driven up to a side door, and endeavored to make my way to my own room unperceived. Mrs. Severne, however, was on the watch for me. She came into the hall, greeted me in the most affectionate manner, and telling me that the ball was as much in my honor as Francisca's, begged me not to disappoint her and her daughter by refusing them the pleasure they would derive from my presence. It would have been churlish in me to refuse, so I promised, and hurrying to my chamber, dressed myself and descended to the drawing-rooms.

"Mrs. Severne and my father met me at the door. The latter was of course glad to see me. He had. always been kind and indulgent to me, and I felt that I owed him a great deal for the opportunities he had given me for improving my mind, when it would have been more agreeable to him to have had me at home during the many lonely years he had passed there.

"Mrs. Severne at once dropped her husband's arm, and taking mine, told me that Francisca was very anxious to see me, and that I must go at once and be presented to her.

We found her surrounded by a crowd of admirers, but as soon as I was introduced she devoted herself so exclusively to me that they all disappeared, and I was left alone with her and her mother. She was certainly very beautiful. Her eyes and hair were black, and her complexion, though dark, was clear and brilliant; and yet her beauty was not the kind I most admired. It was too dazzling, too bold, for the ideal of female loveliness I had formed in my mind. There was nothing subdued about it, nothing quiet, nothing of that calm and gentle spiritualism which my ideal possessed, and which reveals so charmingly, and yet so truthfully, the nobility and heroism of the soul.

"It was not long, however, before I felt the influence of her spell. Her manners were graceful and winning; she showed that she had been well educated, she expressed herself in language that was free from fault, and she gave utterance to ideas which made me believe her to be a paragon of virtue. I had never mingled much in the society of women; those I had been thrown with were of the most commonplace kind, and I was but twenty years old. Can it be wondered at therefore that I lost my senses, and that when she asked me to walk with her on the lawn, I went out of the hot and glittering rooms vain of the distinction that the most beautiful woman in that brilliant throng was on my arm?

"She treated me with the utmost confidence, told me all her little troubles, appealed to me to be her friend, begged me to remember the ties that already bound us to one another. She was apparently so artless, so free from guile, so winsome in all her ways, that I wondered why I had not seen all her goodness in her face at the first glance; I looked at her again, long and anxiously, by the light of a splendid lamp that hung over our heads, and that lit up the avenue in which we walked. She was very beautiful; I could not question that. But I did not see the expression I had expected to find. There was a want of harmony between her face and her words which troubled me. It was unnatural that there should be this want of accord, and I was annoyed, as I was and am still, at all incongruities. Still my disappointment was not of long duration: I forgot it all in the pleasure I experienced in her society; and when, after an hour passed outside, we returned to the house, I had become her devoted admirer.

"After that I saw her daily, almost hourly. We took long walks through the woods, and along the beautiful lake that lay hid among the hills not far from the house; we rode through the paths which led to the most unfrequented spots; we read out of books we both liked, and we did many other things which served the one great purpose of bringing us together. All this was very pleasing to Mrs. Severne, and I saw also that my father was satisfied.

"And yet I did not love Francisca Sefton. I was pleased with her, and felt lonely if I was not almost constantly in her society. I never thought of marrying her, and therefore when my father one morning told me how gratified he and his wife were with my attentions to her, and that they had both set their hearts on our marriage as the one thing needful to complete their happiness, I received the information with a surprise I could not conceal, for I was not conscious of having done anything to warrant the belief that I was attached to her by any warmer tie than that resulting from my connection with her as the daughter of my father's wife.

"However, when I came to reflect upon the matter, I was forced to admit that I had given ample grounds for the opinion my father and his wife had formed. Two months had elapsed—two months of uninterrupted association with Francisca. I knew she liked me, and it was possible she entertained a stronger feeling still for me. What was I to do? To break off suddenly in my intercourse and go away from Severne Hall, would be cowardly; to remain and shun the society which was so pleasant to me, would be unjust to her and myself; to keep on as I had done, without knowing that she did not look upon me in any other light than as a friend and agreeable companion, would be dishonorable. I determined therefore to have an understanding with her, and to be governed accordingly.

"I reflected fully upon all the possible contingencies of the interview I had resolved upon. If I found that Francisca's feeling for me was no stronger than mine for her, then I should be very well pleased, and we could continue the companionship which had been so agreeable to us both, till the time came for me to go to Germany. If, on the contrary, I found she loved me, there was but one thing I could think of to save my honor and secure her happiness, and that was to ask her to be my wife. I did not look upon this alternative as at all a disagreeable one. I had a high regard for Francisca, I believed thoroughly in her goodness, and I did not doubt that she would be to me a true and faithful wife. It would be my duty to try to make her life a happy one, and with God's help I would do my part justly and conscientiously. Besides, nothing would have given my father more pleasure. He had often mentioned to me, in no obscure terms, how happy it would make him to see Francisca and me married; and as to her mother—whose wishes were, however, a matter of perfect indifference to me —her joy, I knew, would pass all bounds.

"So one evening, just as the sun was sinking behind the hills among which the little lake was almost concealed, I asked Francisca to take a walk with me. She consented with evident marks of pleasure, and we bent our steps toward the bank, amid the foliage of which we had so often strayed in our wanderings. I had never seen her look more beautiful than she did that evening, as she walked quietly by my side, scarcely raising her jet-black eyes from the ground, and seeming to my eyes the very incarnation of modesty and truth. She was born in Spain, and had lived there till she was sixteen years old. The warm southern sun had left its impress upon her, which the four years of her residence in our bleak climate had not been able to efface. How my opinion of her beauty had changed! I remembered then what I had thought of it the first time we met, and I wondered how I had ever been able to form so erroneous an opinion of a face which now seemed to me almost perfect in its loveliness.

"We walked on, scarcely speaking a word till we had turned an angle in the narrow path, which brought us in full view of as much of the little lake as it was possible to see from any one point. There was a rustic bench close by the water, and to that we directed our steps. We sat down, still in silence. My mind was too much preoccupied to talk upon indifferent topics, and she, seeing that such was the case, forbore her attempts to lead me into conversation. The water almost touched the hem of her dress; the place was deep in the shadows of the approaching night. It was ominous of the darkness that was to fall upon my life, and bury it in gloom for so many years.

"At last she spoke :

"'You are very silent this evening, Robert. Have I done anything to offend you, that you will scarcely speak to me ?'

"'Nothing,' I answered. 'I was thinking how much longer we should be together.'

"'Is there any reason why we should part ?' she said, looking earnestly into my face.

"'You know I go to Germany in a few weeks.'

"She made no answer, but looked down at the water which flowed at her feet.

"'We have been very happy,' I continued. 'I have never passed two months so pleasantly in all my life before, and I will always regard you as a dear sister.'

"'I have been happy,' she murmured, 'but I cannot look upon you as a brother.'

"'As a friend, then,' I resumed ; 'and when, in other days, you come to this spot——'

"'I will never come here after you are gone,' she exclaimed, interrupting me. 'It will have no charms for me then.'

"She still continued to look down at the water, but I saw that her eyes were filled with tears.

"'I am glad you like me, Francisca,' I said. 'I shall go away with the consciousness that I have left a dear friend behind me who, amid other associations, will not altogether forget me.'

"'Robert,' she said, in a voice tremulous with emotion, 'do you wish to break my heart ?'

"Then I knew she loved me. I told her that we would never part, and taking her hand, said, that if she would be my wife I would cherish and protect her through all her life and mine. She laid her head on my breast, and revealed to me how dearly she loved me, and that there could be no happiness for her in this world away from me.

"I drank in with a wild delight the words of love she gave me. Already I felt the influence which springs from the consciousness of being beloved ; and by the time we had reached home, I felt that I loved her fondly in return.

"I led her into the drawing-room where my father and his wife sat awaiting our return before going to dinner. I

informed him of what I had done, and received his blessing.
Francisca threw herself into her mother's arms and wept for
joy.   My father kissed her tenderly, and told her how thankful he was that his prayers had at last been answered.   We
were a happy party that night,—happier far than we ever
were afterward.

"Everything went on well, and before our marriage took
place I had become so warmly attached to Francisca that I
looked forward to the day that was to make her mine with
emotions of unalloyed pleasure.   Three weeks after our engagement we took the vows that made us husband and wife.

"It was arranged that we should spend a month at Severne Hall, and that then we should take up our residence in
London.   This plan was agreeable to both Francisca and
myself.   She had never lived in a large city, and was anxious to see something of the world as it is found in one so
vast as London, while I was not only desirous of contribut-
ing to her happiness, but also wished to further objects
which I had in view, and which could only be carried out
successfully in a place where access could be had to large
and complete libraries.   Our stay in the country passed
without the occurrence of any material incidents, till the
day before the one upon which we were to take our departure.   Up to this time I had no cause to complain of Francisca's conduct.   On the contrary, her words and actions
had been uniformly considerate and affectionate.

"I had been fishing, and had returned, with a severe headache, earlier than I had expected.   I was lying down on a
sofa, which occupied an alcove in the library, trying to get
to sleep, when I heard the rustling of dresses, and the
voices of Francisca and her mother.   They had just come
into the room, and had seated themselves in the next alcove.
I paid no attention to them, as my head was aching violently, and I wanted to be quiet in the hope of getting rid
of my indisposition before dinner.   I gave no heed to their
conversation, and they had been talking for several minutes
without my hearing a word they said, when the sound of my
own name, spoken by Francisca, struck on my ear.   She
repeated it, and in a tone of the utmost contempt.

"'You think I love him?' she continued. 'You ought
to know me better by this time.'

"'You did love him once, whatever you may feel for him now,' said her mother.

"'I never did, I tell you. My dear madam,' she continued, with a light laugh, 'I have been too apt a pupil of yours not to be able to make a man think I love him when I really despise him.'

"Her mother laughed. 'There is no use in your getting angry about it, Francisca,' she said. 'I only thought that if you did, it would not be so very bad. He will have a large fortune at his father's death, and the old fool cannot live much longer. He told me this morning that Sir Willoughby Hatfield had detected an organic disease of the heart. You know he can leave me very little, and your fortune is not enough to enable you to live as you would wish. If you do not love your husband, at any rate, try to keep on good terms with him.'

"'It's as much as I can do to treat him civilly,' she answered. 'I have always had the most thorough contempt for him. I hate men who are what are called learned, and who are constantly talking of books. I ought not to have married. I have made a slave of myself; but when I get to London I shall make a bold strike for freedom. I think, though, you ought to give me credit for being a most dutiful daughter, whatever I may be as a wife.'

"I could bear no more. I rose from the sofa and stood before them. 'I have heard all,' I said. 'I know how thoroughly wicked and depraved you both are. I knew your character long ago,' I continued, addressing the mother, 'but I did not think you, Francisca, were as vile as your language shows you to be. You have deceived me for your own base purposes. You may reap some material advantage from your falsehood, but there is an end to even the appearance of love between us.'

"The two were confused for a moment at being detected in their iniquitous schemes. It was only for an instant, however, that Francisca was deprived of her presence of mind, for she came toward me with a look of surprise on her face, and said :

"'My dear Robert, what do you mean ? You must have been dreaming.'

"'No,' I answered; 'I was never wider awake than I am

31

now.   I have been lying down in the adjoining alcove, and
have heard enough of your designs to convince me of the
utter corruption of your nature.'

"She looked at me fixedly and anxiously for a moment,
and then, in an excited manner, and with every appearance
of feeling, said :

"'My God! Robert, you are ill! Ring, mother, for assistance.   Quick! quick! do you not see that he is ill?'

"I shook off her hand which she had laid on my arm.
'You cannot deceive me any longer,' I said.   'I know you
now for a wicked and heartless woman.'

"She burst into a flood of tears, and throwing herself on
the floor, continued to sob violently.

"'You have killed her!' said her mother, addressing me.
'She loves you with her whole soul, and you are treating
her in a way that will break her heart.'

"I made no reply, but walking away, met the servant,
who had come in answer to the bell, and sent him back.   I
could not bear the thought of exposing my wife's conduct
and my own shame to him, and thus making her name a by-
word ere we had been married a month.

"That night I asked my father to give me a few moments'
conversation.   I saw, as soon as we were alone together,
that he knew all that had occurred, and I supposed his wife
had been beforehand with her version.   I inquired if such
was not the case.   He replied in the affirmative, but added
that he did not believe what she had said, for that he also
had heard their conversation, having been in the bay-window
near them writing. He begged me, however, for God's sake
not to insist upon a separation; to try and live with her
while he should live; that it was true his heart was seriously
diseased, and that the physician had warned him against all
excitement.   'Remember, too, Robert,' he said, 'that she
is your wife.   Do not expose her; try to reclaim her; she
is young, and may not be beyond the influence of your counsel; and when she is removed from her mother's control, she
may do better.   If you cast her off, she is lost.   I shall have
a heavy cross to bear likewise, but I shall do so in silence
and secrecy.'

"I heard him through, and resolved to follow his advice.
I went to Francisca, and offered her forgetfulness and for-

giveness. I told her I asked for no explanations, and I begged her to look upon me as her husband and friend, as one who would be her guide and protector in all the trials and dangers that might befall her, and as one who still loved her. She listened to me with tears in her eyes, and then threw herself into my arms, and implored me to take her once more into the heart she had so cruelly bruised."

Severne ceased speaking for a few moments. His friends were full of sadness, but they said nothing. John Holmes wiped his eyes, and Sarah, overcome with the recollection of her own acts, which were recalled by Severne's story, could not restrain the emotion which swelled within her. And Margaret? Her face showed what she felt, even though she shed no tears. And when Severne looked at her anxiously, almost imploringly, as if to ask her sympathy, she returned his glance lovingly and proudly, and put her hand in his in token of her unchanged love and trust.

"I may have been weak," resumed Severne, "but if I was, my error was on the right side. I reflected that she was a woman, and that I had sworn to love and cherish her as my wife. True, I had been deceived; but did that fact release me from my vows? If she was faithless, was I thereby justified in casting her off without making an honest effort to lead her to the right path? I did not think so, and thus it was that I once more gave her my confidence, and resolved to devote my life to the attempt to make her a good and faithful wife, a true and virtuous woman.

"The next day we departed for London. We took lodgings while the house which my father had bought for us was being furnished and put in order for our residence. During this period Francisca's conduct was everything I could wish it to be. I went with her to places of amusement, and gave nearly all my time towards endeavoring to make her happy. She seemed to appreciate my attentions, and for awhile I hoped that all would yet go well with us.

"Six months had elapsed since we had come to London. I had gathered about me a number of persons whose society I liked, and Francisca had also made many acquaintances, among men and women of excellent position. Our means were ample: my mother had left me fifty thousand pounds, and my father had settled a handsome sum on Francisca at our marriage.   We were therefore enabled to live not only in comfort but in style.

"Among our visitors was a gentleman whose friendship I valued, because he was not only correct in his deportment, but was of pleasing manners, and endowed with talents of a very high order.   He frequently dined with us, and made no attempt to conceal his liking both for me and Francisca. With her, however, he never lost a certain gentlemanly reserve, which did him great honor.   Although she made no secret of the pleasure she derived from his society, I never perceived that in the slightest point his conduct passed beyond the strictest limits of propriety.   He was an American, and it was from him that I obtained the ideas of the United States which caused me afterward to make that country my home.

" I had noticed no change in Francisca's manner toward me in all the time we had been in London until one evening, on returning from a meeting of a learned society of which I was a member, I found her walking her chamber in a state of intense anger and excitement.   I inquired kindly what was the matter.   She stopped in front of me and said, while her face expressed the full force of the passion she felt:

" ' I'll tell you what is the matter, Robert Severne.   The matter is that I am tired of keeping up this sickening show of pretending to love you, and I intend to do it no longer. I hate you, thoroughly hate you ; always did hate you, and expect to do so till I die.   There is no person in this world whom I loathe so utterly as I do you ; and I never would have consented to the slavery I have endured since my marriage but to please my mother, who, for objects of her own, made a tool of me.'

" I could scarcely believe the evidence of my senses, but without giving me time for reflection, she continued :

" ' There must be an understanding between us.   I am willing to remain in your house if you do not expect me to make a fool of myself in endeavoring to conceal my real feelings for you.   Reject this and I go out of it to-night to a place where I will be allowed to do as I please.'

" ' Francisca,' I said, ' if you are not mad, I will answer you.'

" ' Mad !' she exclaimed, with a laugh of contempt.   ' I

will show you.' She sat down, and at once became perfectly composed. 'Now I am ready to hear what you have to say. My pulse, I believe,' she continued, as she felt her wrist, 'is as calm and slow as it ever was in my life.'

"'I have no reproaches to make to you,' I said. 'You have chosen your course and I shall acquiesce in it. I have endeavored to make you virtuous and to gain your love, but without success. I shall try no longer. Still, I do not forget that you are my wife, and that it is my duty to treat you as kindly as I can, and as you will allow me. It is impossible that we can live together in future. I will not ask you to go, but will go myself. I will see that you want for nothing; I only beg you not to destroy your reputation. As to all else, I have nothing to demand.'

"'Very well,' she answered. 'That is sensible. I accept your terms. Now leave me, if you please.'

"In regard to the circumstances which led to this interview, I knew but little till the volume of Calderon de la Barca's poems came into my hands. How this book got to my library is explained by the fact that after Francisca's death, her mother took possession of all her effects, and I suppose it was taken to Severne Hall, and placed in my father's library without attracting especial attention, where it remained, till at his death it was sent to me. There is no title on the back, and thus I never noticed it particularly.

"In this book," he continued, taking the volume from his pocket, "I find a full explanation of the motives by which she was governed, and the most bitter expression of her hate for me. I will only say in regard to her, that she states that the gentleman whom I have referred to, had been that evening to the house, that she had asked him to elope with her, and that he, with a consideration for his friend which has never faltered, and a regard for his own honor which has never deserted him, had refused her infamous proposal. When I tell you that he is here among us, and that his name is Edward Lawrence, you will bear me witness that what I have said of him is true. I never heard from him one word of this. Even his love for his friend was not sufficient to make him break his word, unwittingly pledged, to my wretched wife.

"I remained in London for a few days, making prepara-

31*

tions for Francisca's support and my departure. I settled upon her all the money I had inherited from my mother, except ten thousand pounds. During this period, she followed strictly the line of conduct she had determined upon, and let no occasion pass without giving me to understand how much she hated me. Her abusive language, however, did not deter me from doing what I had resolved upon, or make me hurry my departure by a single day.

"Finally, when I had completed all my arrangements, I took my leave of her. She merely bowed her head, without taking my hand or thanking me for what I had done to insure her comfort.

"I afterward wondered if she was insane or not. So far as I could ever discover, there was no cause for her dislike of me. I had always been kind to her in words and actions. In fact, the more I showed my affection for her, the more she seemed to concentrate her hate upon me. I thought it would be charitable to attribute her conduct to mental aberration, and I tried to persuade myself that such a condition existed, but the effort was in vain. She was so systematic, so calm and logical in her judgments, so cool and collected in her demeanor, that I could not in my conscience give her the benefit of this supposition. I saw too clearly that her conduct was the result of bad principles, which had been instilled into her from childhood; that the art of deception had formed a prominent feature of her education; and that the precepts and example of a wicked mother had been all-powerful in corrupting a heart that might have been naturally good. She was totally devoid of all sense of honor; the truth was not in her; there was no generosity, no confidence, no love. She knew her conduct was wrong, she admitted it to me on several occasions; she says so repeatedly in her journal, and yet she willfully persevered in her depraved and reckless course. She cannot, therefore, escape the condemnation of all right-minded men and women. And it would be folly in me to affect an extenuation of her wicked, her very wicked behavior.

"I went to Germany, and endeavored to seek relief from the troubles that weighed heavily upon me. It was then that I first met de Hutten. I soon discovered that there was solace to be found in the contemplation of the laws of our existence; in the study of the operations of the mind ; in the investigation of those works of God which teach us both our littleness and our greatness; and in the consideration of those learned treatises which the great minds of past ages have given to us. I was making for myself a new world, and experiencing no small degree of happiness, when a letter from Lawrence informed me that my wife was so ill that she was not expected to recover.

"I hesitated whether I should return or not. Finally I determined to go. I thought that perhaps on her deathbed she might do me justice, and die with her sins forgiven; and I found, too, that the love I once lavished upon her was not yet dead in my heart.

"I went to my house at once on my arrival in London. I found Francisca suffering under a severe attack of typhus fever. She was unconscious, and her life evidently hung upon a thread. Many things which reached my ears convinced me that her course had been down, down, till she had reached a level from which it was impossible she could ever be raised so as to recover my respect. Still, she was sick and helpless; I pitied her; I remembered what I had once felt for her, and therefore I watched by her side, night after night, hoping that the scale would turn in her favor, and that she might yet be enabled to live a virtuous life. It did turn. Through the efforts of Dr. Maxwell and Lawrence, and perhaps in some degree through the careful nursing I gave to her, her disease began to yield. As soon as she became conscious, I spoke to her, and told her I had come back to take care of her till she recovered. She was too weak to make any reply, but I saw that she recognized me, and that her dislike was as intense as ever. Day by day she got stronger, and day by day her hatred grew in violence. Whenever I came near her to ask how she did, she took especial pains to express her aversion, and frequently threatened to kill herself as the only effectual means of getting rid of my presence. I stayed away from her, therefore, and went to live with Lawrence, who resided not far from my house. I came every day, however, two or three times, to inquire of the nurse her condition, but I never saw her again till I stood by her death-bed.

"This idea of suicide seemed to grow upon her, I should

judge from the perusal of her journal, but she took pains to conceal it from all her attendants. She told them that I had repeatedly threatened to murder her, and she even told some of them that I had attempted it twice. When she had, as she thought, poisoned their minds against me, she put her scheme into execution. I was in the house at the time, having sat up in the room adjoining hers all night, in consequence of a slight relapse she had suffered the previous day. I went to her room as soon as I was called, and found her suffering great pain. I saw at once that her symptoms were like those produced by poisoning from strychnia, and sent immediately for Dr. Maxwell and Lawrence. As she lay there, writhing in convulsive agony, she repeatedly accused me of poisoning her. My attempts to win her to the truth, and to make her see the evil of her life, were all in vain, and she died with the lie on her lips.

"No one knew that she had committed suicide but Dr. Maxwell, Lawrence, Ellen Whiting, and myself. Ellen had been the unconscious instrument of the crime. I begged them all, for the love they bore me, to keep the secret locked in their own breasts. I desired to spare her name the disgrace which attaches to self-murder. She had enough to bear without this being superadded. She was not buried before I was half suspected of having killed her. It was thought by some of her friends that there ought to be a post-mortem examination. It was known that I had purchased a quantity of corrosive sublimate shortly before her death, and this substance was sought for. It was not found; but at my request an examination was made for strychnia, and a large quantity was discovered. This fact, however, was not mentioned. It was known but to the four persons who knew she had destroyed herself.

"The suspicions against me, therefore, took no active form, but still I was suspected. Men whom I had counted as my best friends shunned me, and many of those who had profited most by my companionship or influence were the first to give me up. Then I learned that a good name borne for a lifetime avails but little with the mass of mankind when suspicion is excited against its possessor, and kept alive by those who are envious of his position. The worst injury a man can do the world is to be successful. It never forgives him.

"None of you know what it is to suffer under the imputation of a crime, the mere contemplation of which would excite the utmost horror in your breasts. I know all the torturing emotions which this great wrong can cause, and I have borne them for many years, snstained only by the friendship of a few brave and devoted friends, and above all, by the consciousness of an innocence which I always knew would, in the end, be made abundantly manifest.

"I resided a year in London after Francisca's death, trying to stem the current against me, and to live down the aspersions cast upon my honor, but it was in vain. If I had been wealthy I should doubtless have sncceeded, but Francisca had dissipated all the money I had given her, and my father having been induced by his wife to give credit to the falsehoods she told him in regard to me, I would not apply to him for aid. The small means I had reserved for myself out of my mother's fortune were almost entirely consumed in paying the debts Francisca had contracted. I resolved, therefore, to shake the dust of England from my feet, and to seek in another land the peace which was denied me here. I went to New York, knowing no one in that great city but Lawrence. He gave me a home, loaned me money, secured me employment, and, above all, tried to keep my heart free from the chilling influence, the cynicism, the contempt of mankind, which, had I been left to my own thoughts, would have changed its nature.

"Within two years after my arrival in that city I heard that my father's wife had eloped with a dissolute nobleman of her country, and shortly afterward my father died. I might then have returned and entered upon the enjoyment of my property, but I decided not to do so. I was determined to achieve success without any other aid than that which my own persevering efforts could give me. I remained there, devoting myself to various kinds of literary and scientific labor, until at last I discovered a new and improved metallurgic process which at once made me independent. Then I sent over to this country and took my property ont of the hands of the executors. The rest you know. When I tell you now that I am happy, you will understand what the word means for me. It is only those who have tasted bitter fruits who can appreciate the full flavor of the sweet. And all this I owe to my friends and my enemies. Without the one, the occasion for proving my innocence would never have arisen; without the other, I should not have attempted to vindicate myself in the only way possible,—the further disgrace of her who was once my wicked and faithless wife; and now, when I look at all this, and recall to mind that it is God's work, I can thank him in the same breath for having given me enemies as well as friends."

*　　*　　*　　*　　*　　*

He was done. The story of his life had been told, and he was left alone with her who had brought the first light to a heart darkened by misfortune. Her head lay upon his breast, and he played caressingly with the golden hair that half concealed her beautiful face. "My darling," he said, as he bent down and kissed her lips, and looked into her violet eyes so earnestly, so trustfully, so lovingly, that her heart bounded with a wild delight, "it is worth a world of sorrow to feel the happiness of this hour. Let us look forward with confidence to the future that God has in store for us. Hitherto he has protected us, and henceforth he will not desert us."

"If he gives me the power to make you happy, and grants me the continuance of your love, I shall be content."

A low knock at the door interrupted her. Severne went to open it, and there stood Sarah as pale as death, and with her eyes filled with tears. He took her by the hand and led her into the room.

"What is the matter, my dear child?" he said, tenderly. "You have been weeping! When we are all so happy you ought to be joyful, too."

"I could not go to bed," she answered, tearfully, "without telling you something of what I feel. You had learned how false one woman had been; you knew I had deceived you, that I was wicked and low—lower even than she who had done you so much wrong, and yet with all this knowledge you took me by the hand, forgave me, trusted me, lifted me up from my sin and shame, found me friends and a dear sister, made me your child, and gave me a father's love. I know that I am not what I ought to be; I still feel that I am unworthy of all your kindness; but I do not the less appreciate it, and I hope in time to prove to you that your goodness has not been altogether in vain."

"My dear Sarah," said Severne, "you have proved that to me long ago. You prove it every moment of your life. Do you think I cannot see how good and true you are? how worthily you have lived up to the promises you made me? how gentle and womanly you are in all your feelings? My dear child, I have had my reward. When I first saw your face, over a year ago, by the light of a street lamp, I said you were at heart a good girl. God put it into my mind to give you the chance to throw off the evil that surrounded you. But you had taken the first steps before I saw you again; here is the one who kindled the sparks that lay hid, even from your own knowledge, and who, by the simple power which goodness can always exercise, has made you what you are. So don't let me see any more tears or pale faces," he continued, with a smile. "You are one of us; we all love you dearly, and we intend to make you as happy as we can."

"My darling," said Margaret to Sarah, in a whisper, "all the love you and I can give him will not be the half he deserves. We have nothing in this world to do but to love him and seek his happiness. He is the noblest, the truest, the bravest man that ever lived."

CHAPTER XXXIII.

IN WHICH MATTERS GENERALLY ARE BROUGHT TO SATISFACTORY CONCLUSIONS, AND THIS HISTORY BROUGHT TO AN END.

THE next morning at breakfast John Holmes thought it time to state the results of his study and perseverance in his chemical pursuits. All were in such excellent spirits, and apparently so disposed to see the ludicrous side of a subject, that he did so a little apprehensively. "It will amuse them at any rate," he said to himself; "and then, I am not at all afraid of being laughed at." Accordingly, in a serious manner, and yet with occasional gleams of sparkling wit and humor which made them all laugh, he told the story of his secret and mysterious labors : how patiently he and Joshua had worked, and how at last he had succeeded in proving that gold was not a simple substance, but a compound of several, a new metal being one of its constituents. "This metal," he continued, "was discovered through the exercise, by a young lady whom I know, of that faculty of the female mind called curiosity. As a punishment, I decided not to name it after her; and then I repented, and concluded to do her a still greater honor,—call it after the man whose name would one day be hers. I therefore christened it Severnium, and a very good name it is, too. This substance is the essential constituent of gold, and with it, as I have demonstrated, gold can be made."

"I am deeply sensible of the honor done me," said Severne, "and in my own behalf and that of the meddlesome young lady for whom I presume to speak, desire to return thanks. I suppose, now, we will all be instructed in the processes necessary to enable us to manufacture the precious metal for ourselves ?"

"Get me plenty of severnium," said John Holmes, "and I will make you plenty of gold."

"Why can't you get it yourself?" said Lawrence.

"That is the great difficulty," replied John Holmes, with a sigh. "Hitherto I have only obtained it from gold. I have separated it from this metal over and over again, and recombined it with the other constituents and made the gold repeatedly; but what is the use of going on *ad infinitum*, unmaking and making the same piece of gold? Unless some one will put me in the way of getting severnium, my discovery is a highly honorable and a very startling one, but is not at all likely to put a grain more of gold into my pocket than is there now."

"On the contrary," said Severne, laughing, "it will take a good many grains out. However, my old friend, you have money enough. You are fairly entitled to the honor of having established a great scientific fact, and you ought to be satisfied."

"I am satisfied. I don't want any more money, and I intend to get rid of what I have very soon. But now that I have told my story, what are we to do with ourselves?

Are we to stay in Europe much longer, or shall we go home as soon as we can ?"

"As far as Lawrence, de Hutten, and myself are concerned," said Severne, "I think I may safely say that we have had traveling enough.   Besides," he continued, glancing at Margaret with the barest trace of a smile on his face, "I have some very important business to attend to at home which will not admit of delay; for instance, I have a new agent to appoint, and——"

"Yes, yes, I understand all about that," interrupted John Holmes, laughing.   "Then we will go immediately; I'll see to-day about the passage by the next steamer. So we'll consider that as settled, if there is no objection."

. This proposal meeting with the approval of all, John Holmes proceeded to get ready for a visit to the office of the steamship company, and the party was about breaking up, when de Hutten, who had been looking for the last half hour as if he had a matter of some importance on his mind, requested a few minutes' conversation with Severne.

"Certainly, my dear fellow," said the latter, "as many as you wish ; come into the next room and join me in a cigar. I think tobacco always gives a finish to a friendly chat."

When they were alone and had lit their Cabañas, de Hutten said :

"You have done me a great many favors. I shall always remember, that but for you, I should never have succeeded in finding the destroyer of my kindred.   I have now a greater favor yet to ask of you."

"I don't know about my helping you to kill your diabolical enemy," replied Severne, with a smile.   "I think your mysterious pentagramme must have influenced me in a way that I could not resist.   But whether that is so or not, you know me well enough to believe that I would refuse you nothing in my power to grant."

"You are very kind, I know, and I trust I do not presume upon your goodness when I request your permission to ask your ward for her hand."

Severne's face grew troubled. "My dear friend," he said, "there is no one I would more willingly give her to than you, for I am sure you would make her happy. Do you know anything of her past history ?"

"Nothing; I have not spoken to her on the subject.   I know she is a virtuous, intelligent, and beautiful woman, and I believe she would make me a true and faithful wife; I love her very dearly, I am not without hope that she loves me; and, besides, I have had the last interview with my great ancestor, who reappeared to me last night, solely, as he said, to urge me to do that which, as I knew before he told me, would of all things conduce most to my happiness."

"It would be wrong in me to let you enter into this matter," said Severne, gravely, "without acquainting you with all the circumstances of her past life as fully as I know them myself. As you say, she is a virtuous and beautiful woman,— beautiful she has always been,—but there was a time, my dear friend, when she was not virtuous. If, after you have heard what I have to tell you, you should still ask me to give her to you, and she should join in the request, I will put her hand in yours and feel that one more blessing has been vouchsafed me."

And then Severne, withholding nothing from his friend, told him all he knew of Sarah. "Now," he said, "you will be able to act with the full knowledge of what she was and what she is. Perhaps you had better not decide at present. Take a day or two to consider the matter. It is one which involves her happiness and yours, and should not be settled hastily."

De Hutten reflected for a few moments in silence, and then he asked:

"Do you love her?"

"Very dearly; I know her to be a sweet, an affectionate, and an honest girl."

"And I love her, too, for what she is, not for what she was. I have decided. I am done with my own past, and do not care to consider hers. I have seen a great deal of her during the time we have been in London. I have observed that you, and Miss Leslie, and Mr. Holmes, and Lawrence respect and love her; I have seen that her thoughts and impulses are all good. What more could I ask? I would rather trust her than many princesses I have met."

"And so would I. You are not deceived in your opinion of her. Go and plead your own cause, and if, when I return in an hour or two, you have come to a satisfactory understanding with her, you will find me rejoiced to learn that she is to have so true and good a man for her husband as my friend, Ulrich de Hutten. By-the-by, de Hutten," he added, returning for a moment, " I do not know that it is a matter of much importance to you, but I may as well tell you that I intend to give her a marriage portion of fifty thousand dollars, and from all I can learn, John Holmes is determined to get rid of some of his surplus funds in the same way."

"Pray keep your money, Severne. What you have already given me is fortune enough. It is as well you should know," he continued, laughing, "that the de Hutten estate is big enough for a prince and princess, and that it was never in a more flourishing condition than now."

And when Severne returned, de Hutten and Sarah came to him, and while the former claimed the fulfillment of his promise, Sarah put her arms around his neck and cried the most joyous tears she had ever shed in all her life.

"He says he knows all," she whispered through her sobs.

"Yes, my dear child, he does."

"And he says he loves me very much."

"I am sure of it."

"Do you think I will make him a good wife ?"

"Yes, a better one than he deserves."

She raised her head from his breast and looked into his face inquiringly.

"Has he told you his life and adventures ?" continued Severne, with a smile. "If not, get him to do so some night when you want your blood frozen with terror, when the wind howls, and when the air may be supposed to be full of demons of all kinds."

"I shall not tell her till we are married. She has put me on probation for a whole year."

"No, Ulrich," said Sarah, "that is not quite correct. I have put myself on probation. Don't you think I am right, papa ?"

"Yes, my dear child, you are right. It will doubtless be trying to de Hutten, but I don't intend to give you up for a year. There was no time mentioned in the bond, my German friend. I have become so much of a Yankee that my wits are as sharp as those of the 'cutest native of Connecticut when a bargain is to be struck."

"I suppose I shall have to make the best of it," said de Hutten, ruefully. "I'll write to my steward to sell Adlerfels to Prince Dagowitz, who has made a good offer for it, and I'll turn Yankee like the rest of you."

"A very sensible conclusion of yours. Now, my dear child, go and tell Margaret what you have done. I don't think she suspects it any more than I did two hours ago. How quiet you have been about it!"

*　　*　　*　　*　　*　　*

"And when am I to reach the end of my probation?" said Severne to Margaret that evening, after he had given her his version of what had taken place between de Hutten and Sarah.

What she answered, and how she answered, need not be particularized, as every one will know that she was as gracious in the matter and the manner as it was possible for any young woman to be, placed in her circumstances. Severne was satisfied, and with that assurance the reader, man or woman, may well be content.

*　　*　　*　　*　　*　　*

"You have settled all your own affairs to your satisfaction," said Lawrence, as they stood together on the quarter-deck of the Arago, as she steamed one fine morning through the Narrows into the glorious Bay of New York; "but I do not see that I am any nearer the haven that every sensible man should wish to reach. I set out over a year ago to get Severne married. He kicked out of the traces and started off on his own track. He went farther and did *not* fare worse. De Hutten too, like an industrious, plodding Teuton that he is, perseveres for a dozen years or more in trying to find a mortal enemy; succeeds when no one else would have dreamed of success, and before one knows what he has further in contemplation, steals off with a matrimonial prize right from under my eyes. I don't see that there is anything better for me to do than to marry Mrs. Markland."

"I am afraid, my dear Lawrence," said Severne, laughing, "that you would not meet with success enough in that quarter to keep your spirits up to a very high point. I think our

friend Joshua has repented of his determination.   He said
as much to me in San Francisco, and I have a letter for the
lady which, I think, contains an invitation for her to go
to California.   My dear fellow, we can do better for you
than that.   Don't you think we can, Margaret ?"

"Grace Langley !" said Margaret and Sarah in a breath.

"Yes," replied Severne, "Grace Langley.   You tried to
find me a wife and I am going to obtain one for myself;
now, while my hand is in, let me get one for you.   I think
I have some influence with her."

"I have thought of her," said Lawrence.   "She is very
pretty, very refined, and I think very good.   Well, well,—
we'll see about it.   I don't know any one who would make
me a better wife.   But there is Goodall; no one seems to
have thought of a wife for him !"

"Goodall will never marry," said John Holmes, sadly.
"He and I will live together, and we shall not be unhappy.
Oh, my friends," continued the good, the noble old man,
"we have all suffered, but by God's help we have triumphed
over our misfortunes and converted them into blessings.
Let us not forget, however, that he gives the victory to
those who with steadfast hearts persevere in the effort to
help themselves.   We have all learned the great lessons
which are taught by adversity,—lessons which unvarying
good fortune can never impress upon our hearts.   We have
obtained a deeper knowledge of ourselves and of our fellow-
men than years of unalloyed enjoyment could have given us,
and I trust our characters have been strengthened, and our
souls expanded by the sorrows we have undergone.   Now,
that our trials are apparently over, and we are looking forward to a renewal of our lives, we know how to value the
teachings of our dearly-bought experience, and we will not
forget to thank our Father, who, in his own good time, and
with his own means, has set all things right."

THE END.

www.ingramcontent.com/pod-product-compliance
Lightning Source LLC
Chambersburg PA
CBHW021721110726
47902CB00005B/1286

9 783337 030575